My Marine and Forever Love

Mike Gillis

ISBN: 978-1-7352619-0-4 (Paperback)
Library of Congress Control Number: 2020911470

Front cover image from Adobe Stock
First printing edition 2020.

OTHER BOOKS BY MIKE GILLIS:

A SIMPLE LIFE IN MAINE

DEDICATION

For my son, Sgt. Joseph T Gillis, U.S.M.C.

CONTENTS

FOREWORD

I loved writing this novel, and I started writing it in the fall of 2019. These writings could maybe be someone's guide to learn how humankind can love and forgive. And live together in harmony no matter how different we are. I'm a Christian writer and filmmaker. All my works are based directly on passages from the Bible, and I do not doubt that you will enjoy it. If this novel can change just one person's life, my job is accomplished. I hope that the words will stay with you for the rest of your life.

God bless you.

Mike Gillis

Chapter One

Marine Forward Operating Base - Afghanistan

Gunnery Sergeant Joseph (Joey) Morris III, is retiring from the United States Marine Corps after twenty years of service. A gunnery sergeant is a service grade above a staff sergeant and one service grade below a master sergeant with a pay grade of an E7. It took Morris nine years to achieve the rank of gunnery sergeant. To obtain the position of a gunnery sergeant, a Marine has to show exemplary intelligence, reliability, and an expert on weaponry. Morris is also an expert in Marine martial arts. Usually, he is called "gunny" inside the Marine ranks. He is currently on his last deployment in Afghanistan and counting down the days when he can rotate back to the states. Let's have no misunderstanding about his service in the Corps.

He has always wanted to be a Marine since he was a child and enlisted on his eighteenth birthday. His father, First Sergeant Joseph Morris II, was a Marine who served in Vietnam for two years and was in the famous siege of Khe Sanh. And his Grandfather, Marine Staff Sergeant Joseph Morris senior, fought in all the major battles in the

Pacific during World War Two. Including Okinawa, Guadalcanal, and the infamous Iwo Jima. Morris went to Moffat County High School in Craig, Colorado, where he was an all-state middle linebacker on the football team. He was offered a full scholarship to Colorado State University. But he wanted to fulfill his dream of being a United States Marine.

Morris is stationed at a forward operating base (pronounced fob) deep in a province in Afghanistan. Morris is winding down his career in a squad that he has been with for two years. His squad consists of thirteen men consisting of four privates, four lance corporals, three corporals, one sergeant. Morris lets his new squad Sergeant, David Lewis, lead the men. Morris is there mainly for an advisory position for Sergeant Lewis. He lives in his squads b-hut (living quarters) because he has always wanted to know his men, and they get to know him. When his squad gets back to the FOB from a mission, he takes a shower and goes to the mess hut.

After eating, he goes to his squads b-hut and sets down at a small desk going over the next day's orders. After about ten minutes, Corporal Johnny Kraite comes to the hut and says to Morris, "Gunny Morris, Lieutenant Anderson wants you and Sgt. Lewis, ASAP." Anderson is a second lieutenant that commands Joeys squad. Morris replies, "thank you, Corporal." Morris then proceeds to Anderson's hut with Lewis. Lewis knocks on the lieutenant's hut. Anderson says, "come in, gentlemen."

Morris and Lewis salute Anderson, and Lewis says, "Gunny Morris and Sgt. Lewis reporting as ordered sir." Anderson salutes the men back and says, "at ease." Anderson then says, "I just got orders for your squad to check out an abandoned village tomorrow. Anderson folds out a map on his desk, and all three men look at it. Anderson points to an area on the map saying, "It's about forty klicks (kilometers) northeast of the base. Intel (intelligence) has it that insurgents (enemy) are hiding caches of weapons there. And we've been ordered for a search and neutralize all weapons and ordnance. I need my best men for this patrol and have your men ready to roll tomorrow morning at zero five hundred. Be prepared to stay in the field for two days." "Yes sir," replies the Sergeants. Then Anderson gives the map to Lewis. Anderson then says, "dismissed." The men salute Anderson and leave his hut. Morris and Lewis go back to their b-hut, but before he enters, he sees Krait and tells him to gather all the squad to meet with him in front of the squads b-hut. Kraite says, "right away, Sergeant."

Later as the men gather in front of the huts, Lewis lays out a map then points to an area saying, "listen up. We have orders to check out an abandoned village. Intel says the bad guys are storing weapons and moving them in at night. We are to destroy such weapons if any are there. And wait around to see if in bad guys bring more presents to their surprise party we have planned for them." All the men start laughing. Then Lewis tells them, "be prepared to stay two days, so have full equipment, and ammo squared away." Private First Class, Lenny Strawn, who is a good Marine, but always seems to be the main "question asker" of the squad, says, "why do we have to have full gear for an abandoned village, Sergeant?" Lewis looks at Strawn with a precarious face, saying to him, "Strawn, why do you always have to question about everything that we are ordered to do?" Strawn replies, "Sergeant, you just said that Intel considers the village abandoned?" Lewis walks over to Strawn and puts his face about an inch from Strawn's face.

Lewis, with an angry look, but calmly saying to him, "Strawn, when Intel says something is not there, I always get an electric shock up my spine, GET IT!" "Yes, Sergeant," replies Strawn. Lewis looks at Morris, and says, "anything to add Gunny?" Morris speaks to the men, "I suggest that you have your equipment squared away ASAP and hit the rack early." Lewis then says, "we'll be moving out at zero five hundred in the morning. That's all. Dismissed."

All the men go too there, hut. Morris goes in and sits at his desk in front of his rack (bed) to get the paperwork ready for tomorrow's mission. About an hour later, Morris finishes up with all the paperwork. He lays down on his rack and receives a book from a small stand and starts to read. There also is a bible on the stand, but it doesn't get read much. Pvt. First Class, Daniel Dawson, who joined the platoon two weeks before, walks up to Morris's rack and says, "Gunny, can I speak to you for a moment?" Morris lays his book back on the stand, then turns to Dawson and says, "of course, Dawson. Sit in the desk chair and tell me what's on your mind." Dawson sits down, then says, "Gunny Morris,

I just heard this morning that you will be retiring soon." Morris lays his book back on the stand and with a big smile. Then nodding his head, saying, "yep, that's right." Dawson replies, "when is this all going down?" Morris says, "in about two weeks, and I'll rotate back to Lejeune. And then I'll be officially retired in about three months. It takes a lot of paperwork to retire." "You'll have twenty-years won't you," replies Dawson. Morris says, "yes, twenty years, but I have loved some parts and hated the other."

Dawson then says, "wow, twenty years. I've been in for two, and it has seemed like forever." Morris then says, "well, I'll tell you what Dawson, you will be a much better man or woman when you get out. No matter what branch of service of the United States you're serving." Dawson smiles, then saying, "Gunny, even though I haven't been around you that long, you're the best gunny I've served with so far. You're somehow different from the gunny's I've served under before. And I heard that you were a Marine Raider." (A Raider is a member of the Marine Corps special operations detachment.) Morris replies, "Yes, I was. I was in a recon (reconnaissance) detachment for ten years then opted to the Second Raider Battalion, out of LeJeune. Dawson lights up, saying, "Marine Raiders are the baddest special operations unit in the world! When did you get out?" About two years ago, I wanted to start winding down to retirement." Dawson looks around then back at Morris and says, "do you mind if I ask you some questions about your life?" Morris says, "sure, go ahead."

Dawson says, "where are you from?" Morris smiles then says, "I was born and raised in Craig, Colorado. My mother and dad had timberland in the surrounding mountains that were in my family for generations. My dad had two lumber mills on the land, and he cut the fine timber to the customer's custom specifications. He sold the lumber to customers all over the United States. We had a weekend, get-away, log cabin on our land. Quite often, some friends and I would go to the cabin to spend at least a week there. When my mother died, she left everything to me, and that is where I'll be taking my permanent retirement" He then says to Dawson, "I sold my mom and dad's home in Craig, and the cabin will be my new address."

Dawson says, "wow, that sounds great. Where did you go to high school?" Morris smiles, saying, "I went to Moffet County High." "I have a feeling that you played football, didn't you," says Dawson. Morris says, "yep, middle linebacker. And we were state-champs my junior and senior years. I got a football scholarship offer from Colorado State when I was a senior, but I always wanted to be a Marine, so I turned it down." Dawson has a small, smirky grin, saying, "I bet you had the pick of the chicks, didn't you. Morris laughs then says, "there were some. But I always thought there was a prettier girl behind the next door." Dawson has a questionable look, saying, "what do you mean by that?" Morris smiles, saying, "what I mean is that I had many sweet, wonderful, Christian girls that I dated. And I let those girls slip through my fingers. But, I went for the most beautiful girl at the school. She was at the time, I thought, was the girl behind the next door. But now I see that it was a terrible decision on my part." Dawson says, smiling, "what was her name, and what happened?"

Morris gets a serene look on his face saying, "her name was Karen Smart. She was a cheerleader and always voted class beauty, class favorite, and our senior year she was the homecoming queen. And man was I in love with her." Dawson, jokingly says, " I know now from experience that's the type of girl I would run and hide from these days." Morris laughs, saying, "I wish I knew that back then, but that's exactly what I should have done. Karen was beautiful and the bad thing about it, she knew it. I also think sometimes about those other sweet girls I mentioned. Dawson shrugs his shoulders, saying, "what happened between you and Karen?" Morris breathes deep, then says, "we seriously talked about getting married after she graduated from Colorado State, and I got out of the Marines.

I was planning on a four-year hitch, and then she would graduate after those same four years. When I came home on leave, we would spend all the time we could get with each other. Halfway through our last year, I stopped getting letters from her. I tried everything to get in touch with her. Every time I got the chance to give Karen a call, her roommate would say that she wasn't there. I even went up to Colorado State when I was on leave to find her, but I never could."

Morris looks down with a saddened face, not saying anything. Dawson then says, "I will understand if you don't want to talk about Karen anymore, but what happened after that?" Morris looks up at Dawson, then says, "I got the dreaded "dear Joey" letter saying she had met someone, and they were getting married immediately." Dawson shakes his head, then says, "you know Gunny Morris, a jerk doesn't always mean a man. Karen proved that women could be jerks also. What did you do then?" Morris shrugs his shoulders then, saying, "what could I do? She was already married when I got the letter." Dawson replies, "well, she made the biggest mistake in her life for not waiting on a good man like you. And not only was she a jerk, but she was also a coward!" Morris looks at Dawson for a few seconds, then says, "I don't know how good a man I am, but thanks, Dawson."

Morris and Dawson don't realize that some of the men that are in their racks or finishing up on preparing their packs are listening to everything they have said. Dawson looks over to the small stand next to Joey's rack and see's a bible laying there. Dawson says, "I see you have a bible." Morris looks at the Bible then turns to Dawson, saying, "I should read it more, but I know that the man upstairs will look after my men and me." Then Dawson says, "my mother gave me that bible when I left for boot camp, and I carry it on every mission." Morris smiles at him, saying, "that's a good piece of equipment to have in your pack Dawson." Joey then says, "you need to hit the rack because I have a feeling we're going to be busy the next couple of days."

Dawson says, "okay, Gunny. But, can I tell you one thing else? Morris replies by saying, "sure, go ahead." Dawson looks around and back at Morris. Dawson, then says, "it's strange, but all my life, I have always had this sense of being able to tell how someone's life will turn out. Or at least come close to it." Morris smiles, saying, "what do you see for me, Dawson?" Dawson has a strange look on his face and says to Morris, "Gunny, don't let go of a lady who would be the best thing to ever happen to you. Even if during that time you don't think it's the right thing to do." Morris looks at Dawson for a moment with a dubious expression on his face then says, "go hit your rack." Dawson replies, "thanks for the talk Gunny." "It was my pleasure, Dawson," replies

Morris. Dawson gets up, walking to his rack.

It's the next morning and all of Sgt. Lewis's squad is lined up in front of their huts. Then Cpl. Kraite walks up to Lewis and says, "all men accounted for, Sgt. Lewis." Then Lewis says, "okay, everybody, saddle up!" The men climb into Hum-Vee's (military support vehicles) that had just arrived for them. Morris and Lewis are in the third Hum-Vee, heading to the sector where the village is located. About two hours later, the squad arrives at the sector and stop about five klicks (kilometers) from the village. Morris and Lewis get out of their Hum-Vee. Sgt. Lewis goes back to the vehicles and says to the men, "fall out!" The men get out of their vehicles and line up in formation by their Hum-Vee's. Lewis looks at the map, then says to his men, "alright, you know the drill. Let's get this operation over quick, so head out." Then the squad hump (walk) toward the village.

A sergeant or staff sergeant is in charge of a rifle squad. That's why Morris is letting Sgt. Lewis lead the men to gain experience. The men start walking into the village in left to right positions keeping vigilant of their surroundings. Looking for IED's (improvised explosive devices) and other hidden ordnance. Dawson takes point (first man in front of the squad.) Cpl. Terry McKey is eight feet to the right behind Pvt. Mike McAuley. Lewis is right behind the first three men. Morris is taking a position in the middle of the men making sure every man keeps his distance from each other.

As they reach about 30 meters from the village, Dawson holds up his fist, meaning for the squad to stop. Then get next to the huts and take a knee. Lewis runs up to Dawson and says quietly, "what's up, Dawson?" He says, "abandoned villages always creep me out, Sgt. Besides, I thought I saw some movement ahead. Lewis says, "I know the feeling. I'm going to signal each man to be extra cautious and to move slower than normal to check and clear each hut." "Copy that," replies Lewis. Lewis looks down at the men pointing to his eyes, which tells the men to be extra diligent. Lewis signals everyone to move out, moving into the village with their weapons ready for any surprise. The men search each hut but find nothing. They get to the halfway point of the village, and again, Dawson holds up his fist, and the men stop and take a knee. Lewis again moves slowly up to Dawson, saying very quietly, "talk to me, Dawson." Dawson says, "maybe Intel was right Gunny. Doesn't seem to be anybody here." Lewis replies, "no one so far, but those openings near the roofs of the huts are making the hairs on the back of my neck get stiff! Keep a watch on those roofs!" "Copy that," replies Dawson. Lewis signals to the squad to watch out for the openings and the roofs then he gives the signal to move out.

As they start to move out, an RPG (rocket-propelled-grenade) hits right in front of Dawson, killing him instantly. McKey, McAuley and Lewis are very seriously wounded. Then the scariest words since man threw rocks at each other are yelled out. "AMBUSH!" The squad immediately takes cover in the huts and starts returning fire toward the roofs. The insurgents open fire with small arms and RPG's. McKey, McAuley, and Lewis are lying in the dirt road seriously injured. Dawson's lifeless body lies about ten feet from the other downed men. The insurgents stop firing, and Morris goes into action. Every ten to fifteen seconds, the enemy fire toward the three men but not hitting them. They're trying to lure the Marines out to pull the injured men to safety. Then they would open fire on the rescuing men.

Morris is crouching behind a hut along with Strawn. Strawn starts to get up to run to the road, and Morris grabs him by his pack pulling him back, saying, "Strawn get your butt back here!" Strawn with a horrified face, says, "Gunny, we've got to get those men out of there!" Morris grabs him by the collar, saying sternly, "that's what the enemy wants you to do! They want us to go get those men, for they can waste us!" Strawn settles down and says, "yes, Gunny." Morris gets on the radio calling Corporal Donny Beard asking what his situation is. Beard replies, "Gunny, I've got four men that are in bad shape and out of action. Stuckey is wounded but can still fight." Everybody else that I can tell is okay!" "Copy that Beard. Give me a few seconds to access this situation and stand by on what we're going to do," replies Morris. Morris sits back with his back against the hut, thinking for a few seconds about what he needs to do.

The insurgents are still firing near the three downed men. Then Morris gets on his radio, and Morris sees McAuley's SAW (squad automatic weapon) lying next to him. And Morris knows he has to retrieve that weapon. Morris gets back on the radio and says, "okay, listen up! I've got to go get McAuley's SAW, so start giving me cover fire, now!" Morris has this before. If he doesn't do something now, the men want have a chance. The men start firing around different parts of the village. Morris runs out and gets the SAW. Bullets are hitting all around him, and then Morris runs into an alley. Morris then gets on the radio, saying, "ceasefire! Save your Ammo!" His men stop firing, and Morris says, "I'm going to outflank the bad guys and go to the front of the village. And when you see me start firing, let them have it!"

Morris moves out of the back of the hut and heads toward the front of the village. He stops at the corner of every hut making sure everything is clear. Morris is getting close to the front row of huts. He pauses again, looking around the edge of the hut and sees an old Nisson pick-up truck driving up. The truck stops at the rear of one of the huts. Two insurgents get out of the back, pulling out caches of weapons, ammunition, and RPG's for a total assault on his squad. The driver of the truck and his passenger get out, helping the other insurgents removing the ordinance. As the enemy starts carrying the weapons to the hut, Morris steps out, firing the SAW killing all four. Joey also puts a few rounds through the engine block and radiator of the truck. He does this to keep the enemy from using it again. Morris looks down at one of the containers housing the RPGs and opens it up, retrieving one of the weapons.

Morris can hear the enemy still firing close to the three downed men. And he knows that the insurgents will eventually kill the wounded men, turning their full attention to the rest of the squad. Morris gets to the last hut at the end of the village, then walks to the front corner of the hut. He looks around the corner very carefully, seeing where the most concentrated enemy fire is coming. The firing is coming from a large opening below the roof of a hut. He aims the RPG at the opening and fires. He hits the opening with a direct hit. As he turns to get behind the hut, a bullet hits him under his body armor through his left armpit. The bullet exits through the top of his shoulder close to his neck. Morris is severely wounded, but his body is running on full adrenaline and determination. Then, he runs to the middle of the road, exposing himself to deadly enemy fire. Then, Morris shouts as loud as he can, "FIGHT ON CAM THE RAM!"

He opens fire spraying bullets to the upper parts of the huts with the SAW. He is concentrating his firing on the windows and openings in the huts. Morris sees an insurgent standing to fire an RPG toward his men. Joey fires at the insurgent, killing him. But when the insurgent starts to fall, he pulls the trigger on the weapon. Firing the RPG into an adjacent building, killing some of the other enemies. At this time, Beard and two men pull the wounded Marines and Dawson's body out of the street. Then they render aid to all the injured. Morris runs out of ammo for the SAW and runs to take cover behind the hut. Morris radios to Beard, saying, "Beard, did you get the wounded out because I damn sure don't want to go out there again!" Beard radios back, saying, "Gunny, we got all the men, including Dawson's body." Morris has a sigh of relief, then radios to Beard, saying, "copy that. I'm heading back." Beard says, "are you okay, Gunny?" "I took a round under the shoulder, but I'm okay," replies Morris. He pulls out his 9mm sidearm and heads back to his men, bringing the SAW with him.

Morris gets back to the men who are still taking fire from the insurgents. He pulls out his map and shows Beard a different route to get the wounded out. And he tells Beard he will stay back to lay down cover fire when they pull out. Beard looks at Morris's shoulder and sees all the blood. Beard, then says, "Gunny, you're hit bad. You have to come with us!" Morris replies, "negative Beard. Get those men out of here now! Beard says, "copy that, Gunny, but were going to have to leave two of the wounded here. And come back to get them." Morris says to Beard, "after I lay down cover fire, I'll get the men out with me." "Copy that," replies, Beard.

Morris loads the Saw with another magazine. He looks at the two Marines that he'll evacuate, saying, "I'll get you out as soon as I empty this magazine." Morris, then yells at Beard, saying, "get the hell out of here!" Morris starts raking the village with cover fire. Beard moves the men out and calls to command for medevac helos (helicopters). He then gives the coordinates to command for the helo landing zone.

Morris fires all the rounds in the magazine and straps the SAW over his shoulder. Morris's actions have allowed all the Marines, walking and wounded, to get out safely. Morris walks over to one Marine and places the man on his back. He then grabs the other man by the collar to drag him to the L.Z. Enemy bullets are hitting all around them, and suddenly Morris is caught in the back by a bullet, knocking him down. But the bullet doesn't penetrate his body armor. He gets up, then picks up the Marine he had on his back. He grabs the other man, and they high-tail it to the L.Z. (helo landing zone). Beard and Strawn run-up to help Morris with the wounded men.

They hear the Blackhawk medivac helicopters coming for them. Morris says to Beard, "give me the radio. Beard hands Morris the radio transceiver, and he calls air command for an airstrike. He gives air command the coordinates to the insurgent village. Morris says to Beard, "I'm going to go back close to the village to make sure the airstrike is on point." Beard says excitedly, "don't get to close Gunny. All that firepower can be lethal from just a few meters from that village." Morris says to Beard, "get these men to the L.Z.!" Beard stuffs gauze under Morris's arm to help control the bleeding. Morris grabs another magazine for the SAW.

Morris also gets a radio then runs back toward the village. Sniper bullets are whizzing past him. About a minute later, Morris sees the medivac helos arrive. The men load the wounded men on the helos. Dawson's body is placed in a body bag, and the men put his body into the helo. Beard and Strawn stay behind to wait on Morris. Then they hear the beautiful, distinctive sounds of the attack helos getting close. Morris sees a UH-1Y "Super Huey" helo first.

This helo will scout the target first, followed by two "Cobra Viper" helos. The Vipers are the attack helos, which will destroy the target. Morris sees the enemy firing at the scout Super Huey with small arms and RPGs on top of the huts. Morris hears the captain of the Huey, (call sign Ghost) radios the major, (call sign Wedge) of the lead Viper, saying, "the enemy is on top of the huts, Wedge. There firing small arms and RPG's at me. So get in here and lite this place up, quick!" Wedge radio's back to Ghost, saying, "bank off, Ghost. We'll be on target in thirty seconds."

The Huey banks off, then Morris calls Wedge saying, "Wedge, you are coming right on target. And I'll keep the bad guys off you till I run out of ammo. Wedge says to Morris in a surprising tone of voice, "who the hell is this! And what is your location?" Morris replies, "Gunnery Seargent Joseph Morris, sir. And I'm about a half-klick from the village. I'm making sure that you're on target. I owe this to my men to see this personally done." Wedge calls back, saying, "keep them off us for as long as you can. Then get your butt out of there Gunny because we're coming in low. Joey then empties the magazine of the SAW at the insurgents.

Joey gets up and starts running the best he can back to the rendezvous area. The Vipers come in so low that Morris can feel their rotor wash (wind from the helicopter blades). The helos start to fire their 20mm cannons and Hell-Fire missiles vaporizing the village immediately. Morris says to Wedge, "great job, sir. Right on target!" After the Viper attack, Morris gets back to the temporary rendezvous area, and Beard and Strawn run to meet him. Then Morris, says, "everybody out?" Beard replies, "everyone out, Gunny." Then Morris passes out from blood loss. Beard and Strawn get him back to the FOB for stabilization and then immediately flown by helo to an aid station. That's where he will receive more extensive treatment for his wound.

Then Morris will be flown to Germany the next day for surgery. Morris is lying in an aid station cot when a corpsman hangs his I.V. fluids. The corpsman asks Morris, "is there anything I can get for you, Gunny?" Morris's head is turned to the side of his pillow, not looking at the corpsman, answering, "not anything right now, corpsman." The corpsman then says, "they're going to fly you out of here to Germany. I'll be right back to get you ready for the flight." He walks off, and Joey buries his head into the pillow and starts to cry uncontrollably. In his twenty years of service, he has never lost a man. Later that afternoon, Morris is flown out of Afghanistan to Germany.

The next day, after his surgery, a Navy Chaplain, Norris White, comes to see Morris. White sees Morris has his head turned. White says, "Gunny, I'm Chaplain Norris White. I was told you did a very heroic thing yesterday. You saved a lot of your men." Morris doesn't say anything, but White knows why Morris is so upset. White also was briefed that Morris never lost a man before until yesterday. Chaplain White then says, "get well, Gunny, and God be with you." If you want to talk, ask for me. Morris still doesn't say anything, and White starts to walk off but stops, turning back to Morris. He walks back to Joey's bed and says, "I know this probably won't help much, but I heard this on T.V. once, and I want you to hear it." White kneels at the head of the bed and seeing the distress in Morris's eyes, saying, "I heard a colonel tell a captain once that there are two rules in war. Rule number one is that fine, young men are killed in war. And rule number two is you can't do a thing to change rule number one."

Morris looks at White with tears in his eyes and says, "thank you, sir." "Take care of yourself," replies White. Then White says to Morris, "oh, one thing else, then I will leave you alone. It's been going around the hospital that you screamed out something when you stood up in the middle of the street. Right before firing at the enemy. What did you scream out?" Morris starts to smile, then says, "I said fight on Cam the Ram. That's the mascot of Colorado State University." White laughs and stands up, saying, "It's been a privilege to meet you, Gunny. Semper Fi!" Morris replies, "copy that, sir."

A naval nurse, Lt. Rachel Berryman, walks up to Morris's bed and hangs an antibiotic bag connecting it to his I.V. She sees that Morris is awake, and says, "how are you feeling, Gunny?" Morris replies, "I don't feel much of anything, Lieutenant." Berryman, then says, "you are on some powerful pain meds right now. Do you know where you are?" "A hospital in Germany," replies Morris. She smiles and says, "that's right. And we're going to get you out of here ASAP."

It's been a month since Morris left Germany. He is back at Camp Lejune with his left arm in a sling sitting behind a desk doing paperwork in a drab office. He is about to go nuts doing this job, but he has to take it easy for his shoulder will heal properly. Captain Lawrence Davis comes into his office, and Morris stands and salutes. Davis salutes back then tells Morris, "at ease, Gunny. Please sit back down." "After you, sir," replies Joey. Davis sits down, and Morris does likewise. Then, Davis says to Morris, "hows that shoulder, Gunny?" "Doing well, sir, but I'm about to go nuts sitting behind this desk," says Morris. Davis laughs, saying,

"I know what you mean, Gunny. And I'm sure you're wondering what I'm doing here personally." Morris smiles, saying, "It had crossed my mind, sir."

Davis, then says, "Colonel Scheffer wants to see you in his office in the morning at zero nine-thirty." Morris, of course, is a little concerned why Scheffer is sending his captain to deliver this message personally. Morris has a questionable look, saying, "sir, can I ask why the colonel want's to see me?" Davis replies, "you will find out everything you need to know tomorrow morning Gunny." Morris then says, "yes, sir." Davis stands and Morris does the same when Davis says, "take care of that shoulder, Gunny." "Affirmative sir," Morris, replies. Then Morris salutes Captain Davis. Davis leaves the office, and Morris says to himself with a frown, "I wonder what this is all about?"

The next morning Morris arrives at Colonel Scheffer's office and greeted by the colonel's assistant, Lieutenant Carrie Madsen. Morris salutes, then says, "Gunnery Sergeant Joseph Morris reporting as ordered Lieutenant." The Lieutenant returns the salute then says, "at ease, Gunny. Colonel Scheffer is expecting you." The lieutenant picks up the phone, saying, "Gunnery Sergeant Morris has reported as ordered, Colonel. The Lieutenant hangs up the phone then says, "follow me, Gunny." "Yes, ma'am," replies Morris. The lieutenant opens the colonel's door, and Joey goes in. Scheffer stands as Morris salutes. Then Scheffer salutes him back, saying, "at ease, Gunny. Take a seat." Scheffer sits back down behind his desk, saying, "hows that shoulder Morris?" Morris responds, "healing on schedule, sir. But to be honest, sir, my back hurts more where I took that round. Scheffer starts to smile, then says, "you don't think I sent for you to ask about that shoulder, did you?"

Morris smiles, saying, "no, sir, I didn't." Scheffer smiles and has a very peculiar gleam in his eyes, saying, "Gunnery Sergeant Joseph Morris, it's my pleasure to tell you that you are being awarded the Naval Cross. For extraordinary heroism for your last action in Afghanistan. We have been flooded with correspondence from everyone that was involved in that fight. Including, Major Dan Rials, call sign Wedge. He was the Commander of the Cobra team you called in. And you went above and beyond the call of duty by saving many Marines, while you were seriously wounded. And at the risk of your own life. Congratulations on this award, Gunny."

Morris is stunned and starts to frown because he starts thinking about Dawson that night before he was killed. Then Morris says, "sir, I just did what any Marine would do to protect his men." "That's right, Gunny. But you exemplified yourself taking on the enemy as you did," replies Scheffer. Scheffer then says, "Brigadier General Carson Moses will present the award to you in about two weeks. I would like for you to have all your family members there for this special award ceremony. My lieutenant will need their names for their dignitary passes." Sir, I don't have any family members except for a few distant cousins I haven't seen in many years. So it will be just me," replies Morris.

Colonal Scheffer stands up, saying, "again, congratulations, Gunny. My Lieutenant will be giving you all the details on the ceremony in a couple of days, dismissed." Morris salutes the Colonel, and Scheffer returns the salute. Morris leaves the office but is not happy to be receiving the award. He keeps thinking about Dawson and Corporal McAuley. Morris found out that Corporal McAuley had died of his wounds when Morris was in the hospital. He dreams about his deceased men and the battle several times a week now.

Master Gunnery Sergeant, Chris Johnston comes to see Morris at his apartment that is located off base that night. Johnston is a great friend of Morris's, where they served together numerous times. Johnson knocks, and Morris opens the door, saying, "Master Gunnery Sergeant Johnston, come on in." They give each other a slight man-hug, and Johnston says, "I thought I would come over and see you. I just got back from Quantico, and I heard you got wounded in your last battle. So I came over to see how you are doing." Morris says, "everything is doing fine." Then Morris points to his head, saying to Johnston, "I'm not so sure about up here, though."

They both sit at a small dinner table, and Johnston looks at Morris's head and says, "what's going on up there, Gunny?" Morris answers, saying, "I can't get that last ambush out of my head. I can't stop thinking about the two men I lost, and I dream about it almost every night. It wakes me up, and I can't go back to sleep. It's like reliving that ambush every time I dream about it. When I wake up from the dream, I'm shaking and soaking wet from sweat. It's taking a toll on my everyday life." Johnston has seen this many times before. He knows that Morris has post-traumatic stress disorder (PTSD). Johnston says, "Gunny, I've been around a lot of men that had the same symptoms that you have. My old friend, your suffering from PSTD." Morris frantically says, "PTSD?" He is still very agitated, then saying, "Chris, you know that I've been in the Marines for twenty years and seen many horrible things! But PTSD?" "Yes, Gunny. You have seen many bad things, but you have never lost men until your last deployment, right?" Morris looks down with a sorrowful facial expression, saying calmly, "you know I didn't, Chris."

Johnston looks at him with a somber face, saying, "Gunny Morris, you are one of my closest friends, and I love ya man. I would suggest getting some help for your issues. Ever since man has been throwing stones at each other, there have been PTSD. They used to call it shell shock ever since the Civil War through Vietnam. But now there are a lot of therapies that the Navy provides to help you lead a normal life." Morris still has the same sad expression, then says's to Johnston, "are you suggesting on me seeing a shrink?" Johnson nods his head with a serious face, saying calmly, "I suggest you see one of the Naval psychiatrists at Lejune."

Then Johnson says, "I heard that they are doing remarkable things with PTSD now. Would you do that for me?" Morris looks down then looks back up at Johnson. With a slight smile and nodding his head, Morris says, "okay, I'll set up an appointment in the morning." Johnson replies by saying, "If you have a problem getting in quick, I have a Naval doctor friend that will get you in ASAP." Morris smiles at Johnson, saying, "Thanks, Chris. I've always have counted on you for good advice." Johnson replies, "don't let me down. Because I will be checking on you." Morris says, "I won't." They both man-hug again, and Johnson says, "well, I need to get out of here because Lisa will have dinner ready in about thirty minutes. Let me know how everything turns out. Okay?" Morris replies, "I will, and say hey to Lisa for me." "Of course I will," exclaims Johnson.

Johnson leaves the apartment, and Morris is pondering on what his friend just discussed with him. Then he goes and lays on his couch, contemplating on should he maybe get his Bible because he needs his faith now more than ever. But, he decides to write the families of Dawson and McAuley.

Chapter Two

Back Home In The Mountains Near Craig, Colorado

Three months later, Joey has officially retired from the Marines. He is back at his log cabin in the mountains around Craig that his parents left him. It's been vacant for three years, and it looks like a lot of cleaning and maintenance. His closest neighbor, Jessie Sneed, lives ten miles from Joey. Jessie watched over his parents and especially took care of his mother when Joey's dad passed away. When Joey's mother died, Jessie looked after the property every day. Joey is glad too have Jessie as his neighbor, even if he does live ten miles away. Jessie is a man that Joey would trust his life. And would have been a pleasure to serve with Jessie within any branch of America's military. Jessie was one of the very few African American Army helicopter pilots to fly combat missions in Vietnam. And Joey is very proud to call him a great friend. Jessie comes up to Joey's cabin to visit at least once a week since he has been back. Joey has told Jessie about his PTSD.

Joey is doing quite well by managing his PTSD now. And he is adjusting well to people calling him Joey. Because it's was a sergeant or gunny for many years. He goes to the V.A. hospital in Grand Junction to see his psychologist every three months. He sees his psychiatrist once every six months. It has done him well meeting with his therapist and especially the group meetings. Now, It's the first week in September on a Tuesday morning around eight-thirty. Joey drives down to Wilson's country store to get a few groceries. It's also the nearest location to get cell phone reception in the area. Wilson's store is about twelve miles from Joey's cabin, and most of the residents in the area still communicate with C.B. radios. Wilson's store has a C.B. base station with a large antenna on the outside. Residents can call the store with their radios if there is an emergency. James Wilson, who has owned the store for over thirty years, can relay messages through a landline telephone if needed.

He arrives at Wilson's store, where you can get almost anything you need to live in the mountains. When Joey was away on his last deployment, Mr.Wilson put in a small deli and hired a young woman, Bailey, to manage it. He also has a few tables where people can eat. You can even call on your C.B. radio for an order, and it will be ready when you get there. Joey parks his Jeep at the side of the store then goes in. He thinks of the beautiful memories when he came here as a kid. He remembers taking a dollar bill and buying all sorts of candy, chips and soda. Then having a quarter left over to play pinball. And you would always hope to get a free game if you scored a lot of points.

There is a pot-bellied wood stove still sitting in the middle of the store. Where old men set around getting warm, drinking coffee, and telling lies. When Joey was a kid, he loved to sit around listening to the men, seeing who could come up with the best lie. City people don't realize that in small communities like theirs, that a grocery store like this was the place to come to find out what was happening. Even in today's modern world. Joey doesn't think that Mr. Wilson even knows how to buy a computer. Everything is handwritten and Wilson calls his orders in on his landline phone. Joey takes a handbasket and goes around picking up the items he needs. Later he walks up to the counter to pay for the groceries.

Wilson comes up from behind the counter, shaking Joey's hand, saying, "well, good morning Sergeant Morris. How are you! I heard you were back, and I'm glad to see you home safe." "It's great to see you, Mr. Wilson, and I'm sorry for not coming to see you sooner," replies Joey. Wilson smiles and says, "you need to call me Wilson now, and I want to thank you for serving this country and also congratulations on your Navy Cross. I hear the Marines are stingy when awarding medals. You must have done something very extraordinary over there." Joey looks down with a sad face, and Wilson notices. With a concerned voice, Wilson says, "are you okay, son?" Joey looks up, smiling, saying, "yes sir, I'm fine. And one thing else I can't call you just Wilson. I have known you too long, and you will always be Mr. Wilson. It's a respect thing, you know." Wilson says, "thank you for that, son. I've been just Wilson all my life. So you calling me Mr. Wilson will be alright with me.

Wilson is putting the prices of Joey's items in an old-style cash register and bagging them in brown paper grocery bags. Joey, then says, "I like the deli that you put in. Looks like your getting modern now." Wilson replies, "so many people were buying sliced meat and bread and trying to make a sandwich here in the store. So, I decided then to put a deli to save them the trouble. And we're swamped because Bailey makes one good sandwich." Wilson looks at Bailey, saying, "Bailey, come over here and meet a real-life war hero." Joey thinks to himself that he wishes people would not bring up anything about what he did while he was a Marine. But in one of his PTSD group sessions at the V.A., the therapist said that your war exploits would follow you all your life. And you must learn how to accept this and manage your feelings because people are very proud of you.

Bailey comes to the counter and Wilson, says, "Bailey, this is Joey Morris." Bailey extends her hand, and Joey takes it, and she says, "very nice to meet you, Joey. And thank you for your service to our country." "Nice to meet you, Bailey, and thank you for your comment," replies Joey. Bailey, then says, "Joey, could I interest you a sausage or a ham biscuit?" Mr. Wilson says, "sure Bailey, fix him whatever he wants. On the house." Joey thanks Wilson and says to Bailey, "okay then. What about a sausage biscuit?" Bailey then says, "what about some coffee with that?" Joey smiles, replying, "yes, that would be fine, and thanks." Bailey produces a pretty smile, saying, "go sit at one of the tables, and I will bring it out to you." "Thanks," replies Joey.

Joey goes to the counter, then saying to Wilson, "how much for the groceries?" How about twenty-eight dollars and fifty-six cents." Joey reaches in his back pocket and gets his wallet, paying the bill. Wilson takes the money and gives Joey his change. Joey notices a big pickle jar on the counter for donations for a wounded veterans organization. He puts his change in the jar. Joey, then pulls out a one-hundred-dollar bill, putting it in the jar. Wilson saw what Joey did and says, "that's very generous of you, Joey. I thank you on behalf of this great organization." Joey nods his head, not saying anything. Joey, then says to Wilson, "I almost forgot Mr. Wilson. I need to get a new hunting license." "Sure thing," Wilson replies.

Wilson gets a metal cash box from below and sets it on the top of the counter. He unlocks it and retrieves a license registration pad out of the box. Wilson then says, "Joey, I need to see your driver's license, please, sir." Joey reaches for his wallet and takes out his driver's license and hands it to Wilson. He writes all the information down and gives Joey his license back to him. Wilson removes the hunter's permit and hands it to Joey. Wilson, then says, "that will be thirty-four dollars and remember that's for pronghorn too." Joey pays him and says, "can I leave my groceries on the counter? I don't want to take up space at one of your tables." "Sure," replies Wilson.

Joey goes and sits at one of the tables waiting for his food when Jessie Sneed comes into the store. Jessie walks to the men sitting around the woodstove, saying, "how much B.S. will Wilson scoop up around this stove when he closes tonight?" All the men don't speak very nice to Jessie after what he just said. Jessie turns and laughs and sees Joey sitting at one of Wilson's tables. Jessie walks up to Mr. Wilson, asking him to grind him some coffee. Jessie walks over to where Joey is sitting, saying, "how is it going this morning, Marine?" Joey replies, "so far, it's been pretty good, Jessie." Jessie then says, "I need to borrow your log-splitter because the hydraulic pump went out on mine yesterday. Joey says, "your welcome to take one of the two that's in the barn." "Thanks, and I'll pick one of them up this afternoon," replies Jessie.

Bailey brings Joey his sausage biscuit and coffee and sits it in front of him. She looks at Jessie, saying, "Good morning, Mr. Sneed. Can I get you something from the deli?" Jessie replies by saying, "Bailey, I know your mom and dad brought up right, but again, please call me Jessie." Bailey smiles and says, "I'll try to remember that next time, Jessie." She looks at Joey, saying with a flirty tone, "enjoy your sausage biscuit and coffee, Joey." "Thanks, Bailey," replies Joey. Joey takes a bite out of his biscuit then nods his head, saying, "man, this is great!" Jessie nods his head and says, "Bailey is a good little cook. You will need to try her Reuben sandwich sometimes. It's great." Jessie looks at Joey with a somber look on his face, then says, "Joey, you don't know this, but your mother kept a scrapbook of everything you did in the Marines. From boot-camp up until when she couldn't do it anymore. She asked me the day before she passed would I keep it up for her till you got out. Then I would give it to you. I told her I would be honored. So that's what I did, kept the scrapbook current till you got home. I want to give it to you when I come to get the log splitter this afternoon."

Joey is little taken back on what Jessie just told him. Jessie sees the expression on Joey's face, then saying, "Joey, I know it will be tough for you to look at the scrapbook, but treasure it in her honor. Look at it when you think the time is right for you." Joey looks at Jessie with a slight smile, saying, "thanks, Jessie. You have always been a special friend to me and my parents." Bailey brings Jessie's coffee, and then she says, "enjoy, Jessie." Jessie looks at her and smiles. Jessie looks at Joey, saying, "I see that Wilson has my ground coffee ready, so I'll see you this afternoon." Joey says, "thanks again, Jessie, for what all you have done for us and be careful out there." Jessie turns toward Joey and says, "It's been my pleasure, Marine."

As Joey is finishing up his breakfast sandwich, an elderly lady named Rea Steen, who is an old friend of Joey's family, comes into the store. Mrs. Steen and Joey's mom were the best of friends. Both families were always at each other's houses all the time. The Steen's were like Joey's second mom and dad. She sees Joey and strolls to him with her arms out. Joey stands smiling at her and they embrace. After a few moments, she steps back, saying, "Joey Morris, I'm so happy to see you." Joey replies, "Mrs. Steen, it has been a long time, and I sure did miss you and Mr. Leo while I was away." Mrs. Steen puts her hand on Joey's face, then says, "both of us prayed for you all the time when you were in the service. We prayed for all the men and women in all the armed forces. And we're both so glad to have you home," Joey, then says, "thanks so much for your prayers. I assure you they helped." Mrs. Steen looks at Joey smiling. Then, she asks him, "Joey, are you planning to go deer hunting anytime soon?"

Joey replies, "yes ma'am. I was planning to go bow hunting later this week." Mrs. Steen puts her hand on Joey's arm, saying, "Leo is not able to hunt anymore, and we don't have any deer meat. I was hoping you could get us one for this winter. I would pay you for all your trouble." Joey takes her arm, then says, "Mrs. Steen, you don't worry about a thing. Since I was planning to go this week, the first one will be for you and Mr. Leo." She hugs his neck and says, "God bless you, Joey." "You don't worry about a thing. We'll have your freezer filled up this week. How about that," Joey, says. She hugs his neck again, saying, "everybody is so happy to have you back on this mountain."

Joey says, with a tender smile, "I appreciate you saying that Mrs. Steen." Joey goes and retrieves his groceries and then steps over to the deli counter, and says to Bailey, "I enjoyed that sausage biscuit, Bailey. It was terrific." She turns around with a lovely smile, saying, "I'm glad you enjoyed it, Joey. Come back for lunch sometimes, and I'll fix you a sandwich!" "I'll sure do that. Goodbye now," Joey replies. He starts to leave the store, saying goodbye to Wilson, and all the men that are there still telling their exaggerated stories. He walks to his Jeep, putting the groceries in the back of the vehicle, and starts back to his cabin.

Later that evening, Jessie arrives at Joey's cabin. He backs his truck to the barn where he will hook-up the log splitter to his trailer hitch. Joey hears Jessie's truck and walks out of the cabin, going out to greet Jessie. Jessie is hooking up the log splitter, then says, "got it hooked up." "Keep it as long as you need," Joey says to Jessie. Jessie then says, "before I go, I want to give you your scrapbook." Jessie walks to his truck door and leans in to get the scrapbook. He walks back to Joey, giving him his keepsake. Joey takes it, then looks down at it with a sorrowful look. Jessie looks at Joey with a compassionate expression, saying, "look at it when you're ready. See you later." Jessie walks to his truck, putting his hand on the door handle. Joey looks up at Jessie, still with a sad expression, saying, "thanks again, Jessie." Jessie looks back at him and smiles. Then, he gets in his truck and leaves.

Joey walks back to the cabin and grabs some wood for the fireplace before he goes into the den. He puts the scrapbook on a home-made coffee table that is constructed out of beautiful cedar. Joey puts the firewood in the wood rack next to the fireplace. He opens a small cedar box getting some kindling wood to start the fire and lighting the kindling with a long match. As the small wood begins to blaze, Joey puts the firewood on top of the fire. Soon he has a roaring fire going. He goes into his kitchen to prepare something for dinner. After his dinner, he goes to his gun case and gets his dad's cross-bow.

It's bow season in Colorado now, and he decides to go for Mrs. Steen's deer first thing in the morning. He will use a cross-bow because he doesn't want to take the chance of hurting his shoulder. He makes sure everything is alright with the bow then gathers up several arrows laying them on his couch. It's nine o'clock that evening, and Joey is sitting in his large recliner that sits to the right of the fireplace. He is listening to a radio station that is broadcasting from the nearby town of Craig, on his Dad's old F.M. radio.

Joey looks over to the scrapbook that he laid on the coffee table. After a few moments, he decides to try to look at it. Joey walks over to the ceder table and picks up the scrapbook. He sits on the couch and then opens it started from the beginning. He sees all his pictures and newspaper clippings about him and all the letters he wrote to her. She always wrote something under everything she glued in it. And tears start to form when he sees over the years that her writing began to deteriorate. Joey saw the last picture that she posted of him, and her penmanship was hardly legible. This picture was the last she was able to put in the scrapbook. And this was when she gave the album to Jessie. Jessie kept it up till Joey got back home. He closes the book because he doesn't want to see anything of his last year in the Marines.

He gets up, putting the scrapbook between some books in a bookcase by his bed. He goes and turns off the radio and puts more wood on the fire. He puts on an old hooded sweatshirt and sweatpants that he had since high school. He has been wearing this outfit to bed when he was home ever since he returned. He then decides that he will buy two more sets of sweats when he goes into Craig the next time. The sweats have become too big for him because he was more massive in high school than he is now. He wants to retire these that he has on now because of the sentimental value. He puts a giant backlog in the fireplace. Then he places split wood on top of the big piece of wood. The backlog will burn all night, keeping it warm in the den. He sets his alarm for four-thirty in the morning for he can get to his favorite hunting area. He pulls a sizeable home-made quilt over him that his mother made for him and falls asleep.

Early the next morning, his alarm clock goes off. He gets up, putting on his hunting clothes plus his hunter's orange vest and stocking cap. Joey doesn't have to wear hunter orange colors in Colorado when bowhunting, but he wears it anyway. Joey goes to the kitchen to get some beef jerky and water that he always carries with him when he hunts. Joey then picks up the cross-bow and arrows and goes to the gun case retrieving a forty-four magnum revolver and ammunition. He never goes into the woods without a large caliber revolver. He hopes that he will never have to use it except in an extreme emergency. For instance, a bear or mountain lion attack. He straps the revolver holster around his waist then puts extra ammunition in his pocket. He leaves out the front door and closes the locked door and looks at the thermometer where it reads twenty-one degrees.

He walks to the barn and hears the snow crunching as he walks to open the barn's doors. He opens the doors and gets in his UTV (four-wheel-drive utility, all-terrain vehicle, with a cab). He puts the bow in the back seat of the UTV. Joey then puts a deer drag sled in the bed of the vehicle. He cranks up the UTV and pulls out. Joey stops and gets out to close the barn doors. He gets in the cab and turns on the heater. His favorite hunting area is located on his land, about four miles from his cabin. They haven't had any significant snow yet, but he knows there will be plenty later in the month.

The sun has come up over the mountains, and he stops his vehicle at his deer hunting area. It's always an incredible pleasure for him to look down into one particular valley. He sees the sizeable rocky brook and waterfall that he played and hunted around almost every day when he was younger. And it never ceases to amaze him how beautiful this place is. And sometimes he walks down to the brook. To sit and take in the beauty and wonder of this special place. And with all its sights and sounds, it emits. Joey doesn't know how much this beautiful place is helping with his PTSD. Joey doesn't know this now. But this is the place where his life will start to change one day. He starts to leave and looks down in the valley again one more time. This time, a strange and wonderful feeling comes over him. He has never felt a sense like this before in his life.

He starts for his hunting area and parks a little distance from his deer stand. He gathers all the hunting gear putting it all on the drag sled. Joey pulls the deer sled to his tree-stand. When he arrives at the stand, he takes a rope that he got from the UTV and ties it around his cross-bow. Joey climbs the ladder with the rope tied around his waist. Then he goes under the safety bar and sits on the stand seat. He pulls the bow up and catches it when it reaches the top. Joey is using all the safety techniques that his father taught him a long time ago. When he gets all settled in, he places four arrows in the arrow holder that's attached to the bow. Joey pulls back the bowstring cocking it in place. He then loads an arrow in the barrel and then looks through the bow's scope sight.

He has seen a few doe's, but he is waiting for something bigger. About an hour later, a large six-point buck walks up into his shooting area. He lifts his bow very slow to aim and waits for the deer to get closer. The deer comes up to about fifteen feet of his stand. Joey centers the buck in the scope then pulls the trigger, releasing the arrow. It's a great shot, hitting the deer above the left shoulder. The deer runs off, and now it's time for Joey to track the animal.

Joey lets the bow drop from the stand with the rope and then climbs out of the tree. He gets the deer sled and tracks the blood trail of the wounded buck. Joey finds the deer about thirty yards from his stand. He pokes the deer with his bow carefully. This practice is to make sure that the deer was dead. Joey loads the buck on the sled and then pulls it to where his UTV is parked. He arrives at the vehicle and uses a winch crane that is attached to the UTV. And loads the deer in the back. Later he arrives at his cabin and backs the UTV up to his dad's truck. He uses the crane to load the deer into the bed of the truck. He gets in and buckles his seatbelt and heads to Craig to take the deer to a meat processor.

Joey arrives at Carson's meat processors and goes into the building. As he walks in, he doesn't see anyone. Joey then shouts, "anybody working today?" A few moments later, Dan Carson walks out with a big smile, saying, "Joey Morris! I was wondering when you were going to bring me some meat. It's sure has been a while!" Joey and Dan went to high school together, and they have always been great friends. They shake each other's hands, then Dan says, "Joey, I heard that you retired from the Marines, and you were back living on the mountain. Great to have you back." Joey says, "great to be back, Dan. Look, I have a six-point in the back of my dad's truck, and I want you to process it special for me." Dan says with a questionable look, speaking, "special?" Joey replies, "Dan, you and your father have always processed our deer. But this meat will be going to someone else this time." Dan says, "who is this person if I may ask?" It's going to be for Rea and Leo Steen. He cannot hunt anymore, and this deer meat will be for them."

Dan walks over to the processing door and tells his two employees, "Jamie, Timmy, go get that six-point out of Mr. Morris's truck." Dan turns to Joey, saying, "are the keys in the truck?" Joey replies, "there is no need. I've already got the truck backed into the alley." Dan turns to the door again and shouts, "the deer is in the truck. And already backed into the alley ." Dan turns to Joey, saying, "how do you want your meat?" Joey replies, "Dan, didn't Mr. Steen always bring his deer to you?" Dan says, "yes, he did, and always got it processed the same way." Joey then says, "do you remember how you processed it?" With a big smile, Dan says, "I sure do."

"Prepare it just like Mr. Steen always ordered it," says Joey. Dan takes out an ordering pad and starts writing Joey's order on it. Then Dan says, "will Friday at one o'clock be okay?" Joey nods his head, saying, "Friday at one o'clock will be fine. I'll see you then." Joey shakes Dan's hand and turns to walk out the door. Dan stops him, saying, "Joey, this is a kind thing you are doing for Mr. and Mrs. Steen. And one thing else, we all thank you for your service!" Joey smiles and walks out the door.

He arrives at his cabin, and he hears Wilson calling him from his store on the C.B. radio. Joey walks into his kitchen, where he has a C.B. base station on the kitchen counter. He picks up the mic, saying, "go ahead, Mr. Wilson." Wilson radios back, saying, "your banker called saying he needs to talk to you asap. Over." Joey laughs because Wilson still uses military radio lingo when he talks on the C.B. This is from the years he was in the Army. Joey, then says, "okay, I will be at the store in twenty minutes." Joey smiles and says, "over and out." Joey takes his hunting clothes off and puts on his comfortable clothes. He walks out to his Jeep and heads for Wilson's store.

When he arrives, Joey takes out his cell phone and sees that he is getting good cell phone reception. He then calls his banker, Jerry Sanders. Jerry's secretary answers and says, "Mr. Sanders office." Joey then says, "Ashley, this is Joey Morris returning Jerry's call." Ashley says, "Oh, hello, Mr. Morris. One moment, please. Jerry answers, saying, "well, hello Joey! It's been a while and good to have you home." "It's good to hear from you, Jerry. What's up," replies Joey. Jerry says, "we need to meet with Mike Richmond. He's the CEO of the corporation that bought the land from your mother last year. Can you come down here at the main bank in Grand Junction as soon as possible?"

"What about," Joey says with a concerned voice. Jerry then says, "well, Joey, to be honest. It concerns a problem that concerns you during a serious computer crash they had. It happened when they were buying the land from your mother. We need for you to meet with us face to face on this matter." Joey has a severe tone in his voice, saying, "Mike, you're getting me quite concerned about what you just said." Jerry, replies calmly, "no, Joey. I assure you that there is nothing wrong. It's an outstanding problem for you. But we need to get together on this." Joey has a relieved expression, then says, "I will be in Grand Junction next Tuesday so we can set up a meeting then. But I need to tell you about my appointment at the V.A. It's at eleven o'clock that morning." Jerry replies, "that will be fine. What about nine o'clock that morning?" Joey says, "I'll have to get up at four o'clock that morning to be at your office by nine. But I'll be there." Jerry says, "that sounds good, Joey, and I'll see you, then…bye." "Take care," says Joey.

Joey is a little hungry, so he goes into the store to get something to eat. He greets the men sitting around the stove. He says hello to Mr. Wilson, then Wilson says, "did you get a hold of your party on your cell phone?" Joey says, "yes, sir. And thanks for getting in touch with me." "No problem whatsoever," replies Wilson. Joey walks over to the Deli counter to get a sandwich. Bailey, with her lovely smile, says, "hey, Joey. What can I get for you?" Joey looks down at all the meats in the meat case then remembers what Jessie told him. Joey looks at Bailey and says, "why don't you prepare for me one of those Reuben sandwiches that you're so famous for." "Coming right up," replies Bailey. As she is preparing his sandwich, Joey goes over to the soft drink case and pulls out a six-pack of cola. He goes back to the deli counter while he waits on his sandwich. Bailey is through preparing his lunch, and she wraps the Reuben up, giving it to Joey. Joey's eyes get real big because the sandwich is massive. He says to her, "wow, Bailey. I don't think I can eat all of this." Bailey leans her head across the counter and whispers to Joey, "I put extra corned beef on your sandwich, but don't tell Mr. Wilson." Joey smiles, saying, "I want sweetheart." He takes the sandwich and cola up to the counter and pays Mr. Wilson. He leaves and gets in his Jeep for the ride back to his cabin.

Friday arrives and Joey leaves for Craig going to Carson's to pick up the deer meat he left there. When he gets to Carson's, the meat is ready and all packaged up ready for the freezer. Joey leaves Carson's and goes to Mr. and Mrs. Steen's house. When Joey arrives at their home, he goes up on their porch and knocks on the door. Mrs. Steen answers the door, saying, "well, hey, Joey. How are you today." Joey says, "I have your deer meat for you. I'll start to bring it in and put it in your freezer." Mrs. Steen is amazed, then says, "you already have it processed?" "Yes, ma'am. Just the way you and Mr. Steen like it," replies Joey. Mrs. Steen says, "Joey, I don't know how to say thank you for what you have done for us." Joey smiles, saying, "you don't have to say anything. The freezer still in the utility room?" "Still in the same place its been for over fifty years," says Mrs. Steen.

Joey goes out to his truck and removes the four large boxes of venison taking it to the utility room. Mrs. Steen tells Joey how she likes the meat stocked. Later, Joey puts the last of the venison in the freezer, saying, "I don't think we can get another piece of meat in that freezer." He closes the lid, and Mrs. Steen, says, "how much do I owe you for the processing and for your time?" Joey gets a pleasant expression on his face, then says, "there's no charge Miss Rea." Rea starts to cry, saying, "Joey, you are the sweetest young man we know. Thank you for what you have done for Leo and me.

Joey takes her frail, wrinkled face in his hands, looking at her with a big smile saying very sweetly, "Miss Rea, you and Mr. Leo were always great friends to my parents and me. And always remember you were part of the best years of my life." Rea hugs him and kisses on the cheek, saying, "I'm so glad that you came back to all of us safely. And like I said before, Leo and I prayed for you every night." Joey looks around with a slight smile then looks back at Mrs. Steen, saying, "well, God heard those prayers, because here I am." She hugs his neck again, then Joey says, "before I go, I want to sit and visit with Mr. Leo." "He's in the den, and I know he will love to see you," replies Mrs. Steen.

As they start to leave for the den, Rea turns to Joey, saying, "Joey, I don't want to pry in your private life. But I've known you all my life, and I'm old, so I'm just going to say it anyway. Joey laughs as she says, "you need a fine, young, Christian woman to stand at your side. You don't need to be on that mountain all by yourself." Joey looks down with a slight grin. Then looks back up to Rea, saying, "Miss Rea, I've been out of practice with women for many years now. I probably wouldn't know what to do." Rea let's out a loud laugh, saying, "Joey, love is like remembering to spit downwind. You never forget how to do it." Joey laughs, then says, "I never heard that saying put that way before." Rea says, "my momma use to say that all the time. She leads Joey to Mr. Leo, sitting in his recliner with a breathing tube under his nose. Joey hugs him and then sits in a chair to talk to him and Miss Rea for a few hours.

Chapter Three

Joey's Trip To The V.A. Hospital

It's Monday night the next week, and it's about eight o'clock in the evening. Joey is in his recliner, reading a book listening to the radio. The announcer at the radio station breaks in the music for a weather bulletin. The announcer is saying that the National Weather Service has issued a winter weather warning for the Craig and surrounding areas for up to six to eight inches of snow. He starts thinking back on what Mrs. Steen told him about being alone up here. Deep down, Joey would love to have a special lady to share his life with that Miss Rea suggested to him. After a few moments, he gets his Bible that is on the second shelf on the stand by his recliner. The Bible is the one that his mother gave him. And it was with him in his years in the Marines. He hasn't read it since he got home, but he wants to look something up. He is curious about what the good book has to say about a wife.

He finds in Proverbs eighteen: twelve, which says: "he who finds a wife finds a good thing and obtains favor from the Lord." Joey starts to think that this might be a little difficult for him to find this lady because he thinks all the real, sincere, Christian women are engaged or already married. And he stays on this mountain most of the time, so he doesn't have the time for companionship with a lady. He looks up with a smirk and kind of smart-aleck voice saying, "okay, God. If you have a lady in mind for me, how about sending her my way, and I will try to lead a life you want me too…deal?" He puts his Bible back beneath the stand and turns the radio off. He gets up, putting on his sweats, getting ready to go to bed. He walks over to the wood rack to get more firewood for the night. He lays a backlog and wood on the fire. He walks over to the bed, but before he gets in, he sets the alarm for the trip to Grand Junction. He climbs in bed, pulling the large quilt over him and falls asleep quickly.

Four o'clock arrives quickly, and the alarm rings. Joey climbs out of bed, getting dressed for the trip. He looks out his window seeing the snow that had fallen the night before. And he says to himself, "the weatherman was right." He walks out of his cabin, where it is still snowing very hard. To Joey, this snowfall is nothing compared to what he has seen most of his life on the mountain. He cranks the Jeep up by the remote key fob to have his Jeep warm for the two and a half hour trip. He is leaving a little early because the snow might make driving a little slow. He goes into his kitchen and gets a tall, insulated cup and fills it with coffee. He set his coffee maker timer last night to have the coffee ready when he got up. Ten minutes later, he leaves out the door and walks to his warmed-up Jeep. Grand Junction is about one hundred fifty miles away. He puts the Jeep in drive and putting the transmission into for four-wheel traction. He heads out down the snow-covered dirt road off the mountain, then about thirty minutes later gets on state highway thirteen. As he is driving, he thinks to himself how excellent the Jeep's traction is on the snow-covered road.

When he got about forty miles away from Craig, the snow has stopped, and he pulls the Jeep to the side of the road. He puts the transmission in the two-wheel-drive then leaves for Grand Junction. He arrives at his destination at eight-thirty and pulls into the State National Bank's parking lot. He sits in the Jeep for about fifteen minutes. Then Joey sees Jerry Sanders drive up and parks in his reserved parking bay. Jerry gets out of his truck, and Joey does the same. Joey then says in a loud voice, "hey, Jerry." Jerry turns around quickly, saying excitedly, "well, look who it is. Joey Morris! It's great to see you!"

Joey walks over to Jerry then both men shake hands. Jerry says, "come on in Joey, and let's get out of this cold." Jerry unlocks the door and deactivates the alarm. They go into the vast lobby of the bank, then Jerry says, "come on into my office. I'm sure you want some coffee." "That would be great," replies Joey. Jerry hangs his coat on his coat rack, then gets his coffee cup, then goes into the employee lounge. The coffee maker has already brewed the coffee, and Jerry opens up a cabinet under the counter. He gets a new bank logo ceramic mug and pours the coffee in the cups. He walks back to his office and hands Joey his mug, then Jerry goes and sits behind his desk. Jerry then says, "you can keep the mug as a small token of our appreciation for you and your late parents for being very loyal customers."

Joey takes a sip out of his mug, then smiles, saying, "you didn't get me down here to give me this mug, did you?" Jerry laughs and replies, "no, I'm afraid this matter of ours is going to be much larger than the mug." Joey has a questionable, curious expression, saying, "what's up then? I'm very concerned about what's going on, especially when it has to do with money. My money to be exact." Jerry smiles and says, "let's wait for Mike, and we'll get started." It's nine o'clock, and Jerry gets a call on his phone. His secretary tells him that Mr. Richmond was here, and Jerry tells her to send him in. Jerry gets up and opens the door, shaking Richmond's hand and welcoming him to the bank. Joey stands as Jerry says, "Joey, this is Mike Richmond. He is the CEO of Richmond Enterprises. His company bought the land from your mother." Joey stands, and Richmond shakes his hand.

Jerry tells all the men to sit down, then Jerry looks at Richmond, saying, "Mr. Richmond, I'll let you have the floor." Richmond looks at Joey, and says, "I'll get right to the point, Mr. Morris." Joey looks at Richmond, then says, "I'm sorry to be a smart-ass, but I think that's a good idea." Richmond says, "I can understand your concern, and no offense is taken. Joey, do you remember when your mother sold us that thousand acres of that pristine timberland last year?" Joey nods his head, saying, "of course I do. I talked to her about it when I was in

Afghanistan. We didn't discuss the price, but she had a good head for business. I said that it would be a good move and to go for it."

Richmond looks down a few moments, then looks up at Jerry. He then looks over to Joey, saying, "Joey, your mother never got paid by my company." Joey looks at Richmond with a stunned expression and calmly says, "why not?" Richmond looks at Joey for a moment, and Joey raises his arms with a concerned look, saying to Richmond, "Well?" Richmond, finally says, "at that time our computer accounting system failed company-wide, and your mother's direct deposit never happened. Even though our system was showing, it was deposited.

When our fiscal year ended, our accountants found surplus money in our land account that should not have been there. And that surplus money was to the penny the amount that was supposed to be paid to your mother. So I called the bank and talked to Jerry. And he verified that a deposit from us was never made in her account. And I'm so, so sorry about this horrible mistake." Jerry looks at Joey, saying, "your mother left you very well off. And when you would look at her finances, I guess you assumed that the payment was deposited last year. Since you didn't know the amount that was agreed upon between your mother and Mr. Richmond."

The next day after your mother signed all the papers, she had her stroke. Never knowing that the money was ever deposited. Joey looks at both of the men. Then looks directly at Richmond, saying, "well, Mr. Richmond, what do you intend to do about this matter?" Richmond says, "the money will be deposited in your account immediately after I make a call to my headquarters. Will you gentlemen excuse me while I make this call?" "By all means," says Joey. Richmond takes out his cell phone, pressing a number and a few seconds later, saying, "Sharon, I need to speak to Bill immediately." There are a few seconds of silence, then Richmond says, "Bill, deposit the funds immediately." After a few moments, Richmond puts his phone back in his inner coat pocket, saying to Joey, "it's done." Jerry checks to see if the funds have been deposited in Joey's account. Jerry turns to his computer and types in Joey's account number. Then he turns to Joey, saying, "it's in there."

Joey looks at Jerry, then says, "okay, what kind of money are we talking about?" Jerry looks at Richmond and says, "go ahead, Mr. Richmond." Richmond replies, "we thought it was the right thing to do by adding interest just as the bank would do if the money were in your account at the right time." Then Richmond reaches in his coat pocket again, pulling out his cell phone. He then presses the note app on his phone. Richmond looks at the total and puts the phone back in his coat pocket. He looks at Joey, and says, "the total, plus the interest, comes to one million, eight-hundred and twenty-five thousand, four hundred and twenty-six dollars and seventy-two cents.

Joey looks at Jerry and then to Richmond with a somber face. Not a face like what you would think that a person would have been told he just got close to two-million dollars. Joey thinks to himself that his great-grandfather bought all the family's land over many years for almost nothing. And I just received a significant sum of money for part of the land. Richmond looks at Jerry then at Joey, saying, "Mr. Morris, forgive me for saying this, but you're not acting like a man that just received over one point-eight-million dollars." Joey looks at Richmond, saying, "Mr. Richmond, my great-grandfather paid almost nothing for all that land. He, my grandfather, and father worked that land very hard to make into a very successful, lucrative timber business. I think it's ironic that I had just a little part in the business when I worked at our timber mills when I was young. And now, I'm getting a great sum of money for hard work from great past family members and employees." Richmond smiles and says to Joey, "that was well-said son."

Joey gets up, shaking Richmond's hand and says, "thank you for what you did, Mr. Richmond." Richmond replies by saying, "thank you, Mr. Morris, for your understanding in this matter. And we thank you for your service to our country." "You're welcome, Mr. Richmond," replies a grateful Joey. Joey walks over to Jerry and shakes his hand, saying, "thanks, Jerry, for what you did for me." Jerry nods his head with a big smile, saying, "Joey, it was my pleasure to help." Joey turns around, heading for the office door, then turning to Jerry and Richmond, saying, "I know I won't see you anytime soon, but enjoy the holidays that are coming up soon." Jerry replies, "and the same to you!"

It's ten o'clock, and Joey decides to go on to the V.A., thinking that he might get in to see his therapist early. Then he shakes his head laughing, saying to himself, "in your dreams Joey Morris. Thinking I will get in early to a V.A. appointment!" He gets in his Jeep, driving to the V.A. He arrives in about thirty minutes early but uses his extra time trying to find a parking space. He has to park about an eighth of a mile down the street and walks to the hospital. He arrives and goes through security and takes the elevator to the third floor. He gets off the elevator, and about ten veterans are waiting to see the same doctor. It's one fifteen that afternoon. Then Joey is called into the doctor's office, where he remains another thirty minutes. His psychiatrist sees him for about ten minutes. Joey then goes to see his phycologist, where he waits again. Later the door opens, and Dr. Stephenie West says, "Joey, would you come in please." Joey walks into her office, and he waits till Dr. West sits, and she says, "please relax and make yourself comfortable, Joey.

Dr. West is writing in her computer tablet and then looks at Joey and says, "how's it been going?" Joey smiles, saying, "it feels like I'm getting better. My flashbacks and night-terrors are subsiding. Dr. West looks at him nodding her head, smiling, saying, "it looks like you are slowly managing to adjust to your PTSD, and that is wonderful. Many veterans are leading an almost normal life now by telling me things like you just said. They still will occasionally have small flashbacks, but nothing like they had when they first came to see me. There is no magic pill out there, but you have to decide that this is not going to defeat you. You have to tell yourself that I have already been in many battles when I served in the Marines. And I'm going to handle those battles the best I can when I return home."

Joey smiles at her then says, "I never thought about my problem like that, and thanks. But sometimes I think to myself, will I have any problems tomorrow? And I get depressed when I think about that." Dr. West looks at Joey with a caring expression, saying, "Joey, always remember that there is no such thing as tomorrow." Joey looks at Dr. West with tears forming in his eyes, saying, "Dr. West, no pill could ever help me like the words you just spoke to me." "Joey words can be wonderful things," she says.

Dr. West then asks him, "Joey, I need to ask you something personal, and you can answer the question if you feel comfortable with it. Are you a man of faith?" Joey takes a deep breath saying, "well, I went to church when I was young, but when I joined the Marines, it got put on hold. I had a bible when I was in the Marines, and occasionally, I would read it. And I talked to God sometimes, especially before dangerous missions. But near the end of my twenty years without any major physical injuries, I thought to myself that maybe God listened." Dr. West smiles and says, "Joey, when I said there is no such thing as tomorrow, do you know where those words are based on?" Joey shakes his head, replying, "no, ma'am, I don't." Dr. West has this smiling but calm look, saying, "I based that on a passage that is in the bible. It's in Matthew six: thirty-four. Christ says, "don't worry about tomorrow. For tomorrow will bring its own worries. Today's trouble is enough for today. In my private practice, I have a faith-based therapy program that works very well for anybody's problems that they might have."

It looks like I need to pick up the bible more often to help me out during troubles. I'm not just talking about my PTSD but everyday life," replies Joey with a slight smile. Dr. West shrugs her shoulders, saying, "It won't hurt anything by checking it out more often, Joey." She types some more in her tablet then says, "have you been keeping up with your medication properly?" Joey smiled and said, "Dr. Townsend is gradually taking me off one of my stronger medications. And I know I will have to take some of my medication for the rest of my life. But I hope that someday, something will happen in my life to help me get off all my meds." Dr. West has a thrilled look on her face and nodding her head then says to Joey, "I'm very proud of you, Joey. I have a strange feeling that someday something wonderful will happen to you. That is if you let it happen." Joey smiles and replies, "thank you for those comforting words, Dr. West, and I hope your right." You have helped me more than you will ever know." "Thank you, Joey," replies Dr. West.

Dr. West stands up, and Joey does likewise. Then she says, "it's time for our group therapy. Are you ready to go?" Joey nods his head, saying, "yes, ma'am. The group session is the best part of my therapy." Dr. West says, "let's go, shall we." Joey smiles and waves his hand toward the door saying to her, "after you ma'am." "Still such a gentleman," replies Dr.

West. They walk down the hall then entering into the group session room. Joey sees his friends that have been in group therapy for months, and they all greet each other. Joey notices three new members of the group. They are all women. He always thought to himself that war-time PTSD only effects men. He knows now that he has been wrong. They all sit, then Dr. West says, "everybody we have three new members of the group if you haven't already noticed. May I introduce Kristen, Melody, and Eva. They served in the Navy as nurses in field hospitals. Let's give them a warm welcome, shall we!" All the men come up to the ladies welcoming them. And each man tells each lady their names. Joey notices that the women are nervous, not knowing what's all in store for them.

After thirty minutes, the group break for snacks that the hospital provides for the meetings. Joey is getting a donut when Kristen walks up to him, saying, "your Joey, right?" Joey smiles and says, "yes, ma'am." Kristen has a scared, concerned look then says, "Joey, does this group therapy work?" Joey puts his donut down and looks at Kristen with a smiling, compassionate look, saying, "sure it does, Kristen. The group session is the best part of my therapy. Sometimes we all go out together to eat or visit different places and have the best of times. This past summer everybody came up to my house having a great time. Kristen, you will find out that all of us have the same problem. We care for each other very much. And that, to me, is the best medicine you can take." Kristen smiles and says, "thanks, Joey, for making me feel better, and I will pass it on to the other girls." Joey has a big smile saying, "can I get you something to eat and drink?"

After the group session is over, Joey leaves the hospital and starts walking to his Jeep. He hears someone calling his name. Joey looks across the street, and it is an old acquaintance that Joey knew once knew in high school. Shawn Bryant. Shawn was just a casual friend who Joey didn't dislike, but he knows that Shawn could be a problem back in the day. Shawn runs across the street and gives Joey a man hug then steps back, saying, "Joey Morris, man, it's good to see you!" "It's good to see you also, Shawn," replies Joey. Shawn then says, "I heard that you retired from the Marines. What were the chances of us see each other here in Grand Junction! What are you doing here?"

Joey replies, "I had an appointment at V.A. hospital. Joey then says, "I heard you married Linda Richton?" Joey looks off, smiling, and says, "boy was in love with that pretty, sweet girl ever since elementary school. But she was one of those wonderful girls I let slip through my fingers. You're a fortunate man, Shawn," How is she, by the way?" Shawn looks at Joey a little strange and says, "ahh…she's doing okay." Joey then says, "how many kids do you and Linda have?" Shawn replies with a laid-back expression and says, "we have two girls, ages ten and seven. We also have a son who is two." Joey then has a strange feeling that comes over him. Shawn is just not acting right when they discussed Linda and their kids.

Shawn lights up, saying, "Hey, let's go for a drink. You remember that old hotel on Main Street in old downtown we used to go to when we were in school?" "Yea, I remember," says Joey. Shawn then says, "a rich investor bought it about ten years and turned it into a very luxurious hotel. They have the best bar in town with gorgeous women always hanging around in there." Joey thinks to himself that Shawn hasn't grown up any since high school. He still has the same attitude toward drinking and women. Joey then says to Shawn, "Shawn, I have a two and a half-hour drive, and I want to get home while the sun is still shining. And I have to get some plumbing supplies while I'm in town."

Shawn points down the street, saying, "Joey, there is a hardware store about three blocks down the street on the left. And you won't miss any time going back. So come on." "No, I need to get going," replies Joey. Shawn gets a disappointed look on his face, saying, "come on, Joey. I get off in thirty minutes, and I'll meet you there at four o'clock. It will be great to reminisce about the great times we had." Joey knows that he didn't spend that much time with Shawn, but he relents feeling sorry for the guy. Joey sighs then says, "okay, Shawn. I'll meet you there at four o'clock but only for a short time. "That's great, Joey, and I'll see you then," says Shawn.

Shawn walks back across the street, going to his office, and Joey says to himself, "I have a good feeling that this is not going to turn out well." Joey arrives at his Jeep, getting in, then heads to the hardware store. Joey sees the store and pulls in a parking space in front of the store. He steps out of his vehicle then walks into the store. He stops right inside the door and sees that the store is stocked with everything at everything you could imagine. The hardware store looks like it was around during the old days. He even notices a horse-drawn plow. At that time, a jovial older gentleman comes up to him, saying, "hey there young fellow I'm Daniel! What can I show you today?" Joey looks around then looks at Daniel, saying, "Mr. Daniel is there something in here that you don't have? I even see a horse-drawn plow." Daniel looks at the plow and then back to Joey, saying, "that's for the Amish that comes to town sometimes. They travel a long way to come to Grand Junction about every three months. They come here instead of Montrose. The Amish men say they come here because of my store." Joey has a questionable look then says, "I didn't know there were Amish in Colorado?" "Sure they are. They settled in the San Luis Valley around the turn of the nineteenth century," says Daniel.

Daniel then says, "what can I get for you today?" Joey burrows his brow then says, "I'm going to need some pipe insulation and heating cord." Daniel smiles, saying, "right this way, sir!" "Oh, I'm sorry, Mr. Daniel, for not introducing myself. I'm Joey Morris," says Joey. Daniel shakes his hand and says, "it's my pleasure, Joey! You're not from around here, are you?" Joey replies, saying, "no, sir. I'm from Craig. I come here for my appointments at the V.A." Daniel shakes Joey's hand again, saying, "what branch?"

"Marines," replies Joey with a smile. Daniel looks at Joey with a proud smile saying, "I was in the Navy during the Vietnam era. I served on the U.S.S Forestal. C-V fifty-nine for the most part." Joey looks down and then looks up, saying, "if I remember Navel history correctly, the Forestal was a very famous carrier with many battle stars." Daniel looks away for a few moments then turns and looks at Joey with a sad face, saying, "I was on her in nineteen-sixty-seven when that rocket accidentally fired from that fighter jet. Starting that deadly fire that killed two good friends of mine." Daniel rolls up his sleeve showing a badly scared arm and hand saying with a very woeful tone, "I was right there when it happened. And I will never forget that horrible tragedy." Daniel looks down, shaking his head, and Joey, with his compassionate heart, puts his hand on Daniels' shoulder, sadly saying, "I know how you feel, Mr. Daniel. I have PTSD, and that's why I come to the V.A." Daniel looks up with a sad face, saying, "at least someone now is out there trying to make a difference with our veterans returning home. We didn't get any help whatsoever."

Daniel realizes they need to get off this subject then quickly smiles, saying, "now let's go get your supplies." They walk up to the plumbing supply area, then Daniel says, 'okay, Joey, what do you need? Joey replies by saying, "I need at least three twelve-foot heating cords. Twenty feet of insulating pipe wrap and three rolls of duct tape. I want the silver-backed tape if you have it." "Not a problem," replies Daniel. Daniel goes to different areas picking up Joeys order. Then Joey asks Daniel, "Mr. Daniel, do you need some help?" Daniel laughs and says, "this is nothing. Meet me at the counter."

Joey and Daniel walk to the front counter, and Daniel passes the barcodes over the code reader. Daniel looks at Joey and says, "that will be seventy-three dollars and twenty-two cents, please, sir." Joey pulls out a one-hundred-dollar bill and hands it to Daniel. Daniel takes the money and says, "your change will be twenty-six dollars and seventy-eight cents." Daniel gives Joey his change and says, "let me help you with that." Joey replies, "Oh, this is nothing, Mr. Daniel." Daniel laughs, and Joey gathers up all his supplies. Daniel then says, "please come back the next time your in town. And thanks for your service." Joey looks at him with a compassionate smile, saying, "thank you for your service, Mr. Daniel." Joey gets to the door then turns back to Daniel, saying, "Is there a coffee shop around this area?" Daniel says, "you're in luck, Joey. There's a shop, two doors down. Just take a left when you go out of my doors. Joey then says, "thanks again." Joey takes his supplies out to his Jeep and puts everything in the back. He looks down the street seeing the coffee shop, then shuts the rear of his vehicle and walks to the shop.

He walks in the coffee shop and sees this massive chalkboard that he thinks has to have over two-hundred types of coffee types. A teenage girl comes up to Joey with a beautiful smile, saying, "hello, welcome to The Daily Grind. I'm Jessica. What can I get for you today?" Joey looks at the massive order board behind her and says, "Jessica, do you have just plain old-fashioned coffee? Jessica replies, "Oh, yes, sir. What size do you want? Joey shrugs his shoulders, then saying, "how about a large. And do you have cups that are insulated well because I have a long trip."

Jessica has a questionable look then saying, "well, the cups are pretty thick, but I tell you what. I'll put two cups together for you, and that should do it." Joey smiles and says, "that's very considerate of you, Jessica." Jessica produces her beautiful smile again and says in a slight, flirty tone, "that will be four-dollars and fifty-two cents. And no charge for the extra cup." Joey gives her a ten-dollar bill and says, "keep the change for being so nice." Jesica smiles and says, "well, thank you, sir, that's so sweet of you." She turns around to the coffee dispenser and puts two cups together then puts the cups under the coffee dispenser. She fills the cups and places a lid on the inside cup. She hands the cup to Joey. She then says, "I think this will keep hot for a good while." Joey takes the coffee, saying, "thanks, Jessica." Joey starts to leave, and Jessica says with her flirty voice, "do please come back and see me now." Joey turns and rolls his eyes and leaves. Then Jessica says to herself, "now that was a nice looking older guy." Joey gets in his Jeep and leaves to go to the hotel to meet Shawn.

Chapter Four

Joey Rescues Amanda

Joey arrives at the hotel, seeing that they have valet parking. He pulls under the canopy in front of the hotel then stops leaving the engine running. Joey gets out of the Jeep where a valet comes up to him, saying, "welcome to the Annebridge Hotel, sir!" The valet hands him a parking stub then gets in the Jeep, driving to the valet parking area. Joey walks to the front door as a doorman opens the door for him, saying, "welcome to the Annebridge, sir!" Joey walks in the large lobby then he looks to his left, seeing the lounge. He walks inside the lounge where a young woman host says, "good afternoon sir. Would you like to sit at the bar or a table?" Joey replies, "a table, please. I'm meeting someone in a few minutes." The host smiles, saying, "then please follow me, sir." She takes Joey to a small table near the front end of the bar, and she then says, "will this be okay, sir?" Joey smiles and says, "this will be fine. Thank you." "Your server will be with you momentarily," says the host.

A few moments past and a server to his table, saying, "good afternoon, may I take your order? Joey says to the server, "I have someone meeting me, but I'll go ahead and order. Do you have lime Perrier water?" The server says, "of course, sir. Do you want me to bring it to you now, or do you want to wait until your guest arrives?" "Bring it to me now, and I'm sure he will order when he gets here," replies Joey. The server says, "I'll have your Perrier out to you right away, sir!" Joey smiles at him, saying, "thank you."

As Joey is waiting, the doorman opens the door, and a beautiful young woman walks in. The young woman stops for a moment looking around the lounge area. As she is looking in the lounge, she makes eye contact with Joey and gives him a slight smile. Joey feels like his heart skipped a beat when she smiled at him. She has long golden blonde hair with curly ends and indescribable big beautiful eyes and wearing a tight-fitting red dress. Joey thinks to himself that he is looking at the most beautiful woman he has ever seen. The woman sees the person who she is meeting in the back. But before going back to meet the person, the beautiful woman looks at Joey again and smiles. But Joey notices there is sadness in her eyes.

She walks to the back and sets down at a table where an older, distinguished-looking man is sitting. His server comes to Joey's table and sets his water in front of him with a glass and ice. Joey sees Shawn coming into the bar and says to the server, "my friend has just arrived, so stick around to take his order." The server replies, "of course, sir." Shawn sees Joey at the table, and Joey says to Shawn, "the server is here to take your order, Shawn." Shawn looks at the server having a broad smile saying, "double scotch on the rocks, please. No, make that two double scotches. And hurry! " "Yes sir," replies the server.

As the server walks off, Joey thinks to himself that Shawn hasn't changed his drinking ways from way back. Shawn looks at Joeys drink and says, "fancy water! Come on, have a drink with me!" Joey looks calmly at Shawn, saying, "I gave up drinking many years ago. Besides, I drank very little when I did drink, so I didn't miss much." The server comes to the table with Shawn's scotch. Then the server says, "enjoy your drinks, gentlemen." Shawn looks around the bar then turns to Joey, saying, "man, it sure is good to see you again, Joey. What have you been doing since you got out of the Marines?" Joey replies, "just getting the old homestead fixed up and looking out over my land. That's about it."

Joey looks over to where the beautiful woman is sitting. He looks at Shawn and nods his head to her table, saying, "Shawn, I wonder who that beautiful woman is over at that back table." Shawn looks at him funny, saying, "where?" Joey nods his head toward the woman's table, and Shawn looks back to where Joey is nodding. Shawn then says, "Oh, that's Amanda. You might say she works here." Joey then looks at Shawn, saying, "what does she do here?" Is she the manager? She has to do something crucial around here being that beautiful." Shawn starts laughing and says, "Joey, what did the Marines do to you, man?"

Joey has a questionable look at Shawn, saying calmly, "what did you mean, Shawn?" Shawn starts to drink his second scotch. He starts to laugh then says, "man, don't you know an escort girl when you see one? You being a Marine should know a woman like that at first glance." Shawn finishes his drink then says, "and I might add that she is a very high priced escort girl at that!" Joey looks down and sadly says, "I can't believe a woman that beautiful could do that."

Shawn is starting to get drunk from the two scotches. Then he says, "I should know. I have been a special friend of hers for about a year now. If you know what I mean." Joey stands and gets extremely angry at Shawn and shouts, "you have a wonderful sweet wife, not to mention three young children! And you do this to them?" Customers in the bar look at Joey, then Shawn says with a smirk on his face, "well, to tell you the truth Joey, Linda can't satisfy a man like me. Know what I mean by that?" Joey shakes his head with disgust, saying to Shawn, "no, Shawn. I don't know what you mean, but I have a pretty good idea, though."

Joey looks at Shawn with an angry expression and says, "you are a cheating, lying, jerk! And for that matter, you haven't changed one bit since high school!" Shawn stands up and sticks his finger into Joey's shoulder, saying, "I don't care if you were a tough special forces Marine. Nobody talks to me like that!" Joey is now very livid toward Shawn on what he said about cheating on Linda. Joey then says, "don't ever touch me again, Shawn!" Shawn sticks his finger in Joey's shoulder again, saying, "there I touched you. What are you going to do about it, hero Marine?"

Because Joey is so angry that Shawn has put his finger in his shoulder again, he goes into the Marine protective mode. He shoves his right fore and middle finger into Shawn's solar plexus. Shawn falls back in his chair, gasping for breath. The bar manager comes quickly up to Joey, saying, "what's going on here! Did you hit him! I'm calling security!" Joey says, "there's no need for that because I'm leaving." Joey reaches for his wallet out and throws a ten-dollar bill on the table. Joey then says to Shawn in an angry tone, "I know to the pit of my soul that when you get a drink in you, you take it out on, Linda. Probably the kids also. And if I ever hear of you abusing her and those kids, there's no place you can hide from me."

Joey leans down at Shawn, saying, "you know me, Shawn. You know my meaning. And everything I just said to you better sink in." Shawn looks up at Joey with a terrified expression saying nothing. Then Joey puts his hand on the manager's shoulder and very calmly says, "you can call security now and get them to get this jerk out of here."

Joey starts to leave but turns back and looks at Amanda, where she looks at him with a sorrowful look. He turns and walks out of the hotel and gives the valet his ticket stub. A few minutes later, the valet drives Joey's Jeep under the canopy, parking it in front of him. The valet gets out, and Joey gives him a tip. He gets in the Jeep, saying to himself, "I'm getting the heck out of this town!" Joey drives out and gets on Main Street, and then he shakes his head, saying, "dang! I forgot something at the hardware store. He drives back down the street and parks in front of the hardware store. He gets out walking in, and Daniel, with a surprised look, says, "wow, that was quick! You forgot something, didn't you." Joey smiles, saying, "yes, sir. I forgot to get about six tubes of outside insulation caulk."

Daniel smiles and says, "alright, follow me again!" They walk to the insulation department, and Daniel points to a particular brand saying, "people swear by this caulk, and it's the cheapest I have!" "Okay, give me six tubes, please, sir," says Joey. Daniel then says, 'do you need a caulking gun?" Joey sighs then smiles at Daniel, saying, "I have one somewhere, but I'm not going to look for it, so let me have one." Daniel picks up a six-pack case of caulk and then a good caulking gun. They walk up to the counter, and Daniel scans the items. Then Daniel says, "that will be thirty-nine-dollars and seventeen-cents please, Mr. Joey." Joey reaches for his wallet and gives Daniel a fifty-dollar bill. Daniel takes the money and says, "your change will be ten-dollars and eighty-three-cents."

He hands Joey his change, and he sees something on Daniels counter that he didn't see on his last trip. It's a donation jar for a local pediatric cancer hospital. Joey puts his change in the jar then reaches in his wallet, pulling a one-hundred-dollar bill, also putting it in the jug. Daniel looks down at the jar then looks back at Joey with a big smile, saying, "may God bless you, Joey." Joey smiles and walks out of the store. He puts his items in the back of his Jeep with his other supplies. He unlocks the vehicle, gets in, and cranks it up to head back home.

As he is driving down Main Street, he sees in the distance, Amanda. The beautiful woman he saw in the bar. There is a "seedy" looking man pointing his finger in her face. There also are four men around standing around Amanda, and it looks like she is crying. As Joey gets closer to the hotel, he starts to pay excellent attention to this situation. The man who had his finger pointed in Amada's face hits her on the side of the head, and she immediately drops to the sidewalk. As she is lying on the sidewalk, the man kicks her. At this time, as one would think, Joey automatically goes into Marine Raider mode. He stops his vehicle, gets out, then runs to where the injured woman is. The man who hits the woman sees Joey coming at him, and the man pulls out a pistol. The thug will soon discover he has made a big-time mistake.

Before the man can aim his weapon, Joey grabs the pistol with his left hand, turning the gun to his left then striking the man with his right forearm. This dislodges the pistol into Joey's hand, and he throws the weapon down a connecting street. Then Joey strikes him under his nose with the palm of his hand. The man is knocked out before he hits the sidewalk. Then two of the men run up to Joey, and one guy tries to though a punch. But Joey deflects his arm, then striking the man with a wrist to the side of his head. Right behind the ear. Then that man is knocked out, and he falls to the sidewalk.

Then Joey grabs the other man by the throat and violently runs him into a parked car. One of the other men runs up behind Joey and gets him in a headlock. Joey steps to the right to gain leverage and pulls his head out of the man's arm, where he gets behind the attacker. As Joey was performing this maneuver, he never let go of the man's arm. Joey runs the attacker's arm up between his shoulder blades, dislocating his shoulder. The man falls writhing and screaming with extreme pain. Joey then looks at the fourth man with a livid "killer" face, and the thug runs off down the street, having nothing to do with Joey.

Joey immediately comes to the aid of Amanda. He then sees that she is unconscious and bleeding out of her nose and ear. Then three men who saw everything that happened also come to her rescue. One man says, "hey, man, can we help? Can we call an ambulance?" Joey says to one of the men, "she can't wait for an ambulance." Amanda's once beautiful face is swelling and turning color. Joey says to the men with a very concerned raised voice, "where is the closest hospital?" One man says, "is that your Jeep out in the street?" "Yes," replies Joey. The man then says, "keep going east down Main Street for two blocks and turn right at North Seventh Street. The hospital is just over a couple of miles, and it will be on the left. You can't miss it!"

Joey picks up Amanda, who is still unconscious, takes her quickly to his vehicle. He manages to open the door and places her in the passenger seat very carefully. Joey puts the seatbelt around her, and she slumps over. He gets in the Jeep and carefully places his hand on her upper chest region to hold her up. Joey starts to the hospital, still holding her up. He is going very fast and even running stoplights. He turns onto North Seventh Street, and about halfway to the hospital, Amanda regains consciousness and begins cry in pain. Joey says to her, "hold on. We're almost to the hospital!" About five minutes later, Joey turns into the emergency entrance to the hospital. He stops at the emergency entrance doors and gets out of the Jeep running to her side of the Jeep. He then opens her door, and she is still crying in great pain as Joey unbuckles her seat belt.

As gentle as humanly possible, he removes her from her seat, and she screams in pain. He carries her inside the emergency room, yelling out, "I need help!" A nurse runs up to Joey then looks at Amanda with a sad face then saying, "follow me, sir!" She leads him into an emergency treatment room and says to Joey, "put her here on the exam table!" As Joey lays her gently down, she screams again." The nurse asks Joey, "what happened to Amanda?" Joey replies, "she was hit in the face then kicked while she was lying on the sidewalk." Joey looks questionable at the nurse. saying, "you know her?" The nurse says sadly, "all too well, sir. I'll go get Dr. Kellum right away!" Joey walks over to Amanda, where she is still crying in great pain. He looks over to the counter seeing some peroxide pads. Joey takes one of the pads, and tears open the wrapper. He gently wipes her blood-soaked hair off her forehead. Joey looks at her, saying in a very sorrowful voice, "how could any man do this to you."

The room's privacy curtain is moved back, and Dr. Bradley Kellum enters with his nurse Kathy Noland. Dr. Kellum looks down at Amanda, saying sadly, "Oh no, Amanda, not again." Nurse Noland inserts an I.V. into Amanda's arm and gives her a shot through the I.V. with a powerful painkiller. Dr. Kellum turns and looks at Joey, saying, "I'm Bradley Kellum." Joey replies, "Joey Morris." Dr. Kellum then asks Joey, "are you the one that brought Amanda here and, did you see this happen?" "Yes, sir," says Joey. Nurse Noland starts to cut Amanda's dress off, but before she begins, she tells Joey, "sir, you're going have to leave while Dr. Kellum examines her. There's a waiting room in the emergency department lobby. Dr. Kellum will come and tell you about Amanda when he completes his examination." Joey looks down at Amanda very concerned, but she is starting to settle down because the pain medication is starting to take effect. He turns and walks out of the room.

Joey finds the waiting room and sits down in a large padded chair. He notices that he has Amanda's blood on his shirt. Joey then looks up, saying with a sorrowful voice, "God…I don't talk to you much, but this prayer is not for me. It's for Amanda. I know she is hurt bad and she needs your help. Please let her be alright…please?" He leans forward and puts his elbows on his knees and chin in his hands. Then he forgot to say something then looks up. "Sorry, God, I forgot to say Amen. So Amen for my prayer." He leans back in the chair and tries to relax but to no avail. Joey gets up and starts pacing the waiting room.

A teenage boy with a freshly applied cast on his forearm asks Joey, "are you, okay man?" He looks at the young man, saying, "no, I'm not, but thanks for asking." The young man says, "if you want to talk about anything, my girlfriend says I'm a good listener." Joey stops and looks back at the young man smiling and says, "thanks, young man, and I can tell that your girlfriend has a great guy." The young man smiles, and Joey starts pacing again around the room. Joey can't understand why he is so concerned about this woman. Joey sits down after about ten minutes of pacing. He sits in a different chair, and then an older woman comes in the waiting area sitting next to him.

He leans forward with his hands clasped, and the lady introduces herself to him, saying with a calm smile, "hello, young man, I'm Vickie." Joey turns to her, saying, "I'm Joey." Vickie notices that Joey is very concerned then says to him, "I've noticed you are very concerned about someone Joey. It doesn't take a dummy to notice that you have someone in here you care very much for." Joey sighs then and looks at Vickie, saying, "Miss Vickie, that's what's so weird about all this. This young woman is hurt very badly, and I don't even know her. I'm feeling concerned as if she is some family member. Vickie puts her wrinkly frail hand on Joey's hand, saying, "Joey, God looks at humanity like we are a large family, even if we don't know that someone personally. You had compassion for this girl, and you are helping her in the best way. Think of how many times Jesus had compassion for his children, which is everybody."

Joey looks down then looks back at Vickie as he says, "Miss Vickie, I prayed for Amanda, but I haven't prayed a lot in the past. I don't know if God heard me." Vickie looks at him with a most reassuring smile and says to him, "Joey, did this prayer for this young lady come from your heart?" Joey nods his head, and confidently says, "yes ma'am, it did." Vickie has that reassuring smile then says, "do you believe he will heal her, and even sometimes he heals people immediately just as Jesus did?" Joey looks down again for a few moments then looks at Vickie, saying, "yes, ma'am, I know he can." She pats his hand, saying with a smile, "I have this on the highest authority that he heard your prayer."

Nurse Noland comes in waiting room looks at Joey, saying, "Mr. Morris?" Joey gets up quickly and walks to where the nurse is standing. Nurse Noland says to him, "Dr. Kellum can speak to you now, so follow me." They walk into the emergency department, and Dr. Kellum is sitting behind a long counter, entering into his tablet notes about Amanda. Dr. Kellum looks up and sees Joey. Then Dr. Kellum gets up, going around the counter to talk with him. Joey immediately asks Dr. Kellum, "how is she?" Dr. Kellum replies, "I sent her upstairs for an MRI for a full body scan and x-rays. But what I'm concerned about is she took a severe blow to the face. Were running diagnostics, especially on her head for possibly bleeding. These words are not what Joey wanted to hear, and he hangs his head. Dr. Kellum puts his hand on Joey's shoulder, saying, " I will let you know as soon as I get the results." Joey looks up, then says, "thanks, Dr. Kellum." Nurse Noland ask Joey politely if he would return to the waiting area.

As Joey is walking back to the waiting area, he wants to sit next to Vickie for her calm and reassuring words. As he enters the waiting room, he doesn't see Vickie. He looks at the teenager with the cast and says, "where did the elderly lady go? Did they call her back to the emergency department?" The young man looks at Joey with a questionable look, saying, "what lady?" Joey looks at the young man with a stunned expression, saying, "the lady that I was talking to right across from you." The young man looks at Joey very strangely, saying, "dude, I don't know what you're on, but you were freaking me out a while ago. You were talking like there was someone there sitting next to you."

Joey gets an exasperated tone with the young man saying, "I'm not on anything, man. I was talking to a lady that was sitting right next to me. You had to see her." The young man looks at Joey with an expression like Joey is having an emotional breakdown. Then the young man decides to back down from this situation by saying, "whatever dude." Joey is wholly baffled because he knows he was talking to a real lady. Joey walks back into the emergency department and sees Nurse Noland. He walks up and asks her, "nurse, when you came to get me a while ago, did you see an elderly lady sitting next to me?" The nurse shakes her head, saying, "no, I didn't see anyone."

Joey thinks he might be having a problem when Nurse Noland says, "Mr. Morris, you need to return to the waiting area now. Joey is entirely perplexed now on what has happened. He shakes his head and goes back to the waiting area. When Joey gets to the waiting room, the young man with the cast is being picked up by a woman who is probably is his mother. As the young man is leaving, the young man turns back, looking at Joey with a peculiar expression. Joey walks over to the chair where he was talking to Vickie. He knows that she was there talking with him.

Nurse Noland comes into the waiting area with a man, and she points to Joey, saying, "that's the young man that brought Amanda in." The man looks at Nurse Noland then says, "thank you, nurse." The man walks over to Joey stopping in front of him and extends his hand. Joey shakes his hand, and then the man pulls out a badge, saying, "Mr. Morris, I'm Detective Paul Staley with the Grand Junction Police. We got a call from this hospital saying they had a woman that had been assaulted." Joey says, "yes sir. I brought her in." Detective Staley asks Joey, "did you see Amanda being assaulted?" Joey nods his head, saying, "yes, sir, I saw the whole thing." Then Staley says, "can you tell me in detail all that happened to Amanda, please?" Then Staley sits down across from Joey.

Joey says, "it looks like to me that everybody around here knows Amanda but me." Joey looks around with a disgusted face, not wanting to tell Staley the details of the attack. But he knows that the police will need the information on the brutal attack. Joey looks at Staley, saying, "I first saw her this afternoon at the Majestic's lounge. When I left, I went to a hardware store. And when I was driving home, I saw her in front of the hotel. I saw a man with four men standing around him and Amanda. He was pointing his finger in her face. Then he hits her with his fist, and she fell to the sidewalk. Then the scum-bag kicked her." Staley says, "what did you do then?" Joey sighs then says, "when I saw him do that to her, I stopped my Jeep in the middle of the street. I don't remember anything after that until I was picking her up to take her to the hospital."

Staley looks at Joey with a solemn face and says, "Mr. Morris Amanda, as you may already know, is a very expensive escort girl. The man who beat her was her employer. His name is Ricky Prince, but he goes by the name is Rico. He runs a very discreet escort service in town. We've busted him many times, but he always beats the charges." Joey, with a confused look, says, "how does he always beat the charges detective?" Staley shakes his head, saying, "his girls never press charges because Rico is a dangerous man. The last time that I came up here after he assaulted Amanda, she told me she was going to quit Rico and start a new life. She probably told him she was quitting. And he did this to her." Joey then says, "have you been able to talk to her yet?" Staley says, "no, but I know she won't press charges against him. She is too scared to do that. Some of Rico's girls have come up missing over the years, and we never see or hear from them again. There is just no hard evidence to convict him."

Joey shakes his head, then says, "I would like to have another fifteen seconds with him!" Staley smiles and says to Joey sternly, "that low-life is going to mess up one day, and he will sit in prison for the rest of his life." Then Staley says to Joey, "Mr. Morris, I've been called to this hospital many times before because of Amanda. And I know from talking to her that she genuinely wants to start a new life." Staley looks at Joey, smiling, then saying, "maybe someone could help her out with that." Joey looks at Staley with a puzzled look on what he just said. Then Staley says, "a word of warning Mr. Morris. Like I said before that Rico is a dangerous man, and you took something from him and not to mention that you kicked his butt. He will want to take back what was once his and take revenge on you for what you did to him. And he will do this with any means possible. Be vigilant!"

Staley stands and then Joey does the same. Staley shakes Joey's hand and says, "thanks for all the information, Mr. Morris. Grand junction is a lovely place to live, but there is always somebody who wants to take advantage of a great place like this." Staley walks off but turns back to Joey, saying, "witnesses said that you put a good whipping not only on Rico but his thugs also. The witnesses said you took those men out in about ten seconds. You military?" Joey looks around then back at Staley, saying, "retired Marine." With a curious look, Staley says, "with those martial arts techniques, you had to be in special forces." Joey looks at Staley for a few seconds and with a somber face, saying, "yes, sir. Marine Recon and Raider." Staley smiles, saying, "I'm sure the Marines hated to see you go, and thanks for your service." Staley turns and walks out of the room. About forty-five minutes later, Nurse Noland comes into the waiting room. Joey stands and she says, "you can come on back now. Dr.

Kellum has Amanda's test results." Joey follows her into the emergency department, where he sees Dr. Kellum standing in front of the long counter. He is putting Amanda's test results on his tablet.

Joey walks up to him, saying very concerned, "what did find you find about Amanda?" Dr. Kellum smiles, then says, "she was a fortunate girl. She doesn't have any internal injuries. But she has two fractured ribs on her right side and a hairline fracture in her left wrist. Her cheek is very swollen and discolored, but there are no fractures in that area. I had two put four sutures in her right eyebrow, where she hit the concrete. She will be a very sore young lady for a while." Joey then asks Dr. Kellum, "can I see her now?" Dr. Kellum smiles, saying, "sure, go on in, but she is on some powerful pain meds." Joey pulls back the privacy curtain, and Amanda looks like she is asleep. Joey looks away for a few seconds with his eyes closed. He gets upset when he sees the extent of her injuries. The left side of her face and right eyebrow are incredibly swollen and discolored. Worse than Joey expected. She has a brace on her right wrist that is wrapped in elastic bandages. The brace and bandages reach to the end of her fingers.

He walks up to the head of her bed and gently lays his hand on her forehead. She slowly opens her eyes as wide as she can because of the swelling. She is very groggy from the medication and stares at Joey for a few moments. She tries to smile and says to him slowly, "I saw you at the hotel today." Joey tells her not to speak. Then she falls asleep again. He puts his hand back on her forehead then she wakes again. Amanda slowly and softly says to Joey, "Nurse Noland said a man saved me today. You are that man, aren't you." Joey says, "yes, ma'am, it was me. She tries to smile but can't. She manages to speak softly, saying, "what's your name?" Joey replies, "It's Joey." Amanda blinks her eyes slowly and tries to say, "I'm Ama…" She can't speak her name because she has fallen asleep again. Joey again puts his hand on her forehead, and Nurse Noland enters the room. She stands next to Joey, saying, "Mr. Morris, may I speak to you please? Joey nods his head and turns to walk out with the nurse.

Nurse Noland leads him to the next vacant exam room and closes the drapes. They stand next to the bed when Nurse Noland says, "first of all, Mr. Morris, please call me Dana." Joey then says, "well, call me, Joey, please." Dana sits on the bed, and she asks Joey to sit down by her. Joey sits next to her then she says, "Joey, I'm going to have to ask you something important, and please consider what I'm going to ask of you." Joey has a bewildered expression and says, "what is it?" Tears start to form in Dana's eyes, and she says, "It's about Amanda. Can you see it your heart to take Amanda to your home for a while, if all humanly possible?" Joey is baffled at what Dana asked him. But Joey remembers what Vickie had told him about compassion. He looks at Dana, saying, "Dana, I live by myself around Craig. Up in the mountains. I know how to take care of wounded Marines but not a hurt woman!" Dana smiles and puts her hand on Joey's shoulder then says, "a hurt woman is just like a hurt man or child. You do your best to take care of them day by day." Dana frowns and says, "I don't know much about this man Rico, but I've seen many girls who work for him come in here worse than Amanda. I have heard that some of his girls have come up missing."

Joey looks around for a few moments, then sighs and looks up at Dana, saying, "alright, I'll try to do my best, but only till she gets well." Dana hugs him and sets back, saying, "thank you so much, Joey, but I have a word of warning for the both of you." Joey has a concerned expression then says, "what's that, Dana?" Dana is distraught now and starts to cry, but manages to say, "Amanda has come to emergency three times in the last two months. Her injuries are always are worse than before. I'm afraid this man, Rico, is going to kill her eventually. And since you hurt him, he will want to hurt you or worse." Joey then says, "that's what Detective Staley told me." She looks down, still crying and upset. Joey cradles her in his arms and holds her for a few moments. There is a suture tray near him with some sponges on it, and he takes one giving it to Dana. She leans back, wiping her eyes, and manages to calm down.

Joey then calmly says, "I live in a place where it is almost impossible for anyone to find us." Dana wipes her eyes again then says, "Joey, that young woman in the next room has had a tough life, and she wants to get away from all this. She wants to go back home and start a new life. She has been in this profession since she was seventeen, and she doesn't know how to do anything else." Joey, with a questionable look, says, "how do you know so much about her, Dana?" "As I said a moment ago,

Joey, she has been here three times in two months. And she told me about her life," replies Dana. Dana gets up off the bed, and Joey does the same, and she says, "Dr. Kellum will want to keep her down here for the rest of the night for observation. You can sit in her room if you would like, but she will be out of it for a while."

Joey says, "yes, I'll do that. Will you have all the things that she will need when we leave?" Dana says, "there will be instructions on her injuries for you to follow, and I will give them to you before you leave." Joey, with a questionable face, says, "doesn't she need bandages and medicine for her injuries?" Dana smiles, saying, "there's no need for that because fractured ribs aren't taped anymore. Dr. Kellum will give her a prescription for pain meds and an antibiotic for her laceration."

Joey then says, "Dana, I'm going to take all the back roads out of Grand Junction, for we won't be seen. I'll get the prescriptions filled in Craig." Joey then asks Dana, "do you think she can make the two-hour trip without any pain medication?" "She will be fine, Joey, and will probably sleep all the way," says Dana. Then she says, "we will give her a pain shot before you leave." Joey smiles then says to Dana, "I'm going to go sit with her now. And thank you for all your compassion and care for Amanda. Dana hugs his neck, saying, "your welcome, Joey." Joey starts to leave, and Dana says, "Joey?" He turns around and says, "yes, ma'am?" Dana walks up to him and says, "Joey, something is telling me that you are going to make some wonderful changes in this girl. Please remember that for me."

Joey looks at Dana with a blank face for a few seconds and then turns, walking to Amanda's room. He pulls Amanda's curtain back and sits in a chair by her bed. After a few moments, he leans his head back and falls to sleep.

Chapter Five

Taking Care Of Amanda

It's about eight-thirty that morning. Dana's shift ended at seven o'clock, but she has stayed on duty until Amanda and Joey leave. She enters Amanda's room and looks at Joey, who is still asleep. Dana turns to Amanda and sees that she is awake. Amanda says to Dana slowly and softly, "has he been here all this time?" Dana looks at her with a lovely smile, saying, "yes, he has." Amanda looks at Joey and says to Dana, "I can tell that guy is someone special." "Amanda, you're going to find out that he is a great guy." "What do you mean," replies Amanda. Dana walks closer to Amanda with a gentle smile, saying, "Joey has agreed to take you home with him in the mountains around Craig. And he's agreed to take care of you till you get well. But he also said that when you get well, you can leave and start your new life."

Tears roll down Amanda's cheeks, and she says, "no one has ever taken care of me. Even when I was a little girl." A tear rolls down Dana's cheek as she looks at Amanda with a little frown. Then Dana collects herself, saying, "I'll go and wake him because Dr. Kellum has released you." Dana walks over to Joey and nudges his shoulder, saying, "Joey?" Joey jumps up with a horrible look on his face. When he does this, it scares Dana, and she puts her hand over her heart with a frightened expression. Amanda groans because she jerked when Joey stood up fast. And not to mention the look on his face.

Dana smiles at Joey and say's in a calm voice, "It's okay, Joey, you're with friends." Joey calms down and says to Dana in a sorrowful voice, "I'm so sorry Dana I scared you like that. I still have a problem when I'm woke up suddenly. Again, Dana, I'm so sorry." Dana puts her hand on his face saying, "I completely understand Joey. I have a brother who was in the army who used to do that." But he stopped doing that. And so will you." Dana walks over to Amanda to see if she is alright for being startled by Joey's actions. Then she says, "Amand, are you okay? I heard you groan when you moved suddenly. Amanda tries to smile and says softly, "I'm okay, Dana." Dana then says to Joey, "I'm going to go get her discharge papers and her prescriptions. I'll be right back." Joey walks up to Amanda, and she looks at him, trying to smile, saying, "Dana told me that you're going to take me to your house and take of me." "Yes, I am," says a smiling Joey. Amanda looks at him with tears rolling down her face saying, "thank you, Joey, for doing this for me." Joey takes his handkerchief out and dries her tears then says, "It's okay, Amanda. I will do everything in my power to never let that man get around you again."

There is a knock on the door in Amanda's room. An arrogant looking man comes in walking up to Amanda. He then says in a sharp, uncaring, arrogant tone of voice, "I'm Rex Laird from the collections department. Ms. Crawford, how do you intend to pay for the services that were rendered to you last night?" Laird looks down at his pad and says, "also you have an overdue balance of three-thousand, one- hundred and thirty-one dollars and sixty-one cents. Can you tell me when you will pay for all of these charges?" Amanda has a frightened look on her face, and Joey sees her expression, and he says to Laird, "hey buddy, would you come outside with me?" Laird turns around with a resolute look, saying to Joey again with his uncaring voice, "are you her husband or partner? Are you responsible for these overdue and current charges, sir? If not, this is none of your business." Joey smiles at Laird, saying, "Mr. Laird if you would step out of the room with me, I'm sure we can clear this matter right up." Laird huffs and walks outside the room with Joey.

When they get outside Amanda's room, Joey turns and gets in Lairds' face with a slight smile. Then Joey's smiling face slowly turns into a stern expression, complete with scary eyes. Joey then says, "listen, you arrogant, little jerk!" Laird's eyes get real big, and he seems to be very nervous now. Joey then angrily says, "I know that you are doing your job, but the way you do that job is very unprofessional, uncaring, and cruel. And I'm willing to bet that you get a lot of complaints about the way you do your job.

You scared her, and that has made me very angry. People like you are the reason why people despise collection departments at any hospital. Show a bit of compassion toward people because you don't know their financial situations. I know there are slackers out there. And you have to collect past due charges. But the manner which you just did was wrong. Be courteous and caring for once in your miserable life, and maybe things will get better. Get It!"

Joey looks at Laird, saying, "give me some paper and a pen." Laird's shaking hand rips a sheet of paper out of his notepad and gives the paper and pen quickly to Joey. Joey goes over to the nurse's counter and writes his name and address on the paper. He walks back to Laird, handing him the paper and pen. Joey then says, "that's my name and address. Send Miss Crawford's overdue bills and last night's charges to me, and I will pay them in full." Joey hesitates for a few seconds and says, "Mr. Laird, I hope you fully understand what I just said." Laird replies to Joey nervously, saying, "yes, sir. And I will take of this matter personally." Joey has a big smile and pats Laird on his face, then calmly saying, "good boy Mr. Laird. Now take your skinny butt back to the hole you climbed out of." Laird quickly leaves.

Joey goes back into Amanda's room, and she says with a slow, low voice, "thanks, Joey. I heard what you said out there. I'm sure that man is headed to the restroom now to clean his pants." Joey laughs and says to her, "okay, stop cracking jokes because it will hurt if you try to laugh." Dana enters the room and gives Joey Amanda's paperwork and prescriptions. Then Joey signs her release documents. She gives Amanda a pain shot and removes her I.V. Amanda looks at Dana and says, "could you please find me something to wear besides this hospital gown?" "I will go get one of some of my scrubs. But I'm afraid that's all I can do," replies Dana. Amanda says, "anything but this gown." Dana turns to Joey, saying, "Joey make sure she does her breathing exercises, and she has to cough lightly. I know it will hurt at first, but we don't want pneumonia to set in." Joey says to Dana, "I'll make sure does everything she is supposed to do."

Dana then says to Joey, "where did you move your vehicle last night?" Joey replies, "I moved it to the first parking lot." Dana then says, "you can go get it now and pull it under the emergency canopy. I will have in her scrubs on when you make it back." Joey says, "yes, ma'am." Joey leaves to get the vehicle, and Dana goes to her locker to get a set of scrubs for Amanda. Joey pulls his Jeep under the canopy, and he sees Dana with Amanda. Amanda is in a wheelchair and a blanket wrapped around her. Joey goes to open the passenger door, and Dana wheels Amanda out to the vehicle. Dana and Joey help Amanda into the Jeep, and she moans in pain. Joey carefully puts her seatbelt around her then covers her with the large blanket. He closes the door and turns to Dana hugging her neck, saying, "thanks for all you have done for her, Dana." As Joey starts to walk to the driver's side of the vehicle, Dana stops him, and he turns to her as she says, "Joey, she had a pretty rough time getting into those scrubs. You're going to have to make some mighty big sacrifices in taking care of her. But I assure you she will get better fast, and I will be praying for you." Joey smiles and goes around, getting in the Jeep.

When Joey gets in the Jeep, he notices Amanda has her head propped against the passenger window asleep. He carefully moves her head and puts part of the blanket against the window, then laying her head back against the window. Two hours later, they arrive in Craig, and Joey stops at a local pharmacy to get Amanda's prescriptions filled. She awoke when they were about ten miles from Craig. He pulls his Jeep into the pharmacy and looks at Amanda, saying, "I'll be a few minutes. And I will leave the Jeep running for you won't get cold. Will you be okay?" She says slowly, "I'll be fine." Joey opens his door then turns back to her saying, "will you need anything else while I'm here?" "No, I don't think so, Joey," replies Amanda. Joey goes into the pharmacy and walks up to the counter, and a young lady smiles and says, "can I help you, sir?" Joey says, 'yes, ma'am. I need to get these prescriptions filled, please." The young lady puts the info of the prescriptions in a computer then says, "does Amanda have her insurance information, sir?" Joey replies, "this will be cash."

Then the young lady says, "sir, she needs to be here personally. And she will need an I.D. to pick up the pain meds." Joey understands the procedure that a pharmacy has to follow when it comes to dispensing pain medication. Joey then asks the young lady, "may I speak to the pharmacist please ma'am?" She smiles and says, "one moment, sir." She goes to the back and tells the pharmacist that Joey needs to see him. Joey sees the pharmacist saying something to the young lady, and she comes back to the counter, saying to Joey, "the pharmacist will be with you after she fills a prescription." Joey replies, "thank you so much."

About five minutes pass, and the pharmacist comes to the counter, saying, "yes sir. You wanted to see me?" Joey sees the pharmacist's name tag then says, "good morning, Lacey, I'm Joey Morris." Lacy smiles and says, "good morning Mr. Morris, what can I do for you." Joey says, "Lacy, I have an injured woman in my Jeep. And she is unable to come into the pharmacy. Also, she doesn't have any I.D. I understand about the pain medication laws, and she needs to have these prescriptions filled, please. Lacey turns to the young lady saying, "Terri let me see the prescriptions, please." Terri hands the prescriptions to Lacey, and she looks at the order." She looks up at Joey, saying, "I see that Dr. Kellum prescribed Percoset." She looks at the prescription then looks back at Joey, saying, "tell you what I can do. I'll call the hospital's emergency department and verify this prescription. Give me a few moments, and I'll be right back." Joey says to Lacey, "thank you so much, Lacey."

As she goes to the back, Joey starts to walk around the pharmacy, going over to the window to check on Amanda. He sees that her head is against the passenger window asleep. Joey walks back toward the counter and seeing a display of Teddy Bears. He picks out a medium-size bear taking it with him back to the prescription counter. A few moments later,

Lacey comes back up to the counter and says with a smile, "I called the attending physician on duty in the emergency department. And he verified the prescriptions and that you signed her release papers. But we will need to see your driver's license, and you must sign picking up the order. Joey has a relieved smile, saying, "thank you so much for being so kind and what you've done for us, Lacey." Patti says, "thank you so much for saying that, Mr. Morris. I'll have these two prescriptions ready for you in a few minutes." "Thanks again," replies Joey.

Joey goes back to the window to check on Amanda, where he sees her still asleep. Joey walks around for a few minutes, and Terri says, "Mr. Morris, your prescriptions are ready." He walks up to the counter, asking Terri, "can I pay for this bear here?" Terri gives him the sweetest look saying, "you sure can." Joey gives Terri his driver's license, and she puts the information on the computer. She gives him his license back then she tells him the total price of his items. Joey pays her, then Terri says, "please sign on the pad that you are picking these prescriptions up, Mr. Morris." Joey signs the electronic pad and picks up the prescriptions and the bear. He then says to Terri, " thank you so much, Miss Terri, for being so sweet." Terri smiles and shakes her head, saying sweetly to Joey, "your so welcome, Mr. Morris, and take care of that lady." As he starts to leave, he waves to Lacey. She smiles, waving back to him.

He walks out to his Jeep and gets in, trying not to wake Amanda. As he closes the door gently, she wakes up, turning to Joey seeing the Teddy Bear. She says to him, "who's the Teddy Bear for?" He smiles and says a little embarrassed, "it's for you. I got hit in the ribs once when I played football in high school. I found out that holding a pillow tightly over my sore ribs, it hurt less when I breathed deep or coughed. I thought this bear would help to do the same thing." He puts the bear in her lap, and tears start rolling down Amanda's swollen face. Amanda then says, "you are a charming, sweet, caring man Joey." Joey smiles at her, then says, "are you ready to get to my cabin and start healing up?" "Very much so, Joey," replies Amanda.

He cranks the Jeep up and starts the trip to his house. They reach Joey's cabin, and Amanda has been awake since they left the pharmacy. Amanda groggily says, "Joey, you have a pretty place here." Joey replies, "thanks, Amanda. Now you hold still until I can unbuckle you and help you out of the Jeep." Joey cuts the engine off, then grabs the medicine and gets out of the Jeep. He then runs up the porch unlocking the door and opening it. He runs back to the Jeep and opens her door. He unbuckles her seatbelt and says, "you hold that bear against your sore ribs."

Amanda holds the bear against her ribcage, then Joey says, "not to tight, Amanda." He puts his arms under her legs and gently turns her body. Joey sees her grimacing, and he says, "okay, Amanda. Getting out will be the hardest part, but it's downhill the rest of the way after you get out." Joey puts his left arm around the lower part of her waist. Then he puts his right arm under her legs and gently lifts her out of the vehicle. He puts her down very slowly and says, "did that hurt much?" Amanda replies, "not as much as I thought." Joey looks at her with a concerned face, saying, "do you think you can walk with my help?" Amanda says, "the only thing we can do is to give it a try."

They walk to the steps and gingerly climb each step one at a time. They reach the porch, and Joey leads her into the cabin. He takes her over to his bed, where he helps her sit on the side of the mattress. Joey then says, "hold on to that bear because I'm going to lift your legs onto the bed." He slowly lifts her legs and places them on the bed. He puts his arm around her shoulders then leans her back slowly till her head is lying on the pillow. Amanda moaned as he laid her head on the pillow. Joey then says with a concerned look, "are you okay?" She says, "that hurt a good bit, but I'm good now." Joey pulls his large quilt over her legs, then says, "are you hungry?" "No, but I am a little thirsty," she replies. Joey then says, "is water okay, or do you want something else?" She speaks slowly, "do you have any milk?" Joey smiles at her, saying, "sure do. Besides, milk will be better for you when taking your pain medicine." Joey gently lifts her and places a pillow under her shoulders that will help her raise her head. Amanda grimaces, and Joey says, "sorry." He turns to the kitchen and takes a few steps. But he stops turning back to Amanda, asking, "do you want the milk cold or warm?" She looks at him with a woeful look, saying, "warm milk…yuck." Joey raises his brow then says, "you just answered my question."

He goes into the kitchen and gets a glass from the cupboard then opens the refrigerator, grabbing the bottled milk. He pours it into the glass, then returns the milk bottle to the fridge. He walks back to the den and picks up her pain medication and antibiotic cream off the dining table. He hands her the glass saying, "drink about half of the milk before you take your medicine. And I have to put the antibiotic cream on your stitches." Amanda lifts her right arm to take the glass, saying, "thank you, Joey." He walks to his bathroom and gets a cotton swab out of his medicine cabinet. When he returns, he sees that Amanda has drunk about half the milk. He stands beside the bed and takes the top off the antibiotic cream.

He puts the cream on the swab and gently applies it to Amanda's sutured eyebrow, saying, "does this hurt?" Amanda says, "not very much because you have a gentle touch, Joey." He opens the pill bottle then says, "okay, I think you can take these pills now, and I'll help you." Joey then says in a very gentle voice, "let's open that mouth, and I'll put the pills on your tongue one at a time." She opens her mouth, and Joey places one of the pills on her tongue. She swallows the pain tablet with a drink of milk. Joey does the same for the second pill. He takes her glass then very carefully removes the pillow under her shoulders. He leans her back to her original position. Joey then covers her completely below her chin with the warm quilt. Amanda never takes her eyes off him the whole time he is doing this.

Joey smiles then says to her, "are you comfortable?" She tears up from the tender emotion that she is feeling, saying, "yes, Joey. More than you will ever know." He puts his hand on her forehead with a smile, saying, "why are you crying, Amanda?" She replies, "maybe I'll be able to tell you why I'm crying one day Joey." He shrugs his shoulder with a questionable look, saying, "I'm going to build a fire, but if you need anything, I'll be in my recliner. So you go to sleep now." He removes his hand from her forehead and turns to go to build a fire. She says slowly, "Joey?" He turns back to her saying, "yea?" She looks at him but doesn't say anything. He shrugs his shoulders again, then with a questionable expression, says, "well?" Amanda frowns and says, "nothing." "Suit yourself," says Joey. He walks over to the fireplace, and later, he has a good fire going. Joey then walks to his recliner and looks at Amanda, who has fallen asleep. He sits down and looks up, saying, "God, please put your healing hands on Amanda's ribs and wrist…Amen." He reclines back in the recliner, and after a few minutes, he falls asleep.

It's later that afternoon, and Amanda has awakened. She looks at Joey, who is still sleeping, but she needs to go to the bathroom. She says, "Joey?" He doesn't hear her, and she takes the biggest breath she can take before her ribs start to hurt. She speaks a little louder, "Joey?" He opens his eyes slowly, then stands up quickly and walking quickly to her bed. He says excitedly, "what's wrong, Amanda!" She has an embarrassed look on her face and then says, "Joey, I need to go to the bathroom, and I'm going to need your help." Joey's eyes get as big as pie plates and embarrassed expression on his face. He looks around then back to Amanda, saying, "I didn't think of you having to use the bathroom." Joey looks around again, scratching his head, then looks at Amanda, saying, "I've never helped a woman go to the bathroom before." She has a slight smile as she states to Joey, "I've never had a man help me to the bathroom before, so I guess we will be winging it together."

Joey sighs and says, "Okay, let's get at it." He puts his right arm around her shoulders, gently lifting her. He takes the quilt off her and puts his arm under her legs. Moving them to the side of the bed as her feet touch the floor. Joey picks up her bear and hands it to her, saying, "hold your bear to your ribs now." She takes the bear, pressing it up against her ribs. Joey puts his hands under her arms, lifting her slowly. "I'm going to hold you by the underarms and guide you the bathroom," says Joey. Then he looks at her, saying, "you tell me if you have to stop okay?" Amanda replies, "I think I can make it all the way." He guides her into the restroom and stands her in front of the toilet. He looks down, sighing, then looks back at Amanda, saying, "I'm going to have to remove your scrub bottoms, you know." Amanda tries not to laugh but smiles, saying, "who else is going to do it, Joey?"

Joey shakes his head with a look of horror on his face, and Amanda sees his expression. She slightly smiles, then says, "Joey, you are so adorable right now." He looks at her for a few seconds, managing a little smile and saying, "I'll have my eyes closed during all of this." He reaches down and unties the scrub bottoms strings. He closes his eyes and turns his head toward the door as he pulls the bottoms down. He then puts his hands under her arms, saying, "now guide yourself down carefully." She looks at Joey with an embarrassed smile, saying, "Joey, you forgot my underwear." Joey shakes his head, saying something under his breath as he reaches up to her hips. Joey pulls her underwear down, still with his eyes closed. Then he says jokingly, "is there anything else your wearing, Amanda?" She replies, "nope, that's it." Now he helps her sit down then says, "I'll be right outside the door. Call me when you're through." Joey turns and opens his eyes and walks out of the bathroom, closing the door behind him.

About two minutes pass and Amada says, "I'm though so you can come to get me now." Joey opens the door with his eyes closed, then goes over and lifts her off the toilet. He pulls up her underwear and scrub bottoms. He leads her to the bed, and she says, "Joey, do you have anything for me to wear besides these uncomfortable scrubs?" He looks at her for a few seconds, then saying, "I don't have anything that will fit you, Amanda. The only things I have that you would be comfortable in are some hoodies and sweatpants. And they are so big, and they would fall off you." Amanda then says, "anything but these things, please?" Joey looks at her then says, "okay, I'll be right back." He goes back to the bathroom that also serves as his laundry room and gets the sweats. He brings the "Colorado State" matching hoodie and sweatpants to her. Joey then looks at her scrubs, saying, "you don't want to keep these scrubs, do you?" She looks at him with a frown, saying, "no way."

He goes to the kitchen and returns with a pair of scissors. Joey tells her, "I think that it would be better for both of us if I just cut this scrub top off." He starts to cut but then says, "go stand and face the front of the fireplace. I'm going to get you a thick long-sleeved t-shirt to wear under the hoodie." Joey leaves for the laundry room, and Amanda turns toward the fireplace. He returns and stands behind her with the t-shirt and cuts the scrub top off. Joey then says, "I have an idea. I'll put the t-shirt over your head first and then the hoodie. Then I'll guide your arms through the sleeves." Joey puts the t-shirt over her head. He then gently guides her arm that is on her injured rib side through the t-shirt sleeve.

Joey guides her arm with the wrapped brace through the left sleeve of the t-shirt. Then he places the hoodie on Amanda by doing the same thing. The bottom of the hoodie reaches down to her thighs. He then puts the sweatpants on the floor, helping her to step into them.

He walks in front of her, pulling the pants up. He then says without thinking, "wow, these pants reach up to your…" Joey didn't finish what he was saying and has an embarrassing look because of what he almost said. Amanda smiles at him, saying in a jokingly way, "you mean my breast?" Joey, who still is embarrassed, nods his head with a mortified look. Joey then says, "you're going to need some socks." He goes back to the bathroom, getting a thick pair of his hunting socks and returns slipping them on her feet. "Now, these thick socks will keep your feet warm," Joey says with a smile.

Joey changes the subject fast, saying, "are you hungry now, Amanda?" She tries not to laugh, but smiles, saying, "yes, I am." Joey leads her to the bed as she says, "Joey, I'm tired of lying around. Do you think we could eat at the dining table?" "Will you be okay," asks Joey. Amanda says, "sure. I think I'll be okay." Joey leads her to his dining table and sits her down gingerly." Amanda looks at him with a strange look, saying, "Joey, when you took me to the bathroom and when you put these sweats on me, I hardly hurt at all. And I thought it would be in excruciating pain." Joey looks at her for a few moments, smiling, then says, "It looks like you're a fast healer or those pain meds are working real good." She looks at him shaking her head slightly, saying, "no, I think it's the caregiver that I have." Joey shrugs his shoulders and replies, "Amanda, I don't know what I'm doing. But everything seems to be working out okay. How would you like some venison stew?" She nods her head, saying, "that sounds wonderful, Joey."

About thirty later, Joey brings two bowls of stew out and sits a bowl in front of Amanda. He then places the other bowl at his place at the table. He goes into the kitchen and returns with two glasses of Milk. Joey smiles then says, "Amanda, when is the last time you have been spoon-fed?" "When I was a baby, I guess," she replies. Joey puts her spoon into her bowl and gets a little bit of stew at the end of it. He puts the spoon up to her mouth, saying, "this is just a test run. I don't want to burn your lips or tongue if it's too hot." She opens her mouth and eats the small portion, then saying, "it's fine, Joey, and it sure is good." Joey puts her spoon back into her bowl, getting a larger amount of the stew. Then he puts the spoon up to her mouth. And as she eats the larger portion, Joey says, "this was my grandmother's recipe for this stew." He puts her spoon down on the table then takes her milk glass, putting it up to her lips. She drinks a little, and he puts the glass back on the table. Then Joey takes a bite of his stew then continues feeding Amanda.

After they get through with eating, Joey cleans the table off, then takes the dishes to the kitchen and starts cleaning up. About every two or three minutes, he asks Amanda if she is doing okay. She replies every time that she is okay. He gets through in the kitchen and walks back to the table, asking her, "do you want to get back in the bed?" She shakes her head, saying, "I would like to sit on your couch and look at the beautiful fire." He walks around and carefully lifts her walking her slowly to the couch. He gently sits her down and goes over to the wood rack and put more wood on the fire. He points to the middle of the sofa, asking Amanda, "can I sit here, please?" She nods her head, saying, "yes, you may, sir." When she said that, Joey noticed the expression of pain on her face. He then says to her, "let me go get your bear for you. You look like your hurting." She replies, "well, a little now." Joey gets up and walks to the bed picking up her bear. He walks back to the couch, putting it under her arm. Joey then walks to the kitchen and gets her another glass of milk. He gets two pain pills and takes it to her, saying, "I believe you made need these."

She opens her mouth, and he puts the pills on her tongue again one at a time. He gives her a sip of milk after each tablet. He puts the glass on the coffee table then sits down on the couch. Joey looks at her with a concerned look, saying, "the nurse told me to get you a doctor's appointment and schedule it in two weeks. I'll drive down to Wilson's store in the morning because that's the only area we can get cell reception." Amanda, with a questionable expression, says, "there is a store around here?" Joey says, "it's about twelve miles down the mountain road, and It's called Wilson's Store. Mr. Wilson has just about everything for everyone that lives up here. He even has a Deli now."

Joey sees that she is clutching her bear tighter against her ribs. Joey, who again is very concerned, says, "Amanda, you need to get in the bed and let those pills take effect." Amanda smiles and says, "okay. But If it's all the same to you, I would like to sit here and talk with you for a while looking at the fire." Joeys says to her, "now let me know when you're ready to get back in the bed." She smiles and turns her head toward the fire. Even when her face is swelled and bruised, Joey can tell that she has a somber look to her face. He doesn't say anything to her while she looks at the crackling fire. She does this for about ten minutes when she looks at Joey saying, "Joey, why haven't you asked me any questions?" "About what," he says. Amanda looks down for a few seconds then back to Joey with heavy eyelids, speaking slowly, "anything about me." Joey notices that the pain pills are starting to work on her. He answers her by saying, "Amanda, you will soon find out that I don't pry. I figured you would tell me when you're ready."

Amanda is about to fall asleep, and Joey says, "it's time for you to get in the bed." Amanda slowly says, "okay." Joey lifts her slowly and walks her to the bed. He lays her down and goes to get her bear that she left on the couch. He walks back to the bed, putting the bear under her arm. Amanda looks at him and speaking slowly with heavy eyes, saying, "Joey, do you think I can take a shower in the morning?" He smiles, saying, "since we got through the bathroom situation okay, I think we can work something out with the shower too." She can hardly speak now but manages to say, "thank you."

Joey then says, "time for you get in the bed now." He helps her off the sofa and they walk to the bed. He carefully puts her in. Then she closes her eyes falling asleep. Joey pulls the quilt over, and he looks at her swollen, bruised face. He moves her hair off her face and puts his hand on her forehead. He looks up and says, "God, this is about the same kind of prayer that I prayed last time. Please quickly heal this woman who I'm sure has had a rough life. She doesn't deserve this. And I can tell she wants to change. So help her out with that also, Amen."

Joey puts a couple of more logs on the fire then goes and sits in his recliner. He picks up a book then reclines back in the chair. Joey looks over to Amanda to see if she is okay and opens the book. He turns to the page that he left off two days ago. Two hours later, Joey is getting sleepy and decides it's time to go to sleep. He gets up out of his recliner and walks over to the bed to check on Amanda. He sees that she is sleeping comfortably, and he goes over to the wood rack again. He picks up three logs and puts them on the fire, and they will burn till morning. He sits in his recliner, and every night before he goes to sleep, he turns on his radio. He listens to the Craig radio station for weather updates. Especially during the fall and winter months. Because the weather can change quickly on the mountain. After he gets the forecast, he leans back and pulls another but smaller quilt over him, then falling asleep.

Chapter Six

Amanda Starts To Heal Quickly

It's the next morning at about seven-twenty. Joey wakes and stretches and gets out of the recliner. He puts four logs on the fire where there are burning coals from the fire last night. The logs will catch fire soon from the hot coals, warming the den back up. He walks over to the bed, where he finds that Amanda still asleep. He decides to go out on the front porch to get wood to place in the wood rack. He drops one of the logs, and Amanda awakes. He looks over to her with a sorrowful expression, saying, "I'm so sorry that I woke you up, Amanda." She smiles, saying, "that's alright, Joey. What time is it?" Joey looks at his watch, saying, "it's twenty minutes to eight. Are you hungry? "yes, I am," replies Amanda.

Joey gets a big grin on his face saying, "how would you like the Joey Morris breakfast special this morning?" Amanda clutches her bear, and with a questionable look, says, "whats the Joey Morris breakfast special?" He breathes deep with a proud looking smile, saying, "pancakes, scrambled eggs, deer sausage. And your choice of milk, orange juice or coffee. How's that sound to you?" Amanda nods her head slightly with a smile, saying, "that sounds wonderful. Do you have any mayonnaise?" Joey scrawls his face, then says, "what do you want mayonnaise for?" "I love mayonnaise on my eggs," says a smiling Amanda. Joey shakes his head and says, "that's disgusting, Amanda. That's so gross!" Joey is still shaking his head, then says, "what do you want to drink with your breakfast?" Amanda looks up with her eyes and says to Joey, "coffee first, then orange juice, please." Joey walks over to the bed, and smirkingly says, "do you want mayonnaise with that?" Amanda then says, "Oh, don't be silly, Joey." Joey takes a deep breath saying, "do you need to go to the bathroom before I start cooking?" She nods her head, saying with a slight smile, "yes, I do." They go through the bathroom routine, and when she is through, Joey walks her out of the bathroom. He then says, "would you like to sit at the table or the couch?" "I'm a little cold, so the couch, please," she replies.

Joey helps her walk to the couch and sits her down gently. Joey then says, "Amanda, the logs should catch fire very soon. And I will go get your quilt and bear." He walks to the bed and pulls the quilt off and picks up her bear. He walks back over to Amanda and gives the bear to her. He wraps the quilt around her, then says, "Is this okay?" She looks up to him, saying, "I'm very comfortable, Joey, thank you." He walks into the kitchen to prepare breakfast, and Amanda stares at the fire. She a sad, surprised look on her face, and tears start to form. Because ever since Joey took her to the hospital, he has treated her like she is a real person for the first time in her life. And she knows this could be a dream that could maybe come true for her. Amanda hasn't fallen in love with him. Because she knows all of this will probably soon end when she gets better. Joey then will expect her to leave.

Later as Joey comes back into the den, he says to Amanda, "let's get you to the table." He helps her up, and Amanda says, "Joey, I want to see if I can walk by myself." Joey, who becomes very concerned, says, "Amanda, are you sure?" She replies, saying, "Joey, I know that I can do it because I'm not hurting as much as I was last night." Joey breathes deep then says, "okay, but I'll be right beside you." Joey gives her the bear, and she walks slowly to the dining table. Joey goes to help her sit, and she says, "let me try to sit without your help." She clutches her bear then very slowly sits without very much pain. Joey looks surprised, saying, "you did it, Amanda! Did it hurt much?" She looks up at him, saying, "It's strange, Joey. I hardly hurt at all. Maybe God heard your prayer about me." Joey looks around, slightly embarrassed, saying, "you heard me pray last night?" She has a loving smile, saying, "I wasn't all the way asleep when you prayed, and I heard every word." Joey, with a red face grins, then says, "I'll go get our breakfast."

Joey goes into the kitchen and bringing back two plates and sitting one in front of Amanda. He picks up her fork, and to feed her, then she says, "Joey, I want to feed myself today if you don't mind." Joey leans back in his chair, smiling and nodding his head, saying, "okay, go for it!" She puts her bear on the table, and Joey gives her the fork. She leans forward slowly and stretches her arm to cut a piece of her egg with her fork. She puts the egg in her mouth. Joey claps his hands and says excitedly, "you did it again, Amanda!" She puts the fork down and picks up her spoon, saying, "would you give me the sugar and mayonnaise please, sir?" Joey places the sugar bowl and mayonnaise in front of her. And she takes her teaspoon, and she then puts a teaspoon of sugar in her coffee, stirring it. Amanda asks Joey to remove the top of the mayonnaise jar. She then covers her eggs with the mayonnaise as Joey takes a sip of his coffee, shaking his head. Then they have a nice breakfast together. And they talk about a lot of subjects.

During their conversation, Joey asks Amanda, "how old are you?" She puts her fork down, then saying, "I'm twenty-eight. What about you?" Joey says, "I'll be thirty-nine next February." Amanda looks at him shaking her head with a big smile, saying, "I'll tell you what Joey you sure don't look your age." Joey leans back in his chair then speaking with a jokingly questionable expression, "Is that good or bad, Amanda?" She laughs and says, "Oh, that's very good, Joey!"

They both get through with breakfast, and then Joey says, "remember I'm going down to the store to make you an appointment with my good friend Dr. Kelvin Bailey in Craig." Amanda then says with a slight smile and raised eyebrows saying, "Joey, also you told me that I could take a shower this morning." He nods his head, saying, "no ma'am, I didn't forget. Are you ready for the shower?" "Please. Because I know

I'm pretty grungy," replies Amanda. Then Joey says, "let me go lite the butane heater in the bathroom for you for it will be warm." Joey gets up and goes and lights the heater. He comes back into the den and sits back down at the table. After about five minutes, Joey points his hand to the bathroom, saying, "shall we?" Amanda gets up very slowly, then Joey says, "Amanda, I need to put a plastic bag around your wrist splint for it won't get wet." He goes into the kitchen and comes back with a small garbage bag and a big rubber band. They walk to the bathroom, and Amanda is doing fine.

They go into the bathroom, and Joey reaches into the bathroom closet, getting a bathrobe. He reaches in the shower stall and cuts on the water. He looks back at her, saying, "do you like your shower warm or a little hot?" She replies, "a little hot, please." He adjusts the water temperature and steps back from the stall. He looks at her sighing then saying, "okay, it's going to be just like last night. I'll remove your clothes with my eyes closed." She laughs a little then says, "Joey, I know you have seen a naked woman before." Joey shakes his head, and his face turns red. He then says, "yes, I've seen a naked woman before. But the problem is I've never seen you like that." Amanda tries not to laugh because she knows he's embarrassed, and it would probably hurt her ribs. Joey says, "are you ready?" "Okay, I'm ready," she says. Joey puts the bag over her brace and then closes his eyes, removing her sweats. He helps her into the shower and closes the blurred shower door and says, "is the water, okay?" She replies, "Joey, you don't know how great this feels." Joey goes and sits on the toilet and says, "I'll be sitting on the toilet in case you need anything" Amanda then says jokingly from the shower, "do I need to close my eyes?" Joey looks down at the floor, shaking his head then says lividly, "I have the seat cover down, Amanda." He then hears her laugh gently.

After about five minutes later, Amanda says, "Joey, you are going to have to wash my hair for me." Joey replies by saying, "there is a bottle of shampoo with a conditioner in it on my razor rack. Do you see it?" "Yes, I do," replies Amanda. Joey gets up off the toilet then says to her, "I'm going to open the door so that you can give me the shampoo bottle. And I'll still have my eyes closed. So turn your back to me." He opens the door, and she hands him the bottle. She stands with her back to him as he puts some shampoo in his hands. He reaches out his hands, finding her long hair. He starts washing her hair, and Amanda has a funny look on her face. She starts thinking to herself what it would be like for someone she loved to shampoo her hair like this. Joey is thinking almost the same thing about how wonderful it would be to wash beautiful hair like this. They both frown and hang their heads, knowing this will never happen between them.

She washes the shampoo out of her hair, then Amanda says, "I'm through now." Joey opens the door, and she steps out, shaking her head. Because Joey still has his eyes closed. He takes off the garbage bag and hands her a towel. She dries off the best she can, but she can't reach her back. She then says to him, "Joey, you are going to have to dry my back and also the back of my legs." He nervously takes the towel, still with eyes closed drying off her back and legs. Joey then helps her put on the bathrobe. He opens his hands and says, "I can dry your hair if you want me too. And I'll open my eyes to do that." Amanda replies, "oh, Joey, would you?" He then says, "sure." He walks to the closet pulling out a hairdryer. He plugs the dryer cord into a socket on the wall and starts to dry her hair. He never took so long to dry hair before. When he is through drying Amanda's hair, he takes a hairbrush and starts brushing her hair. As he brushes her lovely hair, he follows the brush with his hand. He has never felt a woman's hair that is so thick, soft, silky, and beautiful all at the same time. Joey gets a strange but good feeling while he is doing this, but he quickly smothers this feeling like it was a flash fire.

She turns around with a smile, saying, "Joey, you could have been a wonderful hairdresser. You have strong hands, of course, but you also have a gentle touch." They look into each other's eyes for a moment. And they both feel something beautiful happening. Joey leads her out of the bathroom then helps her sit on the couch, and she sits down slowly. Joey goes and puts his coat on, then turning to Amanda, saying, "I'm going down to Wilson's store, and I'll only be there about thirty minutes. Will you be okay?" Amanda looks at him with a slightly embarrassed expression, saying, "Joey, I'm going to be needing some undergarments."

Now Joey is embarrassed and with an embarrassed tone of voice, saying, "Ahh…what kind of undergarments are you talking about, Amanda?" She shakes her head and, in a jokingly voice, says, "a bra and some panties silly. I know that a person like you can't possibly be that naïve." Joey looks around the den then looks back at Amanda, saying, "I will have to go into Craig for those things." Joey sighs then says, "alright. But I'm sure their different sizes for those things. So give me yours." Amanda gives him the sizes, as Joey says to her, "since I'm going into Craig. I will get you two pairs of sweats. And also some lady's socks. Also some slippers and a housecoat. I assume you wear small in the sweats and housecoat sizes." Amanda says, "yes and a size eight in a lady's slipper."

Joey produces a small smile, saying, "since I have to go into Craig, I will probably be over an hour. Are you positive you will be okay?" Amanda, with a calm expression, says, "yes, I will be fine, Joey." Joey picks his jacket off the corner of the couch, putting it on. He pulls the keys out of his pants pocket and remotely starts his Jeep with the key fob. The Jeep will be all warmed up when he gets in to leave. Joey starts to turn to the door but stops then saying, "if you need anything, you call Mr. Wilson at his store on the radio that's in the kitchen. The channel he uses is on the radio." He then looks at Amanda for a few moments without saying anything. She has a concerned look, saying, "what is it, Joey?" He walks over to the gun case and gets a loaded three-fifty-seven revolver out and takes it to Amanda. He says very carefully, "I will feel much better with you having this revolver close by you." Joey lays the weapon on the coffee table.

Amanda has a frightened expression, and Joey deescalates her fear by saying with a smile, "you need to keep that revolver by you at all times. For mountain elephants and water buffalo who will want to come in to get warm." Amanda's expression on her face turns immediately from fear to a small smile. He also says, "if someone knocks on the door, be sure to ask who they are. But since no one knows you here, I'm sure nobody will. But when I get back, I will knock, and you ask if it's me. Because I don't want you to mistake me for that mountain elephant or buffalo. She giggles, nodding her head.

Joey says, "by the way, have you shot a weapon before?" She shakes her head, saying, "no." He walks over and picks up the revolver and points to the hammer. He then says, "this is the hammer that strikes the ammunition. With your good hand, pull the hammer back with your thumb back till it clicks." He points to the trigger, saying, "don't put your finger on the trigger until you are ready to fire. And never, never point the weapon at anything you don't intend to shoot." He empties the revolver of its ammunition and gives it to her. Joey then shows her how to hold it. He says, "alright, let's practice all of this." He hands her the gun and shows her how to hold it with one hand. After he teaches her how to hold the firearm, she says, "Joey, it's so heavy." He nods his head laughing, saying, "I could have given you my forty-four magnum, which is the original hand cannon. But I assure you that this weapon will do the trick. Even though your other hand is in a splint, you can balance the weapon on it. Now look straight down the barrel and point it to whatever you intend to shoot."

Joey then says, "before you shoot, hold your breath when you fire. Then squeeze the trigger." Amanda looks at Joey, saying, "what do you mean by squeeze the trigger?" Joey replies, "squeeze the trigger like you are squeezing a lemon. It keeps the weapon steady and on target. If you jerk the trigger bullets, won't hit your target." He then looks at Amanda with a reassuring smile, saying, "now try everything I told you." She lifts the revolver and puts her splinted hand up to balance it. But she can't pull back the hammer with her thumb. He says, "Okay. It looks like we need to change weapons. He takes the gun from Amanda and goes back to the gun case. He gets a semi-automatic nine-millimeter handgun out.

He then says, "Amanda, this is a nine-millimeter sidearm. It's very simple to fire." Amanda looks at the gun with a confused expression. Then she looks at Joey, saying, "this gun doesn't have one of those things you pull back." He says, "this type of sidearm wouldn't." Joey releases the magazine and pulls it out of the gun. Joey then says, "you put ammo in the magazine and then put it back in the handgrip. And you pull this slide back to put a round in the chamber." Joey gives Amanda the gun, and she says, "this gun is lighter than the other one. How do you shoot it?" Joey takes the gun from her and pulls back the slide. Then presses the small safety lever up in the safe position. He gives Amanda the weapon and says to Amanda, "when you saw me pull back the slide, that loaded a round in the chamber." He shows her the safety lever then says, "when I pushed this safety lever up, the weapon can't fire. Just push the lever down to fire it. And when this weapon is fired, another round is automatically put in the chamber. Until you run out of ammo, of course."

He gives the gun back to Amanda and says, "see if you can push the safety lever down." She puts her thumb on the lever and quickly pushes it down. She looks at Joey with a big smile. Joey then says, "now push the lever back up. She pushes the lever up and says, "I can do this, Joey." "Always keep the safety lever up to keep the weapon in safe mode. Then push it down when you're ready to fire it," says Joey. Amanda looks at the gun and says, "Joey, I'm still nervous about these guns." Joey laughs and says, "Amanda, if someone has the intent to hurt you are worse, I do not doubt that you will have the courage to fire it." Joey then says, "make sure you use these same things with this weapon that I told you with the revolver." Joey puts his hand on her swollen cheek very carefully and looks at her with a smiling, calm expression saying, "I'll be right back. And don't forget your breathing exercises." Amanda smiles and says, "okay."

He turns and walks to the door and opens it. He locks the door from the inside and closes the door. Some snow had fallen the night before, but this light snow is nothing to Joey. He walks to the Jeep and reaches for his keys. He realizes he has left his keys on the coffee table. He walks back to the cabin and knocks on the door. Joey hears Amanda say, "who is it?" Joey shouts, "it's me, Amanda. I left my keys on the coffee table." She says, "Just a second." She opens the door, smiling and hands Joey the keys. He says, "this is better than breaking the glass on a window and climbing in." Amanda looks at him with a sweet smile, saying, "be careful, Joey." He walks back to his Jeep and heads out to Craig.

He arrives in Craig, going straight to Corsauts Womans Apparel store. He pulls in and parks near the front of the store. He walks in, standing for a few moments as a friendly young lady comes up to him with a pretty smile, saying, "hello sir. And welcome to Corsauts. I'm Holley. What can I show you today?" Joey stands there embarrassed and red face, saying,

"Holley, I'm looking for some sweat outfits, thick socks, a housecoat and slippers. And…ahh…some undergarments. All for a lady." The young woman smiles then says, "that's why we're here. So follow me, sir."

Joey follows her, and soon they arrive at the sport's apparel section. The young woman takes him to where the sweats are. She waves her hand over the sweats, saying, "we have a large selection and designs as you see. What design and size will she wear?" "She will wear a small size and give her some sweats that are trendy for relaxing in," replies Joey. Then she says, "what color will she prefer, sir?" He looks at the large selection and says, "Holley, I'm going to let you decide on what you would buy for yourself." Holley looks around and picks out two outfits, then turns to Joey, saying, "this is what I would pick for myself, sir." Joey smiles and says, "this will be fine." Holley says, "great. Let's go to the shoe department now." Joey follows her to the shoe department, and when they arrive, he says, "again, pick what you would want in a woman's size eight." She immediately picks up a slipper that is on display, saying in an excited tone, "this is what I would get for myself in a minute, sir!" Joey smiles at her excitement, then saying, "those will be fine also, Holley."

Holley then says, "give me a second go to the back and get those slippers for you." She looks inside to get the stock number and goes through the curtains in the back of the shoe section. A few moments later, she returns with a box with the slippers in it. Then Holley says something Joey has dreaded, "now let's go to the lingerie department." As she turns, Joey stops her, and she turns to him. Joey says, "Holley, I'm embarrassed and uncomfortable about where we are going." She looks at him with a pretty, warmhearted smile, saying, "sir, you don't have to be embarrassed. I do this for men every day. Especially at Christmastime." Joey feels much better after what she said. Holley then says, "are you ready?" Joey smiles at her for a few seconds, then says, "I'm ready." They soon get to the lingerie section, then Holley turns to him shaking her head and says, "sir, lingerie is a little difficult with her not here. She might not like what I would buy."

Joey gets embarrassed then says, "well, is there anything listed as maybe general undergarments for women then? Like boxers or briefs for men." She smiles, saying, "you can never go wrong with this type, sir. A lot of ladies, including myself, use these." Joey nervously says, "how do you buy them?" Holley replies, "they come six to a pack." "That will be fine then," Joey quickly says. Holley starts to smile at his embarrassment and says, "I assume you want me to pick the colors then?" Joey shakes his head, saying in a relieved tone, "for goodness, sakes Holley, please do!" Joey tells Holley Amanda's size, and she picks out a pack with different colors and says, "is there anything else, sir?" Joey gets his embarrassing red face again, saying, "she will need a bra." Holley says, "do you happen to know her size?" "yes, I do," replies Joey. Holley then says, "follow me over here, sir." When they get to that section, she asks for Amanda's bra size. She then asks the most horrible, terrifying words he has ever heard in his life! Holley asks Joey, "does she want one that attaches from the back or the front?" Joey has a look that would scare a ghost but thinks for a few moments. He thinks about Amanda's injuries, then he says in a calm voice, "just guessing, I think the one from the front would be the best."

Holley turns the rack and picks out the right bra. Joey then says, "do you have two of them, Holley?" She gets another one and says, "will that be it?" Joey sighs and smiling, saying, "yes, for goodness sakes, that will be it, Holley. Thank you so much for your help with this uncomfortable situation." Holley smiles, replying, "it has been my pleasure, sir! Now let's go to the front to check out your items." Joey pulls out his wallet and tries to give Holley a tip. She has an expression of concern, saying, "sir, I don't know if we can accept tips, so I better not." Joey smiles, saying, "Holley, you went over and beyond to help a very embarrassed man. And you deserve it. Please?"

Holley is still hesitant about a tip and says, "I better not, sir." Joey then asks her, "I'm going to give you a tip one way or another. Is your manager here?" Holley replies, "no, sir, but the assistant manager, is here." Joey then says, "would you go get her for me, sweetie?" "Okay," replies Holley. Holley walks to the front of the store and starts talking to a young lady that must be the assistant manager. Holley and the lady then walk back to where Joey is standing. Holley says to Joey, "sir, this is my assistant manager, Bettie. Bettie then says, "can I help you, sir?

Joey smiles and says, "Bettie, Holley has been wonderful help for me today. And I want to give her a tip. And I'm sure it will be alright with you." Bettie looks at Holley then back at Joey with a big smile, saying, "sure you can. Holley is our best salesperson!" Joey says, "thanks, Bettie." Bettie walks back to the front of the store. Joey reaches into his pocket, pulling out some cash. Joey hands Holley a one-hundred-dollar-bill and hands to Holley. She stands there with a surprised expression and saying, "are you sure, sir?" Joey nods his head, saying, "you went beyond the call of dutty young lady. You saved me from a lot of embarrassment from your kindness."

Holley hugs Joey's neck and says, "thank you so much, sir." Joey replies, "defiantly my pleasure Holley." She then says, "let's walk upfront and check you out."Joey takes the clothing and slippers to the cashier, where he pays for all the items. He takes his purchase out to his Jeep and puts the bag in the passenger seat. Joey walks around the Jeep and gets in. He heads to Dr. Kelvin Bailey's clinic that is down the street from the woman's store. Joey arrives at the clinic, pulling in. He parks then gets out walking to the front door of the clinic and walks in. He goes through the waiting area, where six patients are waiting to see one of the three doctors here. He arrives at the receptionist window, and the receptionist says, "may I help you, sir?" Joey says to her, "I need to make an appointment with Dr. Bailey for a friend of mine." The receptionist says, "Is this friend a patient of Dr. Bailey? "No, she's not," replies Joey. The receptionist shakes her head, saying, "I'm sorry, sir, but Dr. Bailey is not seeing any new patients." Joey then says, "I understand, but can you please tell him that Joey Morris is here?"

The receptionist frowns, saying, "again, I'm sorry, sir, but I cannot do that." When the receptionist says that, Dr. Bailey's nurse walks into the receptionist's office. Joey says to the nurse, "hello, Teresa." Teresa turns around and starts to smile. Then saying excitedly, "Joey Morris!" Teresa walks out of the office and gives him a big hug. She then says, "what are you doing here? Are you sick?" Joey has a concerned expression, saying, "no, I'm fine, but I need to make an appointment with Kelvin for a friend of mine." "Well, follow me because Dr. Bailey will want to see you," exclaims Teresa. Teresa takes him to Dr. Bailey's office, then saying, "have a seat, and I will go get him." Teresa walks back to where Dr. Bailey is entering data on a computer. Teresa says, "Dr. Bailey, Joey Morris is in your office." Dr. Bailey says with an excited voice, "Joey is here?" "He's in your office now," replies Teresa. Dr. Bailey gets up and walks to his office to see Joey, who he hasn't seen in a long time.

Dr. Bailey walks into his office and looks at Joey with an animated expression saying, "Joey Morris!" Joey replies, "Kelvin Bailey!" They give each other a man hug, then Kelvin says, Joey, I'm so proud of you for your service to this country! Especially that Navy Cross you were awarded!" Joey says, "thanks, old friend." Then Kelvin says, "when is the last time you picked up a football? Joey says, "We used to throw one around when we got bored on deployment. What about you?" Kelvin produces a broad smile, saying, "the last time I picked up a football was our state championship game. Man, we had a great team back then. And it was led by our high school All-American linebacker. You!" Joey then says, "we also had a great quarterback. And that was you!" They both smile at each other with an expression of comradery because they were the best of friends and teammates in high school.

Kelvin then says, "what are you doing around here?" Joey sighs, and then saying, "Kelvin, three days ago, I had to go to the V.A. When I was leaving, I saw a woman who I had seen before that afternoon being assaulted. I helped her out and took her to the emergency room." Kelvin has a concerned expression, saying, "what was the diagnosis?" Joey replies, "she has two fractured ribs and fractured left wrist. She also has a badly swollen face. The nurse at the hospital told me that she needs to see a doctor in two weeks. And that's what I'm here to see if you will see her." Kelvin says, "sure. I definitely will take a look at her. Do you know the attending physician's name?" "His name is Bradley Kellum at the hospital's emergency department in Grand Junction," replies Joey. Kelvin gets on the phone and calls Teresa to come back to his office.

Kelvin says, "what we will do is get her x-rays and diagnosis sent to us from the hospital. I will take new x-rays to see how much she has healed." Teresa comes into Kelvin's office, saying, "yes, sir?" Kelvin looks up at her, saying, "we need to set up an appointment in two weeks for a friend of Joey's. We will be taking x-rays for a fractured wrist and ribs." Teresa looks at Joey, saying, "what's the lady's name?" Joey says, "Amanda

Crawford." Teresa writes Amanda's name on her pad. She then asks Joey, "do you know her birthdate?" Joey shakes his head, saying, "no, I don't, Teresa." Then she says to Joey, "can you tell me how old she might be?" Joey says, "she's twenty-eight. Teresa writes that information down then saying, "I will go to the front and get an appointment scheduled for Amanda."

Teresa walks out of the office, and Joey looks at Kelvin with a very concerned expression saying, "Kelvin, I need to tell you something in confidence about Amanda." "Of course," says Kelvin. Joey takes a few seconds, then says to Kelvin, "Amanda, putting it nicely, was a very expensive escort woman. And she was beaten by her employer because she wanted to quit the business. Kelvin shakes his head, saying, "where is she now?" Joey says, "she's at my cabin, and I'm taking care of her." Teresa comes back to Dr. Bailey's office and gives Joey an appointment card. Then Teresa says, "we have you down for September twentieth at nine o'clock that morning. Is this okay?" Joey smiles, saying, "that will be fine, Teresa." Joey and Kelvin stand up and shake hands. Joey smiles, saying, "thanks, old friend." Kelvin nods his head smiling and says, "my pleasure Joey. Now go take care of that lady."

Joey leaves the clinic going back to his cabin. When he arrives at the cabin, he retrieves all the items he has bought that morning and walks up the steps to his porch. He knocks on the door, saying, "Amanda?" She replies, "is that you, Joey?" Joey then says, "yes, Amanda, it's me. I'm coming through the door now, so don't shoot me!" He unlocks the door and steps in the den. Amanda is sitting in the same place on the couch when he left. Joey sits down and says, "this is for you." Even though the things that Joey bought her seem trivial to him, he sees the happiness in Amanda's face. She pulls the sweat outfits out of the bag then says excitedly, "these look so comfortable, and the colors are beautiful! Did you pick these out yourself?" Joey shakes his head and says, "I'm sorry, but a very nice young lady picked everything out for you. And that includes the undergarments."

She pulls the undergarments out, then says with an excited voice, "all of this is going to feel so great to have on!" Joey's face turns red and says, "I've never seen somebody so thrilled over underwear before." She looks at her socks and slippers, saying, "did the young lady pick these out also?" Joey nods his head and says, "yep." Then Amanda says, "Joey, I want to try on my new stuff right now, and you will have to help me out again." Joey starts to laugh and says, "this is nothing new, so let's go." Joey still closes his eyes while he helps Amanda with her new clothes. After she gets everything on, she goes into the den. She sits on the couch while Joey puts her socks and slippers on. Amanda sighs, then saying, "Joey, this clothing is something I would have picked out myself. You and the young lady did a good job." Joey can't get over the happiness this woman has for these simple clothes he just bought her. He knows in his heart that Amanda hasn't had very many new things in her life. She pulls her bra's out of the bag, looking at them when Joey says with another embarrassed look, "ahh…I got you two sets of those… things." Amanda sees that Joey is in trouble by trying to describe the bra's and helps him out by saying sweetly, "Joey, these are just right. Also, these are the styles that I wear." Joey lets out a big sigh of relief, saying, "thank goodness." Amanda shakes her head, saying, "as I said before, you are so adorable when you get embarrassed." Joey then grins and shrugs his shoulders then says, "Amanda, tell you what. When you are better, I will take you to Denver, and you can get you some new clothes." Amanda lights up and says, "Oh, Joey! That would be wonderful! Thank you so much!"

Later that night, as they are eating dinner, Joey looks up to Amanda saying, "Amanda, I forgot to tell you today about your doctor's appointment I scheduled for you." She looks up with a questionable expression then saying, "when is it?" Joey leans back in his chair, saying, "it's on the twentieth of this month. At nine o'clock that morning. The appointment is with my good friend, Kelvin Bailey, at his clinic in Craig. We were teammates when we played football and basketball in high school. His nurse is going to get the x-rays from St. Mary's that they took when you were in their emergency room. He will compare those to the new ones he will take and see what kind of progress you have made since then." She smiles, saying to Joey with a slight, excited tone, "Joey, I know in my heart that I'm healing faster than I have ever had before! Besides, I don't need those pain pills anymore either! They helped a lot, but they made me feel so strange." Joey has a concerned expression on his face saying, "are you sure about those pills, Amanda? It might be a little early for you to get off them." Sure, I'm sure," replies Amanda.

They go back to eating their dinner, then Amanda looks up with a sweet smile, saying, "Joey, no one has ever taken care of me ever since a was little girl. I always have had to take care of myself. And you will never know what that means to me." Joey leans back in his chair, smiling and appreciated what Amanda said to him. He also notices that the swelling on her face has drastically reduced. She is regaining her beauty, almost looking like the first time he ever saw her. They finish dinner and later are sitting on the sofa together. They're not sitting next to each other just looking at the fire Joey has built. Amanda looks over at the stand next to his recliner.

She sees Joey's Bible on his stand, saying with a questionable expression, "Joey, what is that book on the second shelf on your stand?" Joey looks over at the stand, saying, "that's my Bible that my mom and dad gave me when I was in school." Amanda looks at him, saying, "do you read it much?" Joey looks down, frowning and shaking his head, saying, "not as I should." Amanda tilts her head with another questionable expression, then says, "why not?" Joey looks at the fire and takes a deep breath then saying, "when I enlisted in the Marines, my faith was on hold. I did read it and prayed when a big mission was coming up. I just haven't taken the time to get re-established with God since I've been home. And that's my fault.

Amanda looks at him with a reassuring smile, saying, "I think you are making a start at getting back to your faith. Remember when I told you that I heard you praying for me? And I know that your prayers were answered. Look how good I'm doing." Joey smiles and says, "yes, I guess that is a small start, but I was angry with God when I retired from the Marines. And I guess I'm still angry with him." Amanda looks at Joey with a dubious expression, saying, "Joey, why are you angry with God?" Joey looks down, saying, "I can't talk about it now, Amanda." She smiles and says, "just like when you told me. When your ready, I will be here for you." Joey looks back at her with a slight smile, saying, "thanks."

Amanda looks at the fire for a few moments then saying, "there was a street pastor that I spoke with one time in Grand Junction. He knew what I did, but said nothing about it. But the pastor did say that God will forgive all the bad things someone has ever done. He quoted something from the Bible that went like this, I think. He said, "If you believe in God's Son, you will never die." Joey looks at her, saying. "I believe what your referring to is one of the most famous passages in the Bible." Amanda replies, "can you tell me the way it goes again?"

Joey has a calm expression, saying, "It's John 3:16. And it says, "For God so loved the world, that he gave his only begotten Son, that whosoever believeth in Him should not perish, but have everlasting life." Amanda says, "yes, that's what I think he said. That passage is so beautiful and reassuring." Joey then says, "that's probably the very first Bible verse I ever memorized in Sunday School." Amanda turns to the fire again, saying, "the pastor gave me a small Bible. But I lost it somewhere. When he said that verse, I felt something happening, and I contemplated quitting my profession. I was going to change for the first time in my life. But I was so scared of Rico that I never did and kept on with what I was doing. And I forgot those words that the pastor said.

Joey turns and looks at the fire, then saying, "Amanda, you're right. I need to brush up on getting my spiritual life back in order." Amanda excitedly says, "Joey, will you teach me things in the Bible? Since I've been with you, the life I've known has changed. I want you to tell me your favorite Bible stories." Joey nods his head, saying, "okay, I'll help you out, and at the same time, you will be helping me out." Amanda smiles at him then says, "can we start tonight?" "sure," replies Joey. He gets up and walks over to the stand and gets the Bible. Joey returns to the sofa sitting right next to Amanda. He turns to a chapter and finds one of his favorite stories.

Chapter Seven

Amanda's Appointment With Dr. Bailey

Two weeks have passed, and it's time for Joey to take Amanda to see Dr. Bailey. They leave at eight o'clock that morning, arriving at the clinic right on time. Joey gets out the Jeep and goes and opens the door for Amanda. They walk in the clinic, going up to the receptionist window. The receptionist opens the window, and Joey says, "Amanda Crawford to see Dr. Bailey." The receptionist replies, "would you sign in, please." Joey signs Amanda in, and they go to the waiting area and sit. About five minutes later, Teresa comes through the door, saying, "Amanda Crawford?" Amanda and Joey stand and walk to the door that Teresa has opened for them. Teresa says, "hello Joey, and also to you, Amanda." When she greets, Amanda Teresa says, "I'm Teresa, and would you follow me please." Then Amanda says, "I'm Amanda."

They follow Teresa to an examining room where Teresa asks Amanda to stand on a scale to get her weight and height. Amanda stands on the scales, then Teresa pulls up the height rod and says, "your height is five-foot-five inches." Then Teresa looks at her weight then shakes her head, saying excitedly, "I'm so envious! One hundred and eight pounds!" Then she asks Amanda to sit on the examination table. Joey helps her up on the table, and Teresa wraps a cuff around Amanda's arm to check her blood pressure. After a few moments, Teresa unwraps the cuff saying, "perfect. One-nineteen over sixty-nine."

Teresa puts the blood pressure cuff back on the wall and enters Amanda's vitals in her computer pad. She looks at Amanda, saying, "Dr. Bailey will be with you in a few moments." Both Joey and Amanda say at the same time, "thank you, Teresa." Teresa then says, "let me look at your sutures while I'm here. I'm sure they need to be removed by now. Teresa looks at Amanda's eyebrow then says, "goodness! These sutures are about to come out on there own. Teresa removes the sutures, and Dr. Bailey comes into the exam room, shaking Joey's hand. Then he turns to Amanda, saying, "Hi Amanda, I'm Kelvin Bailey." Amanda says, "very nice to meet you, Dr. Bailey." Kelvin looks at the x-rays and the diagnosis that the hospital in Grand Junction sent him. He looks at the x-rays very carefully then says, "It looks like you have fractures of the six and seventh right true ribs." Then he looks at the wrist x-ray, saying, "you have a fracture of the scaphoid carpal bone in your left wrist also."

Dr. Bailey lifts her sweat and t-shirt to expose where her rib fractures are. He looks at Amanda, saying, "don't worry, sweetie, I'm not going to hurt you." He feels around where the fractures are, and he puts a little pressure with his fingers saying, "does that hurt Amanda?" She shakes her head, saying, "no, sir. Not at all." He takes off the splint on her left wrist, applying a little pressure where the fracture is. Kelvin says, "does this hurt?" Amanda says, "just a tiny bit but nothing like before." Kelvin looks over at Joey then back at Amanda, saying, "we're going to take pictures of these fractures, and Teresa will take you back in just a bit. So sit tight, and I will be back in after I view the new x-rays." Amanda says to Kelvin, "thank you so much, Dr. Bailey." Kelvin smiles, saying, "your most welcome, Amanda." Kelvin walks out of the room, then Joey says, "by Kelvin's reactions, Amanda, I would say your healing fine." She smiles then replies by saying, "I know I'm getting better every day, Joey!"

Joey looks at her for a few moments, and Amanda says, "what?" Joey has a big smile saying, "I'm sure Kelvin will want to see you again. And if he says your okay, we're going to go on that day trip to Denver to get you some proper clothes, girl!" Amanda lites up extremely happy, saying, "do you mean that Joey?" Joey tilts his head with a jokingly stern expression saying, "Amanda, I'm just like Superman. I never lie." She starts to tear up, saying very emotionally, "Joey, you are the sweetest, caring man I've ever known." Joey nods his head a little with a small smile.

Teresa comes back to the exam room, saying to Amanda, "let's go get some pictures, Amanda!" Joey gets up then helping Amanda get off the exam table. He starts to walk with her, but Amanda looks at him smiling then says, "Joey, let me try to do this on my own if you don't mind." "Of course, I don't mind. Go ahead," replies Joey. Teresa and Amanda walk out of the room, walking to the x-ray department. Teresa is looking down the hall with a little whimsical grin saying, "that's a pretty good guy you left back there in the exam room Amanda. You know Joey is the kind of guy you would marry."

They reach the x-ray department then stopping at the door, then Amanda looks at Teresa with a melancholy expression, saying, "I've thought about what you just said more than once, Teresa. He is the finest man I have ever known. And yes, he is the type of man I would marry in a minute. But I don't know if Joey has the same feelings for me. I'm surely going to pray about that situation." Joey, who is still sitting back in the exam room, has a sad expression when he says to himself, "I hope I'm reading this wrong, but I think Amanda is getting too attached to me. And if I'm right, I can't let that happen."

Ten minutes later, Amanda returns to the exam room, and Joey helps her up on the examination table. Joey then says, "how did it go?" Amand produces a big smile saying, "it didn't hurt at all. The X-ray technician was named Perry. And she was sweet and gentle with me." Later Dr. Bailey comes back into the exam room, saying, "okay, I got your pictures, and frankly, I'm amazed." Both Amanda and Joey have questionable expressions, then Amanda says, "Dr. Bailey, why are you amazed?" Kelvin puts his computer pad on the exam table and calls Joey over to look at the pictures with them. Kelvin brings up Amanda's x-rays he got from the Grand Junction hospital that was taken over two weeks ago of Amanda's wrist and ribs. Then Kelvin says, "look at these fractures that were taken two weeks ago."

He points to the fractures saying, "look at this." Amanda and Joey and can see the breaks in her wrist and ribs. Then Kelvin changes the screen that compares those x-rays to the ones just taken, saying, "now look at this." He points to fractures from the new pictures and compares them to the older x-rays. With an excitable voice and expression, he says, "these fractures almost look like they have healed! I've never seen anything like this in my twelve years of practice. These new X-rays look like its been months since that happened to you."

Amanda looks at Joey with a sweet smile, saying, "I know now that God heard those prayers you said over me when I was in the emergency room." Joey nods his head with a slight smile, saying, "I think your right, Amanda." Kelvin puts Amanda's brace back on her wrist, saying, "you can take this off when you go to bed, but I want you to wear it during the day. And I will set up an appointment for you two weeks from now. I'll be right back." He leaves out of the room, and Amanda starts crying. Joey asks her what's wrong, and she says, "Joey, I know in my heart that God worked through you to take care of me. And he brought you to me to change my life." I feel like a whole different person since I met you." Joey looks around the room, thinking about what he said to himself when Amanda was getting her x-rays. He then looks down with a sad look on his face. Amanda has a concerned expression saying, "Joey, are you okay?" He looks up at her, saying, "I'm alright, Amanda."

Dr. Bailey comes back into the room and hands an appointment card to Joey, saying, "the appointment is for October fourth at ten o'clock. "is that okay?" "Yes, that's fine, Kelvin," replies Joey. Kelvin turns to Amanda and says, "it's been my pleasure to meet you, Amanda." She extends her hand to him, and he takes it. She then says, "thank you so much for all you've done for me, Dr. Bailey." Kelvin replies, "it's been my pleasure, Amanda, and I will see you in two weeks." Joey shakes Kelvin's hand, and Kelvin says to him, "take care of this lovely lady Joey." Amanda then says with a big smile, "you don't have to worry about that, Dr. Bailey" Joey helps Amanda down from the exam table, and Kelvin says, "Amanda, I want to speak to Joey for a moment if you don't mind." "I don't mind at all. I'll wait in the hall," replies Amanda.

Amanda leaves the room, and Kelvin puts his hand on Joey's shoulder and, with a broad grin saying, "Joey, the way Amanda has been talking about you, I think that she might be interested in you old friend. That's because you are making a big difference in her life. And I know deep down in my soul, she has changed because of you. She looks to me like she could be marrying material. No matter what kind of past she has. Know what I mean?" Joey looks down then back at Kelvin with a frown, saying, "Kelvin, I think you might be right about Amanda being interested in me. But I can't allow this infatuation she has for me to go any further." Kelvin has a perplexed expression, saying, "for goodness sakes Joey why not?" Joey says, "Kelvin, I can't talk about it right now. I hope you understand." Kelvin smiles, saying, "if you want to talk about it, give me a call or come to the office. Even come by the house if you like." Joey shakes his hand then says calmly, "thanks for understanding. We'll see you in two weeks." Joey walks out of the room, and he and Amanda walk to the receptionist window. The receptionist opens the window, then Joey says, "what do I owe you, ma'am?" She says, "we'll send you a bill, Mr. Morris, and thank you." Joey smiles at her, saying, "thank you."

Amanda and Joey walk out to his Jeep as Joey opens Amanda's door and helps her in. Joey walks around, getting in the vehicle, and they leave the clinic. Then Joey says, "let's get a pizza from Big Toney's for lunch. Amanda smiles, saying, "Joey, I love pizza!" Joey looks to her for a moment then says, "what do you like on your pizza?" "Everything! Plus, extra cheese! But no anchovies," says Amanda. Joey produces a big smile and saying, "that's the pizza I like!" As they are driving down the street, Amanda says, "Joey, can we stop at the pharmacy where you got my medicine?" Joey says, "sure, it's right down the street." They arrive at the pharmacy and Joey parks by the front entrance. He opens his door, then Amanda says, "Joey, you might not want to go in with me." Joey looks at her with a dubious expression, saying, "why not?"

Amanda pauses a bit and, with a slightly embarrassed look, says, "Joey, I need to get some female items, and I'm hoping you understand what I'm talking about." Joey looks at her with wide eyes and a petrified look, saying very fast, "yea, I know what you're talking about." He stares at her with the same look as before then reaches for his wallet. He pulls out forty dollars, saying, "will this be enough?" She tries not to laugh at Joey's embarrassing predicament, and he gives her the money. Amanda hands back one of the twenty's and says, "this will be enough." Joey composes himself a little bit and manages to create a small smile, then says, "you keep all of that. You might see something else you might want to get."

Amanda nods her head, saying, "I'm going to get a little make-up with it then. Thanks, sweetie." Amanda immediately gets a slight panic look on her face because she realizes she just called Joey sweetie. She opens her door then turns to Joey, saying, "I'll be right back." She gets out of the Jeep. Then she starts to walk to the front door of the pharmacy, and Joey is watching her every step. Before she enters the pharmacy, Joey lowers his window, saying, "I'll order the pizza while you're in the pharmacy." She smiles at him, then enters the pharmacy. Joey folds his arms and puts them on top of the steering wheel. Then he leans forward, laying his forehead on his folded arms. He then says to himself, "man, you sure can tell I haven't been around a woman in a while."

Twenty minutes later, Amanda comes out of the pharmacy, and Joey gets out. He walks around the Jeep and opens her door, helping her in. He walks around, getting back into the vehicle. Then Amanda opens the shopping bag and takes out her make-up showing them to Joey. Then she excitedly says, "look at this make-up Joey. They have an excellent selection of the make-up I use." Joey looks at the make-up, and Amanda says, "I know that guys don't think about make-up very much. But think how it makes us look when we have it on." Joey smiles and shrugs his shoulders, saying, "I'll admit that some of you gals can doll up very pretty. But Amanda, to me, you don't need that much to make you pretty." She looks at him with a loving smile, saying, "Joey, that was so sweet. Thank you." Then Joey says, "to the mountain now via Big Toney's?" "Big Toney's and the mountain, sir," replies Amanda.

They get near Wilson's store, and Joey looks at Amanda, saying, "I'm going to stop at Mr. Wilson's and get a couple of sandwiches and chips for tonight's dinner. Amanda smiles, saying excitedly, "Hey! That sounds great Joey" They reach the store, and Joey pulls in then turns around to Amanda, saying, "come in with me and meet everybody." She says, "alright, then." Joey still always the gentleman walks around and opens Amanda's door then helping her out of the Jeep. They reach the entrance of the store, and Joey opens the door. They both walk-in, then stopping inside the door. All the customers look around, and Joey, in all his thirty-eight years, never heard the store become so instantly quite. All the men stand up, staring at Amanda with enormous smiles on their faces.

They have never seen a woman this beautiful to ever come into this grocery store. Amanda looks at everybody with her what beautiful smile. Joey notices all the men staring at her. He then jokingly says, "okay, guys, you can stop ogling now." Then Joey smiles, saying, "everybody may I introduce my friend Amanda." Amanda thinks to herself how nice it would be if someone one day would say this is my girlfriend. Or better yet, fiance or wife. Everybody says, "Hello, Amanda." Amanda waves then says, smiling, "Hey everybody."

Amanda and Joey walk up to the counter where Joey introduces her to Mr. Wilson, saying, "Amanda, this is James Wilson. Mr. Wilson, this is Amanda Crawford." Amanda reaches out her hand, then shaking Mr. Wilson's hand, saying, "very nice to meet you, Mr. Wilson." Mr. Wilson then says, "if you would like, you can call me just Wilson, Amanda. Most everybody does anyway." Amanda looks at Wilson and says, "when I'm around you to you, it will always be Mr. Wilson." Joey looks at Amanda, saying, "I've been coming to his store since I was a kid." Amanda looks at Wilson jokingly, saying, "you never had to run him out of here for being bad, did you?" Wilson smiles, saying, "of course not Miss Amanda. Joey was a great kid. I wish I could say that about some of the other kids." Amanda looks at Joey and, with a loving smile, then says, "Mr. Wilson, Joey is still that great kid."

Joey quickly says, "we're going over to the deli two get a couple of sandwiches from Bailey. Joey puts his hand on Amanda's back and leads her to the deli. They reach the deli counter, and Bailey turns around, saying with a slight flirty tone, "hey there, Joey." Then Bailey looks at Amanda, saying, "who do you have here?" Joey says, "Amanda, this is Bailey." Then Bailey says, "nice to meet you, Amanda." "Very nice to meet you, Bailey," replies Amanda. Joey looks at Bailey, then back at Amanda, and says, "this lady makes great sandwiches." Amanda gives Joey a slight, jokingly, resentful look, saying, "I'm sure she does Joey." Joey looks at Amanda with a scrounged up face and rolling his eyes.

Bailey smiles at them both saying, "what kind of sandwiches would you two like?" Joey says, "I want another one of your Reubens, please." Bailey looks at Amanda, saying, "and for you, Amanda?" Amanda looks at all the meats and says, "I would like a turkey on wheat with lots of mayonnaise. With lettuce and tomato, please." Bailey writes the orders down then saying, "I'll have your sandwiches ready in just a moment." After a few minutes, Bailey hands the sandwiches to Joey, saying again in a flirty tone, "It's great seeing you again, Joey. And nice to meet you, Amanda." Joey has a sheepish grin, saying, "see you next time, Bailey." "Looking forward to it, Joey," replies Bailey in the same flirty tone. As they walk to the counter, Amanda starts to laugh at Joey, and he says, "what!" Amanda jokingly says, "It looks like to me that a cute, young lady has a crush on you." Joey turns to Amanda with a sour face, saying, "she does not Amanda. Besides, she is just a kid." Amanda, who is still laughing a little, says, "It doesn't matter how old you are to have a crush on someone Joey. As they walk to pay for the sandwiches, Amanda says, "besides you're a great guy and ladies can easily get crushes on you. You never know who could have one on you now."

Joey looks at Amanda with a questionable expression, and they walk to the counter. Mr. Wilson says, "will that be all?" Joey says, "yes, sir, that's it." Mr. Wilson rings up the purchase, and Joey pays him. Amanda says, "again, it was very nice to meet you, Mr. Wilson." Mr.Wilson says, "the pleasure is all mine, Amanda. See you two later." They walk out of the store, and Joey opens Amanda's door, helping her in. Joey gets in and cranks up and heads to the cabin. As he is driving, Joey is thinking about what Amanda said in the store. When she told him you never know who has a crush on him now.

They arrive at the cabin when Amanda says, "Joey, let me try to get out of the Jeep on my own. I know you're such a gentleman always opening my door and helping me out. I want to give it a try." Joey smiles and says, "alright, but be careful. Don't get in a hurry." Joey grabs the pizza, sandwiches, and Amanda's pharmacy bag and gets out walking around to Amanda's door. She opens the door and steps out slowly and stands next to Joey. He nods his head, smiling, then says, "well?" Amanda has a proud expression, saying, "Joey, that didn't hurt a bit!" Joey looks at her for a few moments then says, smiling, "I'm proud of you, Amanda. And I'm so surprised at how fast you are healing." He looks around with a gentle, smiling expression, saying, "Vickie was right." Amanda looks at him with a questionable expression then says, "who is Vickie?" Joey smiles and says, "let's get out of this cold, and I will tell you about Vickie when we get inside the cabin." He puts his hand on Amanda's back, and they walk up the steps to the porch. Joey puts the food and Amanda's bag down and unlocks the front door. Joey picks up the food and the bag, and they walk into the cabin.

Joey puts the pizza and bag on the table and goes into the kitchen, putting the sandwiches in the refrigerator. He walks back into the den, walking to the wood rack and places three logs on the smoldering coals in the fireplace. Amanda then says, "I'll be right back. I have to use the bathroom." "What do you want to drink with your sandwich," Joey asks her. Amanda says, "milk will be fine." Joey starts to laugh and jokingly says, "Milk. The best white wine for Pizza!" She shakes her head, smiling, then turns walking to the bathroom as Joey says, "do you need some help? Or do you want to try this yourself?" She turns, smiling at Joey, saying, "I think I can handle this from now on, but thank you anyway."

She turns, then walks into the bathroom, and Joey goes into the kitchen to get Amanda's milk and for himself bottled water. He also gets some paper plates and napkins and places everything in their prospective places on the table. Then Joey sits in his chair. Amanda comes out of the bathroom, and Joey stands up, pulling out her chair. Amanda sits then produces that lovely smile of hers, saying to Joey, "Joey, I know that you're a gentleman, but you don't have to do that every time." He looks at her with a jokingly, stern expression, saying, "I think I told you this before. But any lady around me is going to be treated like a lady."

Amanda shakes her head with a lovely, but questionable expression, then says, "God didn't make many guys like you, did he, Joey." Joey shrugs his shoulders with a nonchalant expression then says, "sure he did. But I'm afraid he is not making any more gentlemen like he used to. Now let's eat!" Joey opens the pizza box where steam and a pleasant aroma comes from the pizza. Amanda looks at him then says, "Joey, let's start giving thanks before we eat from now on. Is that okay?' Joey nods his head, then says, "okay, go ahead." Amanda is a little embarrassed, saying, "Joey, I'm ashamed, but I don't know how to pray. And I want you to teach me how to do it properly. Will you do that for me, please?" Joey looks at her for a few moments with a calm expression then says, "there's no need to be ashamed, Amanda. Just speak from your heart, that's all. I'm a little out of shape on praying properly, but I will do my best."

They both bow their heads as Joey says, "God, we thank you for this pizza, which I'm sure will be delicious you have provided for Amanda and me." Joey pauses for a few seconds then says, "but most importantly, thank you for your healing of Amanda so fast, Amen." Amanda looks at him, saying, "that was nice, Joey." Joey then says, "as I said, you speak to God from your heart. That's all there is to it." Joey looks at her, then saying, "after you, Amanda." Amanda carefully gets a slice of the pizza then Joey takes a slice. Then Amanda says, "Joey, you were going to tell me who Vickie was."

He puts his slice of pizza down, then takes a drink of his water. He looks up at the ceiling then says, "I met Vickie in the emergency waiting room while you were there." He looks at Amanda, then says, "now this when it gets bizarre. Vickie was an elderly lady who came into the waiting room and sat next to me. She noticed that I had a very concerned expression, then she introduced herself." Amanda then says, "you had never seen her before?" Joey replies, "I never saw her until I went and sat in the waiting area after the nurse ran me out of your room." Joey puts his elbow on the table and puts his chin in his hand. He then says, "now get ready for this, Amanda. It gets strange from here. I told her about your injuries then Vickie put her hand on mine. She asked me if I believed in my heart that God would heal you. She also said that God sometimes heals people very fast. I said to her that I did believe that he would heal you." Then she said, "I have this on the highest authority that I didn't have to worry because God would hear my prayer."

Joey looks directly into Amanda's eyes, saying, "then I had this peaceful feeling come over me knowing you would be okay." Amanda smiles and says, "wow! Then what happened?" Joey says, "the nurse came in telling me that Dr. Kellum had some news for me. I went back to the emergency department, and when I came back to the waiting room after talking to the doctor, Vickie wasn't there. A teenage boy that had a cast on his arm was sitting directly in front of Vickie and me. I asked him where the elderly lady that I was talking to had gone. The kid looked at me weird and said, "what lady." I said the lady that was sitting next to me. Then the kid said, "I'm telling you dude there was no one sitting next to you." Then the kid said, "I heard and saw you talking to an empty chair, but an old lady was never there! You were freaking me out, man!" Amanda has this surprising look on her face, saying, "Joey, that is amazing! What did you do then?" Joey says, "I thought the kid was messing with me. So I went and found the nurse asking her did she see the lady who was sitting next to me when she came to get me. The nurse shook her head, saying she didn't see anybody sitting next to me. I went back to the waiting room, thinking I had some emotional breakdown!"

Amanda shakes her head, looking at Joey with an unusual expression, then says, "Joey, I think Vickie was an angel who came to comfort you." Joey shakes his head, saying, "I been through a lot of strange things, but that was the most peculiar thing that has ever happened to me. I have no explanation for that experience." Amanda then says, "do you believe in angels, Joey?" Joey sighs, then smiles and says, "Amanda, I've never thought that much about angelic beings. I've read about them, seen them in movies, and there mentioned throughout the bible. And like I said, I couldn't explain what happened in that waiting room. So I say…yes, I do believe in angels." "Well, so do I. And I believe they are all around protecting us. Just like you saved me from Rico," says a smiling Amanda. Joey gets embarrassed and shakes his head but has a slight smile, saying, "I'm no angel, Amanda, I assure you." Amanda looks at Joey with the most delicate smile saying, "I think you are Joey." Amanda takes a bite of her pizza then takes a drink of her milk. After a few moments, she says, "Joey, that is why I want you to teach me all that you know about the Bible. I know that it will help me to turn my life around." Joey then says, "okay, we will start tonight.

They finish eating, and Joey starts to clear the dining table. Amanda stops him by saying, "let me do this, Joey." She takes the plates, and her glass off the table then goes into the kitchen to wash them. Amanda hears Mr. Wilson call Joey on the radio, saying, "Wilson's store calling Joey Morris…over." Amanda calls out to Joey, saying, "Joey, Mr. Wilson is calling you on the radio." Joey walks into the kitchen, saying, "yes, I heard. Thanks." Joey presses the microphone tab, saying, "this is Joey Mr. Wilson. What's up?" Mr. Wilson says, "Joey, I just heard on the weather radio that we are under a winter storm warning starting this afternoon." Joey looks at Amanda, and sarcastically says to her, "like we never have those warnings in the mountains of Colorado." Amanda smiles, saying, "Be nice, Joey." Joey presses the tab on the microphone, saying, "thanks for the heads up, Mr. Wilson." Then Wilson says, "they're saying we could have over a foot of snow by tomorrow morning, so be prepared." "We're fine up here. Just got to split some firewood to be on the safe side," replies Joey. Wilson then says, "be safe…over and out."

Joey looks at Amanda smiling then saying, "Mr. Wilson not only has the closest store around but he is also our local weatherman. Amanda smiles then says, "you should feel thankful to have a friend like Mr. Wilson." Joey goes into the den then puts his coat and gloves, then saying to Amanda, "better get out there and spilt that wood if we're going to have a big storm." Amanda says, "be careful, okay?" Joey nods his head, leaves out the front door. Amanda walks over to the bookcase to see if there is anything she would like to read. After a few moments, Amanda sees the scrapbook and takes it out of the case. She sits on the couch and starts looking through it. She smiles as she sees all the pictures and clippings from Joey's career in the Marines.

She comes to the last of the book and sees where Joey was awarded the Naval Cross for heroism in his last deployment in Afghanistan. She reads the clippings and sees all the pictures when he received the award. She is amazed and very proud to know a real American hero. Especially a Marine hero. She looks up and thinks that she knew there was something special about him. Later, Joey comes in and brings four armloads of firewood in and putting it on the wood rack. He takes off his coat and gloves, saying to Amanda, "Mr. Wilson was right about the storm. It's starting to snow hard out there now."

Later that afternoon, Amanda goes and takes a shower. Joey is putting more wood on the fire, and he hears, knocking at the front door. He goes to his gun cabinet and retrieving the forty-four magnum revolver. He goes up to the door, saying, "who's there?" Jessie Sneed says in a concerned voice, "it's me, Joey…Jessie! Open up!" Joey opens the door, and Jessie sees Joey's weapon in his hand. Jessie becomes very concerned, saying, "what's wrong with you, Joey?" Joey says, "just being a little cautious these days, Jessie, that's all." Amanda comes out of the bathroom with her bathrobe on and sees Jessie then says, "hello." Joey, who is a little embarrassed, says, "Amanda, this is my closest neighbor, Jessie Sneed." Jessie takes off his cap, and Joey says, "Jessie, this is Amanda Crawford." Amanda walks across the floor, reaching to shake Jessie's hand. Jessie takes her hand, then Amanda says, "so nice to meet you, Mr. Sneed. Joey has told me all about you. What brings you up here?" Jessie says, "I brought back Joey's log splitter before it gets bad out there. So I better get going before it hits."

Amanda smiles, saying, "you come back and stay awhile when this storm passes, okay?" Jessie looks at Amanda and Joey, then says, "I'll do that, Miss Amanda. So I will see you two later." Joey opens the door, and he steps out on the porch with Jessie. Joey says to him, "Jessie, it's not what you think about Amanda and me." Jessie frowns, saying, "I'm not concerned about the girl. I'm concerned that you met me at the door with that hand cannon of yours. What's going on, Marine?" Joey takes a deep breath, saying, "Jessie, I cannot get into it right now. But do keep an open eye for strange people and vehicles that might come up this mountain."

Jessie shakes his head and has a deeply concerned look on his face and says, "you're getting me quite concerned about this, Joey. But I'm not going to say anything else. I'll talk to you later." Joey replies, "thanks, Jessie." Jessie walks to his truck, and Joey goes back into the cabin when Amanda says, "Mr. Sneed seems to be a good neighbor and friend to you, Joey." Joey looks at her for a few seconds then smiles, saying, "the best Amanda."

It's about two-thirty A.M. the next morning, and Joey wakes up. He carefully gets out of his recliner, trying not to awake Amanda. Joey goes into the kitchen and opens his refrigerator to get a bottle of water. He opens the bottle taking a large drink out of it. Joey puts the top back on the bottle then places it back in the refrigerator. He walks back in the den then quietly sets more firewood on fire. Joey then walks to the back window of the cabin. He turns on the floodlights illuminating his land in the back of the cabin. It is snowing hard, and Joey estimates over a foot of snow have already fallen. He says to himself quietly while he is still looking out the window, "the snow is probably going to be around two feet by morning."

He walks to his recliner and sits quietly. Joey is not very sleepy and decides to read to see if this will make him relax to help him fall asleep again. He picks up the book of the stand he has been reading for a couple of weeks. He starts to read, and Amanda turns over in the bed and breathes deeply, holding on to her bear. Joey looks over the top of the book seeing if she is okay. He looks back in his book, and about ten seconds later, he looks over the book again, staring at Amanda. Joey realizes what he is doing and quickly looks back at his book. A few moments later, he looks over the book, staring at her again. He realizes what he is doing and looks back to his novel and quietly says to himself, "Joey, get a grip, man! You've seen beautiful women before!" He settles back in his recliner and determines he is going to read this book. Then after a few moments, he puts the novel on the stand and says to himself quietly, "oh what the heck." He props his arm on the recliner arm and puts his chin in his hand. He has a relaxed, peaceful look on his face as he stares at Amanda.

Later Joey has to clear his throat but does it quietly as possible, trying not to wake her. He is looking at her when Amanda slightly moves her head and slowly opens her eyes. Joey quickly grabs the book off the stand, pretending to have been reading. She smiles at him and says, "what time is it?" Joey looks at his watch, saying, "it's three-fifteen." Joey lifts the book back up, acting like he is reading, then Amanda smiles, saying, "Joey?" He puts down the novel and replies, "yes, ma'am?" She produces her lovely smile and says, "Joey, when I opened my eyes just now, you were staring at me." Joey gets embarrassed, then says, "I was checking on you. That's all." Amanda again beams her beautiful smile, saying, "Joey, when you were looking at me, I have never seen you with such a warm, heartfelt expression that you had on your face. So tell me why you were staring at me...please?"

Joey decides he's lost this battle with her and concedes. He looks around the den and with an awkward expression. He then looks at her and smiles, saying, "Amanda, this will be corny and awkward. One time I heard what I'm about to say in a movie. I thought it was cheesy, but I see now it can be a real feeling that can happen." She shakes her head with a questionable expression then says, "what can happen?" Joey says, "okay, promise me you won't laugh?" She looks at him shaking her head, smiling, then says, "I promise not to laugh because I know it's going to be something adorable."

Joey looks at her with the most serene face that Amanda has ever seen him produce. He shakes his head, smiling, then says, "Amanda, what I was staring at was the most beautiful woman I have ever seen in my life. Your hair was across your cheek, and your face had a soft, pretty glow. I just sat here watching you. And listening to you breathe." He pauses for a few moments then says, "I told you it was corny. And maybe be a little creepy." He looks down, embarrassed, and says, "I never said anything like that before to any woman." Amanda then says, "that is a big relief to me, you never said that to a man." Joey looks at her and starts to laugh, saying, "me too." He looks down again, not saying anything.

Amanda has tears in her eyes, and calmly says, "Joey." He doesn't look up, and she says again softly, "Joey." He looks up at her, "yes, Amanda?" Joey notices her tears, and she says, "come and lay with me?" Joey's eyes get huge with a horrified expression on his face, saying, "Oh no, Amanda, you know I can't do that! It's too dangerous!" She smiles, shaking her head and says, "Joey, it's not what you think. Please do this for me." Joey sits there for a few moments and looks around. He then gets out of the recliner and walks over to the bed, petrified. Amanda says to him, "Joey, I'll have my back to you." He's still hesitating, and she pats the bed behind her. He finally gets on the bed, and she turns her back to him.

He lays down behind her on top of the covers with a little space between them. Amanda then says, "Joey, aren't you going to get under the covers? Want you get cold?" Joey takes a deep breath and closes his eyes, saying, "I assure you, Amanda, I will not get cold." Amanda smiles then says, "you can get close because I want to feel you next to me. And I don't bite that hard." Joey rolls his eyes, then says, "getting bit is not what I'm afraid of." He scoots close to her, and she reaches and takes his arm, putting it around her.

Joey can't resist by taking in the terrific scent of her beautiful hair. They lay there for a few moments when Amanda says with a calm voice, "Joey, at this moment, I have never felt so safe and secure in my life." Joey starts smiling then saying, "well, I can tell you one thing, Amanda, about us laying together." She says softly, "what's that?" Joey says, "this is sure better than laying around with a bunch of Marines." They both start laughing, and Amanda takes his arm and squeezes it against her body. She closes her eyes but soon opens them with tears running down her cheeks. She knows now without a dought that she has fallen in love with Joey.

Chapter Eight

Amanda Experiences Joey's Vast Land

Morning arrives, and Amanda awakes. She gets out of the bed, making sure she doesn't wake Joey. Amanda gets up, seeing sunshine coming from the back window of the den. She walks to the window and sees the fresh snow that fell overnight. Amanda thinks to herself that this is the deepest snow she has ever seen. She goes into the kitchen and pours her some coffee in a mug she got from a cabinet above the coffee maker. Amanda puts her coffee mug on the dining table then picks up a chair from the table carefully. She sets the chair in front of the window then she gets some small firewood from the wood rack. Amanda places the wood on the coals from the fire the night before. She gets her mug and sits in the chair that she put in front of the window.

She looks out the window, and the first thing that catches her eye is the multi-colored finches and sparrows and other birds under the snow-laden trees. She is in amazement at how bright it is out there from the sun hitting the snow that she has to squint her eyes. She can't take her eyes off this portrait that nature has painted. She sits there for a while when Joey wakes up, saying, "good morning." Amanda turns to him, smiling and says, "good morning Joey." Joey then asks Amanda, "what are you looking at?" She turns to him, saying, "Joey, you have to come to see this beautiful sight!" Joey reluctantly gets off the bed because he has seen beautiful snow most of his life. But he's not going to dampen Amanda's excitement. He walks to the window and looks outside, then says, "wow, that is beautiful." Amanda, who is still looking at the snowy spectacle, says, "I especially like all those pretty colored birds hopping around out there." Joey looks at the fireplace saying, "I see you built up the fire. Amanda, it looks like to me you are becoming a real mountain girl."

Joey then says, "are you hungry?" Amanda looks at him, and she quickly says, "starving!" "Okay, let me go rustle up some chow then," Joey says with a big smile. Amanda looks at him with a puzzled expression, saying, "Joey, what is chow?" Joey laughs, then says, "chow is the name for food in the military." Amanda says jokingly, "I guess you might consider that comment a blonde moment because I didn't know what chow was." Joey laughs and walks into the kitchen to prepare breakfast as Amanda looks out the window. Later as they are eating, Joey asks her, "Amanda, would you like to take the snow-track out and let me take you around showing you my place." Her eyes open wide and excitedly says, "oh Joey, I would love too!" Then she looks at him with a questionable expression, saying, "Joey, what's a snow-track?" Joey replies, "its all-terrain vehicle that has wide, hard rubber tracks instead of tires. It has a cab, and it kind of glides across deep snow."

After they finish breakfast and clean off the table, Joey says to Amanda, "you're going to have to wear some of my outdoor gear. It will be big, but it will keep you toasty while we're out there. I know you will want to walk around while we are out." "Sounds great," exclaims Amanda. Joey starts to think that his mother's outdoor clothing should still be in the close cabinet. He finds some of the clothing deep inside the closet. Also, he sees his mom's snow boots. It brings a smile to his face to see Amanda will be wearing his mother's outdoor clothes. Joey puts on his parka then takes a parka, gloves, and boots to her, then says, "Amanda, these were my mother's parka and boots." She looks at him with a questionable face and says, "are you sure, Joey?" He smiles and says, "It will be great to see you in them. But I'm afraid they will still be large on you. She puts on the parka over her sweats and puts her boots and gloves on. She stands up, saying to Joey, "how does it look?" He says, "wow, that looks great, but you need one more thing." He walks to a closet that is in the den and gets a stocking cap then walks over her, putting the knit cap on her head.

Joey thinks to himself that right at this moment, he has never seen Amanda so adorable. Joey feels butterflies in his stomach. Plus, a strange warm feeling when he looks at her with all those oversized outdoor clothes on. But he quickly puts those warm feelings out like it's a flash fire. He then looks up at a smiling Amanda, saying, "let me go out and pull the snow-track out of the barn to have it warmed up for you." Amanda then says eagerly, "I'll be right here waiting!" He walks out the door to get the snow-track ready. He walks out to the barn and cranks the vehicle then turning on the heater. He pulls the snow-track to the front of the cabin then gets out. He leaves it running to warm up the cab.

Joey enters the den and walks to the gun case opening it. He gets his forty-four magnum out with a holster. He gets a box of ammunition, putting it in one of his pockets on his parka. Amanda has a dubious expression, saying, "why are you taking your big gun for?" Joey can't let this "golden" opportunity to tease Amanda. He looks at her very seriously then says, "always carry a weapon when you go into the woods. I hope I never have to use it. But I have it in case of a bear or mountain lion attack." Amanda's eyes open wide and with a frightened expression, says, "bear and mountain lions are around here?" Joey still has a serious expression, saying, "Amanda, you have to remember that you are in the mountains. Bear and mountain lions are all over the place here."

Amanda still has the frightened expression on her face when Joey says in a stern tone, "bears and mountain lions I don't worry about too much. It's the bigfoot that scares me." Amanda gets a panicked look on her face, saying, "bigfoot?" Joey looks directly in her eyes with a serious look saying, "yes bigfoot. They are very elusive, but we know they're around here by all the large footprints in the snow and mud. They say the male bigfoot prefers human women. There have been multiple abductions of women up here that were hiking. And were never seen again." Joey looks up, saying, "it's so strange, but all those women were young, pretty and blonde. They seem to have no interest in other women."

Amanda, who now is terrified, says, "Joey, tell me the truth. Do you think it's safe to be going up in the mountains?" Joey looks down with the same serious look, but he can't hold it back any longer. He slowly starts to smile then burst out in laughter. Amanda looks at him strangely, saying, "Joey, why are you…" She doesn't finish her sentence because she knows now that he is teasing her. She slaps him on the shoulder with a smiling, ridiculed look, saying, "Joey stop teasing me! I didn't know! I've never been to the mountains before!" Joey keeps on laughing, and Amanda says jokingly, "Joey quit laughing at me! But I have to admit you had me quite scared!"

Joey starts to calm down from his laughing, then says, "Amanda, there is no bigfoot up here. And bear and mountain lion attacks are sporadic. Does that make you feel better?" Amanda puts her hands on her hips, smiling and says, "yes, it does! And I'm glad you found it so hilarious at my expense!" Joey puts his arm around her shoulders but still laughing and says, "you ready? The snow-track should be warm now." She nods her head, smiling, then says, "I'm going to get you back for that scare Joey Morris." Then Joey says to her, "let me go into the kitchen and get some hot dogs for we can eat on the trail. What do you like on your hot dogs?"

Amanda smiles and quickly says, "mayonnaise only." Joey looks at her with a revolting expression then says, "who puts mayonnaise on a hot dog Amanda. That's disgusting!" She looks at Joey with a jokingly unpleasant look and says, "for your information, sir. I know many people like mayonnaise on their hot dogs. And I eat it with a lot of other things too that you would probably find revolting." Joey looks at her shaking his head, saying, "okay, suit yourself." He walks into the kitchen and puts everything, including the mayonnaise, in a shopping bag. He walks back into the den and says to Amanda, "shall we go?" "Ready," replies Amanda. They walk out of the cabin, and Joey opens her door to the snow-track and helps her in. He walks around the front of the vehicle getting in, and they start on their adventure.

They start on a trail that goes past the barn heading into the woods. Amanda looks at Joey, saying, "Joey, how much land do you have?" Joey is looking straight ahead as he says, "over seventeen-hundred acres of prime timberland." Amanda has a questionable expression then says, "Joey, I don't know how much land that is." Joey still is looking forward and says, "I'm sure that you have seen a football field before." Amanda huffs and with a tenacious expression and voice, saying, "yes Joey, I know what a football field is." Joey laughs, then saying, "seventeen-hundred acres is about the size of seventeen-hundred football fields." Amanda's mouth drops, and her eyes get big. Then she turns, looking forward, saying, "wow, that is a lot of land!" Joey then says, "we had about twenty-seven hundred acres, but my mom sold a thousand acres to a big timber company a couple of years ago.

He takes her around, showing her where the old sawmill was. And tells Amanda the history of when his family logged the land. Joey then says, "that's why the sawmill was so important. The wood was cut here at the mill, and the lumber was sent all over the world. They then travel into an area that has beautiful cedar trees. The trees are laden with heavy snow that they are bowing over into each other. As they are going through the cedar trees, Amanda smiles, thinking to herself that it looks as if they are traveling through a snow tunnel.

They spend about three hours going over a small portion of Joey's land. Then they start to head home. They get about a quarter-of-a-mile from the cabin, and Joey says, "I've saved the best for last for you, Amanda." They travel to a high ridge that has a breathtaking rocky stream at the bottom. Joey looks at the stream and says, "this is where I spent most of my time when I was younger." He looks at Amanda, saying, "let's get out and cook those hot dogs, shall we? I'm starving!

He gets the bag with the hot dogs and condiments in it. He then gets out, walking around opening Amanda's door and helping her out. She walks to the ridge, looking down at the stream. She hears the relaxing sound of the water passing over the rocks. The water seems like beautiful crystals flowing over the stones. The deep snow and snow-covered trees enhance this beautiful view. Then she gets a somber expression on her face, and tears are rolling down her cheeks.

During this time, Joey has been collecting wood and then clears the snow where he will build a fire. He walks over to the snow track and gets dryer lint and metal hot dog rods out of a small toolbox. Dryer lint is very flammable, and he will use it to start the fire. He puts the lint under little sticks and lights the lint. The fire quickly burns, and he puts larger pieces of wood on top.

He walks over to where Amanda is standing. Then he looks down at this beautiful spectacle of nature at it's best. After a few moments, Joey turns and looks at Amanda smiling, later saying, "what do you think?" After a few seconds, she turns and looks at Joey, saying, "Joey, I didn't know that there were places like this on earth." Joey sees that she is crying and says with a concerned voice, "Amanda, are you alright?" She walks a few steps toward Joey, then saying, "Joey, I'm doing wonderful."

He looks at her with a strange face, and he pulls out his handkerchief and dries her tears. Joey then says, "let's cook those hot dogs." They walk to the fire and begin roasting the hot dogs. "Amanda says, "I've never roasted weenies over a fire before." Joey looks at her with a broad grin and says, "well, you're in for a treat. I love weenies cooked over a fire. And I like mine a little burnt too." He gives a bun to Amanda, and he puts a hot-dog in the wienie bun for her. Then Amanda proceeds to drown the hot-dog in mayonnaise. Joey looks at her, saying, "gross, Amanda."

Joey walks back to the snow track a gets a small cooking pot out of the toolbox. He walks back to the fire then scoops up snow in the pot. Joey holds the pot over the fire for a moment where the snow melts. He takes the pot and puts it in the snow to cool off the melted snow. After a few seconds, he hands the pot to Amanda and says, "take a drink. There's nothing better than drinking Colorado snow water." Amanda takes the pot by its handle and takes a drink. She looks at Joey, saying, "that is the most delicious water I've ever drunk before! That is if you can call water delicious." Amanda hands the pot to Joey as he says, "I can't think of a better word than to call this delicious water, Amanda." Joey finishes the water then says to her, "do you want me to melt some more snow?" She shakes her head, saying, "no, thanks. But we will have to do this again."

Joey says, "Oh, I will look forward to that! Now let's get back to the cabin." He puts out the fire, and he opens the door for Amanda, and she gets in. Joey walks around and getting in the vehicle. He cranks the motor and heads to the cabin. Amanda looks at Joey, saying, "how far away is the cabin?" "About fifteen minutes," replies Joey. Then she says, "walking distance then." He looks at her with a concered expression, saying, "only in the spring, summer or fall. It's too dangerous in the winter."

As they are driving to the cabin, Amanda looks at Joey, saying, "driving this thing sure looks like fun." Joey looks at her with a big smile, saying, "do you want to drive it the rest of the way home?" Amanda looks at him with an excited face and says, "can I, Joey!" "Alright then," says Joey. He stops the snow track then gets out and opens Amanda's door. They walk around the vehicle, and Joey opens the driver's door for her. He shuts her door then walks around and gets in the passenger side. Amanda looks at him with an uncertain expression, saying, "what do I do now?" Joey says, "have you ever drove a car?" She looks at him with an exasperated expression, saying snidely, "yes, Joey, I have driven a car." Joey points to a lever on the dash, saying, "put your foot on the brake and put the lever in drive. Then slowly step on the accelerator and away we go." She carefully carries out Joey's instructions, and they head to the cabin. Amanda then says's "Joey, this is so much fun! As you said, it feels like we are gliding over the snow!"

Later she drives up to the front of the cabin and stopping. She puts the lever in park, then says, "okay, what's next?" Joey reaches into his pocket, pulling out the door key handing it to her, saying, "go let yourself in while I will park this thing in the barn." Amanda knows by now that Joey will always open doors for her. He comes around, opening the door, and she gets out. Joey says, "go in and put kindling wood in the fireplace. Amanda questionably says, "what's kindling wood?" Joey smiles, saying, "it's the smallest wood in the rack. They look like sticks. It's for starting a fire." Amanda walks up the steps on to the porch unlocking the door going in. Joey parks the snow track in the barn.

Later that evening, they are sitting at the couch, looking at the fire. Joey looks at Amanda, saying, "Amanda, where are you from?" She says,

"Mountain Home, Arkansas." Then he asks her, "how in the world did you end up in Grand Junction?" She looks at him with a sorrowful expression, saying, "Joey, I just spent the most wonderful days of my life with you today. I don't want to go into any details on that right now." Joey gently smiles, saying, "Amanda, when you think the time is right, you can tell me then."

"Thanks," replies Amanda. Joey then says, "In less than two weeks, I'm going to be taking you back to Kelvin. And I hope he gives you a full release. Then we can plan that trip to Denver to get those clothes for you." Amanda excitedly says, "Oh Joey, I can't wait till that day!" Joey gets up then turns to Amanda, saying, "what me to show you in the Bible some of my favorite stories?" Amanda produces her lovely smile, saying, "I would love that, Joey." He walks over to the stand next to the recliner. He gets his Bible and walks back to the couch, sitting next to Amanda.

Over two weeks have passed, and Dr. Bailey has released Amanda. On one Thursday night, Joey is teaching Amanda how to play poker. Amanda is losing every hand, and she jokingly blames him for cheating. Joey then produces a slightly comical, evil grin then says, "Amanda, if this were a different time and place. The only time I would ever cheat if I were playing strip poker with you." Amanda looks at him with a questionable face, saying, "what's strip poker?" Joey laughs out loud, and Amanda says jokingly, "Joey don't laugh at me! I can't help it if I don't know what strip poker is!" Joey tries to stop laughing, and he eventually says to her, "Amanda, strip poker is when you lose, you have to remove an article of clothing." He starts laughing again because he sees the embarrassing red expression on her face. Amanda then jokingly says, "Joey Morris, you should be ashamed of yourself! Your such a nice guy. I can't believe you would ever do that with a girl!" Joey shakes his head with a funny looking face saying, "you're right, Amanda. I would never do that to a girl!"

Amanda looks at her with a comical expression, saying, "Joey, you are such a liar. I don't believe that for one bit." Joey laughs, then says, "your right, but I never had to cheat at it. I was very good at that kind of poker." Amanda looks at him shaking her head, smiling, then saying, "yeah, right." When they get finished, Joey says, "are you ready for our

Bible study?" Amanda looks at him with a strange expression then jokingly says, "I can't believe that you want to have Bible study right after you told me about strip poker." He looks at her then says, "well, Miss Crawford, there's not a better place to go than the Bible for forgiveness for past things that displeased God." Amanda has a gentle smile saying, "your right, Sgt. Morris. What we have studied in the last few weeks, I agree with you a thousand percent."

After their Bible study, Joey asks Amanda, "how about some hot chocolate?" She says, "that sounds wonderful." "Go sit back in front of the fire, and I will bring it to you in few moments," says a smiling Joey. Amanda goes and sits in front of the fireplace listening to the crackling fire. And she has grown to love the light, smokey aroma that the fire produces. A few minutes later, Joey comes into the den with the hot chocolate. He hands Amanda her mug saying, "be careful. It's hot."

She takes her mug, and Joey sits down very carefully, and they stare at the fire. A few moments later, Joey says, "I can't think of a better place where I would want to be than here." Amanda smiles at him, saying, "yes, it's so peaceful and cozy." Joey looks at her then smiles then turns back to the fire. Then he says, "and I'm content sitting by this fire all alone for the rest of my life." Amanda gets sad because he didn't mention anybody else being with him. Amanda then thinks to herself that she is probably overly sensitive about this situation. And she is thinking that maybe she needs to stop assuming things about Joey's feelings for her. But anyway, she says a little prayer asking God that he will speak to Joey, and he will listen to what God says. And hopefully, God will tell him to let go and to have some feelings toward her.

A few moments later, Joey looks at Amanda and says, "I've changed my mind because you are doing so good. How would you like to go to Denver this Saturday for that day trip I promised you?" Amanda smiles and says excitedly, "Joey, that sounds great!" Joey looks at the fire and says, "we will have to leave early that morning because it's about three and a half hours to Denver. And I know exactly where I'm taking you." Amanda says, where?" Joey says, "it will be a surprise." She says, "Joey, don't do that to me!" Joey, who is still looking at the fire, says, "do what to you?" She says, "making me wait till Saturday to find out where we're going in Denver." Joey laughs a bit, saying, "sorry, that's the rules." Amanda huffs and stands up, then says jokingly, "I don't like you at the moment, Mr. Morris. And I'm going to the bathroom." She walks off smiling. Joey then turns, watching her walk off with a big smile on his face.

Saturday arrives finally arrives. Amanda and Joey leave for Denver at six o'clock that morning. The drive to Denver is so pretty that Amanda still can't believe how beautiful this state is. They stop at a small restaurant in Silverton for breakfast. Then they plan to drive non stop to Denver. Joey later stops at a convenience store off the main road for gas and bathroom breaks. They finally arrive in Denver about ten-fifteen, and Joey drives to the largest shopping mall in the city. He looks at Amanda, saying, "well, here it is, Amanda!"

Amanda is amazed at how large the mall is, saying, "I didn't know there were malls this big." Joey says, "our mission is to walk around the mall looking in all the women's stores. Then when your ready, we'll go back to stores that you liked the best. How does that sound?" "Sounds great, Joey," says an excited Amanda. Joey then says, smiling, "ready, Miss Crawford?" "Ready Mr. Morris," replies Amanda. Joey gets out, walking around to open Amanda's door. Then they walk to the enormous mall for their great women's clothes adventure.

Chapter Nine

Rico

Meanwhile, back at a seedy bar in Grand Junction, Rico and three of his men are doing some hard drinking. Rico has a splint on his nose, covered by medical tape. Joey shattered Rico's nose when he hit him when he came to the aid of Amanda. Rico has had to have two surgeries to repair his nose. One of the other men named Bud has his right arm in a sling where he had to have surgery on his shoulder. That's because of when Joey drove his arm up between his shoulder blades. Another one of his men who's name is Chris, is rubbing his left cheek. It still hurts because Joey broke it when he hit him with the elbow strike. Then there's Benny. The one that ran away during the beatdown.

Rico takes a drink and sets the glass down hard on the table, just staring straight forward. Chris looks at Rico and says sternly, "Rico, when are we going to find that guy that beat us down?" Then Bud says, "yea, I want to take care of that hero punk as soon as possible." Rico looks at Bud sarcastically, saying to him, "Bud, with your arm in a sling it is not much you can do. Right?" Bud says, "I still have one good arm, and I can assure you that one arm can do a lot of damage." Rico laughs and says, "no, Bud, you're sitting this one out like Jimmy. Remember that's the guy that fractured Jimmy's skull when he ran him into that car. Bud looks at Rico and says, "that leaves you, Chris and Benny. That guy went through us like we were wet paper, and there were five of us." Bud looks at Benny and says, "I take that back, the four of us." How do you think that the three of you can stand up to him?"

Rico smiles and looks at the men, saying, "now Chris and Bud. I would love to hear your plans on how to catch up with this man? And what to do when you find him? Huh?" Chris and Bud look at each other but don't say anything. Rico again smiles, saying, "that's what I thought. You know our friend Benny ran like a rabbit when he saw us getting beat down." Chris looks at Benny with an angry face, saying, "yea Benny! Thanks for helping us out!" Rico looks at Chris, saying, "now Chris, don't be so hard on Benny." Chris looks at Rico, saying, "why the heck not!" Rico looks at Chris and with an evil smile and says, "yes, Benny, the rabbit did run, but he did something for me that caused me to forgive him of his sin." Bud looks at Rico, saying, "what did he do?" Rico looks at Benny and says, "tell Chris and Bud what you got for me, Benny."

Benny holds up a piece of newspaper then says, "I got the guys tag number." Chris and Bud look at Rico, saying, "have you found out who he is?" Rico smiles at the men, saying, "not only did I get his name. I also got his address." Chris says, "who is he then, and how did you get your information?" Rico taps his finger on the table, looking at the men, and they can't believe that he is acting so calmly. Rico then says, "I have a resource around town, and he found who he is and where he lives. And I'm for certain that Amanda is with him." Rico looks at Benny and says, "Benny enlighten these men who he is and where he lives."

Benny looks at everyone, saying, "his name is Joseph Morris, and he lives in the mountains near Craig. We were able to pinpoint his house through a GPS map." Chris then growls out, "what the heck are we waiting for then! Let's go get him and get Amanda back!" Rico, who is still very calm, says to Chris, "have a little patience, Chris. We have to plan this out carefully." An angered Chris says, "to heck with that. I want him now for what he did to me, not to mention everybody else!"

Rico takes the last shot of his whiskey then slams the glass down on the table. He is angry now. Then with a raised voice, he says to Chris, "I told you that we have to plan this out, or do I have to explain it to you again, Chris!" Chris is shaken up and takes a deep breath and swallows hard then says, "I'm sorry, Rico." Rico leans back in his chair, saying, "this guy Morris is very dangerous. I heard the witnesses said he took all of us out in a matter of seconds. They also said he beat us down with some martial arts they have never seen before. I'm sure that Morris is some military ex-special forces guy." Chris looks at Rico with a questionable face, saying, "how do you plan to take him out then?" Rico smiles and says, "he hit us when we were not expecting it. But this time it will be me who will attack first. And when he least expects it."

Rico then motions for the server to bring him another shot of whiskey. She brings it over, and he throws it back fast, then slamming the glass on the table again. The men notice an expression on Rico's face that they have never seen before. The look is pure sinister, and he says, "I'm going to take care of that…hero permanently for what he did to me. And taking something that wasn't his. Rico produces a wicked smile, saying, "I also have special plans for Amanda too." The men finish their drinks and leave the bar going to Rico's office to work out the atrocious plans they will have in store for Joey and Amanda.

Back in Denver, Joey and Amanda have visited all the women's stores in the mall. They sit down in the food court, and Joey goes up to one of the vendors and orders two lemonades. He walks back to where Amanda is sitting, and Joey hands her one of the lemonades. They both take big sips, and then Joey says, "did you pick a store that you liked the best?" She looks at him with a smile, saying, "Joey, to be honest, I liked all the women's stores we went too. But the large store we visited last was my favorite." Joey then says, "alright, Miss Amanda. When we finish our lemonades, we will go back to that store. Because that place was pretty fancy, and I'm sure they don't allow drinks in there." They finish their drinks and put the cups in a waste can, and they walk back to the store. Joey is touched because he can see the excited expression on Amanda's face.

They enter the famous store, and a snooty looking salesperson meets them as soon as they walk through the door. Since this is a glamorous store, the salesperson looks at Amanda's clothing she's wearing. Amanda has her bright orange stocking cap pulled down over her ears and is wearing Joey's mom's large camouflage jacket. The woman looks down at Amanda's boots. It looks like the boots are three times larger than she would wear. Then she looks up at them then says with a very vain tone, "may I help you?" Joey and Amanda look at each other because they know now that this woman is arrogant and snooty.

Joey looks at her name tag and leans in a bit to her, saying in his snooty tone, "yes, Denise. You can help us." This young woman standing next to me wants to buy some designer clothes. So could you give her a few moments of what I'm sure is your precious time to help her?" The saleswoman senses Joey's condescending tone. Then she says in a very uppity voice with a smirky smile, "I'm so sorry, sir, but I'm going on my break in five minutes." Joey then goes in for the kill saying sarcastically, "on no! We were looking so forward to you helping us with your caring, sweet attitude."

She gives Joey a very nasty look then says, "I'll get you someone that would love to help you, sir." Amanda then decides to take a shot at her, saying, "you've been so sweet Denise. And I hope you have a peach of a break." Denise huffs and turns to leave as Joey says to Amanda, "excellent, Amanda! You are becoming a true, old-fashioned Colorado smart-ass." Amanda then says, "she wasn't very nice, was she Joey. She treated us like mud." "No, she wasn't. But she will soon find out that she has made a huge mistake with that attitude," replies Joey. Denise walks up to counter where a young woman is folding clothing. Denise says to the young lady, "Ms. Dalton, there are a couple of mountain people at the front of the lobby needing help. See to them, please." The young lady says, "yes, ma'am. I'd be happy to."

Michelle walks up to Amanda and Joey with a pretty smile, saying, "hi, I'm Michelle. What can I show you today?" Joey has a big smile looking at Amanda then back at Michelle, saying, "Michelle, I want you to help Amanda with a whole new wardrobe, please. And I want you to help her with anything she wants. I'll just be following you two." Michelle looks at Amanda, saying, "Miss Amanda, you are so pretty. And I know under all those clothes, you have a cute figure. So we won't have a problem with your new wardrobe." Amanda looks at Joey with a smile then looks back at Michelle, saying, "thank you for your compliment Michelle and please call me Amanda." Michelle says, "where do you want to start, Amanda?" Amanda thinks for a few seconds, saying, "jeans and leggings first, please." Michelle replies, "that sounds great. Because jeans and leggings are a specialty of mine, so follow me, please." Amanda and Joey follow Michelle though the enormous store, and they come to the jean and leggings section of the women's department.

Michelle says, "well, here you go, Amanda. Have fun and pick out want you want to try on." Joey smiles and says to both ladies, "I got a feeling that this will take a while, so I'm going to sit in this chair." Joey looks at Amanda and see how happy and excited she looks. He thinks back on what his dad said one time and starts to laugh. His dad said, "she looks happier than a dog rolling around on a dead opossum."

Amanda is has picked out about six pairs of jeans and three pairs of leggings. When she picks up the clothing, she gives them to Michelle. Amanda looks around for a few minutes more then looks at Michelle, saying, "okay, let's try on the ones I picked out." Amanda goes into the dressing room, putting on the jeans. Every time Amanda puts a pair on, she comes out to show Joey and saying, "how do they look?" Even though Amanda looks fabulous in each pair, Joey always says, "those are nice." Amanda repeats the process with the leggings, and Joey says the same thing, "those look nice." Even though Amanda looks unbelievably fabulous in those leggings, he suppresses all those tender feelings toward her.

Amanda decides on one pair of jeans and one pair of leggings and gives them to Michelle, saying, "okay, let's go to the sweater and winter top section now." Joey then says, "what are you doing, Amanda?" She has a questionable look saying to Joey, "going to the sweater and top section, why?" He looks at her with a slight smiling then says, "your forgetting something." "Forgetting what," replies Amanda. A big smile appears on Joey's face, and he says, "all those clothes you picked out. You forget them." Amanda and Michelle's eyes get big as pie pans. Then Amanda says, "Joey, are you for real?" Joey nods his head and with a slight smile, saying, "yes, Amanda, I'm for real." She runs to Joey, very excited, and hugs his neck tight. Michelle says, smiling, "I have a feeling we are going to need a stock cart. I will be right back."

Michelle leaves for the stock room, and Amanda starts to cry and looks at Joey, saying, "why are you so good to me, Joey? I don't deserve it." Joey takes out his handkerchief and dries her eyes. He looks at her sternly, saying, "Amanda don't you ever say that again. You deserve nice things, just like any other woman." Joey smiles and says, "besides, you are the only woman I want to spend my money on." Amanda still has tears rolling down her cheeks and leans in, putting her hands on Joey's face. Then she gives him a light kiss on his lips. Michelle comes up with the stock cart and puts Amanda's clothes in it. Then Michelle says, "let's go." Amanda is still looking at Joey with a lovable expression, then turns and walks with Michelle. Joey gets up with a frown, saying under his breath, "I wish Amanda wouldn't have kissed me. That makes the situation with us even worse." Even though he knows that was the sweetest kiss he has ever experienced in his life.

They all arrive at the woman's top clothing section, and Michelle shows Amanda all the latest styles. Joey looks and sees there have to be a thousand tops on the racks in this section. And he doesn't have the slightest clue how Amanda is going to pick something out all of these. Michelle says, "what kind of tops are you looking for, Miss. Amanda?" Amanda is looking at all the selections then says, "of course the ones that will match my jeans and leggings. But I like pullover sweaters and flannel shirts. Michelle shows her all the flannel shirts and sweaters that the store offers. Michelle then says, "you would look fabulous in the sweaters down this rack." Amanda follows Michelle, and they stop at the most gorgeous sweaters Amanda has ever seen. Michelle says, "these are all cashmere."

Amanda looks at Michelle and says, "excuse me, Michelle, I need to speak to Joey a moment." "Go right ahead," replies a smiling Michelle. Amanda walks over to Joey, saying, "those are the most beautiful sweaters I have ever seen. But their cashmere." Joey looks at her with a nonchalant expression, saying, "so." Amanda looks at him with a surprised face. She then says, "Joey, I don't know about many things, but I know that cashmere is very expensive." Joey sighs and still has the nonchalant expression, saying, "Amanda get what you want…please?" She smiles then goes back to the racks. But before she picks out the sweaters, she turns to Joey saying, "v-neck or crew?" Joey looks at her verily seriously and says, "are you nuts? Low v-necks for you." Both Amanda and Michelle look at each other with big smiles. Amanda picks out her choice of sweaters and flannel shirts. Joey then says, "Amanda, get as many as you want. Okay?" Amanda then asks Michelle if she could wear the jeans and one of the sweaters she picked out before paying for them. Michelle lights up, saying, "of course you can, Miss Amanda! Just pull off the tags and give them to me."

After Amanda makes her choices on what to wear, she goes into a changing room. Michelle then puts the remaining tops in the cart. Later Amanda comes out with her new jeans and sweater on. Joey thinks to himself, "why does she have to be this beautiful." Michelle shakes her head, saying, "Miss Amanda, you look stunning." Amanda looks at Joey and says, "what do you think, Joey?" He doesn't want to give her the wrong impression and just says, "looks very nice, Amanda." Now Amanda thinks to herself about what he just said. She was hoping Joey would be very excited for her and say something extraordinary pretty. Amanda looks at him with a small smile, then Michelle says, "what can I show you next?" Amanda looks at Joey, and he shrugs his shoulders. Amanda turns to Michelle smiling and says with another exciting voice, "shoes first, then sneakers." This time Joey speaks up, saying sarcastically, "of course women and their shoes." They all reach the shoe department, and Amanda looks at all of the shoes on display.

Joey sees a display shoe on a display table. Then he walks over to the table and picks up the shoe and says to Amanda, "Amanda, I like these." Amanda's mouth drops and, with a stunned expression, says, "Joey Morris. You of all people picking out lady's shoes?" Joey says, "yea, I think they would look good on you." Amanda is shaking her head, smiling as Joey asks Michelle, "what kind of shoes do you call these Michell?" Michelle produces a sweet smile saying calmly, "they're called ankle strap pumps. And they go perfect with the leggings she picked out. He looks at Amanda, saying, "what do you think, Amanda?" She smiles, saying, "I love them, Joey. Joey then says to Michelle, "she will take these

Michelle, and any other shoes she wants."

Amanda picks out ankle booties and flats as she tells Michelle, "I'll be wearing these flats with this outfit." Michell smiles and says, "sure thing." Michelle walks to a lady's shoe associate, and they write all the stock numbers down. Then they walk to the back to get all the footwear Amanda has picked out. Amanda sits next to Joey, saying, "Joey, when will I have the chance to wear all these clothes?" Joey replies, "all ladies need pretty clothes. You never know when you are going to need them."

Later Michelle and the associate return with all the footwear that Amanda selected. Then Amanda slips on the flats, and Michelle puts the rest of the shoes and boots in the cart. Then says to Amanda, "what's next?" Amanda hesitates a moment, saying, "the lingerie department please, Michelle." They start to walk to lingerie. Then Joey stops them, then says, "I'm going to sit here while you go to that department if you don't mind." Both Amanda and Michelle laugh at what Joey said as they turn heading to lingerie. About thirty minutes later, Amanda and Michelle return from lingerie. Amanda looks at Michelle with a mischievous smile then looks at Joey, then jokingly saying, "I want to show you something very sexy, Joey." Joey gets a look of terror on his face because he thinks Amanda is going to pull out some provocative lingerie. Amanda reaches and pulls out some sleepwear and says, "look, Joey. Old fashioned flannel pajamas." Joey sighs as Michelle tries not to laugh at him. "Very nice, Amanda," says a relieved Joey.

Michelle says, "anything else, Miss. Amanda?" Amanda looks at Joey smiling, then looks back to Michelle and says, "I think that's it." Michelle says, "okay, lets head to my register, shall we." As they follow Michelle to her work station, they pass through the fine jewelry section. Amada glances down at one of the cases and sees a beautiful tennis diamond bracelet. She stops and looks at Michelle, saying, "that has to be the most pretty bracelet I have ever seen." Joey looks down at the bracelet. Then looks up at Amanda, saying, "what to try it on?" She says, "sure...well, I guess." Joey looks at the jewelry associate, saying, "she wants to try on that bracelet, please ma'am." The jewelry associate says, "certainly, sir." The associate unlocks the case and takes the bracelet out and says, "may I see your arm, that you would wear it on madam?" Amanda gives the associate her left arm for her to place the bracelet. The associate smiles at Amanda, saying, "very lovely, I may say. It matches your skin tone perfectly." She shows it to Joey, and he nods his head. Amanda looks at it, smiling and gives her arm back to the associate. The associate takes the bracelet off and starts to put it back in the case.

Joey asks Amanda, "do you like it? It sure looked pretty on your arm." Amanda sighs then says, smiling, "what woman wouldn't, Joey." "We'll take it," says Joey to the associate. The associate says, "excellent choice, sir." Amanda looks at Joey very surprised, to say the least, then takes him by the arm. They walk a few steps away from the counter, and she says vividly, "Joey, I can't let you buy me that bracelet!" "Why not," replies Joey. She says in a solemn tone, "that bracelet cost over fifteen hundred dollars, and that's the sale price for goodness, sakes!" Joey smiles and says, "but do you like it, Amanda?" Amanda looks around, then looks at Joey sighing, and later saying, "well, of course, I do! Are you nuts!" Joey laughs and speaks to the jewelry associate, "box it up for her, please." The associate puts the bracelet in a pretty jewelry box, and while she is doing that, Joey walks over to the next jewelry case where the cross necklaces are. He looks at Amanda, saying, "Amanda come over here for a minute, please." She walks over to Joey and says, "what is it?" He looks at Amanda with a sweet expression, saying, "Amanda, will you do one special thing for me?" She answers, saying, "of course, Joey, what is it?" Joey points at the case, saying, "I want you to get one of these cross necklaces."

Amanda smiles and looks at the necklaces and sees one immediately that she would like to have. She looks at the associate and points to a small delicate cross necklace saying, "I would love to have that necklace." Joey looks at her with a confused face, saying, "that necklace is kind of plain, Amanda." She looks at Joey with a sweet, calm face and says, "that's the whole idea, Joey. Jesus was nailed on pieces of old wood that weren't worth anything." Joey looks at her shaking his head, smiling, saying, "Amanda, your right. And I understand your meaning. Those words you just spoke were beautiful." Joey is looking at Amanda, and he tells the associate, "we'll also take this cross necklace, and that should be it."

The associate puts all the jewelry in separate boxes and the rings up the sale. She tells Joey the price of all the jewelry, and he places his debit card into a chip terminal." The associate puts the jewelry and receipt in a small fancy bag and hands it to Amanda. The associate looks at Joey and Amanda, saying, "this lady of yours, sir, is going to be beautiful wearing this fine jewelry!" Joey has a small smile, then says, "thank you for your help." Amanda thought it was nice what the associate said, thinking that she and Joey were a couple. They walk to Michelle's station, and she starts billing out all of Amanda's other items.

Joey pays for all the merchandise and puts his card back in his wallet. Then he pulls out a one-hundred bill handing it to Michelle. Michelle looks at the bill then looks at Joey with a surprised expression, saying, "this is not necessary, Mr. Joey." Joey looks at her, saying, "Michelle, you helped out a lady that hasn't had anything like this in her life. And you looked like you had fun doing this for her. And you were truly sincere about it all." Michelle says, "thank you, Mr. Joey. This money will be going into my college fund."

Michelle pushes the cart out to the Jeep, and Joey loads all the bags in the back. Michelle hugs both Amanda and Joey, saying, "thanks for making my day." Michelle walks with the cart back inside the store, taking it into the back. She returns to her work area. Denise, the snooty associate, asks Michelle with the smart-alec tone, "did you take care of those mountain people?" Michelle shakes her head with a big smile, saying, "those mountain people as you called them Denise, just walked out of here spending over four-thousand dollars. And the mountain man gave me a one-hundred-dollar tip." Denise looks at Michelle with a surprised look with her mouth open wide. Then Michelle says in snooty tone and looking up, "I wonder what my commission will look like this week?" She looks back at Denise, saying, "imagine Denise, all those sales could have been yours. Thanks!" Denise huffs then walks back to her work area.

Joey is driving down the street, and Amanda has a giant smile on her face. Joey then says, "Amanda, I'm going to stop at this sporting goods store. She looks at him, saying, "Joey, I hope you are not planning to buy anything else for me in this sporting place. You've bought me enough already. And you will never know how grateful I am." Joey parks and looks at Amanda with a smile, saying, "you are so right, Amanda. The clothes and shoes I just bought for you are for the inside. The stuff I'm about to buy for you is for wearing outside." Amanda looks at him with an enthusiastic expression on her face, saying, "well, let's get at it then." He gets out and walks around the Jeep and opens her door for her. They walk across the parking lot, going to the main entrance to the store.

As they go in, an associate of the store greets them, saying, "hi there, folks. What can I show you today?" Joey looks at the associate's name tag then says, "Kenny, I'm Joey. And this is Amanda." I want you to fix this lady up with the best camouflage outerwear you have, please, sir." Kenny says, "very nice to meet you both. Follow me, please." As they are walking to the outerwear section, Kenny says, "what is she interested in today, Joey?" Joey looks at Amanda, and she shakes her head, saying, "now Joey, you know I don't know anything about that type of clothing." He smiles then looks at Kenny, saying, "she will need insulated coveralls. A hooded parka, goose down vest and gloves. She will also need insulated snow boots." Kenny then asks, "what color do you prefer?" Joey says, "she will only be here for a few more months. So do you have something nice that she can wear when she goes back home?" Kenny nods his head, saying, "we have something for ladies you might be interested in that's in stock."

Amanda is a little depressed that Joey has mentioned to Kenny about her leaving. But she thinks to herself that she has a few months to work very hard at maybe changing his feelings toward her. They reach the cold-weather outerwear section as Kenny shows Joey all the lady's outerwear that he told him that the store stocks. Joey looks at Amanda and says, "pick what you want, Amanda." Kenny says, "let's look at the insulated coveralls first." Amanda, with Joey's help, picks out all the clothing and boots that he told Kenny he wanted.

Then Kenny says, "is that it folks?" Joey looks at Amanda, and she says to Kenny, "I'm sure this will be it, Kenny." "Alright. Let's go to the front to checkout," replies Kenny. As they start to walk to the front, they pass some pretty, brown, ladies canvas jackets. There's one that Amanda particularly likes that has a long, matching scarf with it. Joey asks her, "it looks like to me that you like that jacket and scarf." Amanda replies, "it sure is pretty." Joey looks at Kenny and says, "we'll take the jacket and scarf also, Kenny." Kenny looks at Amanda and says, "we just got these in. There called barn jackets, and they're very trendy." "We'll take the jacket and scarf," says Joey.

They walk to the front counter. Joey then pays for all the items. Kenny takes all items to Joey's Jeep, loading everything in the back. Joey tries to give Kenny a tip, and he says, "thank you so much for your generosity, Joey. I own the store, and I love to help people. But I will donate this money to the Children's Cancer Center in Denver. My daughter was a patient there when she was a little girl. Now she is fourteen and healthy as a horse. And boy crazy!" Joey smiles and reaches into his wallet and pulls out two more large bills, then says, "you were great help, Kenny. And donate all this money to the children's cancer hospital in your daughter's name."

Tears come to Kenny's eyes and shakes Joey's hand then say's, "God bless you and your wife. Will you two please come back to see me?" "Sure we will," Joey says. Joey closes the back door then goes to open Amanda's door. She climbs in. Then he walks around, getting in his doorway. He starts the engine then pulls out of the parking area. As they are driving down down the main thoroughfare, Joey looks at Amanda then says, "I know a great steak place down the road here. Are you hungry?" Amanda looks at him with a big smile, saying, "Joey, I'm famished!" "So am I," Joey says, smiling.

They arrive at the steak house, and they enter the enormous restaurant, then Amanda says, looking around, "Joey, this is the largest steak restaurant I have ever seen in my life." Joey looks at her laughing a bit, saying, "oh, this place is nothing, Amanda. There's a steak restaurant in Amarillo, Texas that serves a seventy-two-ounce steak. And if you eat it all, plus all the trimmings in an hour, it's free. Amanda laughs and says, "you know what they say, everything is bigger in Texas."

A greeter comes up to them, saying, "hello! How many?" Joey says, "two, please." The greeter says, "follow me, please." They walk to a table, and the greeter says, "Is this okay?" Amanda smiles, saying to her, "this will be fine. Thank you." "Your server will be right with you," says the greeter. A few moments later, a server comes up to Joey and Amanda's table, saying, "hello, I'm Brianna, and I will be your server. What would you like to drink?" Joey says, "coffee for me, please, Brianna." Brianna looks at Amanda, saying, "and for you, ma'am?" "Ice water with lemon for me, please," replies Amanda. Brianna looks at them then says, "I'll be right back with your drinks and menus."

Amanda looks at Joey, then saying, "I can tell that Brianna is very sweet." Joey looks at Amanda, saying, "I hope she brings those menus quick. I'm about to eat these napkins plus the holder." Brianna returns and places their drinks in front of them. Then Brianna hands the extensive menus to both of them. Then she says, "I'll be back in a few moments to take your orders." Brianna walks off. Then Joey sees right away what he wants. Amanda is looking at all the selections saying to Joey, "they have so many selections. What do you suggest, Joey?" Joey says, "you do like steak don't you?" She replies, "sure, I do." Joey points at the menu then says, "It looks like here they have a ten-ounce rib-eye I'm sure you would like. Plus, get one of their big baked potatoes and a side order of steamed broccoli." Amanda has a sour expression, saying, "broccoli. Yuch. That is so gross, Joey." Joey laughs then says, "well, why don't you put a pile of mayonnaise on the broccoli, and then you might like it." Amanda leans in close to Joey smiling and saying, "shut-up Joey."

Brianna returns and asks Amanda, "have you made your decision, ma'am?" Amanda says, "I would like the ten-ounce rib eye steak, medium well, and a baked potato." Brianna asks Amanda, "would you like a side vegetable?" "No, just the steak and potato, please," replies Amanda. Then Brianna looks at Joey and says, "and for you, sir?" Joey smiles then saying, "I want your twenty-four-ounce sirloin, medium rare, with a loaded baked potato. And steamed broccoli, please." Briana takes their menus, then says, "I'll have your steaks out in a few moments." Amanda looks at Joey with a surprised expression and saying, "Joey, will that giant steak you ordered come with the hooves?" He laughs and jokingly says, "oh, that size steak is an appetizer for me." Amanda shakes her head smiling.

They finish their meals, and soon they are back on the road. After about fifty miles, Amanda leans her head on her window, falling to sleep.

Joey drives extra careful, trying not awake her because she has had a long and exciting day. Amanda doesn't even wake-up when Joey stops for gas. About two hours later they arrive back at the cabin. Joey gently shakes Amanda's shoulder and says softly, "Amanda wake up. We're back at the cabin. She awakens but is very sluggish. Joey gets out of the Jeep walking around to open her door. She gets out, and he hands her his keys, saying, "go unlock the door and go on in. I'll get everything out." She walks to the porch and unlocking the door. She then walks into the cabin. It takes Joey two trips to the Jeep to unload everything he bought for Amanda.

Later that evening, Joey is sitting on the couch, going through an extended fashion show. With Amanda modeling all her new clothing. Every time she models an outfit, she asks Joey, "how does it look?" And Joey always says, "looks nice, Amanda." But when she comes out wearing a different outfit, Joey thinks to himself that Amanda looks so indescribably amazing in all her outfits. But he will not tell her these thoughts because he doesn't want to give Amanda any inclination of her staying here. But Joey doesn't realize that Amanda is saving the best for last. After a few moments, Amanda comes out of the bathroom wearing her barn jacket and scarf.

Joey looks away and closes his eyes. He can't think that a woman can be this adorable wearing a coat and scarf. Amanda sees Joey look away, and she says, "Joey, you don't like the coat and scarf?" Joey turns and looks and Amanda and says, "Amanda, you just modeled all of your new clothes for me. And you were so pretty in all those clothes. But when I saw you in your coat and scarf, you took my breath away." The only thing Amanda can do is shake her head and smile. She turns and walks back to the bathroom and changes into her new flannel pajamas. When she comes out of the bathroom, she tells Joey, "these pajamas are the most comfortable thing I've had on tonight."

She sits on the couch, looking at the fire dancing in the fireplace. Amanda comes up with her first plan of maybe getting Joey to have feelings for her. She looks at says, "Joey?" He looks at her, saying, "yep?" She hesitates a bit, getting up the nerve to ask him her question. She takes a deep breath, then says with a questionable expression, "Joey, will you mind if I can stay with you over the holidays. It would be wonderful to spend Thanksgiving and especially Christmas with you." He looks at her with a broad smile, saying, "I wouldn't have it any other way, Amanda." She cries happily and hugs Joey. He pushes her back gently then says with a smile, "you better stop all your crying. You're going to dehydrate. Amanda smiles at him then Joey dries her tears with his handkerchief. Then she says, "Joey, you've made me very happy!" Then she hugs him again. Joey thinks to himself that he would love to hold Amanda for the rest of his life. If only if she could be someone else.

Joey then says, "we've had a long day, and I think it's time I hit the rack." Amanda looks at him with a questionable, wide-eyed look, saying, "Joey, what kind of rack are you talking about?" Joey starts laughing out loud. Then he says, "Amanda, It's not what your thinking. A rack is what we call beds in the Marines." Amanda is very embarrassed about the question she asked Joey about what a rack is. Then Amanda says sweetly to Joey, "I'll see you in the morning." She turns toward the bed, and Joey says, "good night Amanda." She gets in the bed, and Joey goes to the bathroom to change into his sweats. He comes out and walks to the wood rack. Joey picks up a backlog placing it in the back of the fireplace. Then he puts split firewood in the front. Joey looks at Amanda, and she is clutching her bear. He can't help by thinking to himself how wonderful it would be to fall in love with her. But he can't let that happen. He looks up and says, "God, please do not let me fall in love with her because you know the reason why, Amen." He lays back in his recliner and soon is asleep.

The next morning Joey is preparing breakfast, and Amanda comes into the kitchen saying, "great! Pancakes!" As they are eating, Mr. Wilson calls Joey over the C.B. Joey gets up from the table, walking into the kitchen, pressing the microphone button, saying, "go ahead, Mr. Wilson." Wilson says, "Joey, there's a winter storm warning out for us starting around lunch. Over." Joey still laughs when Mr. Wilson says, "over." Joey presses the microphone button saying, "always grateful to you for the weather reports, Mr. Wilson, but we're fine up here." Then Wilson says, "I always like to check on everybody so over and out." As he starts to walk out of the kitchen, he hears Wilson checking with all the people on the mountain.

As he returns to the table, Amanda says, "I heard Mr. Wilson say that a storm will be here by noon. Are we okay?" Joey replies, "just need to split a little firewood after breakfast." Amanda gets excited, saying, "Oh, Joey, let me help! Because I can wear all my new outdoor clothes for the first time!" Joey shrugs his shoulders, smiling, "sure you can. You can keep me company because it gets boring, splitting wood." "Thank you so much, Joey," says a grateful Amanda. She runs and gets her outdoor clothing and goes to the bathroom to change. Joey smiles as he shakes his head. Later she comes out of the bathroom and sits on the bed, putting on her boots. Joey has already has his coat and stocking cap on, and Amanda stands and says, "let's get at that wood, shall we Joey!"

They arrive at the barn, and Joey opens the doors then goes in and pulls out the log splitter. Amanda sits on a large log when Joey cranks the motor. Then he walks to the side of the barn where a large stack of cut logs are stacked. He starts splitting the wood into small pieces, then Amanda asks him, "what can I do, Joey?" Joey looks at her, saying, "why don't you go get the snow track out of the barn and bring it here. You can start loading the split wood in the back if you think your ready for this kind of work. The key is in the ignition." She stands up quickly off the log then saying, "really Joey, I feel as if I was never hurt. So split firewood is nothing!" Joey starts to laugh at her excitement, then says, "okay then." She walks inside the barn, and after a few moments, Joey hears the vehicle start. She pulls the snow track close to the pile of split wood. She gets out and starts to load the wood into the back of the vehicle.

After Joey finishes splitting the wood, Amanda pulls the vehicle close to the porch steps. She gets out and starts to carry small amounts of wood to the porch and to stack it up. After Joey puts the log splitter back in the barn, he walks up and helps Amanda with the wood. After they finish, Amanda says, "what's next?" Joey smiles, saying, "why don't you back the snow track in the barn for me and lock the doors. The key code is seventy-five-zero-eight." She gives him a big smile and jumps back into the vehicle. She pulls the snow-track to the door and backs in slowly. She cuts the engine off and closes the doors. Then she puts in the door lock code. She walks back to wear Joey is standing and asks, "can we go walking around a little?" He says, "sure. That's a good idea."

They walk down the trail by the barn, and it begins to snow. Amanda still can't believe the beauty of Joey's land. The falling snow adds to the grandeur of her surroundings. They talk about everything as they walk down the different trails. About ten minutes later, Amanda asks Joey, "Joey, do you ever go to church?" He looks at her with a big smile and answers by saying, "Amanda, I consider where we are right now is a church. I've come here many times to talk to God. All this is God's creation. And I believe you don't have to be in a human-made building to glorify God.

Amanda has taken in everything in her heart what Joey just said. She then asks Joey, "Joey, what you need up here is a small chapel where anybody can come to worship God. Especially during the freezing months." She looks around when she starts to tear up, saying, "just imagine someone getting married there." Joey then says with a gentle expression, "Amanda, how would you like me to build you a small chapel? Maybe down the trail a bit from the barn." Then she starts to tear up as she replies, "Joey, you would do that for me?" Joey takes his handkerchief out, drying her tears. Then he smiles and says gently, "yes. I will do that, Amanda. And before you leave, I will have the chapel finished." Joey then says, "let's head back to the cabin and get some coffee." As they are walking back, Amanda is feeling hurt because Joey mentioned her leaving. Joey then asks Amanda, "if you don't mind me asking you Amanda, is there a reason why you always cry at the simplest things?"

She looks at Joey with a delicate smile then looks forward again, saying, "Joey, I don't really know. I wasn't never this emotional before until you came into my life. I guess my emotions are out of control. But, it's a good out of control if you know what I mean by that." They stop walking, and Amanda looks at Joey and says, "I know these new emotions are from your kindness and compassion to me. And I can feel the love from you also." Joey doesn't know what kind of love that Amanda is referring too, and he quickly changes the subject. Joey says, "let's get to that coffee, shall we." Amanda has a melancholy expression on her face as they walk to the cabin.

Chapter Ten

Amanda Comes Close To Death

They arrive at the cabin, and they brush the snow off each other and stomping their boots. They each get an armload of the split firewood and go into the den. They put the wood into the wood rack, then Joey asks Amanda, "would you put some wood in the fireplace, and I'll go make the coffee." Amanda walks over to the wood rack then puts the wood on the fire. She goes walks to the bed and gets her teddy bear. Amanda then walks over to the couch and sits there, staring directly into the fire, hugging her bear. She has a subdued expression on her face now. She can hear Joey rustling around in the kitchen, then he comes out of the kitchen, saying, "we're out of coffee. I'll go down to Mr. Wilsons and get some. Want to go?" She looks up at him with the subdued expression, saying, "no, I'll stay here." Joey notices her sad look and that she is holding her bear. Then he says to her, "Is everything okay, Amanda?" She smiles then says, "I'm okay, Joey. I want to be alone for a little bit, that's all." "Alright then," he says. He puts on his coat and goes to the gun case and gets the pistol out that he showed her how to use. He puts the gun down by her then says, "remember what I taught you about this weapon." She doesn't say anything or even looks up at him.

He turns to leave as Amanda says in a calm voice, "Joey?" He turns to her, saying, "yes?" She says, "Joey, I just want to tell you that you that you have changed my life." He looks at her then says, "Amanda, you have also changed my life for the better." She looks at him with a questionable but smiling expression, saying, "how have I changed your life, Joey?" He walks over and sits next to her, saying, "mainly, you have restarted my faith in God. Like reading and studying the Bible with you. But mostly, I loved telling you the wonderful stories that are throughout the Bible."

She looks at him with the sweetest smile, saying, "Joey, I want to be like you, and I want God in my heart. Can you tell me how? Joey smiles, saying, "you already know how to receive God, Amanda." She looks at him with a surprised face, saying, "I do? He puts his hand on her face saying, "do you remember what that street preacher said to you. Then I explained to you what it meant?" She smiles, nodding her head, then Joey says, "Ask him into your heart and believe he will do it. Then he will move into your hearts apartment building, and he will be your main tenant." Amanda starts to laugh at how Joey phrased that last comment, saying, "that was clever when you said my heart was an apartment building. When can I do that? And do I have to be in a special place?"

Joey takes his hand off her face, then saying, "Amanda, you can be anywhere for this to happen, but being in a special place that you love would be kind of cool." Amanda puts her hands on his face then leans in kissing him lightly on the lips. He looks at her with a slightly shocked expression for a few moments. He smiles at her then gets up, saying, "I'll be right back." He walks out the door, saying to himself, "dang it. I knew this was going to happen. I'm beginning to like it when Amanda kisses me. But I have got to stop that feeling from happening again!" The snow is coming down hard, and he gets in his Jeep. Then he realizes he doesn't have his keys.

He walks back to the cabin then knocks at the door, shouting, "Amanda, I forgot my keys." She unlocks the door, and Joey goes to the coffee table and picks up his keys. Amanda says, "be careful out in that snow." He smiles and nods his head and walks out the door. He gets in and heads to the store. About thirty minutes later, Joey returns from Mr. Wilson's store, and he gets out of the Jeep and walks up the steps unto the front porch. He knocks on the door, saying, "Amanda, it's me, and I'm coming in." Joey doesn't hear a response and knocks on the door again and says in a raised voice, "Amanda!" Joey gets very concerned and unlocks the door and sticks his head in the door, saying, "Amanda?" Joey still gets no response and goes through the cabin looking for and calling her name.

He stands at the bathroom door, looking around with panic in his eyes. He sees all of Amanda's outdoor clothing on the couch. And he knows there's no other place she could be is outside. He walks over to the gun case and gets his revolver and straps the holster around his waist. He also pulls his high-powered rifle out of the gun case. He loads his pockets with extra ammunition for both weapons. He puts the sling of the rifle up around his shoulder walks out the front door. He only sees his footprints in front of the cabin. He then walks to the back door. He opens the door and sees small footprints leading down the trail next to the barn.

He starts down the trail with the revolver in his hand, calling her name. He looks all around the path, still calling her name, but there is no answer. He is terrified for her because the snow is starting to come down hard, and the temperature has fallen drastically below freezing. This snowstorm will quickly cover her footprints, and she will be hard to track. He follows her tracks and loudly calling her name but to no avail. Later he comes upon the ridge above the beautiful stream where they roasted hot dogs. He looks down and sees Amanda standing next to the stream. He yells out, "AMANDA!" He quickly goes down the slope of the ridge. He slips halfway down the hill and rolls to the bottom. He gets up and runs to Amanda. She only has on her flannel shirt, jeans and her insulated boots. She has her arms crossed on her chest, shaking violently. Joey knows she is very close to being hyperthermic. He takes his coat and wraps it around her and putting his stocking cap on her head. He picks up Amanda in his arms and says, "Amanda, put your face against my neck." She slowly puts her arms around him and puts her face against his neck. Joey looks at her face, and it's beginning to turn a pale, light blue.

She starts to close her eyes, and Joey says very loud, "AMANDA DON'T GO TO SLEEP!" As he begins to carry her out, Joey tells her, "Amanda talk to me. Tell me about something you like to do!" She is talking to him incoherent, but at least she's talking. But he does understand her when she mumbles that she was in love with him. He climbs the slope and runs with her in his arms back to the cabin without stopping. He burst through the front door, laying her down very close in front of the fireplace. Then he throws more wood on the fire.

Joey knows that Amanda is close to dying. Joey runs to Amanda's bed pulling off the quilt. Joey then grabs his recliner quilt. It never enters his mind about being embarrassed or shy about what he's about to do. Joey removes all of Amanda's frozen clothing and wraps the two quilts around her. He stands up and hurries to the den closet removing a military-style first aid bag. Then Joey goes quickly to the bathroom and getting five large washcloths. He returns to where she is lying and, with a terrified expression, says to her, "Amanda stay with me! Talk to me, Amanda! She is still incoherent and still mumbling.

He unzips the first aid bag retrieving five chemical heat packs. After he does this, he places a thermometer under her armpit. Joey crushes all the packs to start the chemical reaction in them to produce heat as he removes the thermometer after it beeps. Joey looks at her temperature, and it reads eighty-four point six. Joey knows that Amanda is moments away from dying, and he needs to get her temperature up slowly, hoping it's not too late. Joey wraps the heat packs with the cloths where they won't burn her skin. He reaches under the quilts and places the packs under her armpits. Then Joey puts another pack on the back of her neck. Then he puts two packs in her groin area. Joey wraps her tight again then runs to the bathroom to get Amanda's hairdryer. He comes back with the dryer and sits her up, drying her hair. Then Joey gets her stocking cap off the couch and puts it on her head. He then lays her back down.

Joey then says excitedly, "I'm going to the kitchen to get you a warm drink." He hurries to the kitchen, saying, "God, please don't let her die!" He puts a green leaf teabag plus three teaspoons of sugar in a mug of water. He puts it in the microwave, turning it on to medium for ten seconds. Then he runs back to Amanda and sees that she is still shivering. He looks at her with a concerned expression, saying, "how are you doing, sweetheart?" She has a small smile then says almost incoherently, "you have never called me sweetheart before Joey."

Joey smiles then puts his hand on her face, saying, "you are not out of the woods yet, but you're making some sense now." The microwave dings and he runs back to the kitchen and carefully brings the warm tea to her, saying, "drink all this warm tea but very slowly." He helps her sit up, making sure she is wrapped tight in the quilts. Joey then says, "keep your arms and legs close to your body for the heats packs won't fall off. And I will hold the pack on your neck." She slowly reaches for the mug, but Joey has to help her. She takes a few sips. Then Amanda closes her eyes tightly, then lowering her head for a few seconds. She looks at Joey and says slowly, "Joey, this tea is luke-warm, and it's so sweet." "I did that on purpose because a hypothermic person needs to drink warm sweet liquids. It's to warm up your core temperature slowly," Joey replies. She finishes the first mug, and Joey helps her lie back down.

He quickly returns to the kitchen, preparing another mug of tea. He puts the mug in the microwave, and Joey returns, asking her questions to see how far Amanda has come along. He hears the ding of the microwave and returns to the kitchen to get the second mug of tea. Joey sets the mug on the mantle of the fireplace and helps Amanda sit up again. He takes the mug and hands it to her. He then say's, "drink all of this too. And again, drink slowly." Again he sits with her talking, and when she finishes that mug, he goes back to the kitchen to prepare more tea. When he returns, Joey sits next to her with both of his arms wrapped around her. She says with a resentful expression, slowly, "Joey, you not going to make me drink some more of that tea, are you?" He nods his head then says, "one more cup, and we'll see."

After the third mug of tea, he notices that her shivering has subsided some. He replaces the heat packs two more times, and after an hour, Joey lays her back down and retakes her temperature. It reads ninety-four point nine. Joey looks at her, saying, "Amanda, your temp is coming up. But I want you to stay by this fire for the rest of the day. Also, keep the quilt wrapped around you and wear your knit cap.

All of this scary situation when Joey started the first aid on Amanda has taken over two hours. Then he looks at her then says, "Amanda, I'm going to retake your temperature." He opens the quilts by her armpit and places the thermometer under her arm. The thermometer beeps, and Joey removes the thermometer and looks at the digital readout. He says, "your temp is nighty-six point nine. It's still a little low, but it looks like to me that you're out of danger." He puts the thermometer back in the bag. Amanda knows now that she messed up bad and says to Joey sadly, "thank you, Joey, for saving my life again." Joey doesn't say anything. He stands up then walks to the bathroom to get Amanda one of her sweat outfits, a long sleeve t-shirt, and thick socks.

He returns to her, then saying, "I'm going to help you stand, and then I'm going to put this t-shirt and sweats on you." He removes the quilts and proceeds to put the sweats on her. Amanda laughs lightly, then says, "just like old times, Joey." He doesn't say anything and helps her sit back down. Joey wraps the quilts back around her then he sits down by her. Later that evening, Joey prepares warm soup and crackers and brings it to her. He walks to the bed and picks up her flannel pajamas off the end of the bed. He puts the pajamas on over her sweats then says, "Amanda, you need to get to bed." Joey helps her up and walks her to the bed, and she gets in. He places the quilt over her and goes to a cedar chest to get a think blanket.

He places the blanket over the other quilt. Then he says in a slightly stern voice, "Amanda, I want you to go to sleep, and I will watch you closely for the rest of the night." She looks up at him with her pretty, green eyes, saying, "Joey, with all that tea I drank, I know I will have to go to the bathroom sometimes tonight." Joey looks at her for a few seconds then says, "I understand that Amanda. But walk to the bathroom with your quilts around you. Don't get chilled. And if you need me, I will be awake. But tomorrow, we are going to have a serious talk on what you pulled today." As Joey starts to the kitchen to get a cup of coffee, Amanda says sadly, "Joey, can you give me my bear off the couch, please?" Joey walks to the couch and picks up the bear. He walks to the bed and hands Amanda her bear. She clutches it, and Joey walks to the kitchen to get his coffee.

He comes back into the den then puts his mug of coffee on the stand next to the recliner. Joey walks to the wood rack, then puts a backlog and then split firewood on the fire. He then sits in his recliner, turning on the F.M. radio and starts to read his book. Joey has stayed true to his word because he never went to sleep. He checks on Amanda every hour. As Joey is reading, he starts to think that why in the world did Amanda did what she did today. He puts his book down on the stand, looking at her. Joey then looks up, saying softly, "God only you and Amanda knows why she did that today. And thank you for not letting her die. You heard and answered my prayer. Thanks again, and I pray this prayer in your loving Son Jesus's name, Amen."

The next morning comes, and Joey is in the kitchen. He is preparing breakfast consisting of scrambled eggs, bacon, toast, and coffee. He goes over to Amanda and nudges her shoulder. She opens her eyes with a slight smile. Joey tells her, "Amanda, breakfast will be ready in five minutes, so you need to get up." She gets out of the bed, then goes to the bathroom. A few moments later, she comes out and walking to the breakfast table. She sits at her place, thinking that Joey is going to bless her out this morning for what she did yesterday. He brings out her breakfast and coffee to her. Then he returns to the kitchen to get breakfast. Joey sits down with his plate and coffee mug and says grace. They start to eat, and Joey starts to say something, and she looks down then softly, saying to herself sadly, "here comes the blessing out." But instead, he is smiling and says, "is your breakfast, okay, Amanda?" She looks at him with a stunned expression, then saying, "ahh…everything is fine ." Joey replies, "well, you need to eat all of it to get your strength back, okay?" She sighs and, with a smiling, relieved expression, says, "okay, Joey."

They finish breakfast, taking their plates and utensils into the kitchen, leaving their coffee mugs on the table. Every morning after breakfast, they sit in front of the fireplace, drinking their second mug of coffee. Amanda picks the mugs up off the table then goes and sits in front of the fire. Joey comes into the den sitting down with the coffee pot and sugar bowl. He pours Amanda's coffee then pouring his. Amanda removes the spoon that is in the sugar bowl, putting one teaspoon of sugar in her coffee. Joey has a little concern on his face saying to

Amanda, "Amanda put an extra half of a teaspoon in your coffee to be on the safe side." She puts the extra sugar in her coffee, and they sit just looking at the fire. Amanda is still concerned and anxious because Joey hasn't said anything about yesterday.

A few moments later, Amanda, who is still staring at the fire, says, "Joey, remember last night that you said that you would talk with me about yesterday?" Joey looks at her then turns his head to look at the fire. He then says, "Amanda, I got to thinking about that when I was watching over you last night. I decided that yesterday was a good learning process that you experienced. And I thought that was better than me fussing at you." Joey looks at Amanda, saying, "but I still want to know why you did that. You came close to freezing to death. You don't play around with winter weather around here."

Amanda then says, "remember when we talked about God coming into your life, and it could happen anywhere?" "Yes, I remember," replies Joey. Tears start to form in her eyes, and she looks at Joey with a somber expression and says, "you also said that being in a special place would be nice when you accept him. That's exactly what I did. I went down to that beautiful rocky stream that has become my special place. And I asked God into my heart. And even though I was freezing, I felt a wonderful peace come to me that I have never experienced." Joey dries her tears again with his handkerchief then looks at her shaking his head with a worried expression, saying, "but God doesn't expect you to die when you accept him, Amanda! But since God spared your life, I know he has special plans for you. I know that in my heart!"

They both turn and look at the fire. And Amanda says, "Joey, you knew exactly what to do when I was freezing to death. Is that something you learned in the Marines?" Joey looks at her, saying, "Amanda, when you are a Marine Raider or in Marine Reconnaissance, you train in every type of climate on Earth. From one-hundred and twenty-degree deserts to way below zero in snowy mountain regions. And everything in between." She looks at Joey with a gentle smiling expression, then saying, "It looks like your Marine training saved me twice." He looks at her, saying, "Amanda, you have said that I have saved your life twice. And I want you to know that you have also rescued me." She looks at him with a questionable expression then says, "how have I rescued you, Joey?"

He says, "when you came into my life wanting to know about God, that got me back on track with him. I will always be grateful to you for that." For the first time, Joey hugs Amanda. Then she thinks to herself that hopefully, he is starting to have feelings for her. But she also knows that just because he hugged her that he's just a wonderful and caring man. They finish their coffee, and Joey asks her, "do you want some more coffee, Amanda?" "No, I have had plenty. Thank you," says Amanda. Before Joey gets up his tells Amanda, "I want you to stay in the cabin for the next two days. I don't want you to take any chances by going back out in the cold." She smiles, nodding her head. Joey then gets up, taking the coffee pot and mugs to the kitchen.

Joey returns to the den and walks to the den closet. He opens the closet door retrieving a laptop computer on the closet's second shelf. He walks to the table setting the laptop down then plugs the charging cord in. Amanda walks over to him, saying, "I didn't know you had a computer? Can you get internet up here?" Joey looks at her then saying, "Amanda, remember I can't get service of any kind up here." "Oh, I forgot," replies Amanda. Joey opens up the top then turns on the computer. Amanda looks at him with a questionable look then says, "then why do you have a computer then if you can't get on the internet?" Joey looks up at her and says, "Amanda, computers can be used for things other than the internet." Joey turns on the computer and logs in. Amanda says, "what are you doing then?"

Joey looks at her smiling then says, "I have an architectural and design program on this computer. And you and I are going to design a small chapel." Amanda lights up, saying, "Joey, this is going to be so much fun! And I would love the chapel to be painted white with a grey roof. And I would like to have six colored windows with three on each side. And, of course, the chapel must have a steeple with four clear windows. And windows in the steeple will always be lit." Joey says, "It looks like to me you already had this chapel designed. She smiles and pulls one of the chairs next to Joey, and they start working on the plans

A week later, on a Tuesday morning, they have finished the design for the chapel. Joey prints the building materials list and downloads the plans to a USB stick drive. Joey asks Amanda, "Miss Amanda, would you like to accompany me into Craig to the building materials store with me this afternoon?" Amanda produces a big smile, then saying, "I would love to accompany you to the building store Mr. Joey." Early that afternoon, they go into to Craig to the building supply store. They reach the store as Joey parks the Jeep. As usual, he walks around and opens Amanda's door and helping her out. They walk to the entrance to the store, and Joey opens the door for her. They walk in and go to the contractor's desk. The materials manager, Randy Stowers, stands up excitedly, saying, "Hey there, Joey Morris! What's on your mind today?"

Joey smiles at Randy and says, "Randy, I want you to meet a friend of mine. This is Amanda Crawford. Amanda smiles and wonders how wonderful it would be to hear Joey call her his girlfriend. She reaches out her hand, and Randy shakes it lightly. She then says, "nice to meet you, Randy." "Very nice to meet you, Amanda," replies Randy. Randy then looks at Joey, saying, "what do you need today, Joey?" Joey reaches in his pocket and gives him the USB drive, and Randy plugs it into the store's computer. Randy sees an architectural print on the front page of the materials list. He looks at Joey with a big smile saying, "a chapel?" Joey looks at Amanda with a sweet smile. He then looks back at Randy. Joey nods his head toward Amanda, then says, 'It was her idea." Randy looks at Amanda, then back at Joey, saying, "where are you going to build it, Joey?" "About twenty yards down the from my storage barn. On the path leading to the woods," says Joey. Randy looks at Amanda with a smile, saying, "Amanda, I know this chapel will be beautiful in those woods of his." Amanda looks at Joey, saying, "I think so to Randy." Amanda turns to Randy and asks, "Randy is there a restroom I can use?" Randy replies, "sure. Just come through my office here, and it's down the hall to your left." "Thank you," replies Amanda.

Amanda walks through the office, and Randy prints up the materials list and says to Joey, "It looks like we are going to have to order the windows and chairs. But I can deliver it all to you next Saturday afternoon. How's that sound?" Joey replies by saying, "that sounds great, Randy." Randy prints a pick order for the men in the warehouse and orders the materials he doesn't have. Randy then says to Joey, "do you want me to send you a bill, or do you to pay now?" "I'll pay now," replies Joey. Randy prints up the bill and hands Joey the USB drive. They walk to one of the cashiers then Joey gets a call on his cell phone.

He answers, saying, "hello?" It's Detective Paul Staley from the Grand Junction P.D., And he tells Joey, "Mr. Morris, this is detective Paul Staley, and I have an update on Miss Crawford's case." Joey is surprised and says quickly, "go ahead, detective." Staley says, "we have had Rico under observation since he assaulted Miss Crawford. He and three men are hanging around in Las Vegas. Las Vegas P.D. has been watching Rico closely, and it looks like he's trying to set up shop there. I called you to ease your minds somewhat." Joey sighs and, with a smile, says to Staley, "thanks, detective, and that will ease our minds a lot!" Staley then asks Joey, "is Miss Crawford still living with you?" Joey nods his head and says, "yes, she is and doing fine." Staley says, "that's good news, and good luck to the both of you. But one thing else, Mr. Morris, don't let your guard down just because Rico is in Vegas." Thanks, detective, goodbye," says Joey.

Joey pushes the end call on his phone. The cashier has Joey's total of all the building materials. The cashier tells Joey the amount, and Joey places his debit card in the chip terminal. Joey turns to Randy, saying, "always grateful for your help Randy." Randy shakes Joey's hand, saying, "It's always my pleasure Joey." Amanda walks up, and Randy turns to her and extends his hand. Amanda takes his hand, then Randy says, "and it's been very nice meeting you, Amanda." "Likewise, Randy," says a smiling Amanda. Joey then says to Randy, "we will be back in a couple of weeks for all the paint. And Amanda will pick the colors out." Randy replies, "well, I'll see you, then."

As they are driving back to the cabin, Joey stops at Jessie Sneed's house. Jessie is splitting firewood, and he sees Joey pull up. Jessie cuts his log splitter off, and Joey gets out of the Jeep. Jessie walks up to Joey, and they shake hands. Jessie waves to Amanda, and she smiles, waving back. Jessie looks at Joey, saying, "whats going on with you today, Marine?" Joey puts his hand on Jessie's shoulder, and with a big smile, saying, "Jessie, I need your construction expertise and help for a new building project of mine." Jessie nods his head, saying, "what are you putting up?"

Joey looks back Amanda then back at Jessie, saying, "I'm building a small chapel down from the barn that Amanda wants."

Jessie looks at Amanda then back at Joey, saying, "a small chapel." Jessie walks to Amanda's side of the Jeep, and she pulls the window down. Jessie says, "how are you doing, Amanda?" She produces her lovely smile, saying, "I'm doing great, Mr. Sneed." Jessie smiles, saying, "Amanda, please call me Jessie." She says, "okay, then Jessie." Jessie then says, "I would love to help Joey build your chapel." Amanda shakes her head with a loving smile then says, "thank you, Jessie. That's so sweet of you." Jessie smiles and walks back to Joey, saying, "when do you want to start building?" Joey replies, "the building supply store will be delivering all the materials this Saturday, then I want to start building next week. The chapel is a small project, and with the both of us, it shouldn't take more than two weeks. We will not have to build any pews or benches because I ordered padded chairs for that." "How many people will this chapel hold," asks Jessie. Joey says, "I ordered twenty chairs, and that's pushing it. I also six stained glass windows and four clear ones for the steeple." Jessie says, "want to start Monday morning then?" Joey nods his head, saying, "that sounds good. Thanks a ton, Jessie."

Jessie looks at Joey with a concerned expression then says, "Joey, this is probably nothing, but earlier this morning, a pick-up drove up the road heading toward your property. Besides delivery trucks, I know that practically no one drives up to your place unless you tell me someone is coming. About five minutes later, I decided to investigate. I went into the house and got my shotgun, and got in my truck to see who it was. After three miles, I met them as they were coming back. I pulled off the road to turn around to catch up with them to get a tag number. But they were going so fast I couldn't catch up with them."

Joey looks at Jessie with a worried expression, saying, "what was the color of the truck?" "Red," replies Jessie. Then Joey ask him, "could you see how many people were in the truck?" Jessie shakes his head, saying, "I know there were two in the front, but I couldn't see if anyone was in the back seats." Joey stares past Jessie. Then after a few moments, he says, "let me know if you see them again." Jessie is very concerned now, saying sternly, "what's going on, Joey?" Joey looks around, and he knows he can confide in Jessie. Joey says, "two months ago, I was down in Grand Junction at the V.A. When I started to come home, I saw Amanda getting assaulted by a man. He had four men around him, and I stopped to help stop it. I must have gone into killer mode because I don't remember anything until I was putting her in the Jeep. I took her to the emergency room, and the nurse and doctor knew her by name. Because she has been there so many times before."

Jessie says, "what happened to the guy that was beating her up and his men?" Joey then says, "a detective that was on the case said that Amanda was a very high priced escort girl. And the guy who was beating her up was a guy named Rico. Her employer, so to speak. And the detective told me that none of those guys were standing when I put her in the Jeep." Jessie looks at Joey still with the same concerned face, saying, "Is that why you met me at the door last month with a weapon?" Joey nods his head, then says, "yes." Jessie looks over to Amanda then back at Joey, saying, "Joey, do you think that there trying to find Amanda and especially you because you put a beating on them?" Joey looks down then back to Jessie, "It's a good possibility, Jessie. But the detective called me when we were in Craig. He said that Amanda's former employer, maybe trying to set up business in Las Vegas. Let Vegas deal with that low life from now on." Jessie looks at Joey deeply concerned, saying, "don't let your guard down Marine. You know what the enemy is capable of!" "You don't have to worry about that, Jessie," says an equally concerned Joey.

Joey then says to Jessie, "the nurse told me in the emergency room that Amanda wanted to quit the business and start a new life. And she was going to tell Rico. And that was probably the reason he was beating her." Jessie puts his hand on Joey's shoulder, saying, "thank our God you were there at the right time." Joey looks at Amanda then back at Jessie, saying, "that girl has changed Jessie since she's been here. And she even accepting Christ. As I was teaching her what I knew about the Bible, it got me back on track with God. I put God behind me when I was in the Marines. I only called him at my convenience, not his."

Jessie looks at Joey with a smile saying, "It looks like God got you two together for a reason. And if I may say this, Amanda is a wonderful girl. Maybe the type of girl you could think about marrying." Joey shakes his head, saying, "Jessie, I just have some problems with Amanda that I think I can't correct." Jessie gets close to Joey's face saying with a calm expression, "Joey, God got you two together for a reason, and we don't know what that reason is right now. As you always hear, He does things in his time, not ours. But when He lets you know the reason, I think it will be something wonderful." Jessie looks at Amanda, then back at Joey, saying, "don't let that girl slip through your fingers. And from what I've seen, your both are good for each other." Joey says, "I don't know Jessie. I'll cross that sector when I get there. See you Monday."

Joey gets in the Jeep and starts heading for the cabin. Amanda looks at Joey as she says, "what were you and Jessie talking about for so long?" Joey replies, "oh, we were just talking about getting the chapel up." "I can't wait till I see that finished chapel," says an excited Amanda. As they are driving, Joey asks her, "Amanda, I know this is a question that will make you uncomfortable, but I was wondering what kind of vehicle does Rico drive?" Joey was right. The question does make her uncomfortable, and she says, "why are you asking me that, Joey?" Joey looks at Amanda, where she has a frightened expression. She then says to him, "Joey, you're not telling me something, are you."

Joey, in a reassuring tone, says, "take it easy, Amanda. While you were in the restroom at the building store, a detective that was covering your case called me saying that Rico has been seen in Las Vegas to start a new business there. Hopefully to stay." Amanda's expression turns to a slightly relieved one, saying. "when I quit him, he drove a new Mercedes sports car." Then Joey says, "what about his men. Do you know what they drove?" Amanda says, "no, I don't, but they were always around him." Amanda looks at Joey with a strange concerned face, saying, "Joey is everything alright. Please tell me if it's not." Joey shakes his head, smiling, then looks at her saying, "Amanda, please don't worry. Let's start thinking about that chapel, shall we?" She brings out that lovely smile of hers, saying, "Joey, that sounds great. Let's do just that."

The next Saturday afternoon, the building material store delivers all the materials Joey had ordered. Even the chairs and the windows. The two delivery men unload the materials and placing the chairs and windows in the barn. Monday morning, Jessie comes over to help Joey, but Jessie has brought his nephew Malachi who just graduated from the University Of Colorado. Malachi graduated last May with a degree in structural engineering. And Jessie thought that Malichi would lend his expertise on the construction of this little chapel.

Jessie and Malichi walk up on the cabin porch then knocking on the door. Joey answers the door and invites Jessie and Malichi in. Joey looks at Malichi and says, smiling, "now who is this, Jessie?" Jessie proudly says, "this is my nephew Malichi Lucas." Then Jessie says to Malichi, "Malichi, this is Joey Morris." Joey and Malichi shake hands as Joey says, "good to meet you, Malichi." "Likewise," replies Malichi. Joey then says, "let's sit down for some coffee before we start." Then men sit at the table, then Amanda comes out of the kitchen, and all the men stand up.

Amanda says, jokingly stern, "oh, you guys sit down." Before the men sit down, Jessie looks at Malichi, saying, "Malichi, this lovely lady is Joey's friend Amanda." Amanda extends her hand to him, and Malichi takes it, and they lightly shake hands. Amanda looks at Malichi, saying, "Malichi, you have a lovely name, and it's also biblical." "Yes, ma'am. And that's why my mother named me that," says a smiling Malichi. Joey looks at Amanda, saying, "Amanda, would you bring us some coffee, please?" Amanda looks around the table, saying, "do you any of you guys like any cream with your coffee?" Malichi says, "just straight up, Miss Amanda." She looks at Jessie, saying, "and for you, Jessie?" Jessie says, "the same." Amanda then says, "I'll have it right out."

The men sit down, and Joey asks Malichi, "what do you do, Malichi?" Malichi replies, "I just graduated from the University Of Colorado last May." Joey gets a big smile on his face saying, "wow, that's great, Malichi. What was your field of study?" Malichi says, "structural engineering and I'll be going for my masters starting in January." Joey looks at Jessie then says, "way to go Jessie. You brought an expert to help us." Amanda brings the coffee pot and four mugs to the table, then saying, "may I join you, gentlemen?" Jessie says adamantly, "of course you can Amanda. You will be a pleasant distraction." Amanda produces her lovely smile, saying, "Jessie, that was so sweet." Amanda starts to sit, and the men stand up. Then she says jokingly, "guys stop doing that everything I sit down."

Jessie looks at her, saying, "Amanda, we all were brought up this way, and there is no changing us now." She looks at Jessie with gentle, smiling expression then says, "Jessie, I will have to get used to all the true gentlemen around here. I've never been treated like this before." "Well, get ready to be treated like a lady for the first time then," says Jessie. The men sit, and Joey looks at Malichi, saying, "Malichi, I don't expect you to work this job for nothing. I'll pay you for your work and ideas on this project." Malichi looks at Joey with a somber but smiling expression, saying, "Mr. Joey, we are going to build this chapel for our Lord. I will not accept any compensation for what I do. This chapel will be for God's glory, not mine." Amanda puts her hand on Malichi's arm then says, "Malichi, that was so sweet and genuine. And I know where your heart lies. And I know you will have a wonderful and fulfilling life." "Thank you, Miss Amanda," says a grateful Malichi.

After their coffee, Joey looks at the men then says, "let's get at it shall we gentlemen." Amanda looks at Joey sternly then says, "oh, know you don't, Joey Morris." Joey has a surprised expression and holds up his hands, looking at Amanda, then saying, "what?" Amanda starts to smile then says to Joey, "I'm going help with the chapel also." Joey looks at the men and then back at Amanda. He smiles then says, "okay, lady and gentlemen, let's get started." Everybody puts on their heavy winter outerwear and head outside to start construction of the chapel.

With Malichi's input and hard work from everybody to construct the chapel, It's finished in eight days. Amanda went and picked out the paint and painted some of the inside parts of the chapel when the walls first went up. They put an electrical service on the back of the chapel, and then three days later, the power company came up to hook up the electricity. Even though Joey had a small central heating unit installed, Amanda wanted to have a wood-burning stove put in. The chapel is now finished, including moving the chairs in. Joey and Amanda prepare a delicious celebration dinner for Jessie and Malichi. After dinner, they are all sitting in the den with their coffee, then Jessie says to Joey and Amanda, "what is the plan for the chapel now you two?"

Joey looks at Amanda with a big smile then looks over to Jessie, saying, "ask her." Jessie looks at Amanda with a questionable expression, saying, "okay, Amanda, what's next?" Amanda looks at Jessie, saying, "I just wanted a special place to talk to God." Jessie then says to her, "then why all the chairs?" Amanda replies, "I would like to have some special occasions where people would come up here. Like Easter, Thanksgiving and especially Christmas Eve. Jessie looks at Amanda and Joey, saying, "maybe we could get Malichi's father David to come up here and speak sometimes. He's an ordained Baptist Minister." Malichi then speaks up, saying, "I know he would love to do that. He already comes up here visiting with people, and he has mentioned more than once that he would like to start a church around this area. Maybe we just planted the seed we needed."

Amanda lights up then says to Malichi, "that would be great!" Malichi then says, "I will mention it to him when I get home. I'm very sure he would do it." It's ten minute's past nine, and Jessie says, "it's getting close to my bedtime, so we need to get going." Jessie and Malichi put on their coats and hats, then Joey and Amanda go over to them, giving them hugs. Amanda says, "Jessie, you are such a good friend to us, and I will never be able to thank you and Malichi enough." Malichi says, "Miss Amanda, I know I can speak for Uncle Jessie, but it has been a definite pleasure to have helped on this project. I will let you know what my dad says." Jessie and Malichi leave, then Amanda and Joey walk back into the den.

Joey goes over to the wood rack and puts a backlog on the fire. He turns around, and Amanda is standing behind him, and she gives a tight, loving hug. Joey can't help this time, not to hug her back. They pull back and look at each other for a few seconds. Then Amanda leans in kisses Joey on his lips. This time the kiss is a little longer from the last time she kissed him. Amanda leans back and in an incredible calm voice that Joey has ever heard from her as she says, "goodnight Joey." She goes into the bathroom to change into her pajamas, and Joey walks over to his recliner, sitting down. He stares at the fire with a slight, sad expression. He thinks to himself that every time Amanda kisses him, they become sweeter than the ones before.

The next morning Joey is preparing breakfast, and Amanda awakes. She gets out of bed then putting on her slippers. She walks into the kitchen, saying excitedly, "good morning Joey!" He looks back to her, saying, "good morning Amanda. How did you sleep last night?" She replies, "I had a wonderful sleep." Joey then asks her, "do you like french toast?" She gives him a big smile saying, "I love french toast! I hope you have powdered sugar?" Joey laughs a bit then says, "french toast without powdered sugar is un-American Amanda!" She laughs at what he just said then she pours her coffee in her mug. She then tells Joey, "I'll be at the table." "I'll have the toast out in a moment," replies Joey.

As they are eating breakfast, Joey looks at Amanda, saying, "you know what Thursday is, don't you, Amanda?" She looks at Joey with a questionable face, saying, "no, I don't." Joey smiles, saying, "it's Thanksgiving." Amanda is surprised. Then says excitedly, "Thanksgiving? Wow, I didn't realize it was so late in the year because of everything that has been happening!" Joey says to her, "how would you like to go grouse hunting with me early tomorrow morning?" She looks at him with a smiling, surprised expression, saying, "what's a grouse, Joey?" "Blue grouse. It's a game bird that lives around here. That's what we are having for thanksgiving instead of turkey," replies Joey. Amanda then says, "I never been hunting in my life." Joey says, "Amanda, you can start hunting anytime. You will love it!" She shrugs her shoulders, saying, "okay then. What time would we start?" "I want to be in the woods at eight o'clock. So we'll be getting up about six-thirty in the morning," says Joey. Amanda smiles and nodding her head, saying, "six-thirty? I can do that." Joey nods his head once and with a big smile, saying, "that's great!"

Six o'clock arrives the next morning, and Joey's alarm goes off. Amanda is still asleep. Then Joey goes into the kitchen for some coffee. He comes out of the kitchen with a mug of coffee for Amanda. He gently nudges her shoulder, and he says softly, "Amanda." She doesn't move, and he touches her shoulder again and speaks a little louder, "Amanda." She wakes, turning over to Joey. She stretches and, with a smile, says, "is it time to go hunting?" Joey replies, "not just yet, but I've got your coffee. She smiles, saying, "thanks." She sits up in bed, and he hands the mug to her. She takes a sip, and Joey says, "did I get your coffee, right?" She looks at him with a big smile, saying, "it's just right, sir."

Joey smiles then says, "this is the first time I have served coffee in bed to a lady. For that matter, I've never served coffee in bed to anybody." "And I have never been served coffee in bed before," replies a grateful Amanda. Joey then says, "do you want something to eat?" She shakes her head, then says, "not this morning. This coffee will be all I want." Joey then says, "you finish your coffee, and I'm going to get ready." Later Amanda goes into the bathroom to change into her thermal undergarments, flannel shirt, jeans and snow-boots. She walks out, and Joey says to her with a joking, sarcastic tone, "be sure to put your coat on this time." Amanda gives him an unpleasant look, then laughs and also saying in an equally jokingly, sarcastic voice, "you're funny, you know that Joey."

He laughs, and Amanda starts putting on her coveralls. As she is zipping her coveralls up, Joey gets a doubled-barreled, twenty-gauge shotgun out of the gun cabinet. He gets bird-shot shotgun shells and puts them in his coat. Joey then straps on the forty-four magnum revolver. Then he starts to smile as he looks Amanda while she is putting on her parka. Then he says to her in a solemn tone of voice, "look, Amanda!" She looks at him, and he is patting the revolver that's in its holster. Joey then says, "I got the bigfoot killer." She looks at him with an unpleasant expression, saying, "shut up, Joey." He starts laughing, and Amanda starts laughing also. Joey puts a box of revolver ammunition in his other pocket then says to Amanda, "you ready?" "Ready," says an excited Amanda.

Chapter Eleven

Thanksgiving

Joey goes into the barn to get the snow-track, and they leave passing the chapel, and Amanda says, "Joey, the chapel is so beautiful. Especially with the snow all around it." She looks up at the steeple on the chapel and notices the four windows in it. Amanda says, "Joey, lets put some electric candles in the steeple windows. Which would remind me of what we talked about one time." Joey says, "what's that?" Amanda looks forward and says, "I don't know all the words to this Bible verse, but it says that we don't need to hide our candle but to put it on a stand for people can see it." Joey looks at her, smiling, and says, "that's Mark four-twenty-one, and what you said is exactly right."

She looks over at Joey then says, "Joey, how do you know so much about the bible?" He stares forward, saying, "well, I don't know that much. But when I was in the ninth grade, we had a Bible drill club at church." Amanda says, "what is a Bible drill club?" Joey replies by saying, "We formed a group of youth, and our youth minister would give us a Bible verse. Then we practiced how fast we could find that verse. We even went to the state Baptist Bible drill contest, and our group came in third place." After a few seconds, Amanda sees a big smile on Joey's face, and he says, "my mom and dad were so proud of me." Amanda touches his shoulder, then says, "I know they were Joey."

Joey stops the snow-track then says to Amanda, "we have to walk the rest of the way because we don't want to scare the birds off." Joey gets out, then goes over and opens Amanda's door, helping her to get out. He gets the shotgun off the back window rack. They walk into the woods, and Amanda starts to hear the strange sounds of nature around her. Limbs falling off trees, deer walking in the woods, and then she hears some howling. Amanda moves closer to Joey, almost climbing on his back. She looks around because she has become frightened of the howls. She is still looking around when she says to Joey quietly, "did you hear that, Joey? "Hear what," says a slightly smiling Joey. She says, "those howling noises." Joey, who is still looking around, says, "oh, that's a bunch of coyote's talking to each other. Don't worry. They won't bother us." Amanda looks at the shotgun then back at Joey, saying, "did you bring enough bullets for that gun?" He knows that she is frightened, and Joey doesn't take this excellent chance to tease her about saying bullets for a shotgun. He smiles, saying, "yes, Amanda, we have plenty of bullets for this shotgun."

They walk deeper into the woods, then Joeys turns to Amanda and says, whispering, "walk real quiet while I call up the birds." Joey starts making a high-pitched type of grunt as he looks around carefully. About a minute later, he stops walking suddenly. Joey looks at Amanda and puts his finger on his lips. He starts walking slowly, still making the grunting sound. Soon two grouse fly up from the ground, and Joey kills both of the birds.

Amanda looks at him, whispering, "that gun was loud, Joey." Joey smiles at her, then walks over where the dead birds are. He picks them up, and before he puts them in his bag, he shows the birds to Amanda. He says to her, "boy, these are some fat ones." She starts frowning and sadly says, "Joey, grouse are so beautiful. It's a shame you have to kill something this pretty." Joey quickly says, "when you eat one of these birds that have been grilled with bacon, you will change your mind how pretty they are." Joey puts two more shotgun shells into his shotgun and says to Amanda, "you want to get the next one?"

She looks at Joey with disbelief, whispering to him, "Joey, I told you before I've never shot a gun in my life." He looks at her confidently, saying, "well, this is a good time to learn on the job." He hands her the shotgun then says, "it's just like the revolver that I showed you how to shoot. But with a shotgun, it's so much easier." Reluctantly she says, "okay, show me what to do." Joey says softly, "put the stock of the shotgun against your right shoulder. Then put your left hand on the forward grip." Amanda looks at the triggers then looks at Joey with a questionable expression and whispers, "Joey, this gun has two thingies." Joey almost starts laughing and says, "those thingies are the triggers. Just like on the revolver, which has only one thingie."

Joey then quietly tells her, "point and look down the barrel at what you want to shoot. Pull both hammers back just like on the revolver. And only put your finger on one of the thingies until you are ready to shoot. To make sure you fire one barrel at a time." Amanda then says, "I think I can do this, so let's go." They start walking, and almost immediately, Joey sees a single grouse on the ground. He looks at Amanda, and he points to his eyes. He points to where the grouse is and motions Amanda to get in front of him. She pulls both hammers back on the shotgun.

She moves in front of him, and Joey points to the bird. She sees the bird and creeps toward the bird. She aims the shotgun at the bird, and it flys off. Amanda aims at the grouse and, in her excitement, pulls both the triggers. The blast from both barrels knocks her back into the snow. She is breathing heavily and dazed from the shotgun blast. Joey walks over to her to see if Amanda is okay. She is lying in the snow, and he asks her, "you okay? She looks at him with a stunned expression, saying, "I'm fine." Joey then says, "you got the grouse." She looks at him still dazed then sits up, saying, "wonderful." Then she falls back into the snow, again with the dazed expression and breathing hard.

Joey goes and picks up the grouse and puts it in the bag. He walks over to Amanda, who is still lying in the snow, reaching down to help her up. She takes his hand, and Joey pulls her up. He walks over to the shotgun that is about six feet from Amanda. The gun flew out of her hands when she took the shot. He picks the gun up, and turns to Amanda, saying in a jokingly, sarcastic tone, "I'm glad this wasn't a triple-barreled shotgun." Amanda responds in an equally sarcastic tone of voice, "that's very funny, Joey." He starts laughing and says, "well, it's time to pack up and hit the trail."

Amanda looks at Joey with a questionable expression then says, "aren't we going to hunt some more?" Joey says, "we've killed our limit. You can only have three grouse in your possession in Colorado. There a protected bird." They walk to the snow-track, then soon there back at the cabin. Joey gets out of the vehicle and walks around and opens Amanda's door. He then asks her, "Amanda, would you go in and put some wood in the fireplace, please? Then get yourself warmed up. Also, would you make us some coffee?" She smiles then says, "no problem." Amanda then says to Joey, "what are you going to be doing?" Joey says, "I'm going to clean these birds. Then put them in putting them in the fridge." Amanda looks at Joey with a vibrant expression, saying, "go right ahead." Joey backs the snow-track to the barn and gets out, opening the door. He returns the vehicle into the barn then gets out, closing the doors. He then starts the process of cleaning the birds.

Later, Joey goes into the cabin and puts the cleaned grouse in the refrigerator. He walks into the den and takes off his coat and coveralls. Amanda comes from the bathroom then says, "want your coffee now, honey?" Both Amanda and Joey look at each other with surprised expressions, and Amanda can't believe she called Joey, honey. She looks down a little embarrassed, but Joey changes the subject quickly. He then smiles and says calmly, "I would love a cup, Amanda." She turns around, walking into the kitchen. Then she quietly says to herself, "I can't believe I just called Joey honey." She pours the coffee into their mugs then saying to herself again, "don't give up, Amanda. You're going to pray extra hard tonight that I'll still have a chance to change Joey's feelings toward me."

She walks back into the den and places the mugs on the table. Joey walks over to the table and pulls Amanda's chair out for her. She sits down. Then Joey walks to his chair then sits. Amanda tilts her head with a lovely smile, saying, "Joey, you don't have to pull my chair out every time I sit down." He looks at her and takes a deep breath then says, "Amanda,

I don't want you to say that to me ever again. You know what I said before about any lady that is around me." She smiles then says, "I promise, Joey. I'll never say that again. She pauses for a few seconds then says to him, teary-eyed and smiling, "Joey, you want to know something?" "Sure," he says. Amanda looks at him for a few moments then says to him, "I love how you treat me like a lady. Forgive me for saying things as I said a moment ago. I guess it's because I'm just not used to so much attention toward me." Joey pulls out his handkerchief and hands it to her, saying, "It looks like I'm going to have to get a truckload of handkerchiefs with you around." Amanda laughs as she dries her eyes, then says, "Oh, be quiet."

Joey looks at her and laughs then, saying, "also, you better stop that crying because you are going to water down your coffee." They both laugh, then Joey asks her, "what kind of trimmings would you like with your turkey for Thanksgiving dinner?" Amanda thinks for a moment, later saying, "it's been so long, but I do remember what my aunt prepared. Not the aunt I lived with but my cousin Marilyn's mother." "And what was that," asks Joey. Amanda says, "she would also have a big turkey. And my aunt always had stuffing, mashed potatoes, gravy, and cranberry sauce. And I think she always had some sort of casserole. Oh, I almost forgot that she had a pie for dessert." Joey takes a sip of his coffee then says, "tell you what Miss Amanda. We'll go to the supermarket in Craig to get all our Thanksgiving supplies this afternoon. I want to beat the crowds." "Sounds good to me," replies Amanda. Joey then says, "I make a great grouse stuffing. You'll love it."

Later that afternoon, they arrive at the supermarket, and the parking lot full of vehicles. Joey sighs and says, "It looks like we're not beating the crowds after all." Amanda says, "it's fine, Joey. Let's go." They walk into the store and grab a shopping basket. They walk around the aisles picking out each item for the trimmings they will prepare. Joey has everything checked off his list but the pie. He then says, "we have everything but the pie. Let's go to the bakery." As they walk to the bakery, Amanda asks Joey, "Joey, can I pick out the pie, please?" He looks at her and says, "just as long it's not pumpkin or rhubarb." "No way," exclaims Amanda. They reach the pie section of the deli, and Amanda has a strange feeling that someone is staring at her. She looks around and sees a man smiling at her in one of the check-out lines. The man is apparently with his wife, then Amanda quickly looks away. Then Joey says, "which pie shall it be?" Amanda doesn't say anything and looks back toward the man. He is still staring and smiling at her. She looks at the pies and says sadly, "cherry will be fine."

Joey has been around Amanda long enough to recognize her sad tone of voice. He looks at her, saying with a concerned voice, "what's wrong, Amanda? She is upset but manages to tell Joey, "that man in the check-out line with the long coat is staring and smiling at me. I think it's someone I know. If you know what I mean." Joey looks over to the man who now has a smirky grin on his face. Joey instantly goes into his Amanda protective mode and starts to go over to confront the man. Amanda starts to cry then grabs Joey's arm, saying, "please Joey don't go over to that man." Joey looks at her with a scary expression on his face saying very sternly, "why the hell not, Amanda!" She pleads with him, saying, "that's probably his wife, and I don't want to hurt her. Please try to understand what I'm saying."

Joey looks over to the man again. He then turns back to Amanda, saying, "alright then. But only because of you." Joey has calmed down some and looks back over at the man who still has that smirky grin. Joey turns back to Amanda and looks at her for few seconds then says, "that scum has to be the biggest jerk in this state. For looking at you like the way he did with his wife right next to him." Joey picks up the cherry pie and puts it in the grocery basket. They go through the check-out line then Joey pays for everything. He pushes the basket out of the store, and Amanda is still upset, not saying anything. Joey opens her door on the Jeep and helps her in. He loads the groceries in the back and gets in the vehicle. They head toward the cabin, and Amanda is still not saying anything. Joey thinks to himself how many times Amanda will go through that situation again. Also, he believes that this is one of the reasons he can't have feelings of love for her. They arrive at the cabin, and Joey says, "go ahead and go into the cabin and put some wood on the fire." She opens the door immediately and gets out for the first time without Joey opening the door for her. Joey goes to the back of the Jeep and starts taking the groceries out. Then he says to himself, "I'm not going to let some jerk ruin Amanda's holiday."

Joey brings the bags of groceries in, and Amanda is on the couch, staring at fire crying. He takes the groceries in the kitchen and puts all the items up. He returns to the den and sits beside her. After a few moments, Joey turns to her, saying, "Amanda, I can't imagine the feelings you are experiencing now." She doesn't say anything but keeps crying, staring at the fire. Amanda's hands clasped together on her legs, and Joey puts his hand on them. Then Joey speaks to her calmly and reassuring voice, saying, "Amanda, I want you to listen to me. What you experienced this afternoon could happen again while you're here. But what that man saw today was not the woman he was with in the past."

Joey gets a little closer to her and says, "you have become a Christian, and God is your protector and guardian. It says in the Bible that you must wear the full armor of God to protect you from the tempter's snares. You still have the same physical body, but your heart and soul belong to God now. Jesus was with his disciples after he rose from the dead. He told them that he was about to go to heaven, and his disciples begged him not to go. But he then said one on the most beautiful, reassuring verses in the Bible." Amanda looks at him and says, "what did Jesus say, Joey?" He looks into her eyes then puts his hands on her face, saying, "Jesus said that he would be with us even till the end of time." Joey lifts his hands with a big smile and excitedly says, "man was that cool or what! That means that Jesus will be with you throughout life. The more I think about it, the elderly lady that I was talking to in that emergency department was a real angel. She spoke to my heart, and in turn, with you being here with me, you became a Christian. God sometimes works in strange ways that we don't understand."

Amanda's chin starts to quiver then she starts crying again. Joey gets his handkerchief out and dries her tears. She starts to laugh because Joey is always pulling out his handkerchief for her. Then Joey says, "now that's the beautiful face I want to see." She leans to him, hugging him tight, and Joey slightly hugs her back. She stops hugging him and says, "Joey, I will never be able to figure you out. You have an amazing gift of always making me feel better very quickly. I have cried from the inside all my life. But with you, that never happens anymore. Thank you from my whole heart." Joey laughs then says, "your very welcome, Amanda. And you sure have proved that you don't hold your feelings inside anymore." Amanda laughs, and Joey stands up, taking her by the hand then says, "now let's go make plans for that Thanksgiving dinner."

Thanksgiving day comes, and all the food is ready. Joey has grilled the grouse on the back porch. Right before they start moving the food to the dining table, Amanda looks at Joey and says, "let's go to the chapel and say grace for everything we are grateful for." Joey nods his head, then saying, "that's a wonderful idea, Amanda. Let's go." They put on their coats and boots and walk through the deep snow to the chapel. Joey puts the security code for the door lock, and they enter the warm chapel. Joey built a prayer altar rail with cushions for your knees. He also made a small pulpit for if anyone who wanted to speak.

They both kneel at the Alter, and Amanda says to Joey, "I'll start my prayer first." Joey smiles and nods his head. Amanda then says, "dear God, the only thing I have to say to you today is to thank you for Joey. Who saved my life twice and led me to you, changing my life. Oh, one more thing. I want to thank you for the wonderful meal we are about to eat. In Jesus's name, I pray, Amen." Joey then says, "our dear Lord, I have only one thing that I'm grateful. And that is, I thank you for Amanda. She led me back to you, and she didn't even know she was doing it. And when she leaves after the first of the year, let her be a beacon for your glory. In your Son's name, Amen."

Joey stands up, then Amanda says to Joey, "you can go back to the cabin and start getting things ready. I'm going to stay here for a few moments." Joey says, "that's fine, and when you lock the door, the security code is the same as the cabins." Amanda then says, "Joey, let's leave the chapel door unlocked from now on. Just in case someone wants to come up here and be close to God." Joey smiles and says, "that sounds nice. Okay, we'll do it." Joey turns and leaves, and she puts her hands together, looking at a small cross that is on the wall behind the pulpit. She calmly prays, "my dear Lord, show me the way about Joey. You know I'm in love with him with all my heart. And I want to ask you if he can start having feelings for me. And I hope I'm not selfish by wanting this.

This prayer might sound a little inconsiderate of me, and I don't know if this kind of prayer is appropriate or not. But it says in the Bible "in faith, ask, and you will receive." I have a lot of faith in my heart that You will let this happen. But I know You will let me know what's best for me. I will be sad if Joey's love for me doesn't happen. But I will accept your answer and live the life you have planned for me. In Jesus's name, I pray, Amen." Amanda stands and walks out of the chapel. Then she walks to the cabin to enjoy her thanksgiving dinner.

When she enters the den, Joey comes out of the kitchen, saying, "Amanda, we forgot to get the cranberry sauce." Amanda replies, "that's okay, Joey. Besides, everything is ready." Joey shakes his head and says, "Amanda, it's not Thanksgiving dinner without cranberry sauce. I'm going down to Mr. Wilson's store and get a can." Amanda looks at him with a questionable expression and says, "Mr. Wilson is open on Thanksgiving?" "Sure! He says it's one of the best days for him because people like me always forget something on Thanksgiving," replies Joey. Joey then says, "everything is in the oven keeping warm, and I'll be back in a few minutes." Amanda smiles, saying, "be careful out there."

Joey puts on his coat and walks out and locking the door. A few moments later, there is a knock at the door. Joey has forgotten his keys and shouts, "Amanda, open the door I forgot my keys again." She looks at the coffee table and sees his keys then picks them up. She opens the door handing him the keys, then says, "remember what I said. Be careful out there. He turns toward the Jeep, and she closes the door. About twenty minutes later, he returns to the cabin, and Joey knocks on the door, shouting, "Amanda, it's me. And I'm coming in." "Okay," she replies.

It's later that evening, and Amanda and Joey are sitting in front of the fireplace drinking hot chocolate. Amanda is holding her bear, and Joey looks over to her and asks, "Amanda, Thanksgiving is almost over, and I want to know what you want for Christmas?" She looks at him with wide eyes and excited expression, saying, "Christmas! Oh my goodness, it's here!" She looks around the den then looks at Joey and says, "do you have any Christmas decorations and lights?" Joey looks at her sighing and saying, "I think there are few out in the barn, but you didn't answer my question." Amanda starts looking around the den again, saying where Christmas decorations should go. Joey shakes his head because she is so excited about the decorations. Then he puts his hand on her shoulder, saying, "Amanda!" She turns to him with a big smile, then saying calmly, "yes, Joey?" Joey says, "you didn't answer my question." Amanda tilts her head a bit, thinking to herself what his question was. She then says, "what did you ask me?" Joey shakes his head and laughs, saying, "what do you want for Christmas?"

Amanda looks at him with her beautiful smile then places her hand on his face saying, "Joey, you have given me everything that I've ever wanted. Including the best gift that anyone could have ever given to me. Joey then says, "and what was that?" She starts to tear up and saying, "Joey, you were the main reason I changed my life. You taught me about God and Jesus. Now I'm a new person." Joey rolls his eyes and pulls out his large handkerchief drying her tears again. He then smiles, saying, "I know what you can get me for Christmas Amanda. A big box, full of handkerchiefs." They both start laughing, then Amanda says, "well, Joey, you know that I get emotional sometimes." Joey looks at her with his mouth open then says, "sometimes! How about all the time!" She laughs, then looks at Joey with a loving expression and then, saying, "Joey, you have been the best Christmas present I've ever gotten. And I want you always to remember that."

Joey looks around, thinking to himself that Amanda could be trying to tell him something. Like how she would want their relationship might go from here. He knows that she has fallen in love with him. And eventually, he will have to break her heart. But he would not dare do that till after Christmas. He looks at Amanda, and she is still looking at him with that beautiful smiling face. Then he says, "do you remember your best Christmas present, Amanda?" She turns and looks at the fire, saying, "remember the time when I said I would tell you some things about me?" Joey says, "yes, I do."

Amanda looks at the fire then says, "I never knew who my father was and my mother died of a drug overdose when I was six years old. She died right before Christmas. I went and lived with my Aunt Crystyl and my Uncle Charlie. And my two cousins, Tyler and Riley, after she died."

Amanda looks at Joey with a slight smile, saying, " I had one present under the tree, and my aunt said that my mother got it for me for Christmas. Joey smiles and says, "what was it?" Amanda looks back at the fire, saying, "it was a small barn with farm animals that came with it. It also had a fence around the barnyard. But the best thing about it is when I opened the barn doors, they mooed like a cow. And I played with it all the time." Amanda then breathes deep, and with a sad tone, says, "but my aunt sold it a garage sale when I was at school one day."

Joey feels so bad for Amanda now and thinks how could anyone, especially an aunt, could sell a child's favorite toy. Joey needs to cheer Amanda up. He looks at her smiling, then says, "Amanda, this is what I would think if the same situation had happened to me." "What would that be," says Amanda. Joey looks at the fire, saying, "maybe some person who didn't have much money got the farm-set for their child for Christmas. And that child loved it as much as you did." Amanda looks at Joey smiling, then says, "Joey, I never thought about something like that." She pauses for a few seconds, then says, "Joey, I have never been around someone who can lift my spirits as you do. And I know that you're a tough Marine. But you have a sweet, kind, and gentle heart inside you." Joey turns red with a slight grin because no one has said anything like that to him.

Amanda then excitedly says, "what was your favorite toy?" Joey looks up at the ceiling then back at Amanda, saying, "it was a toy steam engine." Amanda smiles, saying, "I've heard that every little boy loves trains." Joey shakes his head, then says, "not a railroad engine but a real engine that produced its own steam. I was fascinated by steam power. That's how my grandfather's sawmill worked a long time ago. You would fill the toy steam engines boiler with water, and you would lite fuel tablets that fit under the boiler. After about five minutes, it would create enough steam to turn a wheel that was next to the boiler. It also had a valve on the steam pipe. And when you turned a small knob on the valve, a whistle would sound. I played with it all Christmas day until I ran out of fuel tablets. It's out in the barn put up in a safe place."

Amanda looks back at the fire with a sad look on her face. Joey realizes that Amanda has never experienced Christmas, as many children should. He is going to do his best to make sure she has a beautiful Christmas this year. He then says, "Amanda, I want you to draw up some plans on how to decorate the cabin and the chapel. And when you make up the list, include a Christmas tree we'll get in the woods. Then we will go into town and get everything you want. How about that?" Amanda says, "that sounds lovely, Joey."

She then leans down, hugging Joey back and forth, saying, "Joey, I never decorated anything for Christmas before. And I'm so happy now that I could give you a great big kiss!" Amanda realized what she just said and gets embarrassed. But Joey is enjoying her happiness so much that he didn't mind what she said. She reaches her hand to Joey, and he stands up. Amanda then says, "let's get to work on those decorating plans!" Joey holds his hands up, saying adamantly, "oh no, you don't, Amanda! Christmas decorating is a "chick" thing." She leans close to him with her lovely smile, saying, "well, Sgt. Morris, you are about to learn how we chick's do these sorts of things." He stands there looking at her lovely, smiling face. And he knows he can't resist her wishes. He salutes her and says, "yes, ma'am, Major Crawford." Amanda burst out laughing then says excitedly, "I can't wait to see what this cabin and the chapel will look like when we have it decorated for Christmas!"

The next morning they have their breakfast and after they clean up the dishes and cookware. They go into the den to put on their winter outerwear when Joey stops and looks around. Joey looks at Amanda as she is coming out of the bathroom, and he says, "Amanda, we need to get that fir first before we get the decorations." Amanda looks at Joey with a very questionable expression then says, "Joey, why do I need to get a fir when I have all these cold-weather clothes and a big coat?" Joey starts laughing as Amanda has never heard him laugh before. He's laughing so hard that he is rolling on the floor. Amanda is confused about why he is laughing like this, and she can't help but laugh also. As Joey is still on the floor laughing, Amanda raises her voice, still laughing at Joey and then says, "what in the world can be so funny, Joey?"

Joey sits up, still laughing, and he puts his face in his hands, shaking his head. Amanda is still perplexed by his laughing, saying, "Joey, tell me what's so funny?" He tones down his laughing a bit and tries to explain why he is laughing so hard. It's hard to get the words out, then finally he says, "Amanda, it's what you said." She holds up her hands, still laughing at Joey, saying, "what did I say?" Joey stops his laughing as best he can and says, "when I said we need to get you a fir, I meant a Douglas fir. It's a tree. Not something you wear, ding-dong!" She looks at him with her hands on her hips. And with a sarcastic grin, says, "well, why didn't you tell me in the first place?" Joey starts laughing again and lays back on the floor. Amanda, still with her sarcastic grin and hands still on her hips, says, "Joey stop laughing at me!" After a few moments, Amanda can't help at Joey laughing on the floor. After a few moments, he stops laughing with his arms and legs spread apart, then saying, "Amanda, I haven't laughed that hard in years! My stomach muscles even hurt!" She walks to where he is lying then looks down at him, saying, "I'm so glad I'm here for your amusement, Joey." He holds his hand up and says, "Amanda, your going to have to help me up after that Amanda moment." She looks at him with a snide expression, saying, "you're going to have to get up on your own after that performance Joey."

He gets up off the floor slowly and still laughing. He looks at Amanda, and she still has that snide look, but soon it turns into a smile. She then say's, "you are right, Joey. I had another one of my famous blonde incidents, doesn't it." Joey says, "Amanda, your blonde moments is one of the things I like about you. So don't stop. I should've been more specific. The Douglas fir to me is the prettiest of all the Christmas trees that people put up. We have a great stand of the trees about two miles away. And I want you to pick our tree out."

She looks at him and says, "you will help me, won't you? I don't know that much about picking out Christmas trees." "Sure I will," replies Joey. He then says, "I'm going out to the barn to get the snow track ready. And also, I'm going to start one of the chain saws to see if it's in good order. Dress up warm now because we will have to walk through the trees to pick out the one you want." He goes to the gun case and straps on his holster that is holding the forty-four magnum and his Ruger rifle. Then he walks out the door to get everything ready as Amanda gets ready to go out in the freezing temperatures.

Amanda goes into the kitchen and pours up two insulated cups of coffee that they will take on their trip. She walks into the den and puts the cups on the table. Then there's a knock at the door. She looks at the coffee table where Joey's keys are lying. She picks the keys up the walks over and opens the door with an outstretched arm putting the keys in his face. Joey has a slightly embarrassed look on his face and starts to say something when Amanda interrupts him. She says, "Joeseph Morris, you are a Marine with many awards, but you can never remember your keys." Then he says in a sort of a concerned voice, "how do you know about my awards, Amanda?" She notices his tone of voice and says timidly, "I saw the scrapbook that was in the bookcase. You should be very proud of all your achievements." He looks at her with a somber expression for a few seconds then says with a smile, "are you ready? I'm going to go and the snow-track." "Let me go get our coffee first," says Amanda.

They walk to the snow-track, and Joey takes his coffee and opens her door for her. He walks around and gets in, saying, "now let's go get your Christmas tree." Amanda looks at him and says, "our Christmas tree, Joey." Joey looks at her, smiling and nodding his head. They drive a different route this time. Amanda sees a big, ice-covered pond down a hill. She looks at Joey and says, "that's a nice pond down there. Joey looks in the direction of the pond then says, "my dad built that skating pond for mother who was a wonderful skater. She won many championships when she was younger. My dad told me there was some talk about her going for the nationals at one time." Amanda looks at Joey with a questionable expression, saying, "did she try out for the nationals?" Joey shakes his head, saying, "when she was fourteen, she was practicing with some other skaters, and one of the skaters ran into her, and mom tore her knee up. She was never the same after that. But she kept on skating after she got well, but couldn't do the hard technical stuff anymore."

Amanda looks forward and frowns, saying, "that is so terrible when your dream can end that quick." Joey looks at her, replying, "my dad built her that pond for her for she could skate on when they would come up here on one of their retreats. It's only about four-foot deep." Amanda says, "I know where the gentleman in you came from Joey. And that was from your dad. And I know that your mom and dad were deeply in love, weren't they. Joey pauses for a few seconds, nodding his head, saying with a big smile, "yes, they were Amanda. And I never heard them say a crossword to each other. If they did, I never heard it." Amanda looks out her side window and softly says to herself, "what a wonderful, beautiful life that would be." Joey looks over to her, saying, "did you say something, Amanda?" She turns and looks at Joey with a gentle smile, saying, "it was nothing Joey."

Joey looks forward as he is driving then says to her, "Amanda, you do know how to skate, don't you?" She laughs and says, "Joey, I have never put on skates before. Even roller skates." Joey then says, "well, you are going to learn how to ice skate then. You can wear some of my mother's skates, and we will have a big fire after we are through. We'll bake some potatoes, ears of corn, and roast some marshmallows. And wash it down with hot chocolate. How's that sound to you?" She looks at him smiling then says, "Joey, that sounds wonderful."

About thirty minutes later, they arrive at the large stand of Douglas firs. Joey stops the snow-track at the edge of the trees. He gets out then walks around the vehicle to open Amanda's door, and she gets out and gazes at the beautiful snow-laden firs. Joey goes into the back and gets the chainsaw and goggles. He walks up to Amanda, saying, "let's go get that tree for you." Amanda is looking at the magnificence of the trees and takes in the wonderful scent they produce. She then says to Joey, "these trees are so beautiful, Joey. I hate to cut one down any of them." Joey looks at Amanda smiling and says, "no need to worry, Amanda. The Foresty Commission every two years plants ten trees for everyone I cut down." She looks up at Joey with her beautiful smile and excitedly says, "really Joey?" "Really," replies Joey. Joey then says, "now let's get that Christmas tree."

They both venture farther into the trees, and Amanda looks around for at least thirty minutes. Amanda walks up to the perfect tree that's about six-feet tall, looking all around it. She then says, "Joey, this fir is telling me it wants to be our Christmas tree. So this will be it." Joey nods his head and says to Amanda, "stand in the back of me about ten feet. I don't want the tree to fall on you if it decides to fall different from how I'm cutting it." Amand gets behind him, and Joey walks up to the tree, saying, "well, Mr. Douglas, I will try to make this quick." Amanda laughs as Joey puts on his goggles and cranks up the chainsaw. He cuts through the tree in a matter of seconds, and it falls into the snow. Then he grabs the trunk of the tree, and Joey and Amanda drag it back to the snow-track. Joey then says to Amanda, "start the track up, Amanda, for it will be warm for us. She does what Joey asks then he puts the chainsaw in the back. Joey then puts the tree on the snow-tracks steel rack. He ties the tree down tight and sees that Amanda is in the driver's seat, probably wanting to drive it out. He gets on the passenger side and says, "Amanda, as we were driving here, I saw the track is low on fuel. So take us to Mr. Wilson's to get some gas."

She looks at him wide-eyed, saying, "you want me to drive this to Mr. Wilson's? Are you sure?" Joey looks at her and says, "Amanda, I wouldn't have asked you to drive to the store unless I knew you could handle this thing." "Thanks," says a grateful Amanda. She drives the snow-track past the cabin then getting on the road heading to the store. They arrive, and Amanda pulls the track carefully to the gas pump. Wilson peeks out the window to see who's at the gas pump, and Joey holds his thumb up. Wilson nods his head and turns on the pump. Amanda is still in the cab as Joey fills the snow-track up. The gas tank gets full, and Joey puts the nozzle back on the pump. He then puts the gas cap on. He walks over to Amanda's door and opens it and says, "pull the track over to the side of the store, then I will meet you here at the front." She pulls the track to the side then gets out, walking back to Joey. Joey smiles and says, "it's close to lunchtime. How about a sandwich and some hot chocolate?" Amanda says, "lead the way, sir."

They walk up the steps and enter the store. Amanda looks around and sees the same older men as she saw once before sitting around the woodstove. When they see her, they stand and take off their hats. Amanda, with a lovely smile, says, "hey everybody." All the gentlemen say, "hello, Miss Amanda." The men are still smiling at her, and she says with a lovely voice, "oh come on guys, you can sit down now." The men sit but keep smiling at Amanda and don't pay one bit of attention to Joey. Joey goes over to the men shaking their hands and saying, "Hello guys, I'm Joey Morris. Glad to meet all of you." One of the old men named Clarence says, "don't be a smart-aleck, Joey." Joey has a smirky grin then says to Clarence, "and it's my definite pleasure to see you, Mr. Clarence." Clarence probably wants to say something not very nice to Joey, but since Amanda is standing next to Joey, he doesn't say anything.

Joey and Amanda wave at Mr. Wilson, and he waves back. They walk up to the deli counter where Baily turns and, with a surprised expression and a big smile, says, "well, hello Joey!" Joey, who is a little embarrassed, says, "hello, Bailey." Amanda looks at Joey, trying not to laugh when Bailey says sweetly to Amanda, "and how are you today, Amanda?" Amanda is still trying not to laugh at Joey but manages to say, "I'm fine, Bailey." Bailey then says, "what can I get for you two today?" Joey says, "Amanda?" Amanda looks in the meat case for a few moments then says, "Bailey, I would like the roast beef this time on wheat with lots of mayonnaise. Also, a little lettuce and tomato, please." Bailey looks at Joey and says a flirty tone, "and for you, Joey?" Joey looks at Amanda, and she is still trying not to laugh. He looks at Bailey, then says, "I'll have the same but not too much mayonnaise. And put some mustard on it too." Bailey smiles then says, "I'll have them for you in a few moments."

Joey and Amanda leave the deli counter, and Amanda starts laughing. Then she says, "It looks like somebody still has a little crush on you." Joey looks at Amanda with a sour look on his face saying to her, "Oh, be quiet, Amanda." They go up to a counter where the coffee and hot chocolate are. They each pour up a cup of hot chocolate. They walk to one of the tables, then sitting down when Jessie Sneed comes through the door. When he walks past the men sitting by the woodstove as he lifts his pants off his boots, jokingly saying, "The horse manure is getting deep around the stove here guys. You must have been here all night." The men mumble some insulting remarks, and Jessie starts to laugh. Jessie sees Amanda and Joey sitting at a table, and he walks toward them. Joey shakes his hand, and Amanda gets up and hugs his neck. She then says, "please join us, Jessie." He smiles then says, "only for a moment, but let me go get a cup of coffee first." A few moments later, Jessie returns with his coffee then sits at the table. Then Bailey says, "Joey, you and Amanda's sandwiches are ready." Amanda says, "I'll get them."

She gets up, then Joey looks at Jessie with a concerned expression, saying, "you haven't seen that truck or anybody else up my way lately, have you?" Jessie shakes his head, then says, "haven't seen a soul up our way since I saw that truck that day." Joey is relieved, then Jessie looks over at Amanda, then back to Joey, saying, "how's Amanda been doing?" "Jessie, I've never seen someone this happy before in my life," replies Joey. Then Joey smiles, saying, "we had a great Thanksgiving yesterday, and she even shot a grouse for dinner. And this morning we got a Christmas tree she picked out herself. And this afternoon, we're going into Craig to get decorations for the cabin and chapel."

Jessie looks at Joey for a few seconds then smiles, saying, "It sounds like to me you are preparing Amanda to be a real mountain girl. Any reason for that?" Joey looks at Jessie with sad eyes and a frown, saying, "no, Jessie. I'm not preparing her for anything. Besides, what you are thinking is not going to happen." Jessie sees Amanda returning to the table and says quickly with a stern voice, "I don't know what your hang-up is with Amanda. But if you would take my advice, don't let her out of your life. She is a wonderful girl. Do you hear me, Marine?" Joey says in a sorrowful voice, "yea. I hear you, Jessie," Jessie then says, "I can look in her eyes, and I can tell she is love with you."

Amanda arrives at the table, then Joey and Jessie stand up. "she huffs, then says, "will you guys stop springing up every time I come close to you." She looks at Jessie then at Joey. She produces her lovely smile and says, "I'm sorry, guys. I'm just not used to be treated like a lady yet." She sits down, followed by Jessie and Joey. Jessie looks at Amanda and says, "Amanda, you are a beautiful young woman, but that is not the reason you are being treated like you are. We do it to all our ladies up here in respect for them." She looks at Joey, and he is smiling, nodding his head. Then Amanda says, "I know that Jessie. As I said, I haven't gotten used to being treated as such." She looks at both the men, then saying, "now, what were you two talking about while I was getting the sandwiches?" Joey and Jessie look at each other. Then Jessie looks at Amanda smiling, then says, "Joey was talking about how much fun you had this week."

Jessie looks at Joey, saying, "and Joey was talking about how a wonderful, sweet woman you are." Joey closes his eyes as he thinks to himself, "why did Jessie have to say that. It will just get Amanda's hopes up." Amanda looks at Joey for a few seconds, then says, smiling, "well, thank you, Joey, that was so nice of you to say that." Jessie stands up, taking his coffee then says, "I'll see you both later. I have to get going." Joey looks at Jessie with eyes that would melt steel. Jessie goes over to the counter and pays Wilson for his coffee then turns walking out of the store.

Amanda and Joey unwrap their sandwiches then start to eat. Later as they are eating, Amanda looks at Joey with a bashful expression, saying, "Joey, did you say that I was a wonderful, sweet woman?" Joey is mortified but doesn't want to break her heart. He knows that will come later. He smiles and says, "yes, I did, Amanda." Of course, she looks at him with her beautiful smile, then says, "I think you are a wonderful, sweet, gentleman Joey for the way you spoke of me." They get through with their lunch, and Joey goes and pays for the gas, hot chocolate, and sandwiches. They walk out of the store, and Joey says to Amanda, "I'm sure you want to drive the snow-track back to the cabin." She looks at him, saying, "now Joey, you know what the answer is to that."

They arrive at the snow-track, and Amanda opens the passenger door for Joey. He laughs and says, "what do you think you're doing, Amanda?" She replies by saying, "I bet no woman has ever opened a door for you. I just want you to know what it's like to be treated like you have been treating me." He smiles and says to Amanda, "no, this is a first, and thank you." Joey gets in the passenger seat, and Amanda walks around the vehicle and jumps in the driver's seat. She starts the track up and heads out toward the cabin.

Later they arrive at the cabin, and Amanda says excitedly, "let's get the tree in the cabin!" Joey looks at her shaking his head, then he says, "I hate to snow, so to speak, on your parade Amanda, but the tree has to thaw out first. If we don't, there will be snow and water everywhere in the cabin. She nods her head then says, "didn't think about that." Joey says, "I'll put it in the barn where it can thaw tonight. Then tomorrow we can put it up. Sound good?" She says, "of course, it sounds good." Joey gets out and opens Amanda's door, saying, "go get a good warm fire going, and I'll take care of the tree.

Later that afternoon, they go into Craig to get all the Christmas decorations. They arrive at a super-saver type store that seems to have everything. When they enter the store, Joey says, "have at it, Amanda." Amanda gets a shopping cart and takes off toward the Christmas decorations section. Joey takes the time to go to the hunting section of the store, stocking up on ammunition for all his weapons. Later, Amanda finds Joey, and he sees her shopping cart is almost overflowing with decorations. He says, laughing, "Amanda, we're not decorating the whole mountain, you know." She looks at him with a scowl on her face, saying, "Oh, hush Joey. I need your help." "With what," he replies. She says, "I'm not through, and I want you to watch this cart while I go get another one." He looks around, sighing, then looks at her, saying, "okay, go ahead." She blows him a kiss, and she turns to get another cart. Joey can't help but smile at her excitement.

Later she returns with another cart full of decorations, and Joey says, "did you leave any decorations for anybody else?" Amanda starts to say something jokingly sarcastic to Joey but suddenly remembers something. She says, "I forgot the electric candles for the chapel windows. Watch the two carts, and I will be right back." She turns to go back to the Christmas decorations department, and Joey says to her, "take your time. We've got a month till Christmas." She goes back to the decoration department and returns with eight electric candles and some C.Ds. She looks at Joey smiling, then says, "twelve windows, so that means twelve candles. Or do you think we need more?" Joey shakes his head, saying, "Amanda, I don't think we have the space to put everything you've picked out." She has a big grin, then says, "I don't think we have enough to tell you the truth. And I saw a C.D. player in the bookcase back at the cabin, and I got some Christmas C.Ds. The C.D. player still works, doesn't it?" Joey nods his head, then says, "I don't see why it wouldn't." Amanda smiles as she puts the C.Ds in the cart. Joey breaths deep, then says, "let's get out of here, Amanda. And if you think we don't have enough when we get home, we can always come back." "You got a deal," Amanda replies.

Chapter Twelve

Joey Falls In Love With Amanda

They arrive back at the cabin, and they unload the decorations then taking them into the cabin. Amanda starts digging around in all the bags and pulls everything out, laying the decorations on the floor. She looks at Joey, saying, "remember, you said you were going to help." Joey says, "I know what I said, and I know you wouldn't let me forget." Amanda smiles and excitedly says, "well, let's get started then!" They start decorating the den, and it takes about two hours to put up everything Amanda got for the cabin. She gets Joey to string lights around the front porch and windows. He comes back in the cabin and takes his big coat off, laying it on the back of the couch. Then he looks at Amanda and says, "I'll be right back. I have to visit the bathroom."

When he returns to the den, he sees some that Amanda has placed a weird decoration on the fireplace mantel. He shakes his head because it looks just awful. Amanda comes out of the kitchen, then proudly says to Joey, "how does everything look?" Joey starts to laugh and points to the strange candle thing on the mantel and says, "what in the world is that?"

Amanda looks at the decoration, then looks back at Joey proudly, saying, "I thought it looked pretty and very original. And particularly, I think it's a work of art. That's why I put it on the fireplace mantel to showcase it." Joey laughs again, then saying, "that thing looks like it fell off one of those floats down in New Orleans during Mardi Gras."

Amanda looks at him with a sarcastic face saying, "Joey, you wouldn't know pretty art if it bit you on the butt." Joey knows he's not going to win another world war over Amanda, so he surrenders and sits on the couch. She looks at him, and Joey sees the wonderment in her face. She sits next to him, and Joey looks around the den, saying, "Amanda, you did a great job on the decorating." She looks at him, saying, "we did do a good job, Joey. And if it's okay with you, can we put the candles in the chapel tomorrow? I'm so tired of everything we did today that I'm going to take a shower. Then get into my pajamas and relax the rest of the evening."

Joey looks at her with a relieved expression, then says, "Amanda, that's the best thing I heard you say today." Take your shower, and I will start up some chow, I mean dinner for us." She looks at him, saying, "Joey, you can say all the words to me that you learned in the Marines. I'm used to it now, and I kind of like it." Joey looks at her with a strange look and says very adamantly, "Amanda, I assure you that you don't want to hear all the words I picked up in the twenty years I was in the Marines." She looks at him with a slight smile, then says, "okay. Maybe not everything you picked up. I'm going to take my shower now, and I will see you in a few minutes." She turns going to the bathroom and goes into the kitchen. He says to himself, "now what can we have tonight besides leftover Thanksgiving food?" He thinks a bit, then says to himself again, "deer meat tacos. That sounds good."

He prepares the taco's and opens up a can of refried beans and puts them into a pot. He heats the beans and shreds some lettuce and cheese." Joey hears the bathroom door open, and with a raised voice, says, "I hope you like taco's Amanda." She replies, "as long as you have hot taco sauce to go with them." Joey smiles because he also loves hot taco sauce with all of his Mexican food. She comes into the kitchen and says, "wow. That smells great, Joey." He turns around to say thank you, but he starts staring at her, not saying anything. Like he is in a daze or something because Amanda looks so amazing and smells terrific even if she is wearing her pajamas. Amanda looks at him with a puzzled expression, but smiles, saying, "are you okay, Joey?" Then he realizes that unknowingly he was staring at her, and then says, "sure I'm fine, why?" Amanda says, "you were looking at me as if it was the first time you had ever seen me." Joey quickly thinks up something to say, "I didn't know I was looking at you like that. I hope I didn't creep you out in any way." She walks up to him and places her hand on his face. And with the most loving expression, she says sweetly, "Joey Morris, you can look at me like that anytime you want."

Joey's face turns red, and he quickly says, "how about placing the plates and utensils on the table. Everything is almost ready." She smiles and turns, reaching into the cabinet for the plates. She then opens a drawer that contains the utensils. She walks out of the kitchen, and Joey says to himself quietly, "you idiot! Why did I have to stare at her like that!" At the same time, as Joey is talking to himself, Amanda smiles as she places the dishes and utensils on the table. And she thinks to herself that the way Joey just looked at her, he might be starting to have feelings for her, finally.

After they finish their dinner and get dishes washed up, they sit in front of the fireplace going through their usual routine of conversation and a hot drink. Then Amanda says to Joey, "what would you like from me for Christmas?" Joey thinks, looks around concentrating, then he smiles and says to her, "I need a new Gerber pocket clip knife. I lost mine at the first of the year out in the woods. So that's what I would like. I always carried one when I was on deployment as one of my last resort weapons." That's not the romantic answer that Amanda wanted to hear, but she smiles, saying, "can you tell me what a Gerber pocket clip knife is and where do you get them?" Joey says, "it's a tactical looking knife that clips on the inside of your pants pocket. One half of the blade is straight, and the other half is serrated. It's for pulling out of your pants quickly, and it has a thumb assist in opening the blade quickly. And Mr. Wilson has a good selection at his store."

Joey then says, "Amanda, you said you didn't want anything for

Christmas. But I'm sorry to tell you, but I have already ordered it." She looks at him, saying, "Joey, anything you get for me, I will keep for the rest of my life." Since Joey was staring at Amanda in the kitchen, he decides this would be an excellent time to ask her about her future plans. He knows this will hurt her, but he has to start the process some time. He looks at her, saying, "Amanda, what are your plans after you leave here after the first of the year?" Yes, this does dampen her feelings, then she turns to the fire, saying, sadly, "I'm going back to Mountain Home and continue with my new life. I have a cousin who is an assistant manager at a catfish restaurant, and she said she could get me on there as a server. And she said that I could stay with her until I got on my feet. From there, it's in God's hands."

He then says, "this cousin of yours sounds like a nice lady. What's her name?" "Marilyn Deaton. And she is my Aunt Jordan's daughter. Not Aunt Crystyl that I lived with when I was young," replies Amanda. They both stare at the fire, and Joey could hear the sadness in her voice. He has never felt a woman's feelings like this before. It's because he is connected to Amanda more than he realizes. But Amanda is not a woman who gives up quickly. She will pray harder now that something will happen that will change Joey's heart. After a few moments, he looks at her then saying, "after we put the decorations on the tree and chapel, let's go ice skating tomorrow afternoon. She looks at Joey and with a big smile as she says, "okay, but you promised you would help me." Joey looks at her for a few seconds then smiles, saying, "don't worry, Amanda. I will be there to catch you if you fall." Joey doesn't know how much he is crushing Amanda's heart every time he says something like that. She wishes that he would say something beautiful like that to her, but in a lovely, romantic way to her.

Later that evening, as they are still sitting by the fire, Amanda says to Joey, "I'm going to bed now, Joey, and I will see you in the morning." He says, "good night, Amanda. I'm going to stay up a little while longer." She stands and walks to the bed. Then she kneels to pray before she gets in. Joey is looking at her the whole time, and he hears her say, Amen. She gets in the bed then pulls the quilt over her. Joey hears her sniffling because he knows that she is crying. After all, they talked about her leaving. Amanda then takes her bear, squeezing it against her chest and turns over with her back to Joey. He gets up off the floor and goes to the bathroom to change into his sweats. As he comes out later, he stops at the end of the bed, and he sees that Amanda is asleep, still clutching her bear.

He walks into the kitchen to get the last of the coffee. Joey then puts wood on the fire. He walks to his recliner and sits. Joey reaches over and turns on the radio playing it very softly. He stares over to the bed, very depressed. Because Joey knows his words that were said tonight had hurt Amanda. But he had to do this because he could never tell her the real reason why he can't fall in love with her. He puts his coffee cup on the stand and continues to look toward the bed. Joey will be cautious not to say anything from now on that could give Amanda hopes that will never come true. He turns the radio off and falls asleep.

Later the next day, Joey brings the thawed out Christmas tree into the den for Amanda can start decorating it. She acts like nothing ever happened the night before. He starts helping her trim the tree, and later that afternoon, they finally get finished. Joey puts a bright star on the top of the tree then Amanda plugs the electric lights into a socket. Then the tree becomes a beautiful sight to behold. Amanda bought both secular and religious decorations for the tree, and the ornaments glow from the lights of the tree. Joey says, "Amanda, I'm not saying this because you decorated the tree. But what I'm saying that this is the prettiest Christmas tree I've ever seen. And that's the truth."

She looks at him smiling, then back at the tree, saying, "well Joey, I'm going to tell you the truth also. Your right. I did do a pretty good job." He starts laughing, then says, "are you ready to go put the candles in the chapel?" Amanda says, "wait just a minute." She walks over to the window that is next to her bed and looks out. She nods her head, smiling because she can see the chapel from the window. She turns to Joey, saying, "I can see the chapel from this window, and at night before I go to sleep, I can look at the candles in the windows." They put on their coats and walk outside. Joey goes into the barn to get a ladder and some extension cords. They arrive at the chapel and go in. Joey then says to Amanda, "go and put the candles in the windows, and I will climb up to the steeple windows. Joey sets up the ladder and the plugs an extension cord in. He climbs the ladder with the cord and candles. Amanda looks at him with a concerned expression then says, "please be careful, Joey." He says, "I will swee…" Joey stops in mid-word then shakes his head and frowns because he almost said sweetheart to Amanda.

Amanda wishes in her heart that Joey would have said sweetheart to her. Then she looks down for a few seconds with a sorrowful expression. But the sad expression soon turns into a smile as she puts the candles in the windows. Joey gets the candles hooked up in the steeple and climbs back down the ladder. Amanda is through with putting the candles in the windows, and then she sits in one of the chairs. Joey comes and sits by her and says, "Amanda, it looks like we got it all done. Everything is going to be so nice." They both start to look at the cross on the wall. Amanda then says, "Joey, let's invite everybody to a Christmas Eve candlelight service here this year to dedicate the chapel. Not only will the electric candles be lit, but I'm also going to put real candles up too. We then can invite everyone to the cabin for a small gathering with finger food and hot punch and coffee."

Joey looks at her then says calmly with a smile, "Amanda, I think that would be wonderful." She looks at back at the cross and excitedly says, "we can get Malichi's father to speak if he's not busy. And we can invite everyone that lives around here. We can even put an invitation for everyone to see who comes to Mr. Wilson's store. I'm sure he would let us do that." Joey looks at her with a loving smile and says, "again, Amanda, that would be wonderful." They sit in the chapel for about an hour, then Joey says, "It's getting late. Let's go get some dinner." Amanda nods her head, and they get up to walk out. Joey picks up his ladder, and they walk out the chapel door. As they are walking to the barn, Joey says to Amanda, "you can go on to the cabin, and I will be there after I secure this ladder." Amanda shakes her head, smiling, then says, "thanks for all that you did for our chapel, Joey." He replies, "your very welcome, madam." Then Amanda gets an excited expression on her face, saying, "I can't wait until tonight to see all the candles lit in the steeple." She turns and walks to the cabin as Joey puts the ladder in the barn and locks the doors.

When Joey is walking to the cabin, he sees Amanda standing near the steps of the back door. Joey walks up to her and says, "what is it, Amanda?" She looks up at Joey and says, "wreaths." Joey then says, "wreaths?" "Yes, I forgot to get Christmas wreaths for the for the chapel doors," says a resolute Amanda. Joey then says, "I'll tell you what we are going to do then. We will go back into Craig tomorrow and stop by a florist shop that makes hand-made wreaths. We need original wreaths to put on the chapel doors. Then later, we can go ice skating." "That sounds good," replies Amanda.

The next day, they drive down to the florist in Craig. Amanda and Joey walk into the shop as an older lady comes up to them with a great smile. The lady says, "hey there. I'm Roben. What can I show you today?" Amanda looks at Roben, saying, "Miss Roben, we heard you have hand-made Christmas wreaths. Is that right?" Roben says, "I sure do, and I make them myself. Come over here, and I'll show them to you." They walk over to where the wreaths are, then Roben looks at Amanda, saying, "here they are." Amanda is amazed at how lovely all the wreaths are that Roben has made. As Amanda is looking at all the wreaths, she sees some that she likes. Amanda points to the wreaths, then says, "Miss Roben, these wreaths right here are beautiful. What are they made of?" Then Roben says, "I made them from vines off of the trees behind my house. And these are my best selling ones." Amanda turns to Joey, saying, "what do you think, Joey?" Joey smiles and says, "they're very nice."

Amanda extends her hand to Roben, saying, "I'm so sorry, Miss Roben, for not introducing ourselves. I'm Amanda, and the gentleman behind me is Joey." Roben shakes their hands, then says, "It's my pleasure to meet both of you." Amanda looks at Roben a few seconds with a slightly peculiar look. Then Roben says, "Is everything alright, dear?" Amanda replies, saying, "I'm sorry, Miss Roben. But I've always had a knack for recognizing special people when we first meet." Roben looks at Amanda with a questionable expression. Joey then says with an embarrassed tone of voice, "Amanda. Don't embarrass Miss Roben." Amanda looks back at Joey, then back to Roben, smiling. Amanda then says, "no, you don't understand, Miss Roben. When I say someone is special, I mean that person is unique in there own special way like the guy behind me. I look at these wreaths, and I can see the heart and soul of you in each one of these wreaths, Miss Roben. Even though I don't know you."

Roben takes her hands and puts them on Amanda's face. Then Roben shakes her head and says with a calm, sweet voice, "Amanda, that is probably the best and heartfelt compliment I've ever gotten in the twenty-seven years in the flower business." She and Amanda hug, and Joey thinks to himself how Amanda can always bring out the best in people. But he won't see it ever again after the first of the year comes. The ladies start looking back at the wreaths, and Amanda says, "Miss Roben, these are so beautiful, but at the same time, they have a simple look to them." Roben smiles and says, "Amanda, you're the first person ever to notice these how special these wreaths are. You noticed the true meaning that I put into these wreaths when I make them. Amanda smiles and says, "really?"

Roben then says, "do you two what to know the story about Christmas wreaths?" Amanda says, "no, ma'am, we don't. Well, at least I don't" Then Roben takes Amanda and Joey's arms and walks them closer to the wreaths and points to a certain one. Robin then says in a very gentle voice, "the vine is to signify the crown of thorns that Christ wore. And the red holly berries stand for his blood he shed for us. The evergreen is to remind us that Christ came to give us everlasting life and love." Both of the women start crying and hug each other again. Joey turns his head and takes out his handkerchief to dry his eyes because he had never heard that beautiful story before. And Roben spoke of the story in the most humble way. The ladies separate, and Roben says with tears in her eyes, "now Amanda, which one would you like to have?"

Amanda also still has tears in her eyes. And of course, Joey hands her his handkerchief to her. Amanda then says, "that's easy, Miss Roben. The one that you told us about with the evergreen and berries. But do you have two?" Joys says, "I've got this one, and I can get one made up for you in about fifteen minutes. How's that sound?" "Just wonderful, Miss Roben," says Amanda. Roben picks the wreath up and says, "I'm going to put you some fresh evergreen and berries on this one when I make the other one for you. And every Christmas, you come back to my store. And

I'll put fresh evergreen and berries on them at no charge." Joey says to Roben, "Miss Roben, you are a very nice lady." Roben replies, "thank you, Joey. That was sweet. I'll be right back."

A few minutes later, Roben comes back with the two wreaths she made up. Amanda looks at them, then shakes her head smiling and says, "Miss Roben, I couldn't ask for anything more beautiful than those two wreaths you made for us." Joy looks at wreaths and back to Amanda, then says, "where are you going to hang these wreaths this Christmas?" Amanda looks at Joey and says to Roben, "we built a small chapel on Joey's land recently." Amanda looks back at Roben, saying, "they will christen the new chapel at Christmas.

Roben says excitedly, "you built a small chapel?" Amanda replies, "yes ma'am. And we're going to have the first service at the chapel this Christmas Eve. And we are going to invite everybody in the area to come." Roben hesitates for a few moments, smiling at Amanda and Joey. Roben then says, "it warms my heart to see a fine Christian couple like yourselves to do something like this." Amanda smiles, but Joey has an awkward look on his face. Roben then says, "is there anything else you would like to go in the chapel or your home?" Amanda looks around for a few seconds and spots some beautiful red poinsettias that Roben has on display. Amanda turns to Joey, saying, "those poinsettias would look nice at the altar in the chapel. And maybe two of them in the cabin by the fireplace?" Joey looks at Roben, then saying in a pleasant tone, "give her whatever she wants, Miss Roben."

Roben then asks Amanda, "how many do you want, dear?" Amanda pauses for a few moments counting the number of poinsettias she will need. Then she looks at Roben, saying, "I think that six will do it, Miss Roben." Roben says, "well, go pick out the ones that you like the best, honey!" Amanda picks out the poinsettias, and Joey starts loading everything up in the Jeep. He then pays for everything. Then they tell Roben what an enjoyable experience they have had with her. Roben says, "I look forward to seeing you two when you're here in town. Just drop by anytime and just say hello."

Amanda looks at Roben and says, "Miss Roben, I would like for you to come to our Christmas Eve service. We don't live that far away, and we would love to have you." Roben says, "thanks for the invitation, Amanda. And yes, I will do my best to come. Give me your address, please." Joey gives Roben the address and draws a small map to his place. Roben says, "I'll just put this address on my phone, and it will take me right to your place." Joey says, "Miss Roben, that is why I drew out the map. There is no cell reception where I live. The chapel is few yards down the trail from the cabin where I live. You can't miss it, and we hope to see you there." Amanda and Joey tell her bye and turn to walk out when Roben says with a broad smile, "hey, you two?" Amanda and Joey turn back to her, and Roben says affectionately, "you two make a darling Christian couple." Amanda and Joey both have slight smiles. But Roben immediately sees some sadness in their eyes.

As they are driving back to the cabin, Amanda looks at Joey and says, "Joey?" He looks at her and says, "yep?" She looks at him for a moment and thinks of the right words to say. She then says, "it's what Miss Roben said back at her flower shop when she said we make a darling couple. How did you feel about that?" Joey thinks very hard not to say anything that would encourage Amanda, and he makes light of the situation. He looks over to Amanda and says jokingly, "well, what do you expect from people, Amanda?" Amanda thinks to herself that Joey might say something romantic about what Roben said. But in the meantime, she is ready to accept anything he says. Then she smiles, saying, "I don't know what you mean, Joey?" He doesn't look at her then says in a jokingly, arrogant tone with a slight laugh, "what I mean is that you are a pretty woman, and I'm a good looking man. People just automatically think we are a couple, that's all."

That is not Amanda wanted to hear. She feels another disappointing crack that Joey has just hammered in her heart. Amanda thinks to herself that there is not much of her heart left for Joey to break. But she knows Joey would never intentionally hurt her. Sadly, Amanda decides that she might give up on trying to get Joey to have feelings for her. And she knows now that you can't make anyone love you. But she smiles and says, "Joey, we are going to have the most wonderful Christmas this year due to you." He looks at her and says, "don't forget you had a part in this too." Later as they are driving down the highway, Amanda says excitedly,

"Joey, let's stop at Mr. Wilson's store and invite everyone there to the Chrismas Eve service at the chapel. And say, six o'clock. Will that be okay with you?" Joey looks at her, smiling and says, "that will be fine, Amanda. And I will get in touch with Jessie to see if his brother-in-law will lead the service. How's that sound to you?" "As always Joey, that sounds great," she says.

As they later arrive at the store, Amanda and Joey go in as all the men that are around the do their routine by standing, removing their hats, and smiling at Amanda. As usual, they pay no attention to Joey. Joey starts talking about the Christmas Eve service to the men, and Amanda walks up to the counter where Mr. Wilson is standing behind. Wilson says, "well, good afternoon Miss Amanda. What can I do for you today." Amanda says, "Mr. Wilson, you did hear about the small chapel we built upon Joey's land, haven't you?" Wilson nods his head, and with a big smile, says, "yes ma'am. I sure did. And I know it's beautiful if you hand in it." She says to Mr. Wilson, "thank-you Mr. Wilson. That was sweet of you to say. We're going to have a Christmas Eve service at six o'clock that evening and a little get-together at the cabin afterward. And we would love for you to come." He looks at Amanda and gets choked up, but manages to say, "my wife and I went to a Christmas Eve service every year at our Church, but since she died, I never went back." Amanda then says, "please, Mr. Wilson, it would do us all good if you came. Please?"

Mr. Wilson could never turn down such a sweet and sincere face and says calmly, "yes, Miss Amanda. I will be there." Amanda says, "oh, thank you, Mr. Wilson. It's going to be a beautiful candlelight service." Wilson looks at Amanda like he is thinking, then says, "I'll tell you what I will do for you, Miss Amanda. I'll put a sign up inviting everybody from around here to come to the service." Amanda leans over the counter and gives him a big hug, then says, "thank you." She then says, "I'm going over to the deli and invite Bailey. See you later, I'm sure."

Later Joey and Amanda are driving to the cabin, and he says, "remember we are going ice skating this afternoon." Amanda looks at him, saying, "looking forward to it." She can't help to remember when Joey said, "I will catch you if you fall." And how wonderful that would be if he meant that in another way. But she knows that will never happen now. But she is determined to have a wonderful Christmas with him. Even though she thinks that God has answered her prayers by not allowing them to be together, and she accepts that. They arrive at the cabin, and Joey says, "I'm going into the barn to get the skates. How about going in and start a fire." Amanda says, "sure thing."

Later that afternoon, they walk down to the ice skating pond. And when they arrive, Joey builds a big fire. They sit on a big log, taking off their boots, and putting on the skates. After they tie the skates up, Joey stands up and reaches for Amanda's hand to help her up. As he is helping her up, Joey gets lip balm out of his pocket and rubs some on Amanda's lips and face. He also does the same for himself. She asks him, "why did you put that on my face?" Joey replies, "your face can get chapped from skating in this cold, just like your lips. Even sometimes worse." Amanda then says, "that's good thinking. Now, what's next?" Joey, who still has hold of her, says, "let's not get to fast, Amanda. But I assure you this will be easier than you think. And believe me, you will have this down at no time at all." Joey says, "just stand here for a moment, and you will see you will not have to balance yourself like you think you will." She stands there, then says, "your right Joey. It's like standing in regular shoes. But only taller. I could look directly into your eyes if you didn't have your skates on."

Joey then says, "okay, I'm going to push you around, for you can get the feeling of the ice." He pushes Amanda in straight lines at first, and she says, "this is not what I expected at all." They stop, then Joey says, "Amanda, I'm going to turn you loose. I want you to stand on the skates by yourself." She nods her head, then Joey, let's go of her, and she stands for a few moments. She looks at Joey to tell him how easy this is. But she breaks her concentration and slips, landing on her backside. They both laugh, then Joey helps her up and says, "I hope you didn't bruise your caboose." Amanda looks at him strangely and says, "what's a caboose, Joey?" He laughs then says, "a caboose is a little railroad car that they used to pull on the end of trains. And caboose is used to describe someone's backside nicely."

She then says, "okay, now show me how actually to start skating. And I want you to skate around for me, for I can see first hand how you do it." Joey says, "you turn the blade of the skate outward from you and at an angle. That's how you push off. And when you get going, you do the same thing with the other skate. And when you want to stop, you put the toe of the skate straight down on the ice. The front of the blades has serrated ends called toe picks. They will dig into the ice, causing you to stop. Look, I'll show you." Joey starts to skate around her, and she observes him. Then he says, "okay, I'll show you how to stop." He skates a little way out and turns coming straight toward her. Joey then puts the toe of one blade into the ice and stops in front of her. Joey then says, "that's all there is to it."

Amanda says excitedly, "I think I got it! Let's go!" Joey smiles, saying, "are you sure?" She says, "I want you to hold me the first couple of times, then let me try it on my own." "Alright then," says Joey. He takes hold of Amanda's waist while she holds on to his arm. Amazingly, Amanda has picked up on the basics of ice skating very fast, but Joey is still holding on to her. A little while later, they stop, and Amanda says to Joey, "I think I'm ready to go solo now." Joey says, "alright, the ice is yours." Joey sits on the log by the fire and watches how she starts. She is going very slow. Joey is surprised at how Amanda has not fallen as much as he once thought. She picks up a little speed, and Joey stares at her with amazement. Because he sees her long blonde hair flowing beneath her stocking hat, also, he sees her face glistening from the rays of the setting sun. He thinks to himself, "is their ever an instance where Amanda isn't gorgeous?" She comes over to Joey, stoping, and saying, "Joey, let's skate together again." "Alright," he says.

He stands up and takes her by the waist. And she puts her arm around his. They skate around for about thirty minutes, and occasionally, Joey looks down at her lovely face just to see how happy she is. The longer they skate, the tighter they hold each other. The crisp, cold air. The evergreens laden with snow. And the setting sun between the mountains gets Joey to thinking. He finally has realized for the first time in his life the beauty and grandeur of his surroundings. He also thinks that Amanda could be the reason for this new wonderful feeling of his. He then says to Amanda, "let's go put some wood on the fire and roast us that corn and potatoes. And marshmallows for dessert." Amanda looks at him and says, "great idea, Mr. Morris. Because I've gotten hungry from all this skating." They skate to the fire, and they are still embracing each other. When they arrive at the fire, they both stand there and look into each other's eyes. And Joey, for the first time, has this incredible urge to kiss this beautiful woman at this perfect time. But he resists this incredible urge because he knows he wouldn't stop kissing her. And that's not going to happen. Joey finally realizes he has fallen in love with Amanda.

Joey releases her, and they sit on the big log next to the fire where they take off their skates. They put on their boots then Joey puts more wood on the fire. Joey has wrapped four ears of corn and coated them with butter with a little salt and pepper. He also puts some water on the corn to make it steam and roast at the same time. Joey wrapped the corn in heavy aluminum foil as the same for the potatoes. He also prepared a vacuum bottle full of hot chocolate.

Joey put the corn and potatoes on smoldering coals at the edge of the fire and covered them with coals with a stick. "Amanda says, "you sure do know how to cook on an outdoor fire." Joey is poking the coals with the stick, and says, "I've been doing this sort of thing since I was a kid. Do you want some hot chocolate?" "I would like that very much, Sergeant Morris," exclaims Amanda. Joey gets two large styrofoam cups out of the bag and pours up the hot chocolate. He gives Amanda her cup and says, "the corn and potatoes should be ready in about fifteen to twenty minutes. You don't want to leave them to long on the coals because the kernels would turn to pop-corn."

Amanda has almost given up on trying to start a serious relationship with Joey. She decides that now is a good time as any to tell him what she has dreaded. She says, "Joey, I want you to get me a one-way airline ticket for Mountain Home right after Christmas. And I'm afraid you are going to have to send me all the clothes you bought me." Joey is still poking the fire, and after a few moments, he looks at her saying with a slightly, sorrowful voice, "okay, Amanda. I will make the reservation sometime after Christmas. They sit there with the most awkward feelings that humans could have toward one another. Then Amanda can't stand this terrible feeling anymore. She decides to save herself and Joey from this misery and change the subject. Amanda says, "Joey, you need to have a name for the chapel. And I can see in my mind the title would be on a lighted sign in front of it.

Joey looks at her, nodding his head, then says, "do you have any ideas on what the chapel should be named?" Amanda looks at him with a big smile, saying, "as a matter of fact, I think I have come up with the perfect name." "What did you come up with," Joey replies. Amanda looks out at the frozen pond for a few seconds. Then turns to Joey, saying, "since the chapel is in the woods and it's on your land, how about Morriswood Chapel?" Joey looks at her for a few moments then starts to smile. He then says, "Morriswood Chapel would be a perfect name for it, Amanda. I'll start working on it tomorrow." He looks at the corn, and steam is coming from the end of the foil, then Joey says, "It looks like everything might be ready."

Chapter Thirteen

Christmas Eve Heartbreak

It's been three weeks since Joey and Amanda skated, and it's two days before Christmas Eve. Everything has been going well, and Joey has made the reservation for Amanda's trip back to her home in Arkansas. He got the ticket for January the third. But the closer it gets to her leaving, Joey thinks of Amanda more often. He also gets depressed about her leaving. But he makes sure she will never know about these feelings. It's getting harder for Joey to suppress all the thoughts that are going through his mind about her. Especially all the wonderful times they have had together. Like the big shopping trip, roasting hot-dogs above the stream, and the ice skating. He starts to smile when he remembers all the times she would say a "blonde moment" when she didn't understand something. But he knows deep in his heart that he can't be involved with her romantically…ever.

It's Christmas Eve morning, and after breakfast, Amanda starts to prepare the finger food for the fellowship after the service tonight. They found out the week before that Jessie's brother-in-law, David will lead the services for tonight's special event. Joey is out splitting wood, and Amanda gets a cook-book that's on the counter and looks up party foods. She decides what she wants and makes up a list of all the ingredients that she will need. Later, Joey comes in the cabin and sets an armload of split wood in the wood rack. Amanda comes out of the kitchen and hands him the food list. She says to him, "Joey, this list is the items I'm going to need for tonight's fellowship. Will you run down to Mr. Wilson's and get them for me?" Joey looks at her, smiling, then says, "of course I will do this for you, madam. But first, let me go to the bathroom. Then I'll go to the store."

Joey comes out of the bathroom, and Amanda is in the kitchen. He says, "Amanda, I'm leaving for the store now. Are you sure this is everything you will need?" "Going by the cookbook it is," she replies. Joey then says, "okay, I will be back in a few minutes." Joey leaves out the door and gets in the Jeep. Heading to Mr. Wilson's store.

He arrives at the store and walks in. And as usual, all the men are sitting around the stove. One man named Jeff asks, "where's Miss Amanda?" Joey looks at Jeff, and shakes his head jokingly, saying, "don't I matter anything to you, Mr. Jeff?" Jeff replies, "not ever since you brought Miss Amanda up here, you don't." All the men around the stove laugh at what Jeff said and Joey walks up to the counter. Wilson says, "Merry Christmas, Joey. Where's Amanda?" Joey replies, "Merry Christmas, Mr. Wilson. Amanda is back at the cabin, starting to prepare the food for the fellowship after the services tonight. Can you get these items for me because I don't know where some of this stuff is." Joey hands Wilson the list, and he looks at it, then he says to Joey, "If you don't mind me saying this Joey, but everything she has written down on this list will not be enough." Joey looks at him with a questionable expression, then says, "why not?"

Wilson says, "Joey, everybody I've talked to around here is coming to your chapel tonight. They haven't been to a Christmas Eve service in years." Joey looks around dumb-founded then looks at Wilson, saying, "Mr. Wilson, we were only expecting maybe six to ten people." Wilson looks at Joey with a tranquil face, then says, "you and Amanda have provided a place that people can worship our Lord's birth. Sometimes the weather is so bad that most of us can't get out. Now we have a place to go without any difficulties." Joey smiles, then says, "Amanda is going to love what you just told me. I can't wait to see her expression on her face when I tell her. So go ahead and double the order then!" Wilson says, "Bailey is not doing anything. She can pull this order. Now go get you some coffee and sit around the stove to hear some good lying." Joey laughs and does just that.

Later Joey arrives at the cabin with all the food Amanda wanted. He gets out of the Jeep and carries one the boxes of food to the cabin. He sits the food on the porch then goes back to the Jeep and gets the second box out. Then Joey closes the back hatch on the vehicle. He walks up on the porch and knocks on the door, saying, "Amanda, it's me. I'm coming in." She shouts out from the kitchen, saying, "okay." Joey unlocks the door and brings in one of the boxes to the kitchen where he sets it on the counter. Amanda looks in the box and says, "where's the ginger ale, Joey?" Joey says, "I'm not through yet." He walks back out to the porch and brings in the second box. He closes the door behind him with his foot and takes the box into the kitchen.

Amanda looks in the second box and says, "Joey, this is more than I wrote down on the list." Joey takes off his coat and says excitedly, "Amanda, I had to double the order because Mr. Wilson said that everyone in the area is coming tonight." Amanda has this beautiful expression on her face, then says, "oh Joey, that's great. Imagine a chapel full of people. And what lovely way to christen the chapel." Joey says, "if we are going to have that many people tonight, we need to get to work." Amanda replies, "yes, we do. But where are we going to put everybody?" Joey scratches his head, then says, "good question. I'll take the chairs from the table and the stools we have in here before the service. And someone will just have to sit on the floor or stand. And for the fellowship afterward, we'll just have to stuff everybody in here the best way we can." Amanda then says, "you will help me all this food want you?" Joey replies, "of course."

It's about five o'clock, and Amanda has everything prepared for the fellowship. She puts on her coat and walks down to the chapel, where Joey has just finished up on the Chapel marque. The marque says,

"Morriswood Chapel…All Welcome." The marque is right next to the steps leading up to the Chapel porch. He has built a small light on the top of the marque, for it will illuminate at night. Amanda stares at the marque then looks at Joey smiling, saying, "Joey, the sign is so beautiful. And the best thing about it, you made it all by hand. It puts the finishing touch on our chapel." Amanda suddenly realizes what she just said about the chapel being theirs. Then quickly replies with a slight, embarrassed expression, "I meant your chapel, Joey." He looks down at her, and with the sweetest voice, says, "this chapel is for everyone Amanda. Not for just one person." "Of course," replies Amanda. She smiles and says to Joey, "now, let's go into the chapel and get everything ready for tonight."

By five-thirty, cars and trucks start to fill the little area in front of the chapel. People are having to park down the road and walking to the chapel for tonight's service. The Chapel is overflowing with everyone from around the area. Roben, the florist from town, has come. And all the men who sit around the woodstove at Mr. Wilson's store are there. Even Mr. and Mrs. Steen, who Joey shot the dear earlier that year, have braved the weather to come. Jessie walks up to Joey and says, "It looks like you should've designed a larger chapel." Joey looks around then back to Jessie, saying, "I believe you're right, Jessie." Joey looks at Amanda as she is talking to some of the guests. Joey, who's is still looking Amanda, says to Jessie, "Jessie, would you look at Amanda's face. Look how happy she is." Jessie looks at her with a big smile, but the smile quickly turns into a concerned look as he looks at Joey. Jessie say's, "after I say this, I will not say anything like it to you ever again. But I have a feeling that you're going soon to break that sweet, wonderful woman's heart. It could be one of those types of heartbreaks that heart might never heal. And believe me, Marine, It will be the biggest mistake of your life." Joey is still looking at Amanda, who is still is having a great time talking to all the guests. Joey then turns to Jessie with a frown on his face saying, "Jessie, thank you for saying that you will not say anything anymore about Amanda and me. You just don't understand this problem that is happening between us." Jessie steps a little closer to Joey, and says, "Amanda doesn't have the problem, Joey. It's you that has the hang-up."

At this time, Jessie's brother-in-law, Rev. David Lucas, walks up to them. Jessie introduces Joey and David to each other. Jessie then says to David, "David, you do know that Joey designed this chapel?" Joey looks at David, then says, "I had some mighty fine help, including Malichi in constructing this building. Joey looks over to Amanda, and motions for her to come over. Amanda excuses herself from her guests. She then walks over to where Joey and the men are standing. Amanda hugs Jessie, saying, "Merry Christmas, Jessie!" Jessie, then replies, "Merry Christmas to you, Amanda." Joey takes Amanda's arm and says, "Amanda, this is Rev. David Lucas, who will lead the services tonight." She extends her hand as Rev. Lucas takes it, greeting her. Amanda, then says to David, "it was a lot of fun working with Malichi. That young man is going to be someone special when he starts his career." David replies, "thank you, Amanda. He told me all about you and Joey." Amanda pauses for a few seconds, smiling, and says to David, "Is Malichi here?" David responds, "no ma'am. He is going to be with his girlfriend this Christmas. And I think you know what I mean by that." Amanda looks over at Joey for a few seconds, then looks back at David with a cheerful expression. Then she says to David, "yes, you need to be with the one you love on Christmas."

David looks around, then says, "It looks to me that everybody is here. So let's get started." Amanda then says to Rev. Lucas, "Rev. David, I printed off four Christmas Carols and put the copies in the seats. There are also some extra in the back. Can you also lead the singing tonight?" He smiles, saying, "of course."

Joey turns off the houselights leaving the electric candles in the windows lit. Then he and Amanda go around the chapel, lighting all the wax candles that Amanda placed around the chapel. After they get through lighting the candles, Amanda stands with Joey against a wall because there is no room left for them to sit. One of the men insists that Amanda take his chair. Amanda thanks the gentleman and sits and looks at the soft glow coming off the faces of the visitors. She sees and feels the peace and solitude from everyone that is here for this blessed night's service. She closes her eyes and says quietly, "thank you, God, for giving me this wonderful feeling for the first time. And may this service be for Your honor and glory, Amen."

Rev. David stands and walks to the pulpit. He then looks at everybody who has come tonight and feels the same feelings that Amanda is feeling. Rev. David then says, "I understand there are some Christmas Carols that Amanda has printed out." He picks a copy of the carols then says, "It looks like to me that the carol's that she picked out are ones we all know by heart. So it seems very fitting that we start tonight's special service with "Silent Night." What a glorious and sublime feeling for someone, even with the hardest of hearts, would feel standing in front of the chapel to see and hear this heavenly service tonight. The singing, the warmth and glow of the lighting, and the smiling faces. Also, adding to the beauty of this service, It starts to snow. No movie or book could begin to describe the sentiment of this moment.

The service was an enjoyable experience for all that came. Later that evening, the guest are starting to leave the fellowship at Joey's cabin. As the guest are leaving, Amanda stands at the door, wishing them a Merry Christmas and thanking them for coming. As Amanda greets the last guests, she sees Joey and Jessie are drinking coffee at the dining room table. Amanda walks over to the table, and the men begin to stand, but Amanda says, "guys, please don't get up. I just want to take a breather before I start cleaning this place up. She pulls out a chair and says, "gentlemen, I think tonight was a glorious success. And I think things like this should not only be at Christmas but for other occasions too." Amanda pauses for a few seconds, then says sweetly, "just think how beautiful a wedding would be at the chapel."

Jessie looks at Joey for a few seconds, then with a smile, he says, "can I help you two clean up?" Joey says, "no, Jessie. You go home and enjoy the rest of this wonderful night." "I'm blessed to have been a part of making this evening happen for everybody," says Jessie. Amanda puts her hand on Jessie's arm, saying, "we could not have done it without you." Jessie pats her hand, then says, "I better get going before the road gets too bad." They all stand up as Joey gets Jessie's coat off the bed. Jessie puts his coat on and says to them, "Merry Christmas Eve, you two. And remember what Judy Garland sang in the movie "Meet me in St. Louis." Amanda has a questionable look and says, "Jessie, I never saw that movie, but what song did she sing?"

With a loving smile, Jessie says, "she sings one of my favorite Christmas songs in that movie. She sings, "Have Yourself a Merry Little Christmas." But it's the end of the song that touches my heart the most." Amanda says, "and what is that?" Jessie puts his hand on Amanda's face and shakes his head smiling, then says, "she sings, and have yourself a merry little Christmas night. I watch that movie every Christmas Eve because it was my wife's favorite at this time of year. And I want you two to have that special Christmas night."

Amanda starts to cry and hugs Jessie's neck. She steps back and says, "Jessie, Joey, and I have something for you to put under your tree tonight." She walks over to their Christmas tree and reaches under the tree for a Christmas gift they have for Jessie. She walks back to him and says, "Jessie, this is from Joey and me." Jessie takes the present and says, "thank you very much, Amanda." Jessie looks at Joey for a few seconds, then back to Amanda, saying, "I want you to have a special Christmas together." Jessie looks at Joey, and says, "do you hear me?" Joey doesn't say anything, but Amanda smiles, then says, "that's my plan, Jessie. And have a safe trip home." Jessie leaves, and Amanda turns to Joey and says, "well, let's get started on cleaning up shall we."

When they have everything cleaned up, Amanda takes a shower. Joey goes out on the porch to restock the wood rack. He sits in his recliner in misery because he is thinking about it's getting closer to Amanda leaving. Joey always thought that when someone says that their heart hurts from sadness, that it was all a bunch of junk. He has never had any pain in this part of his body before. But every time his heart beats now, Joey can feel real physical pain. But as always, he crushes those thoughts because he knows that he and Amanda can never be.

He knows that she will be leaving after the first, and she will leave with a broken heart. Deep down in his soul, there's a feeling for Amanda that want go away. But Joey is determined to fight this feeling he has for her. He hears Amanda drying her hair, then later, she comes out of the bathroom with her flannel pajamas on. She also gets her bear off the bed to hold. Amanda sits down in front of the fire next to Joey. And Joey always loves the sweet, warm, lovely scent that she emits after her shower. Joey then says, "Amanda, while you were in the bathroom, I made us some spiced tea. It was my grandmother's recipe, and we always drank it on Christmas Eve. Do you want some?" Amanda says, "I would love some, Joey."

Joey goes into the kitchen and pours the tea into their mugs. He returns to the fire and hands Amanda her mug. As he is sitting down, she takes a sip and says, "Joey, this tea is so good." He says, "thanks. But I do cut down on the cinnamon a bit because I think the recipe calls for too much." Amanda takes another sip, then says, "Joey, I have never had spiced tea before. And this will be on my Christmas drink list from now on. Thank you."

They sit for a few moments when Amanda looks at Joey and says, "Joey, I almost forgot about the Christmas C.D.'s I bought. Would you mind if I play one now?" "Sure, go ahead," replies Joey. She stands up and walks to her bed and pulls out a plastic container where she keeps different items. She opens the top and pulls out three discs. Amanda decides on the "Carpenters Christmas Portrait" C.D. She walks over and to the C.D. player then tries to unwrap the cellophane around the disc. Amanda finally gives up and walks over to Joey. She hands the disc to Joey, saying, "I don't see why they wrap these things like this. They're so hard to open." Joey reaches in his pocket and pulls out a small pocket knife, and opens the disk case, and hands it back to her. She looks at the cover of the disc then looks at Joey, saying, "do you like the Carpenters?" Joey says, "who wouldn't like the Carpenters. Karen had the prettiest and mellow voice that I ever heard." Amanda looks back at the cover and says, "I never heard that much about them, but this disc has every Christmas song that I love. So that's why I picked it."

She walks over to the player and inserts the disc, and it begins to play. She sits in front of the fire, and Joey asks her, "do you want some more tea?" "Please," says Amanda. Joey takes her mug and walks into the kitchen. As he is in the kitchen, Amanda looks down the list of songs that is on the back of the C.D. case. She sees a song listed that she has never heard before. But, somehow, the title of the song touches her heart. The song that is affecting her heart is "Merry Christmas, Darling." And she sees a familiar song that precedes this particular song. She thinks to herself that she will give it one last try for Joey to have feelings for her, even if it breaks her heart. She also believes that the atmosphere, tenderness, and solitude of this night could affect Joey. Amanda starts the song preceding Merry Christmas Darling. And she decides that she will ask Joey to dance with her before Merry Christmas Darling starts to play.

Joey returns from the kitchen with their mugs, and hands Amanda's hers. He puts his mug on the fireplace mantle and sets more wood on fire. He gets his mug, then sits next to Amanda. After a few songs, Joey tilts his head smiling, and says, "Amanda the last time I heard this C.D. I was on deployment in Afghanistan. One of my corporal's wife sent him this disc. And he played it on Christmas Eve. The whole hut got quite when one particular song started to play. After the song had finished, I saw some of the toughest men in the world crying. I imagined to myself what it would feel like too long for someone special you miss back home on Christmas Eve." Amanda smiles and looks at Joey, saying very gently, "what was the name of the song Joey?" Joey looks at the fire and says, "Merry Christmas Darling was the name of the song." Amanda lowers her head smiling and closes her eyes. She thinks that God has answered her prayers about Joey because this could not be just a coincidence on what he just said.

As they are drinking their tea and listening to the music, the song before Merry Christmas Darling starts to play. Amanda says a prayer under her breath, "please, God let this be true." Before the song ends, Amanda looks at Joey and says, "Joey, will you dance with me when the next song starts to play?" Joey has a surprised expression and says, "no, I better not Amanda. I'm not that good of a dancer." Amanda smiles, then says quickly, "neither am I, so come on." Amanda stands up and reaches out her hand to Joey. He takes her hand and stands. She puts her arms around his neck, but there is still a little space between them. Joey is thinking to himself that this is not a good idea to dance with Amanda. He might not have the will to fight off what he knows what will probably happen.

Merry Christmas, Darling starts to play, and they start swaying to the right and left. Amanda pulls closer into Joey, then lays her head on his chest. Amanda then says softly, "Joey, listen carefully to the words of this song." In the middle of this beautiful song, Joey lays his head on

Amanda's head with his eyes closed. He thinks to himself that he hasn't forgotten what it's like to dance with someone special. Joey knows in his heart that this is a very different feeling that he has never experienced. The woman that he is slow dancing with now is so different, and he doesn't have the words or thoughts to describe this beautiful moment. He holds Amanda closer to him until the song ends. They are still dancing after the song ends, then Amanda looks at him with her indescribable beautiful eyes. When they stop dancing, they look deeply into the eyes of each other. They slowly lean into each other and have a long, emotional, passionate kiss. They both have never experienced a kiss that came directly from deep inside a person's heart before.

Joey pulls back with his hands up, and looks down at the floor, saying, "Amanda, that shouldn't have happened." Amanda starts to get slightly upset, then says, "why not Joey? I'm still feeling that kiss that you just gave me. And I don't care what you think about what I'm about to say. That kiss that you gave me was from someone who was in love with me." Joey still stands there with his head down, not replying to what she said. Then Amanda says in a sad tone, "Joey, did hear what I said?" Joey looks up at her with a sad expression, saying quietly, "yes, Amanda, I heard what you said." Amanda holds her hands up and says, "well?"

Joey looks at her, then says, "Amanda, I was hoping it wouldn't come to this, and I will admit that I do have feelings for you." Amanda begins to smile, but Joey turns her smile into a frown when he says, "Amanda, I can't fall in love with you." She starts to cry, then says, "why not Joey?" Joey looks around, trying to think what he can say without hurting her more. He looks and says, "well, one thing I'm too old for you. And also, I suffer from post-traumatic stress disorder." Amanda is still crying and says, "your first answer, I don't care except about you being too old for me. I think you're coming up with stupid, lame excuses for your holding back your love for me." Joey, then says, "Amanda, I don't know how I would react with a serious relationship with someone. I just think that a relationship would deter me from my recovery process right now."

Amanda then says snidely, "another lame excuse Joey." She is not only crying, but she is also outraged now, and she starts nodding her head. Enraged, she says, "as I said, those are just lame excuses, Joey!

There has to be something else why you won't love me. I wouldn't have ever known you have PTSD until you told me! And I'm sure you've had a lot of help to cope with your distress!" Joey nods his head and says, "yes, I have Amanda." Joey breathes deep, and says in a slight, self-assertive tone, "Amanda, you don't know what it's like to experience what I have. The counseling and medication do wonderful things, but they're no magic cure. You have to do the rest."

Amanda stands there, looking at him with a sad expression. She still is crying, but manages to compose herself to say, "Oh yeah? I bet you think that the only people who get PTSD are in the military!" Joey shakes his head frowning, then says, "of course I don't Amanda. I guess in general, that's what people think who have the disorder are veterans."Amanda shouts, saying, "well, let me tell you something that you don't know, Joey Morris. I also have PTSD!" And I never got any help for it until I met you. Joey is in a state of shock for what Amanda just said. He never knew that she suffered from a PTSD problem. He then asks her, "Amanda, I know you are very angry with me, and I don't have the right to know this. You know my problems started from my last deployment in Afghanistan. Did you start getting your emotional problems for something in the past?" Amanda turns and stares at the fire for a few moments. Still very upset, she says, "you're right, Joey. You don't have the right to know. But I'm going to tell you because I don't want you to be a jerk to someone else."

Do you remember when I told you I had to go live with my aunt and uncle when my mother died?" "Yes, I do," replies Joey. Amanda speaks in a cold, dark tone of voice, saying, "when I was fourteen, my cousins started to molest me almost every night." She starts trembling, then says, "when I was fifteen, my uncle started to do the same thing. But he did things…" She stops talking suddenly for a few seconds, then says, "I can't talk about what he did to me." Joey says in a very caring voice, "did you tell anyone?" Amanda looks at him, saying, "I told my aunt about it, but she said I was dreaming." Amanda pauses for a few moments. Then she starts to tremble even harder now. She then turns around and screams at Joey, "HOW COULD ANYBODY DO THAT TO A CHILD!" Amanda turns back to the fire and says, "then when I had a chance, I ran away with the help of a friend. I hitched rides with anybody I could. Mostly truckers. I ended up in Grand Junction, and that's where I met Rico. And you know the rest of the story."

She puts her face in her hands and starts to cry again, and Joey gets up and holds her. But he doesn't say anything. Just holding her and pulling out his handkerchief from his pocket. He lets her cry as long as she wants, and a few minutes later, she stops crying. She pulls back from him, and he attempts to dry her eyes as always. But she stops him, then sadly says, "I believe that one handkerchief won't help me tonight, Joey. Since I've been here with you, I didn't need any help with my problem. I never even thought about it. Believe it or not, Joey, not only did you save me physically but emotionally too. I know from the center of my soul there is something your not telling me. The age difference and PTSD were just a decoy to try not to tell me the truth. Please tell me why you can't love me. Please?"

Joey turns away from her and walks toward the kitchen, saying, "Amanda, I can't tell you now. I've hurt you enough tonight to tell you why." She says, "you might as well because I know you don't want me anyway. So what's the difference?" Joey turns around and says, "please, Amanda, please, you don't want to know." She gets enraged and shouts, "I WANT TO KNOW NOW! YOU OWE IT TO ME!" He turns around quickly and says, "alright, Amanda. What I'm about to tell you will be the hardest thing I've ever had to say to anyone." Joey looks around a few moments then says, "I can't forgive or forget your past Amanda. Especially, all the men you've been with." Amanda is so shocked at what he said, that she sits on the couch, speechless. He starts to sit on the couch, and she says lividly, "don't you dare sit on this couch with me, Joey Morris!"

He stands in front of the fire, and Amanda stares straight forward. She then says with a blank face, "these three months I've been here have been one, big lie." Joey turns back toward her and says, "what do you mean by that, Amanda?" She looks up at him, "everything we've done together these past months has just been erased from me." Joey then says, "Amanda, from day one, we both knew you would be leaving someday. And we discussed you would leave after the first of the year.

What's changed about that?" Amanda walks up to him and sadly says, "I didn't know I was going to be with the most wonderful man I have ever known. I fell in love with you, Joey. And I tried my hardest to get you to love me. And deep down, I know that you are in love with me. A woman can tell when a man is in love with her. But since you can't forgive me of my past, all hope of that is lost."

She then says, "I don't want to look at you or hear from you for the rest of the night. I can't imagine why I've not had a fatal heart attack because you have crushed my heart probably beyond repair. But, I will say this one last thing. You are a coward and a hypocrite Joey. And I want you to know that." She walks to the couch and grabs her bear and walks toward the bed. But Joey stops her before she gets in the bed, saying, "why do you say I'm a coward and a hypocrite Amanda?"

She stops for a moment, then turns around towards him, and says with an angry tone, "it's from all the Bible studies we did." Joey has a questionable expression on his face, then says, "I don't understand what you are talking about, Amanda." She walks a few steps toward him, then stops. And still, with the same angry tone of voice, she says, "everything that you taught me from the Bible and when I became a Christian. What I got from all the things we studied is that I concluded that the Bible is full of love and compassion. And it's like a handbook on how we were supposed to live a Christian life. But what has stuck in my mind most is on how we are supposed to forgive one another." Joey hangs his head down because he knows what she is saying is true.

Then she says, "of all the stories that we read about in the Bible, there is one that is my favorite." Joey looks up and says sadly, "which one is that?" She says, "it's about the woman who was caught in the act of adultery. And men were chasing her in the street, saying, "this woman was in the very act of adultery. And we have to throw rocks at her and kill her according to the law." The woman runs and kneels, facing a wall waiting to die. A man with a rock went over to Jesus, who was sitting nearby and ask him, "Jesus, this woman was caught in the very act of adultery. And by the law, it says we should throw rocks and kill her for her sin. What should we do?" Jesus looks up at the man and says, "any man here who has not sinned let him throw the first rock." The men all look at each other, and one by one, they drop their rocks and leave.

Jesus walks over to the woman who is crying and terrified. Jesus then says, "woman, where are the men who want to condemn you?" The woman looks around and sees no one. The woman then says, "there's no one here." Then Jesus says, "neither do I condemn you. Now go and sin no more." Joey looks down, and Amanda says, "Joey, I know in my heart that women is in heaven now because she did what Jesus told her to do. Just like me. But what I'm getting at Joey, that Jesus can forgive, but you can't. Now sleep on that tonight." Amanda walks to the bed and gets in where Joey can hear her slightly sobbing as she clutches her bear. Joey goes to the wood rack and puts wood on the fire for the cold night and walks to his recliner. He sits with the most depressing feeling he has ever felt. He thinks to himself of all he has done in his life, especially his time in the Marines, that nothing has ever been this difficult for him.

Chapter Fourteen

Rico Reappears

Christmas morning arrives, and Joey wakes up to blue skies and the sun shining through the window. He gets up and puts wood on the fire and goes into the kitchen to make him some coffee. He comes back and sits in the recliner, looking at Amanda sleeping. About an hour later, he goes over to the bed and nudges Amanda's shoulder and says, "Amanda, wake up, it's Christmas morning." She doesn't move, and he pokes her again when she says, "leave me alone, Joey, I don't want to get up." Joey has a discouraging look on his face and says, "Amanda, would you please come open the gift I got for you. Please?" Amanda replies, "I don't want anything, especially from you, Joey." Joey takes a deep breath, then says sadly, "please?"

She huffs and throws the quilts back and gets up, walking to the Christmas tree. Joey says, "will you sit down in front of the fire, please?" She huffs again and sits in front of the roaring fire. Joey reaches under the tree and picks up her gift and hands it to her. She sits there holding the present, and Joey says to her, "would you please open it, Amanda."

She breathes deep and opens up the gift. When she unwraps the gift and opens the box, there is a leather-bound Bible with her name on it. She just stares at it and starts to cry. Joey then says, "it's a "New International Version" of the Bible. I got it for you because it's a lot easier to read and understand for new Christians."

She stares at the Bible for a few moments, then looks at Joey with teary eyes, saying gently, "thank you, Joey. You can open your gift from me, but you already know what is." Joey reaches under the tree and gets his gift. He opens it, and it's the Gerber knife he wanted and says, "thanks, Amanda, it's exactly the one I wanted." They sit there for a few moments without saying anything to each other. Then Amanda, still with the teary eyes, turns to Joey and says, "Joey, I'm sorry the way I reacted last night. I was thinking to myself before I went to sleep, that you can't make someone love you. Also, last night, you said you couldn't forgive me for my difficult past. I have forgotten my past because I know I have been forgiven by God. And please forgive me for saying what I said to you. And I have forgiven you for what you said to me. But there's one thing that I said last night I want you to remember forever." Joey says, "what's that, Amanda?" She pauses, then says, "I said God could forgive, but you can't. I never want you to forget that because what I said is the truth. And I still feel the same way this morning, and I hope you understand what I mean." Joey looks down and says in a sad tone, "I know what you mean, and I will never forget Amanda."

Again they just sit there, not saying anything to each. Later, Amanda turns to Joey and says, "Joey, would you get my plane ticket tomorrow because I want to leave as soon as possible." Joey looks at her sadly and says, "Amanda, you can stay to after the first of the year. But what happened last night, I don't blame you for wanting to leave as soon as possible. Amanda shakes her head, and with a despairing look, then she says, "Joey, I can't stay around any longer. It would be too painful, and I know you understand what I'm saying." Joey nods his head, then says, "I will go down to the store tomorrow morning and make the plane reservation. "Thanks," replies Amanda. They go through the rest of the day without saying anything to each other.

The next morning Joey starts his Jeep remotely to have it warm when he leaves for Wilson's store. He puts on his coat and asks Amanda if she needs anything. The only thing she says is, "just reserve the ticket, please." He nods his head and turns, walking out the door. A few moments later, there is a knock. Amanda gets exasperated with her eyes closed because she knows he has forgotten his keys again. She picks up the keys off the coffee table and walks over and jerks the door open and hands him his keys. She closes the door, and he walks out to his Jeep to leave.

Joey arrives at the store, then looks up the website of the airline and reserves a one-way ticket to Mountain Home, Arkansas. After he makes the reservation, he walks into the store to get some coffee. He pours up the coffee and takes the cup to the counter to pay. Wilson comes up and says excitedly, "how was you and Amanda's, Christmas Joey?" Joey looks up at Wilson with a sorrowful expression, saying, "Mr. Wilson, the only thing I can say that it was not very pleasant." Wilson knows that he doesn't need to discuss Joey's dilemma, then says, "that will be the usual price of a dollar and twenty-five cents." Joey pays him and walks out of the store without saying anything to anyone. He gets into the Jeep and starts back to the cabin. As Joey is driving, the memories of the fun he had with Amanda keep pouring into his mind.

He arrives back at the cabin and walks up the steps and unlocks the door. He walks in and takes off his coat, laying it on the couch. Amanda is sitting on the bed, holding her bear, and Joey can tell she has been crying. He walks up to her and says, "the earliest ticket I could get is the day after tomorrow. But you will have to leave from Hayden and fly into Harrison with one stop in Dallas. Can you get your cousin to pick you up in Harrison?" Amanda says, "I'll call her this afternoon and see if she can."

Amanda and Joey keep their distance from each other and talking to each other when necessary. The next day, Amanda starts packing a few clothes, and Joey says, "Amanda when you get to Mountain Home, send me your address, for I can send the rest of your clothes to you." Amanda looks at him sadly, saying, "I don't want you to do that, Joey." He looks at her with a questionable expression and says, "why not for goodness sakes?" She turns to him with tears in her eyes, saying, "I don't want anything to remind me of the most wonderful, magical time in my life.

The clothes that I will be wearing when I leave will be bad enough." Joey looks down and nods his head. Then he walks to the kitchen.

The next day all that Amanda can do is stare out the cabin window and cry. Joey spends the day cutting and splitting wood. And only comes into the cabin to warm up and eat. He is cutting more wood than usual. He does this because he doesn't want to be in the cabin with Amanda with all the awkwardness. And experience the horrible anguish and anxiety that they both will suffer. Later that evening, Joey takes a shower and puts on clean clothes. He walks through the den, and Amanda is sitting on the couch. He looks Amanda, and he can see the results of a face that has been crying all day. Joey asks her, "are you hungry?" "No," she says in a sad tone. He walks into the kitchen to make coffee and looks in the cabinet and discovers there is not enough coffee to brew. He calls Wilson's store on the radio, saying, "Morris to Wilsons store, come in, please." A few seconds later, Wilson answers him, saying, "this is Wilsons, what can I do for you, Mr. Morris?" Joey replies, "Mr. Wilson, I know you are about to close, but could you wait a few minutes. I need some coffee. Can you grind me some up? Wilson says, "sure thing, come on." Then Joey says, "Morris out."

Joey goes into the den and tells Amanda, "I'm going to the store to get coffee. Do you need anything?" Amanda, who is staring into the fire, says, "I don't need anything, Joey." Joey puts on his coat and leaves out the front door. Amanda starts to cry again, thinking to herself if she will ever get over Joey. Amanda is still very much in love with him with all her broken heart. Even after the terrible thing, he told her last night. And Amanda also realizes that she will never meet another man like him. But she asks God to help her through this horrible ordeal. Amanda knows that Joey will never be with her, so she will lead a Christian life, knowing that God has forgiven her. Amanda is still staring into the fire when there is a knock at the front door.

Without thinking about her safety, Amanda jumps up and walks to the door. As she is walking to the door, she shouts lividly, "I don't know what you're going to do when I'm gone, Joey, about you forgetting your keys!" She jerks the door open, and to her extreme horror, it's Rico with his henchman Chris behind him. She screams and runs to the back door.

And when she opens the door, it's Rico's other thug Benny standing there. She runs back into the den, screaming Joey's name. Chris grabs her and throws her violently on the bed. She is so terrified she can't say anything.

Rico walks over to her and says with a sinister smile, "hello, Amanda, it's been a while." Amanda finds the strength to say, "Rico, Joey will be right back at any time." Rico leans into her face, saying, "that will be just fine, sweetie, because we have a plan to deal with your hero boyfriend. Then later, I'm going to show you what I do with one of my girls who quits me. Where is your jacket Amanda, because we're leaving. We don't watch you to catch a cold on this freezing night." As Amanda cries, she says, "Rico, Joey will track us through the snow." Rico puts his hands on her face, saying again with his sinister expression, "that is what exactly what we want him to do, baby. Now, where is your jacket?" She doesn't say anything when Benny grabs her hair and angrily says, "where is your coat for the last time, Amanda?" She nods to the den closet, and Benny walks over, opening the door, getting her coat. Benny then asks her, "Is this it?" She nods her head, and he throws the jacket at her, saying, "put it on!" Amanda puts the coat on and zips it up. Rico takes her by the arm and says, "now, let us start our new adventure I have planned for you, Amanda."

They walk out the back door heading into the woods. About ten minutes later, Joey pulls up to the cabin and walks up on the porch. He yells out to Amanda, saying he is at the door. There is no response, and he and he repeats what he said. Still no response. Joey quickly unlocks the door. He goes in, and he doesn't see Amanda. But he sees the closet door open and the bed in disarray. He goes to the bathroom and knocks on the door and says, "Amanda?" He then feels a cold draft that seems to be coming from the kitchen. He walks into the kitchen and sees the back door open. He runs to the door and looks outside and sees footprints leading into the woods. He gets an extreme expression of anger and says. "Rico!"

He runs to his closet and puts on his snow camo coveralls. Then hurriedly, he reaches to the top shelf of the closet and gets military-grade snow boots, called "bunny boots." The boots allow you to walk very fast in deep snow. He puts them on and goes to his gun case and gets his forty-four magnum revolver in its holster and straps it around his waist. He also takes his snow camouflaged, high-powered rifle. He gets extra ammo and puts on a special head-worn LED flashlight. It emits a special dull red beam, that to the enemy is hard to see. Rico is seriously underestimating Joey's Marine Raider skills in warfare during snowy situations.

Rico has Amanda by the arm, pulling her through the snow. He is taking her to a truck that they parked on the abandoned log road. Rico looks at Amanda, saying, "If you have any ideas of breaking free. I have something in my pocket that won't allow you to take three steps. I think you know what I mean by that." His men are not keeping up because of the heavy snow. Chris yells out, "Rico, this new way we are taking has deeper snow. So slow down, will you?" Benny, then yells, "will all of you slow down? I can't keep up for all this snow!" Rico and Amanda are getting farther away from Chris and Benny, but Joey is catching up very quickly. And Joey did hear Benny yell out. Suddenly, Joey sees Benny's flashlight glow and decides to come at him from a different angle know as "outflanking" in the military.

Benny is still struggling in the snow, and Joey walks up behind him silently. Joey is standing right behind him and taps Benny on the shoulder. Benny turns around quickly. And before he can make a terrified expression of Joey being there, Joey strikes him with his elbow. Joey strikes him so hard that Benny takes about five steps behind him before he hits the snow. Joey runs over to where Benny is lying and picks up his head by his collar. He makes sure Benny is out. Joey sees that Benny is knocked out and pushes his head back into the snow.

Joey looks at the direction of the other footprints and starts to follow. He soon sees Chris's flashlight beam and uses the same tactics to outflank him as he did with Benny. Joey slowly creeps on him as he stands right behind Chris. Then Joey makes the sound, "psst." Just as Benny, Chris turns around quickly, and Joey grabs him around the throat tightly with one hand, for he can't yell out. Joey pushes him into a large Douglas Fir where Chris hits his head violently against the tree. Chris falls quickly into the snow, but Joey doesn't have to check him. He knows that Chris is not much of a threat anymore by the way he looks. Joey then follows the two sets of footprints that will lead him to Rico and Amanda.

Later, Rico and Amanda come to a small opening in the woods. Then Rico yells out, "Chris, Benny, come on!" Rico waits a few moments, then yells again, "Chris, Benny!" They don't answer, then Rico looks around and pulls out a pistol from his coat pocket. He puts the gun against Amanda's head. She gasps as Rico looks around and yells out, "Alright, Morris, I know you are out there. And I know that you are some kind of special forces Marine. But I have the advantage here, and you're special fighting skills won't be able to help you. If I even hear a twig break or snow falling off a tree limb. I will put a bullet in your girlfriend's head.

Amanda yells out through her, crying, "Joey, please! If you are out there, don't do what he says. If Rico kills me, I'll be in heaven before I fall." Rico grabs Amanda's hair pulling her head back and shouting in her ear, "I don't believe your God is going to help you two tonight. You see, Amanda, I have some special plans for you for what you did to me. But I won't hesitate to kill you just the same. And Morris will not allow that to happen." Then, Rico yells out again, "did you hear that Morris? Don't underestimate what I'm capable of doing!" Rico then yells out, saying, "well Morris, how about it? Do you want your girlfriend to die?" A few seconds past. Joey then yells, "alright, Rico, I'm coming out." Amanda screams out, "no, Joey, don't!" Rico starts to have that sinister smile of his and says to Joey, "alright, Morris come on out. But you better be as slow as pouring axle grease out of a cup and your hands up. Do you understand?" "Yes, I understand," replies Joey.

Joey walks out of the woods with his hands up. Rico says, "stop! Get rid of every weapon you have on you. Including the hidden ones." Joey throws down his rifle then unbuckles his holster, dropping it in the snow. He takes his Marine Ka-Bar knife from the back of his pants. Joey also drops the knife that Amanda got him for Christmas. Rico, then says, "that better be all, Morris." Joey replies, "that's all I have." Rico starts to move with Amanda, and says to Joey, "I know that you are very fast with all those special fighting techniques of yours. But your not faster than a bullet." Rico points his pistol to a tree and points it back at Joey, saying, "get over next to that tree over there." Joey moves over to the tree, and

Amanda says, "Joey, I'm so sorry I got you into this." Amanda looks at Rico and says, "you have what you came after, and that is me. I'll do anything you want me to do, just don't kill Joey." Rico looks down at Amanda with a wrathful expression, then says, "I'm afraid you don't have anything to say in this matter, Amanda. He took something from me that was not his and not to mention he broke my nose." Rico looks at Joey, saying, "nobody does that to me! NOBODY!"

Joey stares at Rico, then saying, "Rico, it's me you want. So let Amanda go." Rico produces his sinister smile again then saying, "oh no, that's where your wrong, Morris. After I take care of you, I have some special plans for this pretty lady. So Amanda, say goodby to your hero." Rico aims the weapon at Joey and starts to pull the trigger. Then Amanda hits his Rico's arm, screaming, "NO!" Rico gets the shot off anyway, and the bullet hits Joey. Joey falls into the snow, not moving, and Amanda screams, "JOEY! NO!"

Rico is very angry for Amanda hitting his arm while firing the pistol at Joey. Rico grabs her hair so tight her head tilts back. He walks her over to where Joey is lying and pushes Amanda on top of Joey, where she thinks Joey is dead. Rico angrily says, "you hit my arm and tried to save your boyfriend, didn't you? So that makes me change my plans for you." Rico smiles and says to Amanda, "you know something, Amanda, you're getting up in years arent you. And I got some younger girls to take your place. And what that means, I don't need you anymore." You'll soon be joining your boyfriend with your so-called God. So good-bye, Amanda. I can't say it hasn't been fun." Amanda looks at Rico bitterly, and says, "before you kill me, you killed those two girls that were working for you. Why?" Rico replies, laughing, "sure I did. Those girls wanted to quit me just like you did. So I'm going to do for you what I did to them. She closes her eyes, and calmly says to Joey, "I'll see you in a few moments, my love."

Rico's smiling expression turns quickly back into his sinister face and points the pistol at Amanda. Suddenly, Rico's face instantly becomes an expression of pure, unbelievable pain because he has just been hit on the head with a large tree limb. Rico drops into the snow completely knocked out. Amanda then sees Jessie holding the big limb. Jessie rushes over to them, and he turns Joey over. Amanda becomes hysterical because she sees blood coming out of Joey's neck. Then she says, "Jessie, please don't let him die!" Jessie sees that the bullet has penetrated the right side of Joey's neck. He then props Joey up against the tree. Jessie sees where the bullet had exited the back of his neck. He puts his hands on Joey's wounds and tells Amanda, "Amanda, take your hands and keep pressure on these wounds now!"

Amanda is shaking and crying but manages to do what Jessie asked her. Jessie removes his coat and takes his two of his shirts off quickly. He takes his hunting knife out and gives Amanda the shirts and the knife, saying, "I want you to cut those shirts into long strips, Amanda. And take my bandana out of my back pocket and give it to me." She gives Jessie his bandanna and tears it in half. Jessie then tells Amanda, "okay, sweetie, remove your hands, and I will take over. He presses the bandana halves in each of Joey's bullet wounds. He then tells Amanda, "hurry, sweetie with those strips."

Amanda cuts two strips off one of the shirts and hands them to Jessie. He folds the two pieces tight to use as extra compresses holding them inside the wounds. Then Jessie says, "Amanda, tie the strips together to make one roll. Amanda starts tying the pieces together and, after a few moments, hands the roll to Jessie. Jessie starts wrapping the strips around his neck then he lifts Joey's left arm. He rolls the pieces under Joey's left armpit and back to his neck. This will cause pressure to help stop the bleeding. Amanda gives Jessie another roll, and he repeats the process. Still, Jessie is applying pressure to Joey's wounds with his hands.

Suddenly Joey has come too, and groggily says, "you don't have to be so rough old man." Amanda is laughing and crying at the same time and lays her head on his chest, saying, "thank you, God!" Jessie says to Amanda, "he's not out of the forest yet, Amanda. But keep on praying. Joey then says to Jessie, "I remember getting shot, but I don't remember anything past that." Jessie says, "keep quiet, Joey. I don't want these wounds to start to bleed worse than they are now."

Joey looks at Amanda, and he puts his hand on her face. Jessie then says as he tends to Joey, "I got Wilson on the radio to tell him to call the sheriff. I told him to tell them where to come." Jessie looks at Amanda, and says, "Amanda, that man, and his men will never bother you again. Because I heard everything, he said. They will be put away for the rest of their lives." At this time, they hear the sheriff's snow-tracks coming through the woods. Jessie smiles and says, "I hear the cavalry coming, so let's get this boy to the hospital before he bleeds to death." Jessie is still holding extra pressure on Joey's wounds until a deputy takes over. The deputies place Joey in the back of one of the snow-tracks. Then one deputy radios to the hospital that there bringing a gunshot victim in and will be at the hospital in thirty minutes.

Chapter Fifteen

Amanda Leaves Joey

The sheriff's deputies arrive E.R., where nurses are waiting for them. The nurses rush the gurney to the deputies SUV, and Deputy Larson Taylor yells out, "GUNSHOT WOUND TO THE NECK!" The nurses lay Joey on the gurney and rush him into a trauma bay where two E.R. doctors run into the room. Amanda has been holding Joey's hand the whole time, and Jessie has been right at her side. One of the nurses tells them they have to leave the room, and Amanda starts crying, saying, "Joey, I'll be right outside." Amanda puts her arms around Jessie's neck, sobbing uncontrollably. Jessie smiles, rubbing his hand down her hair and says, "don't worry, sweetie. I assure you that Joey has been through worse than this."

Amanda is still clutching Jessie and starts to pray, saying, "Joey is in your capable hands God, so please don't take him away from me. In Jesus's name, Amen. Jessie looks at her, smiling, and says, "Amen." An orderly walks up to them with two chairs and a compassionate expression on his face. The orderly then says, "I'm not supposed to do this, but you can sit in these chairs for you can be close to him." Jessie looks up at the young man and says, "thanks for your kindness, son."As one would think, Amanda is still holding on to Jessie with a despairing look. About an hour later, one of the doctors comes out of the trauma room.

Amanda and Jessie stand up, and the doctor says, "I'm Dr. Clayton. You have a fortunate young man in there. The bullet nicked his carotid artery, but it missed the outer region of the three c vertebrae. If the bullet had hit that vertebrae, there would have been paralysis. The bullet exited out the backside of the right quadrant of his neck. We have got the bleeding temporarily stopped, but he will be going to surgery to repair the artery now." Dr. Clayton looks at Jessie with a questionable expression, then saying, "did you administer the first-aid to Mr. Morris, sir?" Jessie nods his head, saying modestly, "yes sir." Dr. Clayton says, "without that type of aid, that man would have bled to death. It looked to me like military first-aid." Jessie nods his head again, saying, "yes, sir, it was." Dr. Clayton puts his hand on Jessie's shoulder, then says, "with those techniques, you saved his life." Jessie looks at Amanda, then back at Dr. Clayton, saying, "in all reality doctor, this young lady is the one that saved his life."

Amanda asks the doctor, "what's next for Joey, Dr. Clayton?" Clayton says, "after surgery, he will have to stay here for a few days. Then in about a month, he should be fine. Only if he takes it easy, of course." I'll see to that personally," says a smiling Amanda. She hugs Dr. Clayton, and Jessie shakes his hand. Then Amanda and Jessie see Joey pushed out of the trauma room on a hospital bed. Amanda runs over to him and lightly kisses him, then says, "I'll see you when you get out." Joey doesn't say anything but puts his hand on her face. Then Amanda starts to cry again, then says, "I'm in love with you, Joey." Then Jessie says to Joey with a smile, "this will be nothing for you, Marine. You've been through worse than this." The nurses take Joey up to the surgery department, and Amanda hugs Jessie as they stand there holding each other. Jessie looks down at Amanda then says, "It looks like God heard your prayers, Amanda."

A month later, Joey has resumed to regular life. But Amanda makes sure he does take it easy. This time it is Amanda's turn to take care of him. Amanda is sitting in front of the fire when Joey returns from the sheriff's office. He opens the door and walks inside. He throws his coat on the couch, and he asks Amanda, "is there any coffee?" She looks at him and says, "I knew you would want some when you returned, so I made a pot." "Great, because it's freezing out there," replies Joey. He goes into the kitchen and pours his coffee into his mug. He walks back into the den and sits next to Amanda on the couch. He takes a sip of his coffee then turns to Amanda, saying, "I have some great news." She says, "what kind of great news?" Joey smiles and says, "Rico has been indicted for attempted murder and kidnapping. And his men are being charged for being accessories to the fact. And the judge set no bail for any of them. Also, they will be extradited to Grand Junction for murder. And that's due to Jessie's statements at all the things Rico said that night. Those scum bags will spend the rest of their lives in prison, and nobody can help them this time."

Joey takes another sip from his coffee and looks at Amanda, saying, "Amanda, I want to take this time to thank you for what you have done for me these last four weeks. I know I delayed you from getting home during this mess. So, I got you another ticket while I was in town. It's for an eleven-thirty flight on Thursday morning. You need to get in touch with your cousin to tell her your itinerary." Amanda has been praying and hoping that since everything that has happened lately, she hoped that Joey would have changed his mind about her. But to her dismay, she finally realizes that this will not occur. She then says sadly, "thanks. I'll call Marilyn this afternoon." Amanda starts to take a sip of her coffee, but turns to Joey and says, "remember when I told you that a friend helped me run away from my aunt and uncle?" Joey nods his head, and Amanda says, "It wasn't a friend, it was Marilyn." Joey smiles and says, "cousins always make the best friends, Amanda."

It's seven o'clock on Thursday morning, and Amanda is packing. Joey is asleep in the recliner, and she walks over and nudges his shoulder very carefully and says calmly, "Joey." He wakes up and says, "Is everything okay?" Amanda nods her head and says, "everything is fine. I'm going to walk down to the chapel one last time by myself. And I didn't want to alarm you if you woke up and I wasn't here." He says in a sad tone, "okay.

I'll fix us some breakfast while you're gone." She shakes her head, saying, "there is no need, Joey. Because I'm not going to be hungry for the next few days." Joey produces a sad expression then nods his head.

Amanda walks down to the chapel and goes in and sits on the front row of chairs and looks around and starts to smile. She remembers how much fun she had helping to build this lovely chapel. She starts to tear up when she sees all the decorations from that beautiful Christmas Eve service they had. Amanda looks up at the cross, and says, "God, in one of our Bible studies, I learned how to listen to you when you speak through the Holy Spirit. And I must obey what you want me to do with my life. And I humbly accept what you have in store for me. And I ask for your forgiveness for being disappointed in your answer to me. When you revealed there wasn't a future for Joey and I. Will, you watch over him for the rest of his life, because he is a wonderful man. He brought me to you, and at the same time, he got right with you again. I love you. In Jesus's name, I pray, Amen."

Amanda sits a little while longer, getting her prepared for what will be coming up later that morning. She leaves the chapel and walks back to the cabin. When she enters the cabin, Joey says, "Amanda, we need to get going. They always say get to the airport one hour before your flight." She looks at Joey, saying, "let me get my bag and my coat." She walks over to her bed and picks up her bag and puts her coat on. Amanda says to Joey, with tears in her eyes, "okay, I'm ready to go, Joey."

Joey takes her bag, and they start to leave the cabin. Amanda starts to cry, saying with a smile, "don't forget your keys." They walk to the Jeep, which Joey has already cranked, and he starts to open Amanda's door. She looks at Joey and says, "wait just a minute." She looks at the cabin and the surrounding area for one last time with her chin quivering and tears streaming down her face. She looks at Joey again and says, "okay." He opens the door for her and helps her in as always. He gives Amanda her bag then walks around the Jeep getting in.

There is not a word spoken between Amanda and Joey when they drive to Hayden. They arrive at the airport, and Joey starts to open his door when Amanda says, "I don't want you to come with me, Joey. I don't think I can take any that terrible, sad emotion anymore." He replies, with a sad expression, "Amanda, please let me come…Please?" She sits there for a few seconds, then Amanda says in a melancholy tone, "it's going to kill me, but okay." He gets out and opens her door for her one last time. He helps her out, and they walk to the entrance to the airport. As they are walking into the terminal, Joey hands Amanda some money, saying, "this will tide you over till you get on your feet. She looks at the money then looks at him, saying, "thank you, Joey. I have to be honest that I didn't know what I was going to do for money when I got back home. But I prayed about it and see what God has provided for me."

They walk to the area where she will be leaving. Amanda sees a waiting room right before you go to security. She looks at Joey, and says, "step in here with me. I want to say one last thing to you. As they enter the waiting room, three teenaged girls are waiting for their flight. There are also two businessmen waiting for their flights also. A teenage boy is also waiting. Amanda and Joey are standing near the entrance when Amanda takes Joey's face with her hands and says, "this will be the last thing I will ever say to you, Joey." All the waiting passengers looked up when Amanda said that. They carefully listen and watch the scene that is about to unfold.

Amanda starts to cry, and with the saddest expression, and saying with the sweetest voice, "Joey, please let someone special in your life. I want this lucky lady to share the wonderful and magical experiences I had with you. If you don't mind me saying this, but you are a beautiful man. And men like you are still around but getting harder to find. When you find this lady, don't ever let her go even if she doesn't have a less than perfect past life. Always remember Joey, that love is forgiveness."

Amanda picks her bag up and leans up and kisses Joey lightly on the lips. Amanda then looks at him with the most heartbreaking expression that a human could ever make. She then says, "I will always be in love with you, Joey Morris. And that love will last for eternity." Joey then hangs his head in sorrow. Amanda smiles and says, "Hey, isn't this the time where the guy comes to his senses and stops the girl from leaving like in the movies?"

Joey doesn't say anything, and Amanda puts her hand over her mouth and runs out of the waiting room sobbing. Joey looks up and sees the three teenaged girls crying. Even though they are trying to hide it, the two businessmen are wiping their eyes with their handkerchiefs. The teenaged boy is shaking his head, looking at Joey. The boy says, "come on, man! I would never let a cool chick like that out of my life! The way she spoke to you, anybody could tell she's in love with you. I wish a girl would say something like that to me. That wasn't cool, dude." Joey looks at the boy, and then he looks at the three girls and the businessmen. They all have mad expressions and nodding there heads agreeing with the boy.

Joey steps out of the waiting area and looks down at the security area where Amanda is waiting to go through. She is still crying, and the TSA agent that is checking her bag sees that she is crying. This agent has seen this many times in her years working in security at the airport. The agent looks toward the waiting room and sees Joey standing there with a sad expression on his face. With compassion, the agent whispers, saying, "I'm not supposed to say things like this on the job, but trust me, honey. I know everything is going to be okay with you." Amanda looks up at the agent and gives her a slight smile through her tears.

Amanda passes through security, and she sits on a bench putting her shoes back on. She gets up and walks to where she will be boarding her plane. But before she turns a corner, she stops and looks back toward the waiting room. Joey is still standing there watching her leave. Amanda stops and smiles. Then she walks to the boarding area disappearing out of Joey's life. Joey stands there for a moment, then turns to leave the airport.

Later, he arrives at the cabin and gets out. He wants to look down at the chapel. But he knows it would be too depressing. Joey walks up onto the porch, and he stands at the door, not going in. He knows that he will be feeling horrible when he enters the cabin. After a few more moments of standing at the door, he finally goes in.

For the first time, the cabin feels like a tomb when he enters. Joey feels like the life and soul of the cabin has died. He stands and looks around, seeing all the Christmas decorations that Amanda never took down. He takes his coat off and throws it over to the couch. Joey goes over to the wood rack and places the wood in the fireplace then starts a fire. When he stands up, he notices the ridiculous decoration that

Amanda loved so much on the fireplace mantle. Joey walks over to his recliner and sits staring at the fireplace, waiting for the fire to start. Joey sits in his recliner for the rest of the day. When Joey goes to his bathroom, he doesn't look at his bed as he passes it. It will be to difficult to see where Amanda slept. And he will do this same routine of not looking at the bed for some time.

Two weeks have passed, and Joey has been trying to get on with his life. But it's not happening. Every place he goes, it reminds him of the wonderful times he had together with Amanda. He goes down to Wilson's store only if he has to. When he does, he gets what he needs without saying hardly anything to anyone. One day while he was there, one of the older men who always sits by the stove, ask him, "where's Amanda been, Joey?" Joey stops and after a few seconds says, "she's gone." Then he walks out of the store going back to his cabin to live in total misery.

The next day, Joey is sitting in his recliner, and he hears a knock at the door. He slowly gets up to answer the door. It's Jessie, and Joey turns from him but leaves the door open Then Joey says, "I'm in no mood for any lectures, Jessie." Jessie walks in and says, "I'm not here to lecture you, son. I just stopped by for some coffee." Joey sits in his recliner and tells Jessie, "there's coffee made in the kitchen." Jessie walks into the kitchen and prepares a mug of coffee for himself. He walks back into the den and sits on the couch. Then he says, "haven't seen you in a while, Joey. Everything going okay?" Joey just looks at the fire, not saying anything to Jessie. Jessie takes a sip of his coffee and then sits the mug on the coffee table. Then he says to Joey, "well, I take it that since you didn't answer my question, everything is pretty lousy for you."

Joey knows the reason why Jessie is here. But he thinks to himself that Jessie is his closest friend and he just wants to help. Joey looks over at Jessie and sadly says, "well, let's just say I'm taking it day by day, Jessie. They don't say anything to each other for a while, and Jessie says, "Joey, I said I was not going to lecture you, and I'm not. I'm here to listen to anything you want to discuss. Not just about things that recently happened." Jessie still sees the depressed expression on Joey's face and tries to cheer him up, saying, "Hey, let's go do some elk hunting in the next couple of weeks. It will give me a chance to try out my new Weatherby six-point-five Creedmore rifle." Joey still is looking at the fire and says, "thanks, Jessie, but I'm not up for any hunting." When Joey says that, Jessie has realized that Joey is still too depressed for any conversation right now. Jessie finishes his coffee then stands, taking his mug to the kitchen. He comes back into the den, putting on his coat. Before he leaves, Jessie says to Joey, "you know where I'm at."

Jessie walks toward the door, and Joey says, "I miss Amanda so much that my whole body aches, Jessie." Jessie turns around and walks back to where Joey is sitting. Jessie looks down at Joey and, with a stern voice, says, "then why in the world did you send her away? That girl was the best thing that ever came into your life!" Joey still is looking toward the fire, not saying anything. Jessie raises his voice, and adamantly says, "say something to me, Marine!" Joey sits up quickly, and he stands in front of Jessie. Joey then says in a raised voice, "I'm in love with her Jessie, but I couldn't forgive her past dammit. A relationship can and will not survive if you cannot forgive."

Jessie calms down and walks over to the couch and sits down. He looks at Joey and says, "sit down." Joey sits back in the recliner, and Jessie starts looking around the den for a few moments. Joey is looking into the fireplace, then Jessie says, "Joey look at me." Joey doesn't look at him, and Jessie says again, but this time quite loudly, "Joey, I said, look at me!" Joey eventually turns his head toward him. Joey knows Jessie will mean all business for what he is about to say. Jessie says, "Joey, I have known you all your life, and I'm saying this from my heart. I was married for thirty-nine years to Shirley before she passed. And we had the best times together. I don't get lonely because we were so in love that she still lives in my heart. And I talk to her every day as if she was still here physically."

Joey looks down sadly as Jessie says, "and don't lie to me saying that you never get lonely. Every man needs a good woman to help him up when he falls off the mountains of life, son. Have you ever asked God for a special lady to come into your life?" Joey is still looking down, then looks up at Jessie, nodding his head, saying, "alright, Jessie. The answer to your question is yes. I have spoken to God about a special woman."

Jessie shakes his head, then says, "do you maybe think that God answered your prayer with Amanda coming into your life?" Joey says, "yes, I have Jessie, but I couldn't get that one thing about her out of my head."

Jessie stands and says, "Joey, I'm not the world's best Christian, but I know that God speaks to us. You have not been listening to Him because of the unforgiveness in your heart. And I know he has been trying to get through to you. Listen and obey God, and he will always show you the way. My Grandmother told me that when I was a kid. And I have never forgotten it." Jessie stands up and walks over to Joey with a calm expression on his face. Joey stands, and Jessie puts his hands on Joey's shoulders and says, "I would suggest you go to that lovely chapel we built and have a good talk with the good Lord. And I assure He will speak to you and will show you the way. Just listen to his answer." Joey smiles at Jessie, then says, "I'm going to do that right after you leave. I promise." Jessie smiles and says, "I'm proud of you, Marine. Now go do what you said you were going to do."

Jessie leaves. Then Joey puts on his coat and boots and walks out of the cabin and walks to the chapel. He stands at the door for a few seconds and goes in. Joey sits in the front chairs there for a while, just looking around this peaceful setting. And with a smile, he starts to remember all the things he did with Amanda while they were building the chapel. And remember how excited she was on Christmas Eve decorating inside this chapel. He looks over to the stained glass windows and sees the electric candles she put up. He slowly looks up at the cross, and soon he begins to talk with God.

With tears in his eyes, Joey says, "God, why couldn't I forgive Amanda? When she told me the story of the adulterous woman in the Bible. And the men who wanted to stone her and what Jesus said to those men. When she told me that story that it shook me to my core, but I didn't tell her. Amanda was right when she said that Jesus could forgive, but I couldn't. But for some reason, I didn't do a thing. Please, Lord, forgive me for not forgiving her." Joey hangs his head in misery then looks back at the cross. Joey then says, " Please, Lord, I miss and love her so much. But still, at this moment, I can't forgive her. Please speak to me and show me the way. And please forgive me for not listening to you. In Jesus's name, Amen."

Joey sits in the chapel for a while longer and later notices that the sun is setting. He leaves the chapel and walks back to the cabin. Joey prepares himself a sandwich and a glass of milk. He takes his meal to the dining table and starts to eat. As he is eating, he glances over to the bed, and a strange feeling comes over him. He gets up from the table and walks over to the bed. He picks up the pillow and presses it against his face. Joey senses the beautiful aroma of Amanda's hair and the light scent of her perfume. Joey doesn't think he can't get any more miserable than he is now. Joey presses the pillow against his face. After a few moments, Joey puts the pillow back on the bed. Then something catches his eye that is on the floor by the nightstand. It's Amanda's bear.

He slowly reaches down and picks up the bear, and this is all his emotions can take. He starts crying, and he rocks back and forth, clutching the bear, saying, "God help me, please!" Later, he lays the bear on the pillow and walks back to the dining table. All of the emotions he has experienced over the last two weeks has finally taken the final toll on him. He takes his glass of milk and unfinished sandwich and puts the sandwich in the garbage can. He washes his milk glass then putting it in the dish rack. He walks back into the den then puts wood into the fireplace. He walks to his recliner, then he sits on it and reclines back. Joey is physically and emotionally drained and wants to go to sleep. He looks over at Amanda's bear and starts to tear up again. Joey then closes his eyes and falls asleep.

He starts to dream about Vickie, the mysterious woman who was in the emergency waiting room. And what she said to him. Then another dream comes to Joey. He dreams about his last deployment in Afghanistan. He is talking to Pfc. Dawson again in the b-hut the night before Dawson dies. Joey can hear him say again, "Gunny, don't let go of a lady who would be the best thing to ever happen to you. Even if during that time you don't think it's the right thing to do."

Joey wakes up suddenly, remembering the dream about Dawson. He sits up and stares straight forward. He thinks to himself, "did God just speak to me?" Joey doesn't know what to do because the only thing that is on his mind is getting Amanda back. He says a little prayer, "God, I know in my heart, you just spoke to me. And what You spoke was for me to go get Amanda." Joey is so excited that he can't go back to sleep. He waits the rest of the night for Wilson's store to open. When Wilson's opens at five o'clock, Joey is waiting in front of the store. He will make important phone calls on Mr. Wilson's land-line telephone.

He sees Mr. Wilson unlocking the doors. Joey goes running to the doors and quickly enters. He startles Wilson, and Joey says, "sorry for scaring you, Mr. Wilson, but I'm going to have to use your land-line phone. I'll pay for everything." Wilson then says, "son, are you okay?" Joey looks at Wilson with a smile, "I'm praying it will be." Wilson then says, "take all the time you need on the phone and don't worry about the charges." Joey takes out his cell phone and searches for all the catfish restaurants in Mountain Home, Arkansas. He finds two restaurants, but they don't open till eleven o'clock P.M. He waits at the store around the stove talking nervously with all the regular men who sit around the stove. Eleven o'clock can't get here fast enough for Joey.

Jessie walks in for some coffee, and he sees Joey sitting by the stove. Jessie walks back to back and gets his coffee and walks to the counter to pay Wilson. After he pays him, Jessie turns around, and Joey is standing behind him. Jessie is a little startled but smiles and says, "you okay this morning, son?" Joey smiles then says to Jessie, "Jessie, God talked to me last night in a dream." Jessie nods his head and says, "no, that's where you're wrong, Joey." Joey looks at Jessie with a stunned and confusing expression, then says, "what?"

Jessie then says, "God had already spoken to you when you first laid eyes on Amanda. Do you think everything that happened between you two was a coincidence knucklehead? He brought you two together for a reason. And you didn't listen to him because you listened to yourself. That's why you were so miserable." They both look at each other, and Joey has his head down, thinking about what Jessie just said. Then Jessie says, "how do you know without a doubt that he spoke to you, Joey?" Joey looks at Jessie for a few seconds then says, "I dreamed about what one of my men said to me the night before he died. And I know God wants me to get Amanda and not to mess things up this time. That's why I'm here at the store to use Mr. Wilson's land-line phone to make sure there are no "can you hear me now" moments on my cell phone."

Jessie then says, "It looks like you have done some heavy-duty praying there, Joey. I know that the good Lord has probably given you a second chance with Amanda. Do you know how to contact her?" Joey nods his head, saying, "Amanda told me she was going to get a job at a catfish restaurant where her cousin is the assistant manager in Mountain Home. I found two catfish restaurants there, and they both open at eleven o'clock. I'm going to try them both." Jessie looks at Joey and says, "how will you know if Amanda's cousin will let you talk to her? Management at places like that usually doesn't give that kind of information out." Joey looks around then back at Jessie and says, "I thought about that Jessie. I'm sure Amanda has told her cousin all about me by now. And I'm hoping that her cousin will have a tender heart and maybe forgive me for what I did to Amanda. I don't think God would have told me to go get her if this was not to be."

Jessie says, "do you know her cousin's name?" "Yes, it's Marilyn Deaton," replies Joey. Jessie then says, " I would suggest you call before they open, though. Joey looks down, nodding his head and saying, "that's a good idea. I'll do that." Jessie then says, "well, I have to get into town. But I do want to know what happens ASAP, okay?" Joey smiles then says, "don't worry about that, Jessie." Jessie has a soothing expression then says, "good luck Marine. You deserve that sweet lady." Jessie starts to walk out, and Joey says, "Jessie?" Jessie turns around and says, "yea?" Joey walks up to him, then says, "how did you know about Rico had kidnapped Amanda that night?" Jessie says, "late that afternoon, I saw some headlights heading up on that old logging road that goes through the back of your land. So I decided to investigate. When I got to your cabin, there was nobody there. And went to the back and saw all the footprints. So I tracked them into the woods."

Jessie starts to laugh and then says, "then I started to see all the knocked out thugs, and I knew I was on the right track. I got there right when he was going to shoot Amanda. Then I knocked the heck out of him upside his head with that big limb." Joey says, "again, thanks. Amanda and I owe our lives to you." Jessie smiles, then turns to walk out of the store. Jessie stops and turns to Joey, saying, "like they always say, Joey, go get that girl now!" Jessie then exits the store. Joey sits down by the stove again. He decides he will start calling the restaurants at ten-thirty later that morning.

Joey is so nervous because time is going so slow. It's now ten-fifteen, and he can't wait any longer. He goes up to the counter and asks Mr. Wilson, "Mr. Wilson, I can't wait for one more minute. I would like to use your phone now." Wilson replies, "sure thing. Come around the counter and take your time." Joey says, "this want interfere with your business in any way, will it?" Wilson says, "of course not. If anyone wants anything, they will get me on the radio." Then Wilson produces a big smile and says, "besides, I think I would call this an emergency telephone call." Joey laughs and says, "thanks, Mr. Wilson."

Joey walks behind the counter and picks up the receiver on the phone. He looks at his cell phone and sees the telephone number for the first restaurant and dials the number to the restaurant. The phone rings at the restaurant, and a lady answers, saying, "Ray's Catfish Kitchen Lacy speaking. How can I help you?" Joey takes a deep breath, then says, "Miss Lacy, may I speak to Marilyn, please?" Lacy says, "sure. Let me go get her." Joey is so relieved that the first restaurant that he called was the right one. A few moments later, Marilyn picks up the phone, saying, "this is Marilyn. Can I help you?"

Joey says, "Miss Marilyn, I can assure you that I'm not a creep, stalker, or anything scary like that. But I have to ask if Amanda Crawford works for you. Marilyn says sternly, "I'm sorry, sir, we don't give out that kind of information." Joey knew that Marilyn was probably going to say that. Joey then says, "please, Marilyn, I have to know, please?" Marilyn is perturbed now and again says sternly, "again sir, we don't give any information like that, and I'm hanging up now." Joey says quickly, "wait…wait. Let me tell you some things that only you would know. Marilyn doesn't hang up but doesn't say anything. Joey then says, "my name is Joey Morris, and I'm sure my name is not very pleasant to you right now. Amanda is a very caring and emotional person. She would probably cry if I swatted at a gnat. Also, I know that Amanda loves to put mayonnaise on everything. And I'm sure she's even tried it on ice cream. And excuse me for saying this, but she has a lot of blonde moments. And that just makes her more adorable."

A few moments of silence pass, and Joey says, "Marilyn, are you there? Marilyn says, "yes, I'm here. But I'm still skeptical about you. And yes, I guess you would be the only one that knows these things about her." Joey says, "thanks for believing me, Marilyn." Marilyn then says in a resentful tone of voice, "so you ao you're Joey Morris. Do you think I would tell you anything about Amanda after what you did to her?" Joey hangs his head and says, "Marilyn, I deserved what you just said to me. But since she left, my life has been a train wreck.

I didn't listen to God, and he is the one who has made my life so miserable for not listening to him. And I see now that I was trusting my feelings and not God's guidance. And I know He wants us together. So I beg of you, please will you help me?" Marilyn is a Christian woman, and she knows now that Joey is sincere. She waits a few seconds and then says, "will you promise me that what you said is sincere and from your heart?" Joey nods his head, then calmly says, "Marilyn, I've never been this sincere in my life. I miss her so much that I didn't know that my heart can physically ache like the way it does. I know now that I'm truly, deeply in love with her."

When Marilyn hears what he just said, she still wants to be on the safe side. Marilyn then says, "okay, Joey, just two more security questions. What branch of the military were you in, and what was your rank? Also, tell me, what was your pay grade? I know these things because my husband was in the Army." Joey says, "I was a gunnery sergeant in the Marine Corps with a pay grade of E-7." Again, there are a few moments of silence, and Joey says, "are you there?" "Yes, I'm here," she replies. Marilyn says, "okay, Joey, I believe you." Joey shakes his fist in the air and says, "Marilyn, I want to come to get Amanda and bring her home. Please tell me where she is." Marilyn replies with a calm voice, saying, "tell you what Joey. We are closed on Mondays, and I will give you my home address." Joey then says, "I've been so heartbroken, I don't know what day this is." "It's Saturday," Marilyn replies.

Joey says, "that will be great! That will give me plenty of time to rehearse what I'm going to say to her." Marilyn says, "Joey, please don't do that. Your heart will tell you what to say to Amanda when you see her." Joey nods his head then says, "your right, Marilyn. And what you just said touched my heart. I will catch the next flight out and be at your house Monday evening." Marilyn then says, "okay, this is my address. Do you have a pen and paper?" "Hold on," Joey replies happily. Joey turns to Mr. Wilson and says, "Mr. Wilson, I need a pen and some paper, please." Wilson takes a pad and pen out of his apron pocket and hands it to Joey. Joey then says, "go ahead, Marilyn."

She gives Joey her address, and he writes it down. Marilyn then says, "Joey, please don't hurt her ever again. Is that understood?" Joey smiles and says, "Marilyn, if she cries around me ever again, it will be tears of happiness. And I will get the next flight out, which will be on Monday."Joey then says, "Marilyn, please don't tell her I'm coming. Marilyn replies, "I won't. And we will see you Monday evening." Joey then says in the most sincere voice, "thank you, Marilyn." She says, "your welcome, Joey. And if you turn out not to be who you say you are, I'll shoot you myself." Joey laughs then says, "there will be no need for that, I assure you."

Chapter Sixteen

Mountain Home, Arkansas

Joey hangs up the phone and looks up the number for the airlines that will get him to Harrison. And most importantly, to get to Amanda, He calls the airline and makes his reservation for Monday. He also calls a car rental company to reserve a vehicle. After Joey hangs up the phone, Wilson says to Joey, "I couldn't help…" Wilson stops in mid-sentence, smiles, and then shakes his head. Wilson says to Joey, "no, I take that back, I was listening on purpose, hoping to hear some good news. And I think that everyone here was listening for a good outcome. Because your sweet Amanda made life around here a little sweeter." Wilson then says, "the only thing that I can think to say to you right now is God's speed. And I know I speak for everyone here. We miss her terribly because Amanda has a special quality about her that can make the most difficult man happy."

The weekend goes so slow for Joey, and he is about to explode with anxiety. Monday finally comes, and Joey arrives at the airport three hours before his flight leaves. Later that afternoon, Joey has arrived in

Harrison. Joey gets in his rental car and puts the directions to Marilyn's house on his phone. He leaves the airport and gets on Hiway 412, and it will take about an hour to get to Mountain Home. As Joey is driving, he thinks to himself that it's not cut in rock that Amanda will take him back. He's never thought about that, and it scares him. Joey starts to get prepared for Amanda, not wanting him back mentally. But he also feels that God would not have allowed everything to fall in place if this wasn't true. Then he says, "I have faith in you God that Amanda will want me back."

Every mile he gets closer to Mountain Home, his anxiety is getting close to reaching the stratosphere. He thinks to himself that he has never had this much anxiety flowing through him. This type of stress is not the same kind as it was during rough times when he was in the Marines. He realizes this must be some kind of love anxiety he is experiencing now. He gets to Mountain Home and stops at a small café to get a cup of coffee, and to get his wits together. He stays at the café for about thirty minutes, then decides it's time to go to Marilyn's house. He pays for his coffee and leaves the café. He gets into the car and sits there for a few minutes. He reminds himself about Marilyn's advice not to rehearse what he is going to say to Amanda. He cranks up the car heading to what either way will be a life-changing event.

Joey is listening to his phone for directions to Marilyn's house, and finally, he arrives at his destination. He sits in his car for a few moments before he walks to the door. Joey takes a deep breath and gets a small digital camouflaged travel case from the passenger seat. He opens the door to the car then walks up to the front porch of Marilyn's house. He rings the door-bell, and he hears Marilyn say to her husband, "I'll get it, Glenn." Marilyn walks up to the door and says, "who is it?" Joey replies, "it's Joey Morris." Joey hears Marilyn unlock the door then opens it. Joey and Marilyn stand there and look at each other for a few seconds. Then she reaches out her hand to him. She says, "I'm Marilyn." Joey takes her hand, saying, "Joey."

They both let go of each other's hands. Marilyn then says with a concerned voice, "Joey, please don't hurt her anymore, because I know her busted heart can't take any more abuse." Joey says in a calm, sensitive tone, "Marilyn, I promise you that would be impossible now." Glenn comes walking into the living room and says quietly, "you must be Joey. I'm Glenn." Both men shake each other's hands, then Joey says, "it's my pleasure, Glenn." Marilyn looks at Joey and says, "Joey, I'm going to call to Amanda that she has a delivery." Joey has a smiling, calm expression and nodding his head. Joey puts his bag down, smiles, then says quietly, "please, will you Marilyn?"

Marylyn walks to the front part of the hall of her house. With a raised voice, she says, "Amanda, you have a package here." They all can hear Amanda say as she walks out of her room, "now who in the world would know where I…" She doesn't get the last word of her sentence out because she sees Joey standing in the den. Amanda stops for a moment, with tears starting to form in her eyes. She very is very apprehensive because she doesn't know precisely why Joey is here. Joey looks at Amanda with a worried expression. He has this expression because he doesn't know if she will take him back. She walks up to him, and they both stand, looking at each other, not saying anything. Glenn leans over to Marilyn, and says quietly, "this scene would be great in a movie." Marilyn turns to Glenn, saying sweetly, "yes, I believe your right, Glenn."

Amanda says to Joey, "how did you know where to find me, Joey? Some of those special Marine things you do?" Joey turns and looks at Marilyn, then turns back to Amanda, saying, "let's just say a wonderful lady had faith in me." Joey picks up his bag and unzips it. He pulls out Amanda's bear and says with tears in his eyes, "you forgot this, Amanda." Amanda's chin starts to quiver, and then she starts to cry. She takes her bear, and she then hugs Joey as tight as she can. As they are hugging, Joey quickly pulls out his handkerchief to dry her tears. Amanda pulls back from him and says, "I hope and pray you didn't come all the way here just to give me my bear." Joey puts his hands on her face and says, "no, Amanda, I came to bring you back home to Colorado. That is if you can see it in your broken heart to forgive me for what I did to you."

She starts to cry again. She shakes her head, and with a lovely smile, says, "Joey, before I left, I said love is forgiveness. And that I was in love with you. Love is the most powerful emotion in the universe that God blessed us with." Joey, then says, "Amanda, I'm so in love with you, that my heart was actually, physically hurting because I missed you so much." Joey brings her face to his, and they have the most loving, compassionate kiss that a man and woman could ever imagine. Marilyn and Glenn smile at each other as they put their arms around each other's waist. Joey and Amanda are still kissing. Joey then pushes her face back very gently. He puts his handkerchief up to her eyes, and she starts laughing. He wipes her eyes, but this time he wipes his also. Amanda says, "we are going to have to get a truckload of handkerchiefs for all my crying. You are my Marine and forever love. But I know my cries from now on will be of cries of happiness."

Joey reaches down into his bag and pulls out a small jewelry box. Amanda's eyes get large and with a shocked expression on her face. She starts to cry again. Joey opens the box and says, "Amanda Crawford, will you marry me?" She quickly jumps up, hugging Joey's neck, saying, "Yes! Yes! Yes!" He takes her left hand and slips the beautiful ring on her finger. Amanda runs over to Marilyn, and they jump around, hugging each other, squealing and crying. Glenn walks over to Joey and shakes his hand. Glenn then says, "well done from one sergeant to another." Joey walks over to the girls and asks Amanda, "Amanda, I want to marry you right now. Let's get a preacher or a Justice of the Peace. As soon as humanly possible." Joey looks at Marilyn and says, "Marilyn, how long does it take to get a marriage license and to get married in Arkansas?"

Marilyn looks at Glenn, and he shrugs his shoulders. She then says, "if I'm not mistaken, you can get a license right away, and it's good for sixty days. And when you do that, you can marry anytime during those sixty days." Joey gets excited and says, "that sounds great, and we…" Amanda interrupts him before he can finish his sentence, saying, "Joey, honey, there's only one place I want to get married." Joey looks at her and shakes his head with a big smile, saying, "our chapel, right?" She smiles, nodding her head. Joey says to Amanda, "what was I thinking. It's the only place it should be."

Joey looks at Marilyn and Glenn and says, "and you two are flying back with us." Amanda looks at Marilyn, and says, "Marilyn, I want you to be my maid of honor." Marilyn smiles and says, "I would be honored to be your maid of honor, Amanda." Glenn says, "when do you plan on leaving, Joey?" "Well, I would at least like to stay here a couple of days to get to know you and Marilyn better," replies Joey. Glenn looks at Marilyn and says, "honey, can you get off work for about a week? I want to see this beautiful place that Amanda has described." And of course, the most important part, be there for the wedding." Marilyn looks at Joey and Amanda, who are holding each other and says, smiling, "even if I have to quit my job, I'll be there for you two. But I don't think I will have to do that, though." Joey looks at Glenn and says, "what about you, Glenn?" Glenn replies by saying, "I have a lot of sick leave. And I think it's about time I get sick."

Everyone laughed when Glenn said that. Amanda then shakes her head, tearing up, and says, "you have just made me and Joey very happy." Joey says, "I don't want no arguments, but Amanda and I are paying all your expenses. I will get our one-way and your round trip tickets tomorrow." Glenn says excitedly, "you won't get no arguments from us, Joey!" Marilyn slaps Glenn's shoulder lightly for what he said. Joey looks at Amanda, saying, "has everyone eaten yet?" "Not yet," says Marilyn. Joey smiles, then says, "Okay, everybody, go get ready because I am taking everybody out for some good, Arkansas, down-home cooking! And it will be my treat!" Glenn looks at the girls, then points at Joey, "now that is my kind of guy." Marilyn looks at Glenn with a distasteful expression, and says, "shut up, Glenn."

The next Wednesday, they take their flight to Colorado. As the plane is making Its descent into Hayden, Marilyn looks out her window, saying in awe, "the mountains in Arkansas are pretty. But they have nothing on the beautiful mountains of Colorado. Joey looks over to Marilyn and says, "Marilyn, I saw a movie that was about a mountain man a long time ago. And one of the characters in the film says, "the Rocky Mountains are God's finest sculpturing." She looks at Joey, saying, "well, he was right." The plane lands and they walk to Joey's Jeep that he left at the airport. He loads everybody's luggage in the back, and they head to the cabin. But they stop at Wilson's Store on the way. They all get out of the Jeep and walk to Wilson's front door. Joey opens the door for Amanda and Marilyn. Then Joey and Glenn enter the store.

All the men and women in the store have the brightest smiles when they see Amanda. They quickly walk to her, hugging her neck. Even the men who sit around the stove all the time walk over to welcome her back. Some of the ladies are crying, and Wilson walks over to Amanda and hugs her. Then Wilson looks at Joey then says, "Joey, thank you for bringing back the sweetest, prettiest thing that has ever been on this mountain." Amanda hugs Mr. Wilson, and she says, "thank you, Mr. Wilson. That was so sweet of you to say that." Joey looks at Amanda and says, "show everybody what we will be doing soon, Amanda" Amanda smiles and holds up her left hand, and everybody sees her engagement ring. Everyone goes over to Amanda and Joey congratulating them. But this time, it's more crying, hugging, hands shook, and pats on the back for Joey.

Amanda looks at Marilyn, and she takes her hand and says, "everybody, I want you to meet the person that is responsible for Joey and me being together again. This is my cousin, Marilyn Deaton, and her husband, Glenn. And Marilyn will be my maid of honor. So welcome them as you did me when I first arrived here. Everybody introduces themselves to the Deaton's, and then Jessie walks through the door. Amanda then turns to Jessie. And with tears in her eyes, she runs over to Jessie, and they embrace rocking back in forth. Amanda says, "Jessie, I'm so glad to see you, and I've missed you so much. And I've got something wonderful to tell you." Jessie raises his eyebrows and with a big smile, says, "now what would that be?" Amanda takes Joey by the hand, then says to Jessie, "Joey and I are going to get married! Isn't that the best news you ever heard!" Jessie looks at them both, saying, "yes, Amanda. That is the best news I've ever heard in my life!"

Then Jessie gives Joey a big man hug and says to him in his ear, "I see that God did speak to you, and you finally did what he said." Joey looks at him, nodding his head and smiling, then says, "Jessie, I want you to be my best man." Jessie nods his head and saying, "it would be an honor, Marine." Mr. Wilson speaks up, saying, "when will all of this take place, you two?" Amanda looks up at Joey with a smiling, questionable expression, then Joey says, "as soon as we go into Craig tomorrow and get our marriage license. Then sometimes this week. And everyone is invited!" All the ladies come up to Amanda offering their help with the wedding and reception.

Amanda and Joey pick next Sunday for their wedding. It's Thursday night, and Joey and Amanda are sitting in their usual places in front of the fireplace. Amanda has her head on Joey's shoulder as he is picking at the fire with a poker. He lays the poker down, then says to Amanda, "when are you going to get your wedding dress?" She raises her head and with the sweetest smile, then says to him, "I'm going to wear my jeans and a flannel shirt if that is okay with you." He smiles and says, "that sounds wonderful, baby." She lays her head back on his shoulder and puts his head on hers.

Amanda and Joey go into Craig the next morning to get their marriage license. As they are walking out of the county clerk's office, Amanda stops and says to Joey, "how about two-thirty Saturday for the wedding?" Joey says, "I'll marry you right now, Amanda, but I guess I can wait till Saturday. I know you need to get a few things organized first. And two-thirty will be fine. They kiss each other, and Amanda says, "let's stop by the hotel and tell Marilyn and Glenn all the details. And as we're heading back to the cabin, we can stop by Mr. Wilson's and tell everybody. Joey kisses her again then says, "let's get this mission started, sweetie!"

Saturday finally arrives, and the Chapel is full of guests. More than was at the Christmas Eve service they had last year. People are standing outside in the cold by the door to see this lovely occasion. Joey and Jessie have on their jeans and flannel shirts. Even Rev. Lucas, who is officiating today's service is in casual attire. All the men are wearing rose boutonnieres with little white flowers around them. Joey has asked an old friend, Tim Busby, if he could play his guitar and sing at the wedding. Tim tells Joey, he would love to play and sing for this occasion.

Before the ceremony begins, Tim plays and sings two songs that Amanda has picked out. Tim starts to play the third song as Joey, Jessie and Rev. Lucas walk to the pulpit. As soon as the men get in place, Marilyn walks down the small aisle. She is wearing jeans and a red flannel shirt and is holding one white rose. She walks to the front and stands across from Joey. When Tim finishes the song, he starts to play and sing a love song that Joey picked out just for Amanda. Tim starts to play and sing, Jim Croce's "Time In A Bottle" as Amanda walks to the front. She is wearing her leggings, blue flannel shirt, and her ankle strap pumps that Joey bought her last year. She carries a single red rose.

Amanda arrives at the front, and she can't help crying because she listens to the beautiful words of this meaningful love song. Joey smiles and pulls out his handkerchief and wipes her eyes, saying, "I didn't forget my handkerchief." Amanda starts to laugh but manages to settle herself down and smile. When Tim finishes the song, Rev. Lucas says, "dearly beloved. We're here in the sight of God and this company, to witness this man and woman to be joined in holy matrimony..."

That night, after the ceremony and reception, Joey and Amanda are exhausted. They look at all the wedding gifts they have received from all their friends. They have had to put some of the presents on the front porch and the bathroom. They decide to go through all of the wedding gifts tomorrow. They just want to sit and relax and stare at the fireplace and reminisce about all that went on today.

Later that night, they are sitting on the couch, holding each other. Joey is wearing his sweats, and Amanda is in her flannel pajamas. Amanda shakes her head with a smile and says, "that was a beautiful ceremony this afternoon if I say so myself." Joey then suddenly says, "Amanda?" She replies, "yes, sweetheart?" Joey looks at her, then says, "we haven't planned our honeymoon due to all this running around we've been doing this week." Amanda puts her hand on his face and, with the sweetest expression, says, "darling, I'm on my honeymoon right now. Here in this cabin with you. That's all I ever wanted in a honeymoon." They smile at each other and sit back on the couch, holding each other even tighter.

Later Amanda says, Joey, how about some hot tea?" "That sounds good," replies Joey. Amanda says, "I want to sit on the floor in front of the fireplace like we use to do." When Amanda gets up to make their tea, Joey gets up and puts more wood on the fire. He then sits down in front of the fire. Amanda comes in with their tea, and she sits between Joey's legs. They rest their tea mugs on the floor, and Joey wraps his arms around her. Amanda lays the back of her head on Joey's chest. Joey and Amanda don't say anything to each other at this moment. Their both extremely nervous about upcoming events that usually happen on wedding nights. Amanda says, "Joey?" He immediately and nervously says quickly, "yea?" Amanda starts to laugh at him, being so nervous. She then says in a sweet voice to him, "Joey, I know there are customary things that newlyweds do on their wedding night. And we have all the time in the world for that. But tonight, I just want to lay in bed with you. And I want you to hold me all night just the way you did like when I was first here. Remember that's when I fell in love with you." Joey gets up, then puts more wood on the fire. He walks back to Amanda and holds his hand out toward her. She takes his hand, and then she stands as they turn and walk to the bed.

Chapter Seventeen

A Wonderful Life

Four years have passed, and there have been many changes around the Morris place. One of the changes is that Joey has built an addition onto the cabin. If one would look to the left of the cabin from the front, you see a two-story addition making the cabin looking like a split-level type house. The new addition was built with the same type of cedar as the original cabin harvested from their land. The latest addition has two bedrooms and a full bathroom on the second floor. On the first floor, there is a master bedroom and a remodeled bathroom. The den has been remodeled with all new furniture. A large dining table with a matching china cabinet is in the corner. All these changes in the den and master bedroom were under Amanda's ideas and creativity. Also, Amanda works three days a week now at Roben's Florist in Craig.

But the most exciting thing that has happened, Joey and Amanda, built a new church. The new church is about fifty yards down from the chapel. The chapel is now used for weddings and other special events, including the Christmas Eve service. People come from all over

Colorado to get married at the chapel. Just as Amanda, one time hoped. Joey and Amanda never charge anyone the use of the chapel. Rev. David Lucas has become the full-time minister of the new church. The church has a sanctuary, fellowship room and kitchen. Also, there are six Sunday School rooms. They have services there every Sunday.

Joey and Amanda sold the new church and land to the board of elders for one-dollar. Joey is a founding elder, and Amanda is the social and wedding director. The church is named Morriswood Mountain Church.

Late in the year, on Christmas Eve afternoon, Joey is driving back from Craig, where he did his last-minute Christmas shopping. He is now wearing a beard that Amanda asked him to grow. He doesn't like it, but it's what Amanda wanted. She said he would look more handsome and "woodsy." He drives up to the cabin where he parks behind Amanda's late-model four-door Jeep. Joey sees all the Christmas decorations on the outside of the cabin are all lit up. He walks to the back of his vehicle and gets the gifts out he purchased.

He walks up on the porch and unlocks the door and walks in. A beautiful, blonde-haired three-year-old girl runs up to him and raises her arms, and says, "Daddy!" Joey picks her and kisses her about six times on her cheek then says, "Abby, how's my little sugar plumb today?" Abby says, "I'm good, Daddy, and I've missed you." Joey kisses her again and says, "and I have missed you and your mommy." Abby speaks very well for a three-year-old. And Joey always tells everyone that is the Marine that is coming out in her. Joey is still holding Abby, and he looks at Amanda, who is sitting at the dining table. Joey says, "Merry Christmas, Mommy." Amanda produces her beautiful smile, then says, "Merry Christmas, Daddy." Abby looks at Joey, saying, "Daddy, mommy let me open a present early!" Joey looks at Abby, and with a surprised expression, says, "she did!" Joey looks at Amanda, and she shrugs her shoulders. "Come over to the table and see what I got," exclaims Abby.

Joey walks over to the table and kisses Amanda. He then sits down with Abby, who is sitting in his lap. Abby, excitedly says, "look, Daddy. All kinds of farm animals and the barn where they live. But listen to this." Abby reaches down and opens the barn doors, and it moos like a cow. Abby starts to giggle, then says, "it moos like a cow!" Joey and Amanda smile at each other, then Amanda says, "I'm going to the kitchen and make me some tea." Joey looks at Amanda, saying, "I'll do that for you, sweetheart." Amanda replies, "no, I'll get it. I need to walk around a bit." Amanda puts her hands on the table and pushes up. She struggles a bit because she is very pregnant.

She walks to the kitchen and fills the tea-pot up with water, then puts it on the stove. She gets the tea out of the cabinet, and suddenly she has a sudden pain. She puts her hand on her abdomen and takes a teabag out of the box. A few minutes later, Amanda has another pain, and she looks slowly down at the floor where she is standing. She looks out into the den with a surprised look saying, "Joey, I think it's time to get me to the hospital. My water just broke!" Amanda turns the stove off, then Joey puts Abby down, and says to her, "Abby, go get your mommy's bag and coat." Joey goes into the kitchen and says, "wow, this came fast. A lot faster than Abby did."

Abby comes back into the den with Amanda's bag and coat. She gives Joey Amanda's coat. Joey puts Amanda's coat on for her and zips it up. Then he says to Abby, "go get your coat on sweetie." Joey puts his jacket on, then says to Abby, "get mommy's bag, sweetheart." They all walk out of the cabin, and Abby says, "Daddy, is mommy going to have my baby brother now?" Joey says to Abby, 'yes, ma'am. It sure looks that way. And this will be our best Christmas present from Jesus." Joey helps Amanda in his Jeep and buckles her in gently. He puts Abby in her car seat and closes her door. He gets in and looks at Amanda with the sweetest smile and says, "I'm in love with you, Amanda." Amanda smiles and responds while having a contraction, "and I'm in love with you, Sergeant Morris. But we better get going now and step on it!" Joey cranks up the Jeep and heads to Craig, saying quietly to himself, "thank you, God, for speaking to me. And I finally listened."

THE END

235

About the Author

Mike Gillis is a filmmaker and Author. His film credits are "Change of Heart," "Around the Next Corner," "When I Loved You," and "Triste Adagio." He is currently in production of his new film, "The Trumpet Player." He authored his first novel, "A Simple Life in Maine" last year. Mike's work is always faith-based and always leans toward real, true love between a man and a woman.

Mike resides in Vicksburg, Ms.